To my sister Jan, who would never
expect me to dedicate a book
to her – surprise! And thanks
for everything.

The Forgotten Children

Anita Davison

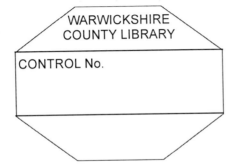

W F HOWES LTD

This large print edition published in 2017 by
W F Howes Ltd
Unit 5, St George's House, Rearsby Business Park,
Gaddesby Lane, Rearsby, Leicester LE7 4YH

1 3 5 7 9 10 8 6 4 2

First published in the United Kingdom in 2017
by Head of Zeus Ltd

A CIP catalogue record for this book is available
from the British Library

ISBN 978 1 51008 078 2

Typeset by Palimpsest Book Production Limited,
Falkirk, Stirlingshire

Printed and bound by
T J International in the UK
Printforce Nederland b.v. in the Netherlands

MIX
Paper from
responsible sources
FSC   FSC® C013056
www.fsc.org

CHAPTER 1

London, September 1904

Flora tilted her hat over her left eye and pouted at her reflection in the mirror above the mantelpiece. Bunny appeared at her shoulder and plucked a sheet of pasteboard propped against the clock.

'That's the third time you've scrutinized that card in the last hour.' She frowned as she returned the grey velvet confection to its original position.

'Don't you find it strange that we've been invited to tour a hospital neither of us has ever heard of?' He tapped the card against his thumbnail. 'Incidentally, I like that hat the other way.'

'St Philomena's Hospital is a charity founded by a wealthy philanthropist to provide medical care for children of the poor.' Sighing, she adjusted the hat again.

'An admirable endeavour, no doubt, but why have *we* been invited?' He pushed his spectacles further up his nose with a middle finger and tucked the card into his inside pocket. 'If Arthur became

1

ill, we're unlikely to take him to a hospital in Southwark.'

Flora suppressed a shiver at the mention of illness in respect of their infant son, who currently enjoyed chubby good health. 'Charities are always looking for funds; maybe they regard Mr Ptolemy Harrington, Solicitor at Law, as a viable proposition?'

'Trust you to get to the bottom of the thing.' Bunny joined her by the front door being held open by their butler. 'Are you sure you wouldn't rather go in the motor car?'

'No, and it's too late to change your mind, the taxi is already here.' She smiled at his downcast expression that was so like Arthur's. 'And Southwark is hardly a suitable place to leave your beloved Aster, no matter how many street urchins you pay to watch it.'

'Taxi it is, then.' Bunny handed her inside the motor taxi that idled at the kerb whilst giving the house a slow appraising glance through the window.

The façade of Portland stone that rose four floors from the street always sent a possessive thrill up Flora's spine. A pair of Ionic columns flanked a shiny black-painted front door with a set of railed stone steps that descended into basement kitchens equipped with the latest innovations Flora had insisted upon. Aware of what life was like in the servants' hall at her childhood home, Cleeve Abbey in Gloucestershire, with its outdated facilities, she had been determined to make her own servants'

2

lives a little easier. She had unwisely expressed this sentiment in the presence of her mother-in-law, the memory of whose contempt still made Flora's cheeks burn.

The taxi headed east along Victoria Street, past the Catholic cathedral and around Parliament Square, past monumental buildings that represented the might of the British Empire.

On the far side of Westminster Bridge, Portland stone and red brick gave way to wood and steel of the industrial area of the city, deteriorating more with each mile. The taxi's route took them in a wide circle and back to the river where the sparkling new structure of Tower Bridge reached into a darkening sky.

'It's hard to believe we're only three miles from Belgravia.' Flora wiped a gloved hand to clear the mist on the rain-streaked taxi window as they entered Quilp Street and passed beneath a wrought-iron archway that displayed the words *St Philomena's Hospital for Sick Children*.

The hospital was a solid, rectangular building with a mansard roof that squatted amongst its less imposing neighbours like an elegant woman who had known better days; the red brick having faded to a dirty russet colour by forty years of coal smoke from the surrounding factories and tanneries.

'Is that baking I can smell?' She sniffed appreciatively at an enticing aroma of burned sugar that seeped into the cab.

'Probably. The Peek Frean's factory is one of the

main employers in this area,' Bunny said, handing her out of the cab. 'They call this place "Biscuit Town".'

Their heads down against a sudden rainstorm, they ran for the entrance, splashing through puddles that soaked their feet, and exploded into the entrance hall laughing delightedly. A group of ladies in wide-brimmed hats and black-suited gentleman gave the newcomers slow, appraising looks, some curious, others of bored disinterest, before going back to their conversations.

Bunny handed the porter who held open the door for them the printed invitation that had so perplexed him earlier.

'Mr and Mrs Harrington, is it?' He squinted at the square of pasteboard. 'As you can see, we have quite a few visitors today, but someone will be here shortly to show you around.'

'I hope we shan't have to wait too long.' Bunny nodded to where a group of four were being ushered through a set of swing doors, their departure making little impression on the remaining crowd.

'Don't be such a stuffed shirt.' Flora cuffed him lightly. 'We've only just arrived, so relax and enjoy a few hours away from your office.' She inhaled the scent of late summer flowers, beeswax and warm bread instead of the disinfectant and carbolic soap she had expected.

'This wasn't quite what I had in mind when I said I needed a break from paperwork.' Bunny adjusted his tie in the reflection of a framed print of Southwark Cathedral on the wall.

'It's quite an impressive building, don't you think?' Flora tilted her head back to where the slate grey sky was visible through a glass lantern four stories above half-panelled walls; a ceramic tiled border set at shoulder height with hand-painted flower designs.

'It's certainly busy.' He indicated the constant procession of neat, efficient nurses, lumbering porters and serious-faced doctors who strode purposefully through a set of double doors and disappeared through others ranged on the opposite side.

Flora paused beside a statue of an adolescent girl in two-thirds scale set in a curved niche in the wall. Her expertly carved alabaster gown fell into loose folds at her feet, a posy of flowers held against her smooth cheek, her eyes cast demurely down, and the words, *Saint Philomena* etched onto a plaque fastened to the base.

'I saw a statue of a girl similar to this one when I visited the Isle of Wight.' Flora eased forward to get a closer look. 'It was of Princess Elizabeth, by Marochetti. I wonder if this is his work.'

'Which one?' Bunny had wandered further along the hall, his attention on an oil landscape. 'There must have been any number of Princesses named Elizabeth down the years.'

'She was a daughter of King Charles the first and died at a similar age. I thought both sculptures looked similar.'

'You are quite correct, it is indeed Marochetti's work,' a low, resonant female voice said from behind them.

Flora swung around to where a woman in a black nurse's uniform stood, regarding her calmly, her slender hands, encircled by stiff white cuffs, clasped demurely in front of her.

'I–I'm sorry, I didn't realize anyone had heard me,' she said, flustered.

She looked to be in her early forties, with slight traces of crow's feet visible beside her blue-green eyes, her delicate, symmetrical features told of beauty in her youth. A memory hovered at the back of Flora's mind she couldn't place. Had she seen her somewhere before?

'The ability to move quietly is a useful skill in my profession.' Her warm smile held a hint of mischief. 'Allow me to introduce myself, I'm Alice Finch, the Matron here.' Her austere black dress clung flatteringly to her still girlish figure; her dark honey-coloured hair worn swept up beneath a stiff white cap from which trailed a strip of linen trimmed with a double row of pleats that fell to her hip.

'Flora, Flora Harrington. And that gentleman over there is my husband, Ptolemy Harrington.' She cleared her throat noisily, drawing Bunny's attention from his study of the poster.

'What an unusual name.' Miss Finch gave his outstretched hand a brief, business-like shake.

'We don't call him that,' Flora began, 'he's known as—'

6

'Quite,' Bunny cut across her, a hand raised to adjust his spectacles. 'I assume the hospital was named for this saint?'

'Indeed. Saint Philomena is the patron saint of children and young people.' She turned a smile on Flora with a question in it. 'I find her quite beautiful.'

'Er–yes, yes, she is – I mean was,' Flora mumbled, suddenly nervous beneath the matron's close scrutiny.

'Her remains were found inside the catacomb of Saint Priscilla in Rome,' Miss Finch continued. 'Legend says she was only thirteen at the time of her martyrdom, and believed to be a fourth-century Greek princess who was tortured and killed for scorning the advances of a Roman emperor.'

The bustle of the entrance hall diminished to a low murmur as Flora tried to unearth where she had heard that lilting, musical voice before, but the memory eluded her.

'Are you all right, Flora?' Bunny broke the spell, making her jump. 'You seem distracted.'

'Sorry, I—' she lifted a gloved hand to her temple, conscious they were both looking at her. 'It's nothing, just a slight headache.'

'May I get you something for that?' Miss Finch's smile became concerned. 'We have an excellent pharmacy here.'

'Th-that's kind, but won't be necessary.' Guilt made Flora's cheeks burn at the lie. 'Do tell us more about your saint.'

'If you're sure, but do let me know if the pain becomes worse.' Her gaze held Flora's for a long second. 'Now, where was I. Ah yes, Philomena's remains were moved to Mugnano, near Naples. A number of miracles occurred there, including a nun who claimed Philomena recounted her entire life story to her in a vision, including her ordeal at the hands of her persecutors.'

'How fortuitous.' Bunny lifted a sceptical eyebrow. 'I mean, that this revelation should have come from a nun.'

'Precisely.' She slid a sideways look at him, their thoughts evidently in accord. 'I'm not entirely convinced of its provenance either. However it prompted the Roman Catholic Church to grant her sainthood.'

'Well, even if it isn't true,' Flora said, relieved to find her voice sounded normal again, 'I quite like the notion of a saint dedicated to babies and children. Is this a Catholic hospital?'

'Not at all. We accept children of all faiths. In fact there's a separate ward and kitchen here for our Jewish children.' A perplexed frown appeared on Miss Finch's face as she scanned the now deserted entrance hall. 'Oh dear, you appear to have missed the last tour group. Never mind. If you have no objection, perhaps I might show you our facilities myself?'

'We'd be honoured, wouldn't we, Flora?' Bunny prompted.

Flora nodded, surprised at how much the idea appealed.

'Splendid!' Miss Finch clasped her hands together. 'Now, where shall we begin?' In answer to her own question, she added, 'The Primrose Ward is for patients close to recovery, so you'll be less likely to be exposed to infection.' She gestured them through a set of double doors and led them along an internal corridor painted a cheerful yellow, apparently to offset the lack of windows.

A man in a dark overcoat strode towards them along the otherwise empty corridor. Solidly built, though not fat, his salt and pepper hair sprouted thickly from a low hairline; a heavy gold watch chain looped across the front of his paisley waist-coat added to his overall air of affluence.

'Ah, Miss Finch.' He lifted his silver-topped cane in salute, forcing them all to a halt. 'I've left my group in the conference room availing themselves of the refreshments.' He directed a neutral smile of acknowledgement at both Flora and Bunny. 'I'm confident I impressed them with our work here and quite optimistic about new subscriptions.'

'That's excellent news. May I introduce Mr and Mrs Harrington? This is Mr Raymond Buchanan, a member of our Board of Directors. Mr Buchanan, Mr and Mrs Harrington.'

'It's a pleasure to meet you both.' He covered the end of his cane with his bowler hat and shook each of their hands in turn. 'Are you interested in becoming a patron of St Philomena's?' His heavy eyelids slanted inwards like a sleepy spaniel, a scribble of spidery broken veins across slightly puffy cheeks.

9

'Er, we aren't sure as yet,' Bunny replied. 'Although I'm interested to hear how the subscription system works.'

'It's quite straightforward. Depending on the generosity of your donation, a cot in one of the wards would carry your name.' His gaze slid sideways along the hallway, evidently eager to be off. 'Miss Finch will furnish you with the details. Now, I'm afraid you'll have to excuse me. I'm late for an appointment.'

'Mr Buchanan, before you go, might I have a brief word?' Miss Finch grasped his arm in a firm grip and drew him to one side, her head bent close to his. He frowned, nodded once or twice in acknowledgement, but his expression remained fixed longingly on the door.

'Come away, Flora,' Bunny urged, his voice lowered. 'They obviously wish to talk privately.'

'Not so much a talk, more like a one-sided argument.' She sneaked a look at them over Bunny's shoulder. 'Whatever they're discussing it's important to her, as she's doing all the talking. He's not saying much and keeps trying to get away.'

'It's none of our business. Now stop staring at her. You've been doing that since we arrived. Which is most unlike you.' His frown dissolved and he blinked as if reconsidering. 'Come to think of it, it's not actually, but you aren't usually so obvious.'

'I know, and it's odd, but I cannot help it. There's something familiar about Miss Finch. Almost as if we've met before but I can't place her – oh, look out, she's coming back.' Flora pretended to study a notice on the wall that explained the dangers of a lung infection from polluted air.

'I'm sorry about that.' Miss Finch re-joined them, her face visibly paler, and her lips drawn together into a thin line.

'Is everything all right?' Flora asked.

Bunny pinched her inner elbow and she stiffened but kept her smile fixed.

'Simply a minor difference of opinion. Now, where were we?' Her gaze moved past them into the distance. 'Ah yes, Primrose Ward.'

CHAPTER 2

Primrose Ward ran across the entire length
of the building, the walls painted pale green
and cream with a row of metal bedsteads
on each side. Large, multi-paned windows ran
along one side, with three sets of double doors
placed at intervals, all of them open.

Three nurses sprang to their feet as the trio
entered, their strained expressions making Flora
wonder how many times they had had to jump to
attention that morning for visitors.

In response to a discreet gesture from Miss Finch,
they resumed their supervision of a group of children gathered on a rug in front of the fireplace; a
row of teddy bears lined up for a tea party. A little
way off, a curly-haired boy who rode a rocking
horse with noisy enthusiasm.

'I've never seen four fireplaces before,' Flora
observed as a porter followed their progress through
the ward and pulled each set of doors closed behind
them.

'This ward is almost a hundred feet long,' Miss
Finch explained. 'When only partly full, like today,
we partition off the separate areas so they can be

heated as necessary. In winter keeping the wards warm is a major concern.'

'How very practical,' Flora said. '

'They don't look ill.' Flora said, though without exception the children who pretended to pour tea were thin and frail looking, with sallow skin; a marked difference to her own son, Arthur, who at six months old was pink cheeked and chubby. Her thoughts went to the nursery, where at this time of day he would be taking a nap in a warm, safe place with his nurse in attendance. She experienced a sudden need to hold him in her arms and resolved to do so the moment they arrived home.

'They're not ill. As far as it goes.' Miss Finch sighed. 'Most are small for their age and not exactly robust. If I had the choice, I would keep them here in order to build them up with clean water, good food and warmth.' She lowered her voice slightly. 'Most live in dreadful conditions; damp and cramped in the majority of cases, with inadequate food, little heating, and unsanitary water. They tend to be malnourished and contract infections easily.'

'Can nothing be done?' Bunny's question was more of a challenge.

'A great deal is being done, Mr Harrington. It's simply never enough. The pollution from the factories and tanneries make full health impossible. Then there's the added problem of cheap alcohol.' She exhaled in a long sigh.

'I cannot imagine how distressing this work must

13

be.' Flora changed the subject, conscious that anything more she said would sound hollow and perfunctory. 'Are the nurses trained here?'

'Indeed, they are.' Miss Finch nodded to a young nurse in a pink apron different from the white ones the other nurses wore. Little more than a child herself, she sat cross-legged on the rug pretending to drink from a miniature cup for the benefit of a small, enraptured girl.

'Sixty years ago, nursing was seen as a disreputable occupation for young women because it was thought to contaminate their minds. Miss Florence Nightingale was reprimanded for dismissing staff who drank heavily and behaved like slatterns.'

'I read about her when I was younger,' Flora said.

'Depending on who you speak to, she was either a "petticoat imperieuse" with a naked ambition, or a heroine who improved hospital practices and saved thousands of lives. I'm sure I don't need to tell you which view *I* favour.' A shadow crossed her features but was gone immediately. 'But don't pay any attention to me, I can be quite a bore on the subject when I get started.'

'Not boring at all, it's fascinating and very noble, if I may say so.' Bunny bent and retrieved a ball that had rolled across the floor and landed at his feet. He held it out to a tiny boy who gazed up at him in wonderment as he accepted it. 'What are the main illnesses you deal with here?'

'Chest complaints mostly.' Miss Finch gently

guided the child back to his nurse. 'Whooping cough, pneumonia, bronchitis and tuberculosis. We also treat a fair number of work-related accidents, like mishaps with machines in factories and delivery boys who fall off carts. Regrettably, it's quite common, and legal, for children of ten to be employed nine hours a day in the factories.'

'Really?' Flora frowned. *Why did she not know that?*

'Are these the youngest patients here?' Bunny smiled down at the boy with the ball, who appeared to have taken a liking to him and had drifted back to his side.

'We treat all ages, although at one time the governors didn't permit patients older than twelve, or under two years to be admitted.'

'Babies weren't allowed?' Flora asked, shocked. 'Why ever not?'

'Infants require constant monitoring and they are unable to explain their symptoms accurately.' She shook her head sadly. 'Fortunately, that rule has been relaxed in recent years.'

'That's reassuring.' Flora found the thought of any child being refused treatment when needed distressing.

'Certain illnesses render us helpless,' Miss Finch continued. 'Diphtheria and tuberculosis, for example. In those cases all we can do is let the disease run its course.' With a final, 'carry on' gesture to the nurses, Miss Finch led them through a set of double doors into a long hallway where a young nurse with vivid cornflower-blue eyes waited. Her distinctive pink apron clashed with a mass of curly red hair caught untidily beneath her cap; her hands twisting nervously in its folds.

'Yes, what is it, Nurse Prentice?' Miss Finch's gaze slid to the unsightly creases in the girl's apron.

'I'm sorry to bother you, Miss Finch.' She released the apron, her face flushed. 'I wondered – I mean could you spare me some time this afternoon?'

Miss Finch gave the hall a swift glance before answering. 'I assume it's connected with what we discussed the other day?' At the girl's swift nod, she added, 'I'm sure I can spare you a few minutes when you go of duty. Perhaps—'

A burst of noisy tears from the ward they had just left drowned out the rest of Miss Finch's reply, combined with the flap of double doors that preceded the arrival of another nurse in the black uniform and white cap of a senior staff member.

Nurse Prentice backed away, her head down, and obviously uncomfortable with the arrival of the newcomer.

'Shall we proceed?' Miss Finch set off along the corridor, where Bunny fell into step beside her, the two of them already in deep conversation.

Struck by the start of fear that appeared on Nurse Prentice's face, Flora halted, as the older woman gripped the student nurse's upper arm, her expression set and angry. The young nurse hunched her shoulders and stared at the floor, offering nothing in return. The woman said something too low for Flora to hear, the exchange ending as quickly as it had begun, and dismissed, Nurse Prentice bobbed a swift, if awkward, curtsey and fled.

The senior nurse caught Flora looking at her, but stood her ground, with neither remorse nor embarrassment on her plain features. She was younger than Flora had first thought, with dark eyes and a sour expression.

'Are you coming, Flora?' Bunny called from further along the corridor where he stood beside Miss Finch, both of them turned towards her.

'Yes, yes of course.' She hurried after them as they continued on down a short flight of steps into a half basement where a row of shoulder-height windows lifted the gloom, the space filled with the savoury smells of roasting meat and the clang of pots and pans.

'The main kitchen is on this floor,' Miss Finch said unnecessarily. 'The door at the end leads to a rear yard containing the wash house, a disinfecting oven, and a post-mortem room.' She stopped short as a young man in a faded waistcoat over a striped shirt, the sleeves rolled to the elbows, stepped smartly into their path.

'Pardon me, Miss Finch. I didn't see you there.' A lock of floppy brown hair in need of a cut slipped over one eye. 'I was on my way to—' He paused and frowned up at the ceiling. 'Oh dear, I appear to have forgotten where I was going.' He thrust both hands into his trouser pockets and rocked on his heels, his slow, confident smile on his lips. 'I see you've brought more visitors to admire my domain.'

'This somewhat fey young man is Dr Albert Reid, our radiologist,' Miss Finch said in response to their combined look of enquiry. 'Don't let his air of distraction mislead you. He's almost a genius and manages an X–Ray room here at the hospital.'

'How intriguing,' Bunny said once the introductions had been made. 'I recently read an informative article in *Knowledge Magazine* about this technique of photographing bones. I would be most interested to see how it's done.'

'Splendid!' Dr Reid ushered him through a door on his left into the room. A bed occupied centre stage beside which a series of poles had been arranged to support a large camera; the contraption allowing its adjustment to the required height. A round glass ball at the top of the poles contained what resembled an oversized cylindrical light bulb.

'Is it not safe?' Taking her cue from the matron, who had not moved, Flora remained on the threshold.

'I have my reservations, Miss Finch whispered. 'I realize progress in medicine is vital, but in the case of these Roentgen rays, there is such a thing as overexposure. Quite literally.'

'It doesn't *look* dangerous,' Bunny said as he examined the contraption more closely. 'How does it work?'

'This glass is vacuum-sealed and electricity is

passed through this tube here,' Dr Reid accompanied his explanation with the use of extravagant arm gestures. 'X–rays – that is, electromagnetic energy waves – are released at the positive electrode. These high-energy rays are synchronized with the camera shutter, so they pass through soft body tissue, but are absorbed by dense material such as bone.' He held up what looked like a sheet of black glass within a metal frame with cloudy white shapes on it. 'That's what the shadowing is on the photographic plate.' He turned a bright smile on Bunny. 'I would be happy to give you a demonstration.'

'That would be excellent, I—' he intercepted Miss Finch's fixed expression and Flora's brief shake of her head. 'Um–perhaps another time.'

'I see our esteemed matron's misgivings have made an impression on you.' Dr Reid sighed. 'Surely, even you, Matron, must be aware this innovation is a major step forwards for the medical profession?'

'I concede that, Doctor,' Miss Finch replied carefully. 'However, I would still advise you to exercise more caution with that light.' Her lips formed a hard line as if she chastised a schoolboy.

'It's quite harmless.' He held both hands up, twisting them back and forth. 'See! Not a sign of disfigurement. And it's not a light, it's a cathode ray within an evacuated glass bulb, that—'

'I'm aware of the science,' Miss Finch cut him off firmly. 'I simply feel we don't know enough about the long-term effects to be complacent.'

19

The doctor's shrug dismissed her. 'Whilst we are on the subject, is there any news about moving my X–Ray department to a higher floor?' His eyebrows rose into his hairline in eager anticipation. 'The damp down here is injurious to the equipment. We have to spend the first hour of every day drying it out.'

'I've submitted your request to the Board of Governors.' Miss Finch's tone implied she had been asked this same question numerous times. 'It's out of my hands now. All I can do is await their decision.'

'Ah well, I suppose I'll have to be patient.' Dr Reid released a long-suffering sigh and brushed back an errant lock of hair that flopped over his eyes. 'However, from a diagnostic viewpoint, it will make the surgeons' lives easier.'

'I cannot argue on that score,' Miss Finch conceded. 'But, please don't let us detain you. You appeared in a hurry to be somewhere a moment ago.'

'Ah yes.' A light seemed to ignite behind his eyes. 'I remember now, I was on my way to the pharmacy. Good day to you, Miss Finch, Mr Harrington, Mrs Harrington.'

'Are you really worried about him?' Flora asked, her gaze on the doctor's retreating back as he loped away, his hands in his pockets.

'Though I'm a lone voice on the subject.' Miss Finch chewed her bottom lip. 'Not in treatment terms, you understand. The ability to take images of bone damage is invaluable. What worries me is the amount of exposure to which men like Reid put themselves. He works with that equipment for ten hours every day and feels he's immune to what has befallen others. Ernest Wilson for instance.'

'Who?' Flora asked.

'I've heard that name.' Bunny held up a hand as if a thought had just struck him. 'He works at the London Hospital. He's had articles published in the *British Medical Journal* about X–rays. Fascinating subject.'

'Wilson is a pioneer of the technique and quite brilliant.' Miss Finch sighed. 'But his methods have become careless and he's gradually losing his fingers.'

'You believe these machines are causing actual physical damage?' Flora eased away from the open door to the X–Ray room behind them.

'Indeed I do. Unfortunately, not everyone agrees with me.'

'I had no idea.' Bunny massaged his chin with one hand. 'That's quite worrying.'

'Are these machines used on the children?' Flora asked.

'Thus far the department is still experimental, so no children are exposed to the rays. Dr Reid has an agreement with the Board to do his research here, but that is all for the time being.'

'Glad to hear it.' Flora suppressed a shiver. 'What of his request to move the X-Ray room to another floor?'

'And allow his damaging rays to infiltrate the

entire hospital?' Miss Finch sliced a sideways look at her. 'Not while I'm matron here. Now, I imagine the other visitors must have left by now, so might I invite you to my office for some refreshment?'

Without waiting for an answer, she set off towards the stairs that led to the main floor.

'I had no idea you knew about X–rays.' Flora said to Bunny as they followed at a distance.

'I know lots of things. By the way, you haven't explained your apparent fascination with the matron.'

'I wouldn't call it that, but she's an exceptional woman, don't you agree? Perhaps I simply admire her dedication.' She glanced to where Miss Finch had paused to wait for them at the end of the corridor, unable to explain the impact this stranger had made on her. 'Come on, or she'll think we've lost interest in her tour.'

CHAPTER 3

Miss Finch's office was located at the rear of the ground floor; a spacious room that still managed to be cosy. A black leaded grate framed by Morris tiles, each decorated with a blood-red poppy, was set at right angles to a window that looked onto a walled garden. A sturdy oak desk sat facing a dresser that took up the majority of the opposite wall, the shelves tightly packed with leather-bound books with gold tooling on the thick spines.

The same woman who had upbraided Nurse Prentice earlier arranged ledgers on the oak desk. She barely looked up when they entered, her bland gaze sliding over them without recognition. Her black hair was pulled into a severe bun from a centre parting, above a heart-shaped face and close-set pebble eyes. The black uniform dress on her angular frame reminded Flora of a spider, her movements awkward as if she was uncomfortable in her own skin.

'Ah, Sister Lazarus, there you are,' Miss Finch greeted her. 'Would you be so kind as to fetch some tea for both myself and my visitors?' She waved Flora into an upholstered chair that proved more comfortable than it looked.

'As you wish, Miss Finch.' Sister Lazarus dropped the last ledger onto the desk with a thud, flint in her swift glance at the matron as she left the room; the first sign of animosity towards the matron by her staff Flora had seen. Or did she regard making tea as a task beneath her status?

'Sister Lazarus can be reserved, but she means well. Most of the time,' Miss Finch said, catching Flora's contemplative look at the closed door.

'I do so admire young women who follow a career.' Flora settled into the chair and arranged the folds of her skirt. 'I'm afraid I took the first post offered to me as a governess and never thought to look further.'

'Where was this?' Miss Finch took her seat behind the large desk, her hands clasped on the tooled leather inlay.

'In the country.' For reasons she could not yet fathom, Flora was unwilling to reveal too much about herself. 'My former charge is now an impressive young man of seventeen.'

'I should imagine you were a very successful governess,' Miss Finch said.

'She was,' Bunny broke off from his examination of a row of certificates displayed on a wall.

'You must be proud of your former charge,' Miss Finch added.

Flora smiled, self-conscious at their combined compliments, although a possessive pride in his

24

achievements and hope for his future was exactly what she felt for the boy she had been responsible for. In any other circumstances, they would have retained contact through polite birthday and Christmas greetings and a sepia photograph on a bureau. However the revelations of two years before meant he was her cousin. Their relationship had grown closer since Flora's marriage, though at times she found it difficult to forget she had once been his main disciplinarian; a fact he reminded her of with good natured teasing when she became too authoritarian.

'Young women these days have more independent spirits than in my day, though at times I fear they venture into dangerous territory,' Miss Finch continued, apparently happy to share confidences. 'Several of my nurses flirt with the idea of joining the *Women's Social and Political Union*.'

'Do you disapprove of votes for women?' Flora debated whether to mention her affiliation with the *National Union of Women's Suffrage Societies*, but decided this was not the time.

Bunny had turned from his scrutiny of the pictures, his arms folded across his chest regarding them both steadily; a clear message that he was interested in what Miss Finch had to say on the subject.

'Not at all,' Miss Finch said. 'I encourage modern thinking, however, most men of my acquaintance regard women as incapable of using the privilege of a vote wisely. They think we would select the candidate purely on a handsome face or a well turned-out suit.'

'I agree, although if the former were true,' Flora said, 'Arthur Balfour would never have become Prime Minister.'

Miss Finch's uninhibited, joyful laugh sent blood rushing through Flora's limbs. It was familiar, as if reminding her of someone or maybe a place and time she couldn't remember. Her inability to recall it one way or the other frustrated her.

'I do feel that the aggressive manifesto of the WSPU causes some concern,' Miss Finch continued. 'Partly because they appear to have commandeered my favourite tea room in Ebury Street where they sit and put the world to right.'

'I think I know of it.' Flora searched her small repertoire of such establishments. 'Is it called Martell's, and is run by a natty little Frenchman?'

'The very same,' Miss Finch replied.

Flora saw anticipation in the look the matron levelled at her across the desk, but perhaps she had imagined it.

'Is your Sister Lazarus one of these militant suffragists?' Bunny braced both hands on the back of a chair, his body tilted forward.

'Not that I am aware. However, now I think about it, her character is entirely suited to throwing bricks through windows. Perhaps I should suggest she join Mrs Pankhurst's ladies?'

Bunny let out a throaty laugh, in which Flora and Miss Finch joined with the easy abandon of old friends, their merriment interrupted by the return of Sister Lazarus with a loaded tray.

'I'm sorry I took so long, Miss Finch.' She split a baleful look between them as if suspecting their laughter was directed at her. 'A valve stuck on the boiler and I couldn't get the pilot lit.' She plonked overfull cups of murky brown liquid haphazardly on the desktop, making the china clatter.

'Er–thank you, Sister.' Miss Finch jerked back her chin, and Flora raised her hand to hide a smile.

Sister Lazarus glared at each of them again before she pulled the door shut behind her with a resounding bang.

'Is she a good nurse?' Flora asked, mainly to fill an awkward silence at the woman's departure. A line of wet footprints on the polished floorboards. The kitchen must be in another building and if a trip outside in the rain had been necessary, no wonder the nurse looked bad-tempered.

'She's efficient and a stickler for the rules.' Miss Finch stirred sugar into her tea but did not meet Flora's eye. 'She tends to lack the warmth I find vital when dealing with children.'

Flora took a tentative sip of the hot, if stewed tea and pondered on why a young woman would choose to work with children if she lacked compassion for them? It struck her as an odd choice of profession. But then she could not know what alternatives, if any, were open to Sister Lazarus.

'Efficiency often makes up for certain weaknesses.'

Bunny peered into his cup, grimaced and set it down again without comment.

'You're probably right, Mr Harrington.' Miss Finch smiled at him. 'And I have no complaints about her.'

Flora was about to set her own cup down when a piercing shriek made it leap in her hand, spilling the tea. 'My goodness, what was that?'

'It sounded as if it came from the rear yard.' Miss Finch rose and opened the door, greeted by the sounds of running feet and a male shout.

Flora exchanged a look with Bunny and, as if in silent accord, they followed the matron to the end of the hall, where a door stood open to a yard surrounded by a jumble of brick buildings.

Miss Finch eased her way to the front of a crowd that had already gathered, issuing increasingly irritated, 'excuse me's' and 'let me through's' as the three of them pushed to the front of the crowd.

A figure in the distinctive pink apron of a student nurse lay face up on the cobbles, her right arm bent gracefully at the elbow and her fingers slightly curled inwards, her left leg bent awkwardly behind her at the knee. A wide pool of blood had gathered beneath her head and had mingled with the rainwater that trickled red rivulets along the seams in the cobbles.

'It's Nurse Prentice.' Flora inhaled sharply. 'The one from Primrose Ward.'

'Don't look.' Bunny pulled her into his side, shielding her, though his warning coming too late as she had already seen the worst and was unable to tear her gaze away.

This was certainly not Flora's first dead body, though the fact this one had been walking the halls less than an hour ago struck her as particularly shocking. The second time she had met Bunny was over a corpse lying on the deck of an Atlantic Liner and she had been surprisingly pragmatic even then. Her reaction now, as it had been then was not horror or disgust, but curiosity as to how they had come to be there – and why.

Two doctors emerged from the main building, both in identical leather aprons bearing ominous stains Flora assumed to be dried blood. The younger one was Dr Reid, who instructed the curious onlookers to stand aside.

Miss Finch bent and lifted the girl's wrist, then laid it down again. 'How did it happen?' she demanded of the closest nurse, who shook her head but did not respond.

'She weren't here when I went to take me dinner,' a man in overalls on the edge of the crowd said, peering over Miss Finch's shoulder to get a better look.

A wide-hipped female with a ruddy complexion shushed him, while gasps erupted from newly arrived spectators. Murmurings went up among the growing crowd and two student nurses comforted a third who had burst into noisy sobs.

'Didn't *anyone* see what happened?' Miss Finch demanded, more firmly. 'Who found her?'

'I did, Matron.' A man in coveralls carrying a hoe shuffled forward. 'I came through the garden gate a few minutes ago, she was just lying there.' He looked up as if inviting further comment, but met only blank stares and shaking heads.

'Looks like she slipped on the wet and hit her head on the kerb there,' Dr Reid pointed to one of the raised stones that formed a border enclosing the yard that bore streaks of blood on the edge.

'Rubbish, man!' The second doctor had squatted beside the body where he prodded the back of the girl's skull with his fingers. 'There's a depressed fracture of the parietal bone. At a guess, I would say she was hit.'

'Hit with what?' Dr Reid lifted both his arms to indicate the plain concrete yard of about fourteen feet square that contained no more than a couple of rain barrels and a small wooden hut. 'There's nothing here. No, I'm pretty confident she must have simply tripped in the wet. Look at her shoes, the soles are thin and quite smooth.'

'Whatever the cause,' the senior doctor straightened, brushing droplets of water from his trousers, 'I will investigate thoroughly when we get the body to the mortuary. Miss Finch, the police will have to be informed.'

Nodding, Miss Finch issued instructions to the porter who had arrived at a run, before easing through the crowd to where Flora and Bunny stood. 'I think it best if you both leave now before the police arrive.'

'Don't you want us to wait and talk to them?' Flora chose not to mention it wouldn't be the first time she had dealt with the police.

'There's no need. You cannot tell them any more than I can. I'll deal with it. Come back to my office and wait there. I'll ask the porter to order you a cab.'

'Don't worry about that,' Bunny said. 'I'll flag one down on the road.'

'You're not likely to find one out on the street.' Miss Finch's raised eyebrow indicated amusement at this suggestion. 'Cabbies don't tend to wait around in this neighbourhood. Forbes will send a runner to fetch one for you.'

She ushered them away from where the doctors' voices were raised in emphatic argument, while gesturing to the crowd to go back inside the building, arms waving as if they directed traffic, and although most complied, some others took more persuading.

In her office, Miss Finch restlessly paced the floor, her jaw clenched tight.

'What a dreadful thing to happen.' Flora closed her eyes and turned her head away, but an image of the young nurse's head surrounded by blood appeared behind her eyelids. She blinked them open again and reached for the back of her chair, conscious that her hand shook.

'Sit down, Flora,' Bunny guided her into the seat. 'You've had quite a shock.'

'So have you. You're quite grey.' She offered him a weak smile that she transferred to Miss Finch, who now stood by the window, a clenched fist pressed to her mouth, deep in thought.

'Do you think she fell, Miss Finch?' Bunny asked. When she did not respond, he added, 'If you need to be elsewhere, we quite understand.' He remained standing, an elbow balanced on the mantelpiece. 'Miss Finch?' he prompted.

'I'm sorry?' She swung to face them with a start, her eyes clouded with inner thoughts. 'I do beg your pardon, and no, of course I'll remain here with you until the police arrive, you are my guests. I don't know if she fell or not, we'll have to wait for the post-mortem.'

'Dr Reid and his colleague seemed to have differing opinions,' Flora couldn't help mentioning.

'Oh, I shouldn't read anything into that.' Miss Finch moved to her desk where she drummed its surface with restless fingers. 'The doctors here tend to lock horns frequently. It's their way of asserting themselves.'

Flora could not shake the feeling there was something very wrong about the scene they had just witnessed. At first sight everything seemed uncomplicated, if tragic. A young girl runs across a rain-drenched yard, slips and hits her head on a corner stone. In most cases it would result in little more than a sore head or momentary unconsciousness, but this nurse had died. She recalled the elderly doctor's assertion that she might have been hit with something, and resolved to look up the term 'parietal bone' in their extensive library when she got home.

'The safety of the students here is my responsibility.' Miss Finch asserted. 'It's unacceptable such a young life should be wasted in that way.'

'It was an accident, surely? You cannot be held responsible.' Bunny's brow furrowed as if he too sensed there was more to Miss Finch's distress than she revealed.

'I know, but—' she plucked at the pages of an open ledger on the desk.

'Wasn't she the same nurse who asked to speak to you on the ward?' Flora asked, convinced the same thought was running through Miss Finch's head.

Bunny's eyebrows drew together and he gave a tiny shake of his head.

Flora knew that look. It warned her not to ask awkward or leading questions. Not that she ever took any notice once her interest was piqued, as it was now.

'Exactly.' Miss Finch sighed. 'Which makes me regret having dismissed her. Nurse Prentice, Lizzie, obviously had something on her mind.'

'Something important enough to get her killed?' Flora asked.

'Flora,' Bunny murmured through gritted teeth.

Miss Finch seemed oblivious of their tense interaction, her own thoughts taking precedence. 'One thing could be entirely unrelated to the other.'

Before Flora could ask what she meant, the door was flung open again with such force, the metal knob banged against the wall, forcing Bunny to take a rapid sideways step to avoid being hit.

'The police are here, Miss Finch,' Sister Lazarus announced, her eyes flat and hard. 'They wish to speak with you. Immediately.' She emphasized the last word, her pointed chin lifted in confident superiority.

'Already?' Miss Finch pushed herself upright. 'That was quick.'

'Forbes went to fetch them. A carriage had overturned on the corner of Marshalsea Road, so they were already close by.'

'Are they in the yard now?'

'Er–no. The body – I mean Nurse Prentice has been taken to the morgue, so they have gone there.'

'She was moved?' Miss Finch glared at the nurse with a mixture of annoyance and surprise. 'Who presumed to give that instruction?'

'I did.' Sister Lazarus' expression held no emotion. 'I simply thought—'

'You shouldn't have done that, Sister.' The matron massaged her forehead with one hand. 'The police need to see where Nurse Prentice died.'

'I apologize.' Sister Lazarus' eyes held no regret. 'Dr Reid said it was an accident. Anyway, it didn't seem right to leave her lying there for everyone to stare at. It would have been . . . disrespectful.' Though her bland expression did not reflect the sentiment.

'I suppose there isn't much we can do about it now.' Miss Finch's jaw clenched as she approached the door. 'I'll come and speak to the detective in charge of the case.'

'There isn't one.' Sister Lazarus shrugged, her gaze sliding away when Miss Finch glared at her. 'Only a sergeant and a couple of constables.'

Miss Finch closed her eyes briefly but said nothing, as if she fought an urge to rail against not only the nurse's incompetence but also that of the police.

'We're quite prepared to speak to them,' Bunny offered, despite the fact he seemed quite rattled too.

'That won't be necessary.' Miss Finch's knuckles whitened as she gripped the edge of the door, lowering her voice. 'Mr Harrington, Mrs Harrington, I apologize for this dreadful turn of events.' Her clear gaze shifted to Flora and held. 'I hope we shall have the opportunity of meeting again. Perhaps at *Martell's Tea Room*? I'm often to be found there on Thursday afternoons.' With a final nod, she pulled the door shut behind her, leaving them alone with Sister Lazarus, who reloaded the tray with a sharp rattle of crockery.

'Are you all right, Bunny? You're quite pale.' Flora gathered her gloves and bag as a prelude to leaving.

'I think so.' He nodded rapidly, his eyes clouded behind his spectacles. 'It never occurred to me before that head wounds bled so much. That poor girl.' Catching Flora's eye, he issued a short, embarrassed laugh. 'I forget you're more used to seeing bodies than I am.'

'The first is always the worst. That man who was

35

killed on the *SS Minneapolis* still haunts me.' She blew out a breath through pursed lips as a long-ago image intruded. Flora saw violent death as something to be fought, not lamented over. Rather than dwell on unpleasantness, she concentrated on the how and why. Belatedly she remembered they were not alone. 'Was that poor girl a friend of yours, Sister Lazarus?' Thus far, the woman had shot them occasional bland looks, but offered nothing to the conversation. Maybe her profession rendered her immune to such sights.

'Nurse Prentice was a student, whereas I'm a qualified ward sister.' She hefted the tray in both hands, a curl to her upper lip, implying Flora had suggested something untoward. 'Fraternization is not conducive to discipline.'

'My apologies, I didn't realize such things were frowned upon.' Flora inclined her head. Did she mean all students, or this one in particular?

Bunny pretended to read a medical journal, though Flora suspected he listened keenly to the exchange.

'Was she good at her job?' Flora asked, adding, 'I assume nursing doesn't suit everyone.'

'Indeed. Nurse Prentice was barely competent and tended to gossip,' Sister Lazarus replied grudgingly. 'I had to reprimand her on several occasions. Miss Finch can be an excellent administrator but tends to be lenient where the students' behaviour is concerned.'

'I see.' Flora concentrated on buttoning her

gloves, having learned from experience that to retain eye contact often stifled confidences. 'I'm sorry we didn't drink your tea after all the trouble you went to.' Flora experienced the odd sensation she was being judged by a critical headmistress. A ridiculous notion as, having been educated in the schoolroom at Cleeve Abbey with her employer's daughters, she had never in her life attended school. The only headmistress she had ever met had turned out to be a murderous spy. Or perhaps it was the severe black uniform that made this woman look menacing?

'It's no bother. The staff kitchen is only along the hall.' She planted her feet in front of the door. 'I'd better go. The police will probably wish to talk to me.' She aimed a look at the door, then swung her gaze pointedly back to Flora.

She considered standing her ground but it seemed hardly worth it, so she stepped aside.

The porter stood outside, his hand raised to knock. Sister Lazarus glared at him and he backed away, both hands upraised as he waited for her to pass. 'Your hackney is here, sir, madam,' he said, as Sister Lazarus' brisk footsteps receded along the hall.

'Are you sure we should leave?' Flora asked as they made their way to the front entrance moments later.

'Normally, no, but we neither knew the victim nor did we see the accident. Therefore Miss Finch might have a point. Discretion is the better part of valour in this instance.'

'I've never subscribed to the premise of that saying. Being discreet means you ignore everything and thus miss all the most interesting events in life.'

'I doubt there's anything interesting in this case.' Bunny handed Flora into a hansom that waited on the front drive. 'It was simply an unfortunate accident.'

Flora adjusted her skirt over her knees, her attention caught by a hackney cab that had drawn up beside them. As Bunny climbed in beside her, the driver of the other cab flicked the rein and pulled away.

'That man in the hackney that has just left, I think it was Mr Buchanan. The man Miss Finch introduced to us.'

'I cannot see him now he's gone,' he relaxed against the wooden seat. 'But I'll take your word for it.' Bunny knocked on the trap above their heads and gave their address to the driver, who closed the flaps over their knees with the handle.

The hansom jerked forward, pausing at the gates for a carter to pass by, by which time the other cab was out of sight.

'I'm sure it was him, though didn't he say he was in a hurry to keep an appointment over an hour ago?' Flora asked.

'I believe he did, yes. Funny that, I'm sure I saw him in the crowd around the body of the nurse when Miss Finch suggested we leave.'

'Did you?' Flora turned her head and stared at him. 'How odd.'

'Not really. Perhaps his "I have somewhere to be" was simply an excuse not to have to stand around in corridors making polite talk.'

'Possibly. But with a death among the staff, wouldn't he have stayed to establish what had happened?' Bunny started to say something but Flora continued, 'And did you notice that Sister Lazarus' skirt and shoes were wet when she brought in the tea? Not all of it, just a few inches of the hem at the front. If the staff kitchen was only a few doors from Miss Finch's office, why did she need to go outside?'

'Give me a chance to answer one of those questions.' He held a hand towards her, palm outwards. 'The going outside part could be because she needed to fetch a handyman to fix the pilot light on the boiler.' Bunny braced his other hand against the door frame as the taxi took a sharp corner. 'Also, it had been raining earlier.'

'I had forgotten about the boiler.' Flora slumped against the upholstery, mildly disappointed there was such a simple explanation. 'She's a strange, cold sort of person though, didn't you find? For a nurse.'

'Sister Lazarus? I imagine it's necessary for survival in that profession. High emotions must be counterproductive with what they must see every day. Especially where children are concerned.'

'I suppose so.' Flora tried to recall if Sister Lazarus' face was among those gathered round Lizzie Prentice in the yard, but couldn't remember.

'Stop looking for shadows, Flora.' He slid his arm around her shoulders and pulled her closer. 'Don't misunderstand me, I enjoy these sojourns of yours into crime, but not everyone you meet is a villain. Accidents do happen on occasion.'

'Yes, I suppose you're right.' She reached up to adjust her hat that he had dislodged. 'Although I don't like unanswered questions.'

By the time the hansom had reached Westminster Bridge, she had resolved to call her friend Lydia when they got home and invite her to tea the following afternoon. One thing she was sure of, was Miss Finch's mention of Martell's tea room was not a coincidence.

CHAPTER 4

'Thank you for taking me to *Elena's* for dinner last night.' Flora planted a kiss on Bunny's cheek as she passed him in the dining room on her way to her chair. 'It was a lovely surprise. And you were right, it did help take my mind off what happened yesterday.'

'Which was exactly my intention.' He looked up and smiled before going back to the sheaf of letters in his hand. 'There's a report on that nurse's death in this morning's edition of *The Telegraph* if you want to look.' He pushed the newspaper towards her, folded open at the appropriate page.

Flora poured herself a cup of coffee before giving her attention to the newspaper, where a column inch on page four announced the death of a student nurse at St Philomena's Children's Hospital. In words that might have come from Dr Reid, the journalist reported that the girl had slipped on wet cobbles and hit her head on a stone kerb. In an apparent attempt to make the story more sensational, the report quoted a police source which suspected she had been attacked by an opportunist thief on the hunt for opiates. Below the article sat a fuzzy drawing of what could have been any young woman.

Flora pushed the paper away and stirred milk into her cup. 'Is there anything interesting in the post?'

'Only a notice about these Motor Car Act rules and the new speed restrictions.' He tapped the letter that lay beside his plate.

'Why do the council need to make so many rules when there are so few motor cars about?' The tantalizing smell of hot bacon announced their butler's arrival with Bunny's breakfast. 'Are you going to camp out all night like Earl Russell?' Why did he do that anyway?'

'He did so because he was determined to secure the first registration number issued.' Bunny chuckled. 'My number twenty six isn't nearly as prestigious as his A1. That this system is in place at all indicates that motor cars are here to stay. I told you they weren't a fad.'

'Indeed you did.' Flora eyed the sausages, bacon, tomatoes and fried eggs glistening with butter loaded onto his plate. With a small sigh she helped herself to a slice of toast from a silver lattice basket. 'Just the coffee and toast for me will be all, Stokes.'

The butler gave her a disapproving look along with his bow of acquiescence as he withdrew.

'Not hungry?' Bunny looked up at her briefly before attacking a sausage.

'About yesterday,' she began, avoiding the question. Since the birth of their son, Flora's clothes fitted too snugly for comfort. If she was to return to her former coltish figure, a little restraint was necessary. 'We should have waited and talked to the police after that nurse was found.'

'Whatever for?' he said between mouthfuls. 'They would have kept us hanging about all afternoon, and for what? Look, I'm not unsympathetic to the plight of that poor girl, but it was an accident after all, and we had nothing to tell them.'

'Apart from her brief but intense argument with Sister Lazarus, which no one saw but me,' she said under her breath and reached for the sugar bowl, but changed her mind at the last second and pushed it away.

'Did you say something, darling?' Bunny looked up briefly from his plate.

'Only that the older doctor didn't agree with Dr Reid, did he?' Flora sipped her coffee, relaxing as the hot, strong brew revived her laggard spirits.

'I think we've been here before.' Bunny looked up, his blue eyes sparkling behind his glasses. 'Reminds me of our first meeting aboard the *Minneapolis*, when the captain said that chap Van Elder had died from a fall, but you insisted he'd been murdered?'

'And I was right about that, wasn't I?' Flora scraped her toast with an almost invisible layer of butter. 'Maybe I am on this occasion as well?'

'It was an unfortunate, even a tragic death, but nothing to do with us.' His tone remained calm, but a pulse at his temple gave a sudden rapid

43

jump. 'Remember what happened the last time you started poking into matters of death and conspiracy? You were very nearly killed yourself.' He put down his knife and fork and reached for his coffee cup.

'But suppose—'

'It's not as if you knew her.' He cut her off with a wave and pulled the butter dish across the tablecloth.

'No, no I didn't.' Flora hadn't known Marlon van Elder or Evangeline Lange either, but that fact had not prevented her taking an interest in their respective murders. A thought which had occurred to her the day before resurfaced, and discarding her toast, she rose and approached the bureau that occupied an alcove beside the fireplace.

'I think this registration scheme is a good one if they can get it right.' Bunny reverted to their previous conversation as he examined the papers again. 'I predict a time when everyone will use petrol-engine vehicles instead of horse-drawn ones.'

'Surely not in our lifetime!' Flora looked up briefly from where she crouched at the bottom cupboard just as a pile of papers, books and a needlework box tumbled onto the floor, none of which were what she sought.

'The world is moving faster than we think. I'm not so sure about these other rules though, like fines for reckless driving.'

'Isn't that a good thing?' Her voice echoed slightly in the recesses of the cupboard.

'Perhaps, but who decides what is reckless and what isn't? The good news is that the speed limit has been increased from fourteen miles an hour to twenty.'

'That's good news?' Flora piled the objects haphazardly back into the cupboard, unbent with a grunt and opened one of the upper drawers.

'What are you doing, Flora?' Bunny twisted to face her with an exasperated sigh. 'Have you lost something?'

'The box of photographs I keep in here. I haven't seen them for a while. It looks as if they might have been moved – ah no, here they are.' She withdrew a pasteboard box from the second drawer and brought it to the table.

'Those belonged to your fath— I mean Riordan, didn't they?' Bunny wiped his mouth on his napkin and pushed his plate away. 'What do you want with those?'

Flora didn't react to his slip of the tongue. On occasion, she too forgot that Riordan Maguire, the man who had raised her as his own, was not a blood relative, so she could hardly chastise Bunny for making the same mistake.

'They called them *carte de visite* when I was a child.' She sifted through a pile of sepia images mounted on thin card, found those she was looking for and returned the rest to the box.

Bunny rose and skirted the table, studying the pictures over her shoulder.

'That's your mother isn't it?' He pointed to the

image of a fair-haired woman perched on a chair in what was evidently a photographer's studio. Lily Maguire met the camera lens with confidence and a hint of a smile, her tightly corseted figure held stiffly upright, her delicate hands demurely clasped in her lap. 'She was a very pretty woman.'

'Yes. She was.' Flora ran a fingernail across an image of the same woman. She sat on a lawn, her legs stretched out in front of her beneath her skirt, one hand on her wide straw hat and her gaze fixed on the far distance; a slightly blurred outline of Cleeve Abbey behind her.

Flora knew every line and blemish of both photographs, but couldn't remember the woman who had posed for them.

'Why keep them in a box?' he asked. 'Wouldn't they be better framed and put on display?'

'These are the only copies I have, and this one is slightly damaged already. In the daylight, they will fade into nothing, and then I will lose her forever.'

'I'm sorry, I didn't think of that. What made you want to look at them today specifically?'

'You'll think I'm being ridiculous.' She looked up into his eyes and summoned her courage, willing him not to dismiss her.

'Oh, I don't know,' Bunny mused. 'Ridiculous, was when you ordered the removal of a perfectly functional kitchen range and replaced it with one of those new-fangled Windsor models. However, if you recall, I didn't say a word.'

'You didn't have to.' Flora lifted one eyebrow in his direction. 'The week-long muttering under your breath was clear enough.' She came to a decision. 'All right, I'll tell you. When I saw Miss Finch for the first time yesterday, I had this strange feeling I was looking at my mother.'

'That's not possible, Flora.' The enquiring light in his eyes faded immediately to scepticism. 'Your mother died when you were a child.'

'No one knows for sure *what* happened to her.' He opened his mouth to speak again but she cut him off, 'Look closely.' She tapped the image with a fingernail. 'There's something about her eyes and the way she held her head which struck me as familiar. They could be the same woman.'

He sighed, took the photograph from her and peered at it as if he hadn't seen it a dozen times. 'This fold in the paper has distorted her features slightly, though I suppose this could be what Miss Finch might have looked like as a young woman. It doesn't mean she's the same person.'

'You think I'm imagining it?' She wanted to make him understand that what she had felt at the time was too strong to be ignored but was unsure how to.

'I concede there's a resemblance, but no more than that.' He handed the photograph back to her, slid an arm around her shoulders and rested his cheek against her hair. 'Have you considered that having so recently had a child yourself, your thoughts naturally turn to your own mother?'

'This was different.' She licked her lips, summoning her courage. 'I'm not saying it's even possible, but just suppose my mother is still alive?' She hugged the photographs to her chest, unaware until that moment how important it was that he not dismiss her too lightly.

'Flora, I—'

'It's possible, isn't it?' She interrupted what she suspected would be another dismissal. 'After all, her body was never found.' She voiced a thought she had had thousand times since discovering her mother had not died when Flora was a child as she had been told, but in fact had gone missing.

'Might you have met Miss Finch before, but have simply forgotten?'

'It wasn't like that.' She shrugged out of his hold, irritated. 'You can rationalize it all you want, but it was like seeing a familiar face in a crowd. You know instinctively it cannot be anyone but them.'

Flora fidgeted beneath his stare, aware he would prefer she put the past behind her where it belonged. However the mystery of Lily Maguire's disappearance was one which had plagued her in the two years since Amy Coombe had told her story.

Now housekeeper at Cleeve Abbey, Amy claimed Lily Maguire had not died when Flora was a child as she had been told, but disappeared after an altercation with Amy's father, Sam Coombe. A child at the time, Amy had witnessed an argument between Sam and Lily when the latter had tried to get Amy into a women's refuge rather than be sold onto the streets by her lout of a father.

'Her body was never found,' Flora insisted. 'Maybe Sam didn't kill her that night?'

'What other explanation could there have been?' He lowered his voice to a sympathetic whisper. 'If she had survived, why would she have stayed away from you for so long?'

'What if she couldn't help it?' Bunny started to interrupt her, but she rushed on, 'Amy said her father was drunk when she left them arguing. Sam Coombe maintained Lily had simply left, and without a body, the police couldn't arrest him. What if she—' she broke off, unable to finish the thought.

'She's dead, Flora. She must be.' Bunny sighed on a released breath, apparently unwilling to go over the same ground they had covered many times before. 'It's not healthy to dwell on what might have been. You must let go of the past.'

'I know, and you're probably right.' Dismayed, she returned the cards to the box and replaced the lid just as a discreet knock at the door preceded the arrival of Milly, their nursery maid, who paused in the door frame, her face as expressionless as a mannequin in Selfridges shop window. Didn't the girl ever smile?

'Master Arthur has been dressed and fed, Mrs Harrington, if you wish to visit the nursery.' She bobbed a brief curtsey and waited, her gaze fixed somewhere above Flora's head.

'Thank you, Milly. I'll be up in a moment,' Flora replied, dismissing her.

'What was that about?' Bunny scowled as the door closed. 'You aren't usually so terse with the servants? Has she done something to annoy you?'

'Nothing I can openly complain about. She insists on set times for my visits to the nursery.' At his incredulous look, she shrugged, 'It's the only way I ever get to see Arthur.'

'What do you mean?' Bunny's brusque tone demanded an explanation. Stokes could have set up a wine shop in the cellar for all he would have noticed, but anything concerning the well-being of their son required his full attention.

'In a way it makes sense. I risk upsetting his routine if I arrive unannounced.' She fiddled with the fringe on a chair back. 'Milly even chooses his clothes and toys. It's as though our son is a new toy I'm not allowed to play with.'

The teddy bear she had bought Arthur was always missing from his crib when she visited, replaced by a surprised-looking bunny rabbit. Its appearance always made her feel rejected, although the baby could not know the difference.

'He's not yet five months old, darling.' Bunny chuckled. 'He doesn't play with toys yet apart from the soft and fuzzy kind.' He returned to the table and shuffled his correspondence into order.

'I took him to the park in his perambulator the other day,' Flora persisted, conscious she sounded petulant. 'When I got back, Milly said I had kept him too long in the London air.'

'Should I discharge her?' He peered at her over his spectacles. 'I could pay a call on Mrs Hunt's Employment Bureau in Duke Street. If anyone can find a replacement, she could.'

'Er–no, don't do that.' The idea had instantly appealed only to be rejected, replaced by practicality. 'Good nursery staff aren't easy to find. Besides, even *I* have to admit that Arthur's thriving.' Bunny had researched Milly's background and training with his usual thoroughness, thus there was nothing Flora felt she could legitimately complain of. If only the girl was more animated; surely babies needed smiles and happiness around them?

'You mustn't let her bully you.' Bunny slid the papers into a leather briefcase that sat on an empty chair. 'Don't we have a habit of engaging slightly unusual staff?'

'I suppose we do.' Sally, Flora's lady's maid had been engaged mainly because Flora's mother-in-law disapproved of the girl's outspoken manner. A decision Flora had never regretted. She couldn't imagine life without the pert and delightful Sally Pond.

Another knock at the door was followed by a cough that preceded the return of Stokes.

'Mr Osborne has arrived, madam.'

'Thank you, Stokes.' Flora's gaze shifted to the ormolu clock on the mantle as the butler withdrew. 'He isn't due for another half-hour.'

'He's your father, not a visiting tradesman. Now where is William taking you on this treat he won't reveal to anyone?' Bunny hefted the briefcase in one hand and made for the door.

'You've just answered your own question. He insisted it was to be a surprise.' Flora moved to the window that overlooked the street where a gleaming motor car stood at the kerb. 'Now I know why he's early. He's come to show off his new acquisition.'

Bunny crossed the room in three brisk strides, giving a sharp intake of breath. 'Good grief, it's a Spyker!' The admiration in Bunny's eyes reminded her of an intensity he normally reserved for her.

'I suppose it is quite pretty with the emerald green and black outlines on the doors,' she conceded, acknowledging the need to show some enthusiasm.

William sat behind the wheel, apparently receiving compliments from several passers-by on the street. He wore a full length camel overcoat, a long yellow scarf wrapped around his neck and a flat leather cap with a pair of driving goggles perched on the peak obscuring his handsome features, but she knew without doubt it was him.

'She's more than pretty. Under that bonnet is an eighteen horsepower engine, a pressed steel chassis with solid axles and an advanced suspension system of elliptic leaf springs.'

'Well, of course, that makes it all *so* much clearer.' Flora rolled her eyes and reached up to plant a kiss on his cheek. 'And now I know you'll be happily occupied with William's new toy, I can spend a few moments with Arthur before we leave.'

'You still can't bring yourself to call him "father", can you?' Bunny asked without looking at her.

His words halted her at the door, but she didn't reply other than to direct a smile over one shoulder as she pulled the door shut behind her.

Through the window on the upper landing, she saw Bunny descend the front steps to where William's motor car stood at the kerb. Together they circled the brand new vehicle, William gesticulating with enthusiasm, greeted with an occasional nod and smile of approval from Bunny.

As he had for most of her life, Riordan Maguire still occupied the role of father in her head and to replace him felt like a betrayal. William was, well, William; the dashing young man who had made flying visits to Cleeve Abbey during her childhood, his arms full of gifts and always with a ready story of adventures in far off lands to tell his three nieces and the butler's daughter. Riordan might not have been her blood, but he deserved the respect due to a loving parent, and that was how she would always remember him.

William had pushed the goggles onto his forehead, the sight of his handsome face making Flora wonder what he would think of her theory about Lily Maguire. If the two came face to face after all this time, would he recognize the girl he had once loved?

'Stop imagining things, Flora,' she murmured, her breath forming an opaque film on the window glass. Perhaps Bunny was right and her unresolved feelings were turning to an obsession. Or perhaps she had been reading too much of Bunny's copy of Sigmund Freud's *The Psychopathology of Everyday Life*. With this thought uppermost, she pushed away from the windowsill and headed for the nursery to cuddle the baby for a few minutes before joining William.

CHAPTER 5

Flora settled into the buttoned seat of the Spyker with its comforting smell of new leather and saddle soap. After several false starts with the starting handle, the engine purred and spluttered into life. William threw up a fist in triumph and dashed around the bonnet and leapt into the driving seat.

'Where are we going?' Flora snuggled into the blanket he had thoughtfully provided.

'It's a surprise.' He pulled his goggles down over his eyes and grabbed the wheel in both hands. 'All I will reveal is that we don't have very far to go.'

The motor car lurched forward into the centre of the road, took a sharp left turn into Lyall Street, narrowly missing the rear wheel of a horse-drawn hansom.

'Manoeuvres well, doesn't she?' William shouted above the discordant honk of an irate driver he had overtaken.

'Do you always drive this fast?' Flora hoped the couple on a leisurely walk through Sloane Square would not choose that moment to cross the road.

'We pass everything so quickly that I cannot focus. I sense a headache coming on.'

'Don't be so grumpy, Flora.' William took one hand off the steering wheel and gave her shoulder a friendly shove. 'Not like you to be so unadventurous. I thought you would love it.'

'Sorry, I don't mean to be miserable, and I'm enjoying the ride. In a way.' Her heartbeat raced as a green and gold Harrods delivery van made a last minute dash for a gap in the traffic. The thought of a resultant tangle of spindly equine legs mixed in with wheel spokes made her stomach knot. London horses led a hard life and were, without exception, lean and nervous looking. One advantage of Bunny's prophesy about motor vehicles was that fewer animals would have to spend their days pounding hard roads for hours, never seeing a field or a hill, only to die from overwork far earlier than they should. 'What prompted you to arrange this mysterious excursion?' A gust of wind lifted Flora's scarf and blew the end across her face.

'It's by way of an expression of my gratitude.' His eyes sparkled from behind his round driving goggles. 'I never imagined that I would become a grandfather. I'm so delighted, I wanted to spoil you a little.'

His words scraped at her heart and an image of Riordan Maguire loomed into her head. She busied herself rearranging her scarf so he wouldn't see the tears that had sprung to her eyes. Whenever she felt her baby's soft cheek beside hers, she was struck again with fresh pain that Riordan would never see him. 'He's watching over you,' people told her, but the words meant little. Death was stark, inevitable and eternal. Riordan was gone. Just like poor Lizzie Prentice.

'Did you hear me, Flora?' William shouted above traffic noise as they idled at a crossroads.

'What? Oh, of course I did.' She forced her thoughts back to the present. 'And it was hardly necessary. Your mother's diamond necklace was thanks enough.' At the time, Flora's first thought had been what William's late mother would have thought of his giving the precious Osborne diamonds to his illegitimate daughter. 'And you do realize that Arthur is five months old?'

'Indeed, but I needed time to arrange something different. Hedges Butler came up trumps in the end.'

'Who is Hedges, and what has his butler got to do with anything?' Flora called to him over the noise of the engine and multiple clops of hooves on all sides.

'That's his name. Frank Hedges Butler.' William laughed as the motor car sprang away from the corner and took another stomach-lurching turn. 'I've said enough already. Wait until we get there. It's not far now.'

'This is Chelsea Bridge Road.' Flora gazed around at the street they had turned into. 'Are you taking me to watch the polo at Ranelagh Gardens?'

'No, I am not, but you are half right. Now be patient. You'll see soon enough.'

They rolled through a set of iron gates and negotiated a long gravel drive, where William brought the vehicle to a halt on an apron of gravel.

'There! Wasn't that a splendid run?' He relaxed against the leather upholstery and removed his gloves. 'What are you smiling at?'

'You.' Flora giggled. His boyish enthusiasm was infectious, making times like these easier. They might lack the shared memories that accompanied a lifetime's parenting, but this occasion was already a special time she could store away to be relived in the future.

'At least the weather hasn't let us down.' William cocked his chin at the sky but offered no explanation. 'Not a cloud in sight and little wind.'

'Which is relevant to what exactly?' Flora began to feel warm in her heavy coat and unwound her scarf from her neck. 'Have you brought me on a shooting expedition? '

'Stop being so impatient, and no one has shot a pigeon here for a long time.' He shoved his goggles onto the peak of his cap, patting her knee through her coat. 'You'll see in a minute. Just watch.'

'Watch what? There's nothing here, apart from those people on the grass over there.' She nodded to where a small group surrounded something laid between them. From a distance of thirty yards or so it resembled a misshapen sheet, large, flat and shapeless. Her idle glance turned instantly to fascination as the sheet billowed slowly from the ground and rippled along the entire length as if it were breathing.

'Goodness, what *is* that?' Her breath caught as the object bulged, filled and lifted off the ground into a massive teardrop shape as it billowed out. An oversized square basket was attached below it by a series of ropes; the entire contraption dragged across the ground for several yards before rising into the air before settling back onto the grass.

William grinned, evidently pleased with himself. '*The City of New York* is Hedges Butler's pride and joy. Welcome to the Aero Club.'

'He gave his balloon a name?' Entranced, Flora gawked at the massive inflatable that strained against a network of ropes slung over it like a giant fishing net. 'How does it just hang there like that in mid-air?'

'The envelope, that's the technical term for the canvas part, is filled with coal gas. It's lighter than air so, as long as it's full, the balloon stays afloat,' William said. 'The view from sixty feet up is magnificent.'

'You intend going up in that thing?' Flora turned an incredulous look in his direction.

'Of course.' He opened his door and leapt onto the ground. 'And you're coming with me.'

'Me?' Flora froze in place, though excitement bubbled in her chest at the sight of the now fully inflated balloon that hovered ten feet off the ground, its elongated shadow spread across the grass. The crowd stood in a semicircle, necks craned as if the object were a divine deity to which they had come to pay homage.

'It's perfectly safe.' William walked around to her side of the car and opened the door. 'Besides, it's tethered to the ground so only goes in one direction. Up.'

'That's precisely the direction I was afraid of,' she murmured as he guided her across grass that squelched beneath her boots after the previous day's rain.

A startlingly handsome man occupied a folding wooden seat set on the grass, his knees splayed and several piles of coiled hemp ropes piled up beside him. He rose when he spotted them approach, and kept rising until he towered over them. Bunny was almost six feet tall, but this man must have been half a foot taller. His thick dark brown hair matched his heavily fringed eyes, lightly tanned skin and a full moustache over a sensual mouth.

'Flora, allow me to introduce you.' William nudged her forward. 'Charles, this is my daughter, Flora Harrington. Flora, the Honourable Charles Rolls.'

'Ah, so this is the lady about whom I've heard so much?' he grasped her hand firmly in his, her skin prickling through two layers of gloves. 'Delighted to meet you at last.'

Flora's cheeks warmed beneath the soft look in his warm brown eyes. She inclined her head, but for some reason, her tongue wouldn't work and she could only manage a garbled, unintelligible greeting.

'Charles is a motor car fanatic, just like Bunny and me,' William said. 'He has a keen interest in balloons and aeroplanes too.'

'Osborne here says you might like a trip up in *The City of New York*?' He clapped his gloved hands together with a muffled thump.

Flora was about to inform him that 'like' wasn't a word she would have used, but he did not appear to expect a response, and instead took her elbow and guided her firmly towards the basket, where a row of sandbags hung at intervals from the top of the rail that almost reached her shoulders.

'Not nervous are you?' he extended a hand to indicate she should mount a short set of wooden steps.

'What an idea.' Her voice shook slightly but she was determined not to show fear in front of this impressive man, nor disappoint William when he had gone to all this trouble. Hitching her skirt, she swung one foot over the rounded edge of the basket and, with as much elegance as she could muster, climbed over and landed heavily on the other side. Now she knew what a cat in a basket felt like.

'Mrs Harrington, meet Frank Hedges Butler,' Mr Rolls indicated the solidly built middle-aged man in an overcoat who occupied a corner of the basket. 'He's the owner of this magnificent example of scientific engineering.'

'Nice to see another young lady take to the sport.'

His fleshy face creased into a welcome smile, widening again when he caught sight of William climbing in behind her. 'Osborne my dear man, glad you made it. And I take it this is the famous Miss Flora?'

'It is indeed,' William completed the introduction.

'Do many ladies go up in your balloon, Mr Hedges Butler?' Flora asked as Mr Rolls leapt in beside them with remarkable grace for such a tall man.

'Indeed yes. My daughter Vera adores sky-sailing, and Charles' sister, Lady Eleanor Shelley, is also a keen balloonist.' He slapped the rail of the basket with something like affection. 'There'll be just the four of us today, my dear,' he continued, and, as if sensing her unease, added, 'don't worry, we shan't be going anywhere. The balloon is tethered.'

Despite hearing this assertion twice since arriving, Flora was still not reassured.

'The atmospherics are perfect, with no ambient wind, so you won't be buffeted about too much.' Mr Rolls' smile revealed even teeth.

'I was hoping not to be buffeted, as you put it, at all,' Flora attempted a light laugh, though no one appeared to hear her.

'Excuse me, my dear, my engineer wishes me to help him check the ropes.' Hedges Butler nodded to a man in workman's overalls and a flat cap who gestured from the other side of the basket. 'Sometimes I think they don't trust me with my own equipment.' His wide shoulders shook with a baritone chuckle as he turned to Mr Rolls. 'Charles, would you help me take a look at the envelope? It's stretched a little on one side.' With a final nod, the pair climbed back down the steps again.

'Don't look so panicked,' William whispered in Flora's ear. 'They're simply being cautious.'

'I wasn't aware I did,' Flora replied, embarrassed that the anxiety she was doing her utmost to hide was so obvious. 'Though I quite like your Mr Rolls.' She indicated to where he stood with Mr Hedges Butler, his impressive frame bent towards the older man.

'He's a remarkable fellow, isn't he? Did I mention he's walking out with Vera Hedges Butler?'

'Why would you feel the need? I'm hardly interested in Mr Rolls. I'm a married woman, remember?'

'No interest eh?' He raised a cynical eyebrow. 'Then why did you blush when he held your hand?'

'Nerves.' Her cheeks warmed as the blush returned. 'And what exactly have you told them about me?'

'Not much, other than when you're around, there's usually a body somewhere close by.'

Flora gasped in protest, but his wide grin told her he was joking, though he had rendered any mention of Nurse Prentice's death out of the question.

'Everyone ready?' Mr Hedges Butler returned to the basket, this enthusiastic inquiry greeted with loud excited agreement from the men, together with a strangled groan from Flora. 'Release the winch!' he ordered the two workmen who guarded the ropes.

Flora squeezed her eyes shut and clung to William's arm with one hand, the fingers of the other hooked over the edge of the rail as the basket gave a sharp sideways jerk as it rose slowly into the air. Flora's heart leapt in her chest and she inhaled sharply at a strange floating sensation and hoped the wicker floor was sturdy enough not to collapse under her feet and send them all plunging to the ground.

'Isn't it thrilling?' William's tone challenged her to contradict him.

'I don't know, I can't bear to look!' She wasn't sure if she loved or hated him at that moment. How could he do this to her with no warning?

William chuckled. 'I haven't spent four guineas on tickets for you not to see anything. Do take a look, it's a wonderful view from up here.' He wrapped an arm around her shoulders and drew her close into a rough hug, so close, she could smell the rich, spicy scent of his cologne.

'So you keep saying.' Bracing herself, she prised open her eyes. Instantly her breath caught at the sight of the wide expanse of green that lay beneath them. Gardens of houses resembled a green blanket crisscrossed with trees and hedges. A grey-brown ribbon wound around the perimeter where cars and horse-drawn vehicles raced along at speed like toys on a nursery floor.

'Well?' William whispered. 'What do you think?'

'I cannot think.' Flora's fear dissolved and exhilaration filled her chest. 'It's amazing.'

Flora's stomach did another lurch but more in excitement than fear as the basket jolted, its upward movement halting sharply as the thick rope tether went taut, leaving the entire contraption suspended above the ground. The wicker creaked beneath their weight, and a cold breeze caressed her cheeks, making her nose run.

Carefully, she craned her neck over the side of the basket and looked straight down to where the basket hovered above the tops of trees, their leaves beginning to change their summer colours to shades of gold, red and brown.

'It's so quiet up here.' Flora peered over the edge of the basket at the ground far below them. 'I've never seen a tree from this angle before, they are like coloured bushes, while everything looks like a toy model.' She lifted her gaze to where barges and tugboats jostled for position on the river between the Chelsea Embankment and the Middlesex side.

A light tap came on her shoulder, making her jump. She turned to see the handsome face of Charles Rolls beaming down at her, a full champagne glass in each hand. She released her grip on the rail and took the glass he held out towards her.

'When I got up this morning, I never imagined I would be drinking champagne in a balloon.'

'Can you think of a better way to spend an early autumn morning,' he asked grinning as he handed the second glass to William.

'I wish Bunny was here!' she whispered once Charles had moved away. 'He would love this.'

'I invited him, actually.' William tapped the rim of his glass gently against hers. 'He said he wanted us to enjoy this first experience together. Perhaps he'll accompany us next time?'

Flora wasn't sure there would be a next time, though to hide her nerves she took her first sip. Her eyes closed as the bubbles fizzed on her tongue and, once settled, the velvety, sweet apple and slightly floral taste followed.

She would have a few strong words for her husband when she got home. Or maybe it was better he had kept William's secret, or she might have found an excuse not to come.

After two glasses of champagne, she no longer felt the sting of the cold wind on her cheeks, and found herself wishing they weren't tethered to the ground and they could sail over the fields and see more of the vast city below them.

A seagull appeared in line with her shoulder, its wings spread and head turned to stare at her in quizzical surprise as it glided by.

'I don't know what I'm doing up here either,' Flora whispered, a giggle in her throat. The bird gave a shriek of protest, banked higher until it resembled no more than a silver 'v' in the distance.

It was with a sense of disappointment when their allotted half-hour passed and the balloon was lowered to the ground.

'I would love to do that again,' she declared as

William helped her climb out of the basket. She staggered slightly but blamed her light-headedness on the experience of the balloon rather than the champagne.

'I knew you would.' William hugged her shoulders before drawing her towards Mr Hedges Butler and Charles Rolls to make their farewells.

The journey home struck her as decidedly less nerve-wracking than their outward trip. In fact, she even encouraged William to go faster and squealed with pleasure when he dodged through traffic, going round Hyde Park Corner as if they were in a race.

'I liked your Mr Rolls,' Flora observed again. 'He's quite an adventurous character. I hope Mr Hedges Butler's daughter is of the same mind.'

'Indeed she is, although I doubt they'll take their friendship as far as marriage.' William turned a corner so fast, he startled a horse pulling a cart on Chelsea Bridge Road.

'Why do you think so? It's not unheard of for young people who share the same interests to forge a life together, you know.'

'Charles is far too focused on his adventures,' William replied, appearing not to catch her sly reference to his own permanent bachelor state. 'He's got a scheme in mind to go into partnership with some chap called Royce. Charles claims he's the best engineer in the world and they plan to build the most luxurious motor car ever seen.'

'He sounds like Bunny. Or at least the way Bunny

used to when he still hoped to make his living from the manufacture of motor cars.' Had they not married and had a child, perhaps he would have been free to follow his own fate.

'I know what you're thinking, Flora.' William took his eyes off the road to glance at her. 'Don't torture yourself. Bunny is the happiest young man I know.'

'Really?' She hoped she didn't sound too desperate.

'He's found his rightful place in that law firm. He told me he would like to move from corporate to criminal law and try real cases. When the next grisly murder takes place, you'll be seeing his name in the papers.'

'Defence or prosecution?' she said with a nervous laugh. With an effort, she pushed away the image of Lizzie Prentice, whose death she was still not convinced was an accident.

'Ah, now *that* I cannot tell you, you'll have to wait and see.'

Flora gasped as a man in a Homburg stepped smartly off the kerb and into the road without looking.

Her hand instinctively reached out and grabbed the edge of the windscreen as William braked hard and brought the vehicle to a screeching halt. He stood up in his seat and shook his fist. 'We no longer have to employ a man carrying a red flag to walk ahead of cars, my good man! Might I suggest you look where you are going in future?'

'William! You don't have to abuse the poor man.'

Flora shocked by how aggressive William had become seated behind a wheel when he was normally so passive. 'I don't expect he sees a motor car in these streets very often,' she ventured as they set off again. She offered the culprit an apologetic smile as they passed, leaving the astonished man staring after them from the pavement.

The rest of the journey passed without further mishap and William pulled into the kerb, where he switched off the engine which gave a final bang before the silence of the street resumed.

'Well, Flora. After the best surprise outing ever, am I going to be invited to luncheon?'

'Of course you are.' She climbed out onto the pavement wondering why everything seemed to be moving. 'Perhaps I should have more adventure in my life?'

'Or maybe less champagne.' William laughed as he guided her up the steps to the front door.

CHAPTER 6

Flora and William settled in white-painted chairs in the conservatory overlooking the walled garden where they took their post-prandial coffee, the intimate space warmed by a pot-bellied stove set at the far end.

'That girl seems to like you,' Flora observed when Milly complied with her request to bring the baby down to see his grandfather. 'She actually blushes in your company and forgets what she's about to say.'

'The fact you refer to her as "that girl" tells me you've not warmed to her.' William lifted the baby level with his face and blew bubbles against Arthur's rounded cheek through pursed lips as he squirmed and babbled excited incomprehensible noises.

'Is it so obvious?' Flora said, dismayed she was so readable.

'Has it occurred to you she's intimidated by you?' William lowered Arthur and attempted to set him on his lap, but the baby's chubby legs refused to bend, leaving him precariously balanced on William's thighs. A small hand gripped the hair behind William's ear and tugged. Wincing, he carefully prised the chubby fingers away, but thinking it a fine game, the baby let out a shout and grabbed at a forelock with his other hand.

'By me?' Flora bit her bottom lip to prevent a laugh. Apparently, all it took was a small baby to render an impressive man like William totally helpless. 'Why would she be? I give her a free hand in the nursery.'

'Yes, silly girl. You. You're her employer, the mistress of this elegant house with every advantage in the world. She wants to make a good impression.' William held onto the wriggling small body as Arthur enthusiastically mouthed his chin.

'He's teething.' Flora had never imagined anyone would be intimidated by her. Even a maid.

'So I see.' He set the baby back on the blanket laid out for him on the floor. Arthur wobbled a little at first but soon righted himself. 'Goodness, he's sitting up on his own.'

'His latest achievement. That and two bottom teeth.'

'I must come around more often.' He bent over Arthur's thatch of surprisingly thick, red-gold hair. 'He grows so fast.'

'You would be very welcome at any time, you know that.'

'You've been quiet since luncheon, Flora. Is something wrong?' He adjusted his jacket where it had been rucked up by the baby's feet. 'Apart from stern-faced nursery maids, that is.'

71

'Have I? I didn't realize. Nothing is wrong exactly, but something has been on my mind. Would you be offended if I asked you to tell me about my mother?'

'Your mother?' He frowned but the look in his eyes was unfathomable. 'What do you want me to say?'

'I know that you intended to marry her, but Lady Vaughn had other plans for her younger brother and persuaded you to leave the country. Which was pretty poor of you by the way, though I have since forgiven you.'

'Glad to hear it.' His gaze slid away from her to rest on Arthur, who banged two wooden bricks together with a loud rhythmic clack. 'I've regretted my actions so many times since, wishing I had possessed the strength to defy everyone and make Lily my wife.'

'You were only nineteen, and my mother was younger. It's easier to do what's expected of you at that age. Few of us have the courage to flout convention. I understand all that. What I'm more interested to hear about are the times the two of you were happy. What was my mother like when she was young and daring enough to seduce her employer's brother?'

'Is that what she did?' A wry smile pulled at his mouth as if he recalled good memories. 'Well, maybe you're right. I was a shy, awkward youth in those days and she was – magnificent.' A shadow crossed his features as his mind drifted back over the years. 'I met Lily during the summer after my second year at university. When I stepped out of the carriage onto the Abbey drive, I looked up and saw this devastatingly pretty, fair-haired girl leaning from an upper window. Our eyes met, and I gave her what I thought was my most charming smile, but she poked out her tongue and slammed the window shut.' He chuckled, his eyes clouded as if he had left her to revisit the moment. 'I was completely smitten from that moment. Lily was impulsive, adventurous, and even rebellious at times. Much like you, in fact.'

Flora's cheeks warmed at what he obviously meant as a compliment. 'And you didn't change your mind when you discovered she was your sister's lady's maid?'

'That never mattered to me. All we both wanted was to spend every moment in each other's company. George was worried about Venetia as she had a rough time with the birth of Jocasta, and was still recovering. Lily's role had been temporarily usurped by a stern martinet of a nurse, so we were largely left to our own devices. I don't think anyone noticed that we spent all our time together. Or if they did, no one said anything to me.' He reached for his coffee cup, but didn't drink from it, simply held it in his slim, tanned fingers. 'The Abbey was a country idyll and in the long, hot summer days we would sneak into town on the governess' cart for afternoon tea, or go for long walks in the woods, making sure we returned separately, of course. There was no need to ask for trouble.'

'When did it end?' Flora's throat grew scratchy at the emotion in his voice.

'Christmas Eve.' William's brow furrowed as if the good memories had turned sour and he released a long sigh. 'The smell of pine needles still makes me sad. George threw a lavish party to celebrate the season and Venetia's recovery. He invited the entire neighbourhood, festooned the house with candles and a massive tree was set up in the front hall. I returned from university to spend the holiday with the family, though I rarely saw Lily during the week before the party. Venetia had put on a little weight, so Lily was kept busy making alterations to her best gowns.'

'Something I have been trying to avoid.' Flora patted her own midriff.

'Rubbish! You're as slight as a schoolgirl.'

'That's kind but not quite accurate,' Flora said, though the compliment pleased her. 'Go on, you were telling me about the last time you saw Lily.'

'It wasn't quite the last time, but anyway, we had arranged to meet in the orangery after dinner, but when I arrived, she had obviously been crying. That's when she told me she was expecting.'

Flora was tempted to ask how he took the news, but knowing what came afterward, resisted.

'I was shocked, of course,' William continued. 'Delighted too, although I knew there would be hell to pay. I told her I would leave university and we could marry and live on my allowance.'

'Which didn't happen.' Flora sighed as she contemplated how different her life might have been if they had. Different but not necessarily better.

'No.' His eyes darkened as he reached for his coffee cup, as if using the pause to prepare what to say next. 'George's mother was still alive then and the old harridan simply wouldn't hear of her daughter-in-law being related to a lady's maid. Venetia was also outraged at the idea, but given time I might have been able to convince her. My sister, however, wasn't strong enough to resist the dowager countess, mainly because she had already disgraced herself.'

'What do you mean, disgraced?' Flora broke off to wrestle a corner of the blanket from Arthur's mouth.

'She had given George three daughters in five years, but no son and heir to carry the title and continue the Vaughn name. That constituted failure as far as the family was concerned.'

'Did you make any attempt to persuade them to let you and my mother marry?'

'Of course I did!' His brow furrowed. 'I argued and cajoled all that holiday but there was no shifting them. They saw it as a youthful indiscretion to be swept aside in order for me to lead the life they had envisaged for me.' He exhaled in a sigh. 'The life I saw for myself too, I suppose. When Lily told me she didn't want any more rows and upset, that she had agreed to marry Riordan and I was to make my own decisions, I was pretty hurt.'

'She was having a child.' Flora couldn't keep the frustration out of her voice. 'She couldn't wait for you to make up your mind.'

'I know that, but I was young, arrogant and stupid.' William's eyes clouded as he followed the progress of a sleepy bumble bee that hovered over a clump of lavender. For a moment it was as if he had forgotten she was there. Finally, he spoke again. 'George suggested I go to Boston to complete my education, after which I would be taken into the family business. I had this misplaced notion I was the victim; the one who had been abandoned and rejected as not good enough, so I jumped at the idea' He propped an elbow on the arm of the peacock chair, leaned his cheek against his hand and slid his gaze towards her. 'Why do you want to know all this, Flora?'

'I thought it was time.' She chose not to explain about Alice Finch for fear of creating an unattainable hope, or maybe destroying her own. Instead, Flora bent to disentangle Arthur's fingers from the hem of her skirt that he had grabbed with both hands. She swapped the fabric for a stuffed penguin, which he immediately attempted to shove into his mouth. 'Would you rather not talk about those days?' she asked.

'I don't know.' William nudged the baby gently with the toe of his shoe, sending Arthur into a paroxysm of delighted chuckles. 'I never have, so it's a new experience for me. I don't come out of it very well, do I?'

'No, you don't.' She injected a hint of rebuke in her voice. 'Mainly because having you as a father means I'm not descended from the Ulster Scots. And just when I had woven this romantic Celtic heritage around myself.'

'Ah, sorry about that.' William chuckled. 'I'm purebred Home Counties and your mother was born in Surrey.'

'Exactly.' Her smile faded as another thought struck her. 'When Riordan died and the truth came out, would you have preferred to have distanced yourself from me? After all, you chose not to have a family of your own.'

'Of course not!' He leaned across the space that separated their twin chairs and grabbed her hand in both of his, his eyes pleading. Eyes so like her own, she experienced a slight shock each time she looked into them.

'Riordan and I came to an agreement. I wouldn't interfere or make any contact with Lily again. She had made her choice. I returned to Cleeve Abbey as often as I could when you were growing up. More so after Lily disappeared.' He didn't elaborate, but the sense he found it difficult to talk about those days sat in his eyes. 'Venetia had to rein me in on occasion, told me to stop spoiling you. She said if I treated you differently to her girls it would be noticed.'

'*I* noticed.' Although his kindness had confused

her at the time. With hindsight, it made perfect sense. 'Why did you never marry?'

'It's quite simple, and maybe even a little ridiculous.' A slow flush crept up his neck. 'The plain truth is I have never met any woman since who could compare to Lily. I've met lots of lovely, accomplished and intelligent women, but none who made me feel the way she did. I think of her often.'

Flora swallowed, sorely tempted to share her fantasies about Alice, but Arthur chose that moment to grizzle. He flailed his arms and crunched up his tiny features in preparation for a full-blown wail. 'Oh dear, I do believe we're in for tears.'

Before she could react, Milly reappeared like a silent ghost and scooped Arthur into her arms. 'It's time for his nap, Mrs Harrington.' The baby's wail did not materialize and murmuring gentle endearments, the nursery maid backed out of the room.

'See what I mean?' Flora whispered when the glazed door clicked shut. 'It wouldn't surprise me if she was waiting outside the door on alert for the first cry.'

William raised an eyebrow but said nothing, drew his half-hunter from his vest pocket and peered at it. 'Much as I relish your company, my darling. I had better be off. I have an appointment at four.'

Flora was about to say she had one too, but resisted.

'By the way, Flora,' William said when Flora

escorted him back through the house to the front door, 'I shall be going away for a while.'

'Really, where?' She held his driving cap in both hands as Stokes helped him into his coat.

'Are you taking a holiday?'

'Uh, no, it's work-related.' He avoided her eyes and tied his scarf round his throat. 'More ambassadorial dinners, I expect. Lots of hand pressing and small talk.'

'This isn't about Serbian spies again, is it?' A pang of apprehension tightened her hands on the cap.

'No, that situation has quieted down since we arrested that schoolmistress. Though the embarrassment of having my assistant turning out to be one is something I have yet to live down.'

'How long will you be gone?' William always dismissed his role in the Foreign Office as a tedious administrative post, but since his clash with Serbian nationalists during a murder case Flora had helped solve the previous year, she knew otherwise. Under the guise of an aristocrat's bachelor brother-in-law with little interest in politics, William delved into a darker side of the government constantly under threat from foreign radicals.

Flora couldn't forget that after the assassinations of the Serbian King Alexander and his unpopular wife Draga, the year before, rumblings about a coming European war still proliferated.

'A few weeks. Maybe a couple of months. And do take that frown off your face. I shall be in no danger.

In fact I plan to be welcomed into some of the best drawing salons in the world.' He took the cap from her, nodded to Stokes and moved onto the front step. 'I'll be back before you know it.'

She waved him off with a smile that hid a niggling worry. Why did he wait until the last minute before telling her, thus giving scant time to ask questions? Was the fact that he was obviously reluctant to discuss his plans because they were going to be dangerous?

CHAPTER 7

The excited dance and jangle of the bell over the door of Martell's tea room welcomed Flora into its comforting interior. Formerly a private house located near the junction of Ebury and Elizabeth Streets, the front window had been replaced several years before with a wide curved bay with bottle-glass panes. An enticing smell of baking wafted through from the back room.

'*Madame 'Aarreengton.*' The proprietor minced towards her, his dark eyes alight with pleasure at the sight of her, both palms upwards in welcome. He wore his black hair slicked to one side with a liberal amount of pomade, a single lock arranged artfully to one side of a wide forehead. He always wore his black frock coat paired with an embroidered waistcoat; which on this occasion was a vivid canary yellow with blue and green birds poking their heads out from green leaves. 'Yet again you honour me by gracing my *'umble* establishment.'

'I find it impossible to stay away, Mr Martell,' Flora replied smiling. 'I'm ashamed to say your delicious madeleines always draw me back.' Her swift glance around the busy room located Lydia at a table for two, though there was no sign of Miss Finch.

'You're so kind, and the *charmant* Mademoiselle Grey awaits you,' he waved an expansive hand to where Lydia occupied a circular table for two that shared a corner with a voluminous fern.

'Please don't bother to escort me, Mr Martell.' Flora halted him with a hand on his forearm. 'I can see how busy you are. I'll have my usual.'

'*Absolument, ma chère madame.*' He clapped his hands theatrically to attract the attention of a pert waitress in a crisp white apron.

'Have you been flirting with our host?' Lydia's laughter-filled voice rose above the clatter of china and the low murmur of conversation as Flora joined her. 'He always makes such a fuss of you. I swear you must be his favourite.'

'He's such a caricature of the archetypical French waiter.' Flora took the chair opposite. 'It's all I can do not to laugh whenever I see him.'

'Indeed, a prince among the teacups instead of the wine cellar,' Lydia said. 'Not that one ever knows what people are hiding.'

'You think he has secrets?' Flora frowned, half joking.

'Not him specifically, but I've heard,' she lowered her voice, though there was little chance of her being overheard above the clatter of crockery and constant hum of voices, 'there's a tea room owner in Piccadilly who runs a brothel in the apartment above the shop.'

'Where *do* you hear such things?' Flora's eyes widened in shock as she tugged off her gloves.

'Here and there,' Lydia shrugged. 'Shocking, don't you think?'

'And distasteful.' Flora didn't know whether to believe her or not, though Lydia seemed to have a firm grasp on the grittier side of London life. They had met whilst Flora had uncovered a pair of Serbian spies the previous year, one of whom had been the headmistress of the Ladies' Academy where Lydia worked. Since the woman's incarceration, Lydia had run the school with an aplomb that had surprised everyone but Flora.

'What about that woman over there?' Lydia cocked her chin at a woman in emerald green who sat below a large gilt mirror. 'She's quite alone and no one has approached her since she arrived. Do you think she's waiting to be chosen by some predatory businessman who—'

'Lydia!' Flora pressed her knuckles to her mouth to hide a smile, only to raise her eyebrows when a portly older woman joined the lady in green.

'Maybe not a lady of the night.' Lydia shrugged in mild disappointment. 'Though our amiable Frenchman does encourage Emmeline Pankhurst's acolytes.' She nodded at a group of women clustered around a table in the bay window, their heads close together in earnest conversation. 'They come in here all the time. I'll wager they're plotting to wave banners outside Parliament and throw eggs at the politicians.'

'I don't approve of the Women's Political and Social Union,' Flora darted the group a quick look. 'They are too fierce with their policy of civil disobedience. If they start doing what they threaten, they'll put the suffragist movement back years.'

'Maybe it's just posturing,' Lydia suggested. 'Though Mrs Pankhurst has been dragged away by the police several times this year for her public protests.'

'I know. Millicent Fawcett must be so disheartened. After all her years of lobbying the government with debate and rational argument, suddenly her cause has been ambushed by these radicals who want to shock the government into submission.'

'I could not bring myself to harass politicians in the street,' Lydia feigned an exaggerated shudder. 'I would die of embarrassment if anyone I knew saw me.'

'Perhaps you shouldn't stare at them like that,' Flora warned. 'They might take us for potential recruits. Or worse, parliament spies.'

'Don't!' Lydia shivered once more. 'Come to think of it, you haven't been to a NUWSS meeting for weeks.'

'I know,' Flora grimaced, apologetic. 'I'm a dreadful slacker.'

'I didn't mean to criticize.' Lydia's hazel eyes rounded in mortification. 'You have little Arthur to look after as well as that delicious husband of yours. It's no wonder you have no time for us suffragists.'

'More like laziness, I'm afraid. It's not as if I am

particularly busy either. I have so much help in the house, I find myself twiddling my thumbs these days.' Milly's disapproving face jumped into Flora's head, but she pushed it away. 'Are you still an avid supporter now that you and Harry are engaged?'

'I could never marry a man who did not support the movement,' Lydia replied. 'Harry wouldn't want me to abandon the cause either, though he's been distracted lately.' Her hand flew to her mouth. 'Oh, I haven't told you, have I? Harry's uncle gave him a house in Kensington.'

'He *gave* it to him? Lydia, how come you have not mentioned it before? That's wonderful.'

'Because Harry didn't tell me until this week. He says it's not that impressive, that his uncle has owned it for years but left it empty. It's in a poor state of repair so he thought I would be disappointed. He was wrong of course, and the location is lovely, right behind the gardens. When I told him I thought it would be perfect, Harry agreed to have it renovated.'

'What about your own house in Kinnerton Street? Won't you miss it?' Flora loved the compact, three story villa Lydia had inherited from her parents. 'Or isn't that grand enough for the Flynn clan?'

Lydia grimaced. 'You've summarized it perfectly. His uncle's house is twice the size of mine, but is very old fashioned. It doesn't even have gas lighting let alone electricity—' She broke off, midsentence, her features sharpening in warning as Mr Martell approached their table, a tray balanced on one hand.

'I've brought your tea personally, *Madame 'Aarreengton.*' He laid the crockery in front of her employing a series of theatrical gestures. '"ow is your husband and that adorable *bébé?*'

'They're both in excellent health, thank you.' His mangling of her name grated on Flora's ears. Also, as far as she could recall, Mr Martell had not laid eyes on either Bunny or their infant son. 'Our son is thriving. How kind of you to ask.'

'I take a keen interest in my clientele, *chère* madame.' His shiny black eyes surveyed the room as he spoke. 'I like to think of you all as more than mere patrons.'

Flora inclined her head in acknowledgment, while Lydia feigned interest in a flower arrangement on the table. An awkward pause developed in which Lydia rolled her eyes as a signal of impatience. 'Um, Mr Martell, could I ask you to aside two of your *millefeuille* cakes to take away?'

'But of course, though not your usual taste, so they must be a treat for that perky little maid of yours who often accompanies you?'

'You *have* been paying attention.' Flora inclined her head at him, but her sarcasm seemed to pass him by, until finally, the Frenchman took the hint, bowed and backed away.

'I wasn't rude was I?' Flora asked, uneasy. 'But he can be quite intrusive at times.'

'Not at all, simply imperious. Like any lady would be. As I said, you're one of his favourites. And another thing, if I ever have to take a post as a lady's maid, I shall apply to you. Cream cakes indeed.'

'It was all I could think of to distract him. Which will delight Sally, though goodness knows what my mother-in-law would say if she knew. She believes servants need little more than gruel and day-old bread to survive.'

Lydia glanced past Flora's shoulder and frowned. 'He's still staring at us. But then I would be bored too taking orders for tea all day.'

'You've been shopping, I see?' Flora changed the subject, dismissing the Frenchman entirely. 'How are the plans for your wedding progressing?' She took a sip of her tea, closing her eyes briefly as the hot, fragrant liquid relaxed her.

After the investigation into the murder of Evangeline Lange that had brought Flora and Lydia together, Lydia had become engaged to Evangeline's fiancé, Harry, a development not entirely unexpected to all who knew them.

'Slowly.' Lydia studied her over the rim of her teacup she held in both hands. 'It won't be a grand affair either. I've no living relatives other than my aunt in Holborn. Besides, Harry's more distant family might not even come to the ceremony.'

'I take it they disapprove?'

'Not openly. But I cannot blame them. I'm not the catch Evangeline was. I'm a schoolteacher, not an heiress.'

'You're a headmistress at an establishment parents clamour to enrol their daughters at. The school could easily have folded after the scandal of the spying incident, but thanks to you it did not. You should be proud of yourself, I know Harry is.' A charming flush entered Lydia's peach and cream cheeks. 'Besides,' Flora said, eager to reassure her, 'Harry's engagement to Miss Lange was arranged by their families. He wasn't passionately in love with her, not the way he is with you.'

'Do you really think so?' Lydia's high cheekbones turned a darker pink, followed by a shrug intended to be nonchalant but which conveyed an air of despair. 'You should have seen how his parents reacted when we considered Caxton Hall for the ceremony instead of some medieval ancestral church in the wilds of Norfolk.'

'Hmm. I can see that wouldn't be received well.'

'We compromised eventually and settled on St James', but there are still some discontented murmurings about the whole thing. That reminds me,' she glanced up at the wall clock above the counter, 'I'm meeting him in half an hour.'

'Don't for a moment intimate you see yourself as not good enough or you'll be lost forever.' Flora lifted the teapot and topped up their cups, aware she was handing out advice she hadn't heeded herself. Beatrice Harrington's frequent asides that blamed Flora's every inadequacy on the fact that she was raised by a country house butler still rankled. That Riordan Maguire was a widower only made things worse, as if this misfortune was in some way Flora's fault. Since the discovery that

88

she was related to Lord Vaughn, albeit tenuously, her mother-in-law's attitude had undergone a subtle change. 'Anyway,' Flora dropped a lump of sugar into Lydia's fresh cup of tea, creating ripples across the surface, 'you have the perfect excuse to buy new clothes, no matter how small the wedding, so make the most of it.' She plucked a shell-shaped sponge from her plate, her attention caught by a chair at the table to her right.

The couple who had occupied it since her arrival had departed, leaving a copy of that morning's paper behind; the page folded open to the sketch of Lizzie Prentice, immediately rekindling Flora's uneasiness about the nurse's death.

'Flora? Are you going to eat that cake or simply wave it about?' Lydia asked.

'What? Oh, sorry.' Flora replaced the sponge on her plate. 'I was thinking about yesterday.'

'Ah yes, I had forgotten. You and Bunny were going to that children's hospital in Southwark. How did it go?'

'We did yes, and it was a most interesting tour, apart from the accident.'

'What accident?' Lydia straightened.

'A student nurse was found dead in the rear yard.'

'Oh my!' Lydia's hand drifted to her throat, the diamond on her engagement ring winking in the light. 'What happened?'

'We don't really know. We were having tea and heard a scream. By the time we got outside, she was just lying there on the cobbles. One of the doctors insisted she had fallen and hit her head, but another one disagreed. What struck me as odd was the way Miss Finch reacted.' Flora bit into a madeleine, almost groaning as the soft sponge melted on her tongue. 'These get better each time I come here.'

'Never mind the cake, I want to hear more about this Miss Flynn.' Lydia's spoon clicked against the china as she stirred her tea faster. 'You wouldn't have mentioned her unless there was more to it.'

'Finch. She's the Matron at St Philomena's who gave us the tour.' Flora hesitated. She had been longing to bring up the subject of the matron since she arrived but maybe this wasn't the time to repeat the conversation she had had with Bunny about her mother. 'I suspect there was something peculiar about the nurse's death. I'm convinced Miss Finch thinks so too.'

'Go on.' Lydia waited.

'I overheard the nurse, Lizzie Prentice, ask Miss Finch if she might speak to her. She said it was important. Urgent was the word she used. Less than an hour later she was dead.'

'Goodness that does sound suspicious.' Lydia's eyes widened. 'Do you know what she wanted to talk about?'

'No, that's all I heard.' Flora paused to wipe crumbs from the corner of her mouth. 'But looking back, I got the impression Miss Finch already knew what it was about.'

'What made you think that?'

'I'm not sure really. After the body was found, she had this look of . . .' she paused, searching for an appropriate word. 'Inevitability. As if she should have done something sooner, and was angry with herself.'

'Definitely intriguing enough to warrant further investigation.' Lydia frowned as if pondering the thought. 'But accidents do happen sometimes, you know.'

'Now you sound like Bunny, and I need a more sympathetic ear for this next part.' She inhaled a deep breath and set her cup down, knowing whatever she told Lydia would go no further. 'This might sound ridiculous, but the second I laid eyes on Miss Finch, I felt I knew her.'

'Knew her from where?' Lydia delicately pulled a madeleine apart with slim, elegant fingers, placing a minuscule piece between her lips. 'And what does this have to do with the nurse's death?'

'Actually, nothing, but please hear me out. Miss Finch looks exactly like a photograph I have of my mother when she was younger.'

'I'm sure lots of people look alike.' Lydia moved the cake away from her mouth but continued chewing.

'It's more than that.' Flora tried to keep the frustration from her voice. 'She looks exactly how I imagine my mother would look now.'

'Flora.' Lydia sighed and replaced the half of her cake on her plate, fastidiously brushing crumbs from her fingertips. 'I love you dearly, but listen to yourself. A woman you have just met looks like your mother might have looked had she lived? That doesn't make sense.'

'Said like that it does sound ridiculous. Thank you for not laughing anyway.'

'I would never laugh at you. You haven't spoken about your mother other than to say that she died when you were young.' She reached across the table and covered Flora's hand with her own. 'Tell me about her.'

'I don't remember much, and no one talked about her when I was a child. I was told she had died, but I discovered a couple of years ago that she disappeared.'

'Disappeared? I assume that means you haven't accepted that she's dead?' Lydia was nothing if not perceptive.

'I find myself thinking about her a lot, wondering what really happened all those years ago. I even questioned William, but he doesn't know anything either.'

'Something tells me these thoughts of yours won't be going away until you have investigated further?' Lydia pressed her index finger to a crumb on her plate and brought it to her mouth.

'You know me too well.' Flora had had become increasingly preoccupied with the matron of St Philomena's hospital. At least she had resisted telling William that she believed his first love might not only be alive, but living and working in London. It was bad enough that her own imagination took flight, like Mr Hedges Butler's balloon, let alone giving him false hope. 'I was strangely tongue-tied during the tour and Bunny told me off for staring at her. Does that sound fanciful?'

'That Bunny would tell you off, oh, absolutely.' Lydia feigned shock.

'You know what I mean.' Flora smiled. 'He thinks it has something to do with my new motherhood. He hasn't been able to put down Dr Freud's *The Psychopathology of Everyday Life* since it came out last year. Whenever I use a wrong word or say something out of context, he snatches off his spectacles with a triumphant "Ah-ha", followed by his theory as to why I have said it.'

'I do so adore Bunny.' Lydia's uninhibited laugh brought enquiring glances from nearby tables. 'His devotion for you shines from his eyes whenever he looks at you. Makes me quite shivery.'

'Harry looks at you like that, I've seen him.'

'Maybe.' Lydia released a heartfelt sight. 'Though sometimes I wonder if he's thinking of Evangeline. He was distraught when she was killed, so much so he and her father haunted the police station for days demanding to know what they were doing to find her killer.'

'That's understandable. They suspected Harry for a while, and he had to clear his name.'

'You don't think it was more than that?' Lydia's eyes pleaded for reassurance. 'Suppose he never gets over her?'

'He already has, Lydia, you mean more to him than Evangeline ever did. Theirs was an engagement of assets, not hearts.'

Harry's engagement to Evangeline Lange had been arranged by their families, one which had been cruelly ended by Evangeline's murder at the hands of her half-brother. A crime Flora had been instrumental in solving and had almost meant disaster for both herself and Sally. Lydia's subsequent grief at having lost her close friend and Harry's guilt at not having protected the woman he was to marry but did not love, had brought them closer together.

'I suppose so.' Lydia helped herself to a second madeleine. 'I can always rely on you to make me feel better, but don't think I haven't noticed the way you keep glancing out of the window every few seconds. Are you expecting someone?'

'No. Not at all.' Flora was reluctant to insult Lydia by admitting she had invited her as a subterfuge. She owed her more than that. 'What did you say earlier about meeting Harry?'

'My goodness, I almost forgot.' Lydia gasped and her gaze flicked to the clock again. 'Oh dear, I'm late and I promised I wouldn't be.' Taking a final bite of the cake, she discarded the rest of it onto her plate. Her chair screeched across the floorboards as she leapt to her feet and gathered her parcels together. 'Let me leave you some money.' She scrabbled in her purse, fumbled and dropped it onto the table.

'Don't worry about that, it's my turn anyway,' Flora waved her away.

'You're so kind, Flora.' She crammed the purse back into her bag and backed towards the door. 'We must do this again – soon.'

The doorbell jangled as Lydia hurried out, colliding with a top-hatted gentleman on his way in, forcing him to swerve in order to avoid her, dislodging his hat.

Flora's stomach performed an odd flip of excited anticipation as Alice Finch entered behind him. An embroidered bag swung from a cord around her wrist as she walked, her head held high and a half-smile on her lips. She wore a pale grey coat, a dusky pink scarf tucked in at her neck, the shade mirrored by the ribbon wound around the crown of her matching grey hat with a jaunty pheasant feather tucked into the side. Buttoned from neck to mid-thigh, the flared hem of the tailored coat swaying with each step as she glided into the room, she was greeted enthusiastically by the effeminate Frenchman, who fluttered his hands as he showed her to a table in an alcove.

Flora debated whether to draw attention to her presence, or wait for Miss Finch to notice her. Undecided, she lingered over her rapidly cooling tea. The low buzz of conversation, the repeated jangle of the shop bell and the clatter of crockery filled the crowded room which had begun to feel uncomfortably hot.

'What are you waiting for, Flora?' she muttered

to herself, picking up her bag and gloves. 'Isn't this why you came?'

Rising, she crossed the room and halted beside the table where Miss Finch consulted the menu. 'Good afternoon, Miss Finch. May I join you?'

CHAPTER 8

Miss Finch looked up from her scrutiny of the menu with a hint of mild inquiry that transformed to warmth. 'Mrs Harrington, how nice to see you.' She indicated the empty chair opposite with an elegant wave of her hand. 'I would be delighted for you to join me.'

Flora sat, conscious their exchange smacked of a performance as she waited for her companion to summon the waitress and change her order, though more tea was the last thing she wanted.

'I hope you enjoyed your visit to the hospital yesterday,' Miss Finch said when the girl had left. 'And your handsome husband, of course, he of the unusual Greek name.'

'He did indeed, and although he interrupted me at the time, we call him Bunny.'

'Ah, I understand.' Her eyes flashed with laughter. 'A schoolboy nickname and now a constant source of embarrassment?'

'Exactly, although most people think it suits him.' Flora busied herself arranging her skirt and bag, while at the same time studying her companion's features from beneath her lashes. Miss Finch had a similar nose to her own and symmetrical arched eyebrows above the same, wide, expressive eyes that confronted Flora in her mirror each morning.

'She looked charming, your friend,' Miss Finch said, making Flora wonder if she had waited outside until Flora was alone.

'She is. And a professional woman like yourself. She is headmistress of an Academy for young ladies.'

'Admirable.' Miss Finch gave the now crowded room a sweeping look that lingered for a second on the beaming face of Mr Martell who still looked their way. 'I do apologize for hurrying you and your husband away from the hospital yesterday, but I thought it best to keep you away from the police.'

'That makes us sound as if we had something to hide, Miss Finch. Though I assume it was because we had nothing to contribute?'

'Exactly, and please call me Alice. I have a feeling we're going to be good friends.' She acknowledged the waitress who lowered a tray onto the table between them, but if she noticed Flora had changed places and was about to embark on another afternoon tea, she gave no indication.

'Do you live near here, Mrs Harrington?' Alice asked once the girl had left, handing Flora a full cup to which she had added milk. 'Oh, I'm sorry I forgot to ask. Do you take milk or do you prefer your tea with lemon?'

'No, this is perfect. Thank you.' Flora sipped the

excellent but unwanted tea. 'I live a short walk away. Yourself?'

'I have lodgings in Birdcage Walk.'

'Really? Isn't that near St James' Park?' Flora's eyed widened. 'That's quite a way from Quilp Street.' In more ways than one, making her a neighbour of the king. 'Does that not present difficulties with travel and so on?'

'It's quite an easy journey by omnibus.' She twirled a spoon in her cup. 'I like the distance it puts between me and my work. The journey also gives me time to marshal my thoughts in the mornings.'

'How long have you been matron at St Philomena's?' Flora asked, unsure as to where this conversation was headed, although a conviction Miss Finch had mentioned the tea room for a reason persisted. Why had she suggested they meet? To swap trivia about their lives, or something else?

'I trained at the London Hospital where I was a ward sister for several years before being offered the post at St Philomena's.'

'Quite an achievement. Do you have a family?' Flora halted, conscious she was prying. 'I'm so sorry, how rude of me to bombard you with questions when we hardly know one another.'

'Not at all. And no, I don't. I have no parents and had I married, I would have had to give up nursing, something I was not prepared to do.' She offered Flora a plate of almond biscuits before taking one herself.

'Actually, there's a reason I wanted to see you

again.' She picked the biscuit into pieces, though none reached her mouth. 'You see, I have a problem at the hospital.'

Ah, here it comes. 'Yes, I know.' Flora plucked a biscuit from the plate and nibbled at the edge, mainly for something to do rather than from hunger. 'One of your nurses died.'

'Indeed.' She discarded a half-eaten biscuit on her plate with a grimace. 'I'm afraid I don't subscribe to Dr Reid's accident theory. I believe Lizzie Prentice was murdered.'

'I'm listening.' Flora returned her cup to the saucer with a click.

'Indeed, and you are remarkably calm. Exactly as you were yesterday.' Her blue-green eyes met Flora's steadily. 'Most young ladies would have a fit of the vapours at the sight of a body, but you didn't so much as flinch.'

'I wasn't completely unaffected, but yesterday wasn't my first encounter with violent death, Miss F-Alice.'

The woman's eyes widened a fraction, but the gesture appeared more contrived than genuine. She exhaled slowly, as if coming to a decision. 'I have a small confession to make, Flora. I hope I might call you that?'

'I should be delighted if you would. What sort of confession?'

'I read about your involvement in the Evangeline Lange case last year. You played a vital role in exposing the killer, I believe.'

'I did, although it was more a coming together of events. I almost misjudged the situation completely.' Flora buried her nose in her cup, giving this some thought. Her name had indeed been in the newspapers, but as she had remarked at the time, it had been included at the bottom of a column on page five of the *Evening Post*. That Alice had not only seen it but remembered her name sent a trickle of excitement up her spine.

'Dr Reid was adamant Lizzie had simply slipped on the wet cobbles and struck her head, although Dr Marsh disagreed.'

'Did you tell the police Lizzie wanted to speak to you urgently a short while before she was killed?'

'I tried.' Alice's perfectly shaped upper lip curled in contempt, her thoughts evidently still on the police. 'They didn't think it was important. The sergeant decided she must have discovered a thief in the process of stealing morphine from the pharmacy, which is about twenty feet from where she was found. That he most likely panicked and hit her to get away before she raised the alarm. They appear to suspect the whole of Southwark of being opium addicts. I understand their dilemma. I mean, who would have a reason to kill a student nurse deliberately?' She chewed a fingernail, though this gesture seemed out of character with her immaculate appearance.

'Was there anything missing from the pharmacy?' Flora asked.

'Apparently not.' Alice sighed. 'Although our

senior physician declared that proved nothing, other than Lizzie must have disturbed the burglar and he ran away empty-handed.'

'That sounds reasonable. And what *do* you believe?'

'That someone knew she had something important to tell me and didn't want it known, so they killed her first.' She massaged her forehead with one hand. 'Oh dear, said aloud that sounds overly dramatic, doesn't it?'

'Not at all. I was there when Lizzie asked to speak to you. I got the definite impression she was nervous. Have you any idea what she was about to tell you?'

'I'll start at the beginning, or none of this will make any sense.' Alice eased forward on her chair, her elegant hands folded on the table in front of her. 'Some of the children brought to St Philomena's suffer from chronic illnesses which cannot be cured in a few days. We offer long-term care, in that when they are discharged from the hospital we see them at a clinic in an effort to help keep them healthy.'

'That sounds like a good policy, does it work?'

'In the main, yes. Some parents find it difficult to keep the appointments, while others don't see the benefit, or simply cannot be bothered. However, recently, Lizzie had alerted me to several instances of children having missed their appointments.'

'Perhaps their parents didn't feel it was worth bringing them back if they were no longer ill?'

'Which is exactly what Mr Buchanan said when I broached the subject with him.'

'I'm sorry, I didn't mean to imply you are being alarmist.' Embarrassed heat spread into Flora's face until she was sure her cheeks burned.

'In a way you're quite right,' Alice waved away her apology. 'I assumed their parents were too indolent or disinterested to bring them in again. Usually, we're too busy dealing with sick children to worry about the ones who have gone home. Excuses I deeply regret now, since six of these children haven't been seen in more than a week.'

'They've been reported missing?'

'No, that's the problem. I contacted the police, but they said no reports have been made.'

'You aren't to blame for what happens when children leave your care.'

'Maybe not, but I'm convinced something strange is going on. Lizzie was too. She told me she had seen the same man loitering outside the hospital these last few weeks.'

Flora's interest sparked and she leaned forward slightly, her tea forgotten. 'Go on.'

'Lizzie was not the brightest of girls, but she had good instincts. She grew up in Grotto Street; a dreadful place where survival to adulthood is a battle in itself.' She took a deep breath before continuing, 'She believed the man's appearance coincided with the children being discharged. Acting on her suspicions, I visited the homes of each of these children, but in each case, I was given a plausible explanation as to why they weren't there. Two of the boys had begun apprenticeships with a builder. A girl of eleven had been taken into service and one was visiting an aunt. I got no response at the other two houses but the neighbours told me the child I asked about no longer lived there.'

'Something tells me this didn't satisfy you.'

'Six children?' Alice raised a sceptical eyebrow. 'All living within half a mile of each other leaving home in the same week? Indeed it didn't. Also, the stories I was given by the families seemed too perfect, as if they recited what they had been told to say by rote. When I asked for specifics, they simply repeated themselves.'

'That does sound odd.' Flora picked at the tiny pieces of almonds on her plate. 'Did Lizzie say what the man she saw at the hospital looked like?'

'That he always wore a brown moleskin overcoat, with deep pockets, that was too big for him. Something about it having lots of pockets; the sort of garment that might hide a multitude of dubious objects, if you see what I mean.'

'No, I'm not sure I do. Lizzie's information seems quite specific.'

'I thought so too, thus I'm not sure she was being quite candid with me. As I said, she grew up locally, so there's a possibility she knew who he was but preferred not to be associated with him. She also said he frequented a public house called The Antigallican on Tooley Street.'

'Antigallican.' Flora tried the name out on her tongue. 'That sounds like a name contrived by someone who doesn't like the French.'

'That's exactly what it is. A number of public houses were called that during the Napoleonic Wars. Most have changed their names to less confrontational ones since, especially now we have an entente cordiale over the French foreign territories.' She gave an irritated wave with one hand. 'But that's incidental.'

'Did you report all this to the governors?' Flora took a sip of her tea and grimaced when she discovered it was cold, aware that Mr Martell watched them from the other side of the counter.

Alice followed her gaze and stiffened. 'Do you think he can hear us?'

'I doubt it. He's too far away,' Flora said in an effort to be reassuring.

'I'm sorry, I'm so jumpy at the moment.' Alice tore her eyes away from the Frenchman. 'What did you ask me? Oh yes, the governors. As far as they are concerned, the police are satisfied Lizzie died in a botched robbery. They will investigate, of course, but I feel they are looking in the wrong direction. And the governors say those children are no longer our responsibility.'

'Alice, what do *you* think is happening to these children?' Flora signalled to the waitress to bring them a fresh pot of tea. Not that she wanted one, but they couldn't sit there with empty cups in a busy tea shop.

'My heart hopes they are still alive. At least, no bodies have turned up in the immediate neighbourhood. That is to say, no children's bodies. There is always the odd drunk who falls into the river,' she added with pragmatic calm. 'What we need is some evidence to make the police view my theory more seriously.'

Her unconscious use of the word 'we' made Flora smile, but Miss Finch made no attempt to retract it or apologize. It occurred to Flora then that joining forces would be a perfect opportunity to discover more about Alice's past.

'I hope you don't mind my asking.' Her apologetic smile made her seem much younger. 'I didn't know what else to do, not after the police dismissed everything I said. When your name appeared on the visitor's list of prospective subscribers to the hospital, I thought I would ask your advice. However, should you prefer to have nothing to do with it, I quite understand.'

'Not at all. In fact I'm intrigued,' Flora mused. 'What do you plan to do next?'

'I'm not sure, although maybe another visit to the homes of the missing children might be in order. Only,' she grimaced, 'I'm afraid I wasn't exactly subtle with my questions a first time. I doubt another would produce better results.'

'I'm not sure how I can be of any help, although—' Flora bit her lip as a thought struck her.

'You've thought of something. I can tell. What is it?' Alice wrapped an errant curl around her middle finger, a gesture that made Flora's heart skip. She did the same thing herself when nervous or agitated.

'What if I volunteered to go in your stead?' The thought was only half formed but when voiced aloud, it made perfect sense.

'You?' Alice blinked, although Flora doubted her suggestion was entirely unexpected. 'That's reasonable. No one in the area knows you. I must say, though, you don't look much like a slum sister.'

'I beg your pardon?'

'That's what they call the Salvation Army nurses and midwives who visit poor and needy families. They swap food for prayers and promises. Are you sure you want to do this? Bermondsey is not exactly Fitzrovia.'

'I'm aware of that, but why not?' The details crystallized in Flora's head as she spoke. 'I could certainly take food with me to help things along. If these families are as poor as you say, they won't suspect my real motive.' She brought a hand to her mouth. 'I'm so sorry, that sounded awful.' Her rationalization had not seemed quite so bad inside her head.

'Not at all, and you're right. As long as you aren't too persistent with your enquiries. They're a wary lot down there and hiding things from those in authority is a way of life to them.'

'I hope you don't think I would treat this lightly.' The last thing Flora wanted was Alice to think she regarded the enterprise as a game. 'I'm also a mother and know how I would feel if my child had been taken from me and no one was looking for him.'

'Yes, you are, aren't you?' Alice blinked. 'A mother, I mean.'

Flora couldn't recall when exactly she had told her about Arthur. Though she must have done.

'It's an excellent idea. But you shouldn't go alone. I would hate to be responsible for anything happening to you.'

'I'll take my maid with me. I also have a friend who might be persuaded to come too.' Lydia would definitely be eager to help if missing children were involved. The mention of Sally also reminded Flora to collect the cakes she had asked for when she left.

'I'm not sure how much you should reveal to your friend. I wouldn't wish to alarm her.'

'You don't know Lydia.' Flora smiled. 'Besides, she'll get every detail out of me in minutes, none of which would discourage her. She's a headmistress of a ladies' academy in Belgravia, and is also a member of the National Union of Women's Suffrage Societies.'

'She sounds a fascinating young woman. I hope to have an opportunity of meeting her. What progressive company you keep, Flora.'

'I do, don't I?' She contrived a smile as it occurred to her that such effusive praise for her friend made her own character less interesting.

'I really appreciate your help.' Alice rummaged

in the small handbag she had placed on the table between them and withdrew a sheet of paper. 'The addresses are here, together with the names and ages of the children.'

'You came prepared, I see.' Flora reached to take the paper, but at the last second, Alice retracted her hand.

'Oh, I have completely disregarded your husband. What would he say about this scheme of ours?'

'Leave Bunny to me.' Flora plucked the page from Alice's fingers, barely looking at it before she tucked it into her bag. That she had been manipulated reinforced her conviction that she shared a bond with this woman that transcended the formality of strangers.

Alice consulted a fob watch attached to her lapel. 'Goodness, is that the time? I must get back to the hospital.'

'Yes, I must get home too.' Flora scraped back her chair, the sound bringing Mr Martell to their side with the speed of a magician, a tiny white box tied with red and green ribbon hanging from his fingers.

'Have you 'ad a pleasant af-ter-noon?' He eyed them both with interest.

'Perfectly, thank you.' Alice's lips did no more than twitch as she continued past him to the counter at the front of the shop.

Flora took the box from him with a weak smile and followed, annoyed when he remained firmly attached to their side.

'I 'ad no idea you ladees were acquainted,' he persisted, unabashed.

'Did you not?' Flora placed a handful of coins onto the counter, refusing Alice's attempt to do the same.

'Such dreadful goings on at the 'ospital, I hear, Mees Feench.' Mr Martell stepped in front of them as Flora reached to open the door. 'One of your nurses met with an accident, did she not?' He inclined his head, so shiny with pomade the surface reflected the overhead gaslight.

'Accidents happen, Mr Martell.' Flora eased past him and grasped the brass door handle. 'Good day to you.'

'That's the last thing I need.' Alice sighed when they gained the street. 'Gossip about the hospital won't help the donations. The slightest scandal can discourage people from having anything to do with us.'

'I wouldn't take any notice of him, he's renowned for his nosiness.' Flora resisted the temptation to look back, though experienced an unnerving sensation that Mr Martell was watching them through the window. Had he overheard their conversation? Or did he read the newspapers like everyone else?

'Ah, here's my horse bus.' Alice approached the kerb, her arm raised to hail it. 'I really must go. If I have to wait for the next one, I shall be very late.'

'Perhaps I could come to the hospital tomorrow and let you know what I find out?' Flora said.

'Excellent. I'll warn the porter, Forbes, to expect you.' She climbed nimbly onto the platform of the horse bus and turned back with a smile that made Flora's breath catch. 'My dear Flora, I do believe we have a plan.'

CHAPTER 9

Agust of frigid air swept along the hall from the rear door which had been left open. When Bunny had insisted on the installation of the telephone at the Eaton Place house, she had imagined reclining on a chaise longue beside a fire to chat to her friends, not shivering in a draughty rear hall. She would have to convince him to buy one of the candlestick models she had seen on her visit to New York four years before and have it located beside a more comfortable chair in the sitting room.

'Lydia, I wanted to ask how you would—' the line crackled in her ear and she broke off wincing. When it cleared she tried again, 'How do you feel about doing some poor visiting?'

'Even with this noisy line I detect a conspiratorial tone in your voice.' Lydia sounded as if she was in a tunnel. 'Is this another of your murder investigations?'

'Not exactly, and it's not dangerous. At least I hope not.' She bit her lip, glad that Lydia couldn't see the lie in her eyes.

Apart from the odd hiss and crackle, the line

went quiet for so long, Flora was convinced Lydia had hung up the telephone. 'Are you still there, Lydia?'

'I'm thinking,' Lydia said. 'Where exactly are we going on this charitable visit of yours?'

'To Bermondsey, it's an area known as St Saviour's.'

'Why would you want to go down there?' Lydia's shock came clearly down the line. 'Those docks south of the river contain some of the city's worst slums.'

'I thought that was the point of offering charity to the poor.' Flora tried not to sound sarcastic but doubted she succeeded. With a start she registered what Lydia had just said. 'Do you know it?'

'I teach a class on the history of London to my pupils, so, naturally, I'm aware of the industrial area of the city. Are you sure that's where you want to go?'

'I'm positive. What do you say?'

'In that case, we'd better take Abel Cain with us.'

'Abel Cain? How very biblical. Who is he, and is that really his name?'

'It is. He's a carpenter who lodges at the end of my street. He does odd jobs for me and my neighbours in exchange for a few shillings. I'm sure I could persuade him to spare us a couple of hours.'

'Why do you think he would be useful?'

'You'll see when you meet him. When do you wish to go?'

More crackles and hisses meant Flora had to repeat the arrangements for the following morning – twice. When she finally replaced the receiver, she turned to find Sally watching her from the doorway to the kitchens.

'You weren't thinking of going without *me* were you, madam?' Sally wiped her hands on her apron, her brown eyes narrowed with suspicion. 'Can't have you going to a place like that on yer own.'

'You're as bad as Lydia. I'm beginning to feel quite naïve for wanting to go at all. I promise to keep my purse hidden and I won't wear any jewellery.'

'If that's all you're worried about, then you are naïve, whatever that means. A well set up lady like yourself will find worse villains in that quarter than the odd pickpocket. Anyway, I wouldn't mind seeing that Abel again.'

'You've met him?' Flora examined Sally's face for clues but the maid kept her head down.

'He was at Miss Lydia's place fixing some pipes when I took that note round last week.' Sally picked at the paint on the door frame. 'He lives with his mam, and makes cabinets and whatnots out of wood.'

'I'm pleased to hear he looks after his mother. What's he like?'

'You'll see for yerself.' Sally concealed a smile behind her hand, just as a high-pitched shriek came from the depths of the servants' hall.

'Sally!' the voice called. 'Have yer brought Miss

Flora's linens down yet? I want them in this tub or they'll have to wait till Wednesday.'

Sally rolled her eyes and turned away, leaving Flora smiling to herself.

'Since when did you take up charity work?' Bunny asked when they adjourned to the sitting room with their coffee after dinner. 'Have you joined some committee that runs ladies' bridge parties and tombolas?'

'I might have.' Flora picked at the silk bookmark on a copy of *Sense and Sensibility* on the table at her elbow. 'Would that be so surprising?'

'Not at all. Immersing yourself in good works is an admirable way for a married woman to spend her time. And my—'

'—Mother would approve,' Flora finished for him. The very reason she had resisted such activities thus far was because Beatrice Harrington liked to pontificate on how Flora ought to spend her time. The last thing she wanted was to give her the satisfaction her advice had been taken. 'I decided to put my spare time to good use.'

'Really, Flora, how long are you going to keep up this charade?' Bunny's glance flicked up at her as he added milk to his coffee. 'This is connected with Miss Finch at St Philomena's isn't it? Did you go to Martell's this afternoon in the hope of meeting her there?'

'I thought you'd forgotten.' Flora pretended to study a hangnail.

'No, but I was hoping *you* had.' Leather creaked as he adjusted his position in the wing-backed chair beside hers. 'Are you still convinced she might be your long-lost mother?'

'Forget I ever mentioned that,' Flora waved him away. 'She's a charming woman and we got on so well, we might have known each other for years. Does that never happen to you?'

'I had the same instinct about my dentist.' Bunny took a mouthful of coffee, swallowing rapidly. 'Amiable chap. We could have been separated at birth.'

'Now you're mocking me.' Her eyes narrowed, she set down her cup without taking a sip.

'Teasing perhaps, but I would never mock.' His tone softened. 'I was simply pointing out that it's possible to feel connected to a stranger without being related to them. And why do you keep fidgeting? You've picked up your coffee cup twice but not drunk any of it. Is something bothering you?'

'Possibly.' She clasped her hands on her lap and took a deep breath before continuing, 'Alice and I decided the police were wrong about how and why Lizzie Prentice died. That it might not have been a fleeing burglar or as the result of a fall.'

'Have the police changed their minds about how it happened?' Bunny searched her features for some seconds. Then realization dawned and he sighed. 'Oh, Flora you aren't trying to change it for them?'

'Why not? There might have been a very good

reason why someone might have killed Lizzie.' Before he could interrupt, she launched into a censored version of her conversation with Miss Finch that afternoon, finishing with details of the missing children. To his credit, Bunny listened intently, with not a sigh or rolling of eyes to betray his real feelings. She liked to think the mention of the children had altered his attitude. Since the birth of their son his perspective had changed as much as her own.

'What is this work she's asked you to do?' he asked when she had finished. 'And how is it connected to Lizzie Prentice and these missing children?'

'We're going to distribute food parcels in Bermondsey tomorrow and see if we can find out anything.'

'I see, and you thought I might forbid you to go?' His expression remained serious, though his lips twitched. 'Is that why you've been as nervous as a cat all evening?'

'I would have mentioned it before, but, if you recall, the telephone rang just after you arrived home and Randall announced dinner. I didn't want to spoil your appetite, so—' His narrowed eyes halted her prattle. 'And I needed to approach the subject diplomatically.' Flora was about to regale him on the fact he had thus far in their marriage not forbidden her to do anything, and it wouldn't get him far now, but decided not to chance it.

'I hope you're taking Sally with you on this excursion of yours?' His voice lowered into lecture mode. 'You know how I feel about you wandering the London streets alone.'

'You make it sound reprehensible. And of course, I'll take her. Lydia is also coming and bringing someone called Abel.' She moved a dish of biscuits into his reach.

'I was about to suggest taking a policeman, but he's more than adequate.' Bunny took one of the wafer thin biscuits dusted with cinnamon and bit into it. 'I doubt even you could get into too much trouble delivering food.' He chewed thoughtfully. 'However, where Miss Finch is concerned, I don't want you to be distraught when you discover she's been married to a banker for twenty-five years and has six children.'

'I won't be, distraught that is, and she's never married, nor has she any family to speak of.'

'My, you have been busy.' His eyes clouded behind his glasses. 'Is being my wife and Arthur's mother not enough that you feel the need to keep looking for Lily Maguire?'

'How could you think that?' The pain in his face brought her out of her chair and to his side. 'I haven't been looking for her. Only seeing Alice Finch at the hospital brought all these unresolved feelings back. You know I like a mystery and now I have two to keep me interested.' She stood behind his chair, locked her arms around his neck and pressed her cheek to his. 'I love being married to you. In fact, I am entirely spoiled, as I have little to do here when the staff run this house and care for our son perfectly well without me. Besides, I'm not the type to sit and embroider all day, or leave cards all over town on morning calls.'

'If you're feeling undervalued, my love, I could always discharge Mrs Cope?'

'Definitely not.' She hugged him tighter, the prospect of losing their housekeeper unthinkable. 'You know I enjoy solving puzzles. I promise to avoid anything that looks dangerous.'

'I wouldn't call murder investigations "puzzles".' He lifted her hand where it lay on his collarbone and planted a kiss on her palm. 'What else did you and Miss Finch discuss apart from children who don't keep appointments and nurses who die in mysterious circumstances?'

'That was about all, really. Anyway, there might be a perfectly reasonable explanation for the children not being at their homes. And Lizzie Prentice's death could have been an accident. In which case, there's no reason for my involvement, so Miss Finch and I will simply spend a congenial hour together.'

'You're going to see her again?'

'I've arranged to visit her at the hospital tomorrow afternoon to give her a report on our charitable expedition into Bermondsey.'

'From most people that would sound a perfectly harmless suggestion, but not where my wife is concerned.' Bunny snapped open the copy of the *Evening Standard* the butler had left for him. 'All I ask is that you take care.'

'Of course, I will.' She planted a kiss on his cheek. 'And thank you for understanding.' She straightened as something he had said came back to her. 'What did you say just now about Abel Cain? Do you know him?' Was she the only one in her own household who had never heard of this man?

'We enjoy a passing acquaintance.'

'What's he like?'

'You'll find out,' Bunny murmured, immediately captured by whatever was on the page in front of him.

'Why does everyone keep saying that?' Miffed, she retrieved her copy of *Lady Rose's Daughter* and settled to read in a room silent apart from the tick of the mantle clock and the rustle of Bunny's paper.

After the first page, Bunny's joke about Alice being married with six children returned, rendering her unable to take in another word of her novel. Suppose he was right, and Alice Finch was just what she purported to be? What if there was no convenient answer to what had happened to her mother all those years ago? Was she tilting at windmills, as Riordan Maguire liked to say? The room seemed a little darker and cooler than a moment before. She released a sigh and rose. 'I think I'll go to bed.'

'Is your novel not interesting?' Bunny asked without looking up. 'I thought Augusta Ward was a great success in America. What's it about?'

'I cannot concentrate right now, although I'm enjoying it. It's about a woman called Julie, the daughter of a couple who left England in order to be together. Her mother was married to someone else, thus they cannot marry, hence putting Julie at a disadvantage. I've reached the part where she takes a position with an aristocrat who hates her.'

'Echoes of your own life perhaps?' His gaze lifted to hers and held.

'Hardly, and I certainly don't have a cruel employer.'

'I wondered if you had cast my mother in that role.' Bunny smirked.

'Your words, not mine.' Flora tapped his shoulder with the book as she passed his chair on her way to the door, whispering, 'I wouldn't dare.'

CHAPTER 10

'Abel Cain, meet Mrs Flora Harrington.' Lydia's eyes sparkled as she made the introduction on Flora's doorstep the next morning.

A young man in his twenties, with wide, expressive brown eyes and a slightly flattened nose that gave character to his regular but unremarkable features, snatched off a brown cap to reveal toffee-coloured hair brushed back from a square brow with what appeared to be little assistance from pomade. 'Pleased to meet you, missus,' he said in a voice softer than Flora expected.

'And I you, Mr Cain.' Flora exhaled a slow breath, though it wasn't his face which made Flora stare, rather the fact he stood over six feet, with shoulders as wide as a door so she had to crane her neck to meet his gaze. A brown and mustard tweed jacket strained over his muscled chest, while hands as big as shovels rested on the stone pillar. In comparison, even Charles Rolls could have been described as being of average size. 'I doubt anyone will give us any trouble with *him* present,' Flora said out of the corner of her mouth.

'Which was precisely the reason I asked him to accompany us.' Lydia beamed.

Sally bustled forward, ostensibly to help Stokes manoeuvre the cumbersome food basket through the gate, her cheeks bright pink as she stammered a greeting to the young man. No wonder she had been so keen to come.

Flora followed Lydia into the cab that waited on the road, glad she had requested Stokes summon a four-wheeled 'growler' with two horses and room for four passengers, instead of a one-horse hansom.

Having stowed the basket beside the driver's feet, Abel eased his rear end backwards into the seat opposite, forcing Sally into the corner, her hunched shoulders pressed up against the window. A minute into the journey, Flora was about to enquire if she was quite comfortable but changed her mind, as from the sideways looks Sally shot at Abel from beneath her lashes her concern was unwarranted.

'I suggest we begin at Wild's Rents,' Lydia read from Alice's list. 'I doubt the driver will take us to the door, so we'll get him to drop us off in the Old Kent Road and work our way from there.'

Flora swallowed, suddenly nervous that even a London cabby might be reluctant to enter a place she intended to go on foot.

Her trepidation increased once they were the other side of Westminster Bridge and crossed beneath the railway line into Borough High Street where the buildings became muted to various shades of brown and grey overlaid with a layer of soot. The pavements were crowded with grim-faced figures who trudged rather than walked, shoulders hunched and their eyes cast to the ground.

'I 'ope you knows what you're doing bringing these ladies here,' the driver leant down from his seat and addressed Abel, but made no attempt to climb from his perch and open the door.

Abel had not uttered a word on the half-hour journey, and now gave a 'what can you do' shrug as he handed the man their fare. He placed the basket on the pavement before helping Flora and Lydia onto a road filled with horse-drawn carts, handcarts and trams that rattled along, their whistles blowing to warn pedestrians to get out of the way.

Sally only just made it onto the pavement before the driver pulled smartly away.

'Charming,' she said with a sniff. 'Good job we didn't ask him ter hang about.'

'Which wasn't at all likely to happen,' Lydia said, setting off away from the clamour of the main road and down a narrow side street lined with high red-brick walls darkened to a sooty black, the street lamps non-existent.

Flora had imagined rows of neat cottages separated by low stone walls, shabby and utilitarian, but cosy. Instead, she was faced with a double row of tall, depressing tenement buildings blocking out the sky on either side of a dirt road filled with stinking rubbish. Between them ran rows of back-to-back houses that resembled crooked paperboard boxes, the streets little more than dirt alleys.

Women stood around in groups with an occasional grubby child at their legs, their shawls clutched over creased, patched skirts, glaring at the small party who passed in morose silence.

'I'm beginning to feel conspicuous,' Flora complained, accustomed to her own neighbourhood. Her gaze remained averted but for a brief acknowledging nod or a raised hat. Instead of stepping aside to let her pass with a polite bow, the women squared their shoulders and stood their ground, or simply glared as she passed; their bold, impertinent stares making her uncomfortable.

'Whatever you do, keep walking,' Lydia whispered. 'Or you'll be missing your bag and probably a pair of gloves before you can turn around.'

'It's that bad?' Flora grimaced with distaste as she skirted a pile of horse droppings that looked so old, even the flies had lost interest.

'Maybe I'm exaggerating, but it pays to be on your guard. Oh, and the discharge from the factories causes that grittiness in the air. Your eyes will be sore after a while.'

'I appreciate the warning.' Flora blinked, though more from anticipation than real discomfort. 'Do most people here work in the factories?' she asked as they moved along a row of scruffy houses, each of three storeys with one level half-below ground.

'Some do. Others try to make a living by casual work on the docks or the railway. Secure work around here is hard to find.'

'The houses aren't very well maintained,' Flora whispered, indicating the paint that peeled from window frames, broken railings and doors that hung lopsidedly from rusted hinges.'

'The landlords don't care, that's why,' Lydia snorted. 'As long as their rent comes in why should they spend money on paint and window glass?' Her voice took on a cynical edge. 'Those fortunate enough to qualify for rooms in The Peabody Buildings have a better life.'

'Peabody what?' Flora picked her way over a pile of debris from discarded packing crates that threatened to twist an ankle. She cast a look behind her to ensure Sally and Abel were keeping pace, the pair engaged in conversation. Abel's loping stride made Sally almost skip along beside him to keep up.

'Blocks of flats built by some American philanthropist about thirty years ago.' Lydia eased round a deep puddle in the cracked and uneven pavement. 'If you have a secure job, are of good character, you could qualify to rent rooms there. Better than many of the private landlords. Oh, yes and you have to be able to prove you're married to the partner you want to live with. Don't look so shocked, Miss Prim. You'd be surprised how many couples here aren't legally spliced.'

'You're right, I probably would be. What are the

Peabody Buildings like?' Flora couldn't imagine they would be worse than the crumbling, shabby buildings she had seen that morning.

Lydia shrugged. 'Fairly basic, though at least they have indoor plumbing, even if it is a communal standpipe in the hall. Most people rent two rooms, but four is not unheard of, though when they were first built two or even three families had to share a sink on the landing. Changes have been made since those days, with proper kitchens being installed in many of them. You have to abide by the rules though. For instance you cannot nail anything to the walls, even pictures, and if a tenant is ever found to be drunk, he's out. The superintendent keeps an eye on everyone and is quick to report rule-breakers. Oh, and no wallpaper as it might harbour vermin.'

'Which sounds sensible.' Flora wondered briefly how Lydia knew so much about them.

'Sensible? Have you got vermin in your wallpaper at Eaton Place?' Lydia shot her a hard look.

'I very much doubt it – oh yes I see what you mean.' Flora swallowed aware she had insulted Lydia in some way.

A group of ragged children stood at the corner, huddled around what at first glance Flora took to be a man slumped in a wooden crate. On closer inspection, she realized it was a pair of trousers and a torn jacket stuffed with rags and straw. The head was a stuffed sack with a face drawn shakily on it, two bushy eyebrows and eyes fixed on a remote point and strands of brown wool arranged to look like hair sticking out from beneath a faded flat cap.

'Penny fer the Guy, miss?' a child with a dirty face pleaded.

'This is a tradition I do know something about,' Flora whispered, delving into a pocket of her coat where she had placed several threepenny pieces and a few sixpences for just such an occasion. 'Where do they burn the Guys, not in the streets surely?' She glanced round at the narrow streets with their dilapidated houses, brick walls and cobbled alleys full of rubbish.

'They'll find a patch of waste ground somewhere to build their bonfire.'

''S'only a penny, miss,' the smallest of the group said. 'Don't need no discussion 'bout it.'

'Don't you go cheeking the lady,' Sally snapped, sending him back a pace.

'It's all right, Sally.' Flora couldn't help admiring the boy's confidence. 'Here.'

His eyes followed the course of the dull brass-coloured coin as it spun in the air towards the hat, his mouth breaking into a wide smile.

'Cor thanks, missus!' He pushed up the brim of his hat and gave her a triumphant smile.

'You're too soft, Flora.' Lydia tucked her arm through hers and pulled her away. 'You'll see a lot of begging before the morning is over. Don't be too free with your generosity, or you'll run out of coins in no time.'

'It's a tradition, and besides, I don't regard a penny for the Guy as begging,' Flora said.

'I suppose you're right, and I used to do it myself when I was young. We put potatoes into the base of the bonfire before it was lit, so by the time the flames burned down, they were cooked to perfection.' Lydia brightened a little at the memory. 'I still don't think baked potatoes without that hint of ash taste quite the same.'

The row of terraced houses on the next street was in a far worse state of repair than the ones they had just left. The plaster had broken away in places, leaving patches of lathe showing through. Windows grimy with dirt made them almost impossible to see through and some had no glass at all, only a sheet of sacking fixed with nails to split and rotting frames. Lopsided steps led to cracked and split wooden front doors offering little or no protection from intruders. Shabby, faded clothes in dull colours hung from lengths of string slung between windows.

The slippery ground underfoot dipped in the middle, where rainwater and rubbish had accumulated and spread. The smell of damp wood, ordure and boiled cabbage dominated, overlaid with more earthy, feral smells that made her eyes water.

Flora's foot slipped in a pool of greasy water and she stumbled, steadying herself with a hand on the nearest wall. Something small and brown scurried out from a hole in a nearby wall and ran close to her foot.

'Is that a rat?' Flora gasped, pointing, though whatever it was had gone.

'Possibly,' Lydia said, cheerfully.

'Have you hurt yourself, miss?' Abel sprang forward, a frown of concern in his brown eyes.

'A minor slip that is all, but thank you.' She waved him away, watching as he dropped back to walk with Sally, her face turned up to him in infatuation. 'I cannot wait to get home and have a hot bath.' Flora shuddered as she picked her way across a dirty puddle. Not a blade of grass or even a weed broke the flat grey buildings. A tree would suffocate among these streets where so many were forced to live in such depressing surroundings.

'A luxury most people down here don't enjoy.' Lydia's voice took on a sharp edge. 'Have you any idea how much it costs to heat coal for hot water? Let alone the price of soap in relation to an ordinary family's weekly income?'

'I didn't mean to suggest anything.' Flora slowed her steps, startled by Lydia's tone.

'This is the first address on your list.' Either Lydia didn't appear to notice Flora's surprise, or chose not to as she pushed open a lopsided gate with its middle spars missing.

The house was narrow, little more than the width of a door and a small window, set between two waist-high walls forming barriers between neighbours. The bowed step bore the indentation of many feet, and in the absence of a door knocker, Lydia rapped her fist hard on the split wood.

'It's very quiet.' Flora looked up at the blank windows, sensing silent watchers on the other side. 'Sinister almost.'

'Most people will be at work at this time of day,' Lydia said, when the front door remained stubbornly closed against her onslaught, its peeling paint showed it had once been a darker colour. 'Those who have jobs that is. Women and children too.'

'I feel it's wrong that such young children should have to work so hard.'

'Children to us, maybe, but to the factory owners, a nine-year-old is perfectly capable of working a ten-hour day at the ovens.'

'I thought the 1880 Education Act put them in school where they belong at that age?' Flora worried her bottom lip with her teeth as guilt made her question why she had not given the matter more thought until now.

'Legally, yes. But plenty are forced to earn a living to help support their families. It's the way of the world.' Lydia heaved a sigh. 'Of this one anyway. It's a different country down here.'

'You appear to know a great deal about life here.' Flora stole a glance at her friend's impassive profile, intrigued, but before she could question her more the door squeaked open on rusty hinges revealing a man in shirtsleeves and waistcoat, his eyes narrowed at them in suspicion.

131

'What do ye want? Me rent's paid up till the end of the week.'

'It's not about your rent, Mr Fletcher, I assure you.' Flora pretended to consult the list Miss Finch had given her, although she had memorized it. 'Is this where Albert Fletcher lives?'

'Bertie is me sister's boy. She passed away three years ago, may she rest in peace.' The scepticism in his voice suggested this was in debate. 'I'm Joe Briggs.'

'My apologies, Mr Briggs.' Flora summoned her most winning smile. 'I was given this address by St Philomena's Hospital. We believe Albert recently suffered a bad case of bronchitis.'

'He did that, but they fixed him up at the 'orspital. What do you want wiv 'im?'

'I'm glad to hear your nephew is better, Mr Briggs.' At her signal, Abel handed her the basket. 'We brought some food to expedite his recovery.'

'Ye'd best come in.' He cast a swift glance at the alley over their heads before he stepped back and nodded them inside.

Sally and Abel remained outside, though even with the three of them the tiny front parlour still felt cramped. The house appeared to consist of one room with a door in the rear left open to reveal a tiny scullery with a cracked porcelain sink beneath a grimy one-paned window. A step in one corner with a rickety wooden door that only just covered the opening led to a narrow staircase that wound sharply upwards. Flora

132

speculated that there was no more than one room above and, apart from the scullery, only an outside privy in a paved rear yard.

A set of uneven shelves had been nailed to the wall above a scarred dresser containing a meagre collection of miscellaneous pots and a pair of dull pewter candlesticks with snubs of burned-down candles. The walls had been papered sometime in the distant past, the ghost of a pattern still visible in the corners.

A scratched wooden table and three mismatched chairs sat under the front window, a home-made rag rug before a tiny grate, now empty. Though the autumn day was mild, damp still leached from the walls to make the room smell musty.

'Take a weight off.' Mr Briggs cocked his chin in the direction of two wheel back chairs in need of some beeswax polish. 'I'd offer yer tea, but this ain't the Savoy.'

'We don't expect it, Mr Briggs.' Flora licked her lips to play for time as she debated how to begin.

'The matron at the hospital told us Bertie had missed his clinic appointment,' Lydia said, displaying no such reticence. 'We trust he hasn't suffered a relapse?'

'He din't need no appointment. Not now he's better and the cough has gone. He didn't go cos I don't have time to tek 'im. I 'as to work ya knows.'

'Of course, although you're not at work now.'

Lydia nodded pointedly at an enamel-faced clock that sat on the mantelpiece.

'Nay, well me shift don't start till three.' His bland expression gave no indication he had just fallen into his own trap. Clinic appointments were always in the mornings, so he could easily have accompanied Albert.

Flora plucked a wood-framed sepia photograph from the tiny dresser; the room so compact, she only had to reach a hand to touch virtually everything in it. 'What a handsome boy?' She studied a fair-haired child of about ten with large eyes and an unsmiling, full mouth. 'Is this your nephew, Mr Briggs?'

'Aye.' His eyes narrowed again, the fingers of one hand flexing as if he would snatch it away from her. 'Everyone says he's a good-looking lad. Most people thought he were a girl until he were five.'

'May we see Bertie?' Flora asked, though she could detect no sounds that a ten-year-old boy occupied the tiny house.

'Nah, he ain't 'ere. He's gorn to stay with me sister.' At Flora's enquiring look he checked himself. 'I mean, me other sister.'

'How nice for him.' She replaced the photograph gently. 'And where does she live?'

'Sussex.' He shifted his feet as if the subject made him uncomfortable. 'I thought the air would do 'im good.'

'That's very considerate of you. And your sister.'

Lydia glared at him, suspicion clear in every plane of her face. 'I know that county intimately. Whereabouts in Sussex?'

'Uh, well.' He performed an awkward twist of his mouth, accompanied by a quick jerk of one shoulder. 'By the seaside it is. He'll get some clean air and be right as rain when he gets back.'

'I'm sure he will.' Flora softened her tone so as to counter Lydia's harsh one. 'When are you expecting him home?'

'I dunno. When me sister sends him, I expect.' He advanced on the basket Flora had set on a shaky table, its surface marked by years of use. 'So, what ye got there?'

'Since Albert, I mean Bertie, isn't here, we might as well go.' Lydia hooked the handle over one arm. 'Good day to you, Mr Briggs.'

The man's face fell and Flora's conscience got the better of her. She halted Lydia on her way to the door, withdrew a brown paper wrapped packet from the basket and held it out. 'Take this anyway, Mr Briggs. And I'm sorry we missed Bertie.'

His expression softened and he muttered his thanks as he shut the door on them.

'Sussex my hat,' Lydia grumbled once they had gained the street. 'I doubt that man has the first idea where the boy is.' She glared at Flora. 'Why did you give him the food after he had blatantly lied to us?'

'I felt sorry for him,' Flora replied, giving the façade of the sad little house a final look.

'Besides, there's not a lot of point taking it all home again.'

'I suppose you're right, and I shouldn't be ungenerous.' Lydia set off at a swift pace down the path, her anger implicit in the set of her shoulders.

CHAPTER 11

The next address on Flora's list was two streets away and even less appealing than the last. The door creaked open on rusty hinges revealing a surly woman who might have been any age between twenty and thirty-five. She smoothed work-reddened hands down a patched skirt gripped firmly by a small child with a face so dirty it was impossible to determine the sex.

When pressed with a combination of Flora's persuasion and Lydia's shortness, she became vociferous in her insistence it was none of their business where her Martha was.

'We were merely enquiring how your daughter fared after she left the hospital,' Lydia trotted out her standard response to open hostility. 'I'm sure some nourishing food would aid her recovery.'

'Martha ain't me daughter. She's me brother's girl.'

'Where exactly is your brother?' Flora asked.

'He went ta find work up north, cos there's been none here for weeks. Not for him anyways, what with his liking for the beer and the foreman at the docks sayin' he ain't reliable. He didn't send me nothing for Martha's keep neither.' She wiped her hands again but it seemed to make no difference to the caked dirt embedded in her ragged fingernails. 'St Phil's fixed her up and when she got home a lady called and offered her a place in service, so I let her go.'

'What lady was this?' Lydia demanded, one brow raised in scepticism.

'I don't recall what she called herself. She came to the door and said she needed a tweenie.'

'And you let Martha go, just like that?' Flora said.

'It were a good position.' She gave the shabby room a cold stare. 'Better'n she gets here.'

'Where did this woman take her, Mrs—' Lydia left the sentence hanging.

'Flaherty's me name. And I dunno do I? Somewhere in the country she said. I've never been further than Deptford so it meant nothing ta me.'

'Surely she told you the name of a town or village?' Flora asked more gently in an effort to dilute Lydia's confrontational tone.

'Don't 'ave an address as such, but Martha promised to write when she could. Now, are you going to give us some of what's in that basket or what? Martha might have fallen on her feet, but I've still got three nippers under four ter feed.'

'Of course.' Resigned but frustrated, Flora beckoned Sally forward. The chances of Martha being able to read or write were slight, but kept the thought to herself.

'That food was meant to be exchanged for information, and thus far we don't have any,' Lydia said when the door was closed smartly on them.

'She looked as if she could do with a decent meal.' Flora looked wistfully back at the house they had just left. 'Even if she did send an eight-year-old to work as a domestic servant.'

'It's not unheard of.' Lydia kept her attention on the list of addresses in her hand as they walked. 'Young girls are often taken on as tweenies and kept below stairs until trained in the ways of the house.' Lydia sneaked a look at her. 'Some don't leave the basement for several years.' She held out the list, a gloved finger pointed at a line of the script. 'Is that a three?'

'Looks like it,' Flora muttered, adding, 'did you notice, that Flaherty woman said "St Philomena's fixed her up"? Mr Briggs used a similar expression in relation to Albert.'

Lydia shrugged. 'It's a common enough figure of speech.'

'Maybe. But Alice said the families she spoke to sounded coached. As if they had been told exactly what to say if anyone asked. The same thought occurred to me just now.'

'I suppose you could be right.' Lydia bit her lip, thoughtful. 'Let's see how we get on at the other places.'

No one answered their knock at the next cottage, but at the subsequent one, a girl of about fourteen opened the door and glared at them with suspicious eyes. In response to Lydia's gentle questioning, she claimed to know nothing at all about a boy named James, roughly quieting a toddler who tried to interrupt. Having contradicted herself twice, she succumbed to panicked nerves and told them she was busy and shut the door.

'Where next, Lydia?' Flora sighed, leaving a parcel of food on the windowsill where she was sure the girl would see it. 'Though I feel we are wasting our time.'

'There are only a couple more. Flora,' she began when they had set off again. 'I'm beginning to think Miss Finch was right. There's something odd going on here.' Flora didn't respond as remorse quickened her steps. What had appealed as an adventure when discussed in Martell's Tearoom now struck her as unforgivably patronising when confronted with malnourished people living in these squalid conditions. Her gaze flicked repeatedly to the buildings while she imagined hostile eyes glaring at her from the corners.

'Did you hear what I said, Flora? Lydia guided her into a tenement building that stank of boiled cabbage and stale urine; the dark stairways so caked with dirt their boots hardly made a sound on the treads. 'I don't believe anything we've been told since we arrived.'

'I heard, and I agree with you. I wish I knew what to do about it.' Flora rapped on a door on the second landing which opened with a creak of rusted hinges by a slatternly girl who denied all knowledge of anything before Flora said a word. She persevered but the conversation did not improve and although the woman acknowledged the existence of the child they asked about, she claimed ignorance to his current whereabouts.

Defeated, Flora turned away, the sound of the door closing behind her like a blow to her self-esteem. 'I must get out of this building, Lydia. I'm finding it difficult to breathe.' The shallow breaths she took to lessen the worst of the stink were making her light-headed.

'This block is worse than some, I agree,' Lydia conceded, their footsteps clattering on the concrete steps. 'I could do with some fresh air myself.'

They passed Sally on the landing below them, having been accosted by three barefooted urchins who, aware of 'Slum sisters' in their building, had come to claim what was on offer, while what Flora took to be their mother observed shyly through a gap in her front door. In response to Sally's pleading look as they passed, Flora patted her on the shoulder. 'It's all right, Sally, go ahead and give them some food. In a way, it's why we're here.' Flora had almost reached the main door, when a shadow detached from the wall and stepped in front of her. She gasped, halting as the shadow turned into a figure of a youth who made a grab for Lydia's bag. She was too quick for him however, and backed away dragging Flora with her.

'Get away from us immediately,' Lydia ordered, unflinching.

'Just give us yer purse and we won't touch yer.'

His voice was younger than Flora had expected, his words slurred together. In fact he couldn't have been more than fourteen. Despite the cold day his coat looked thin, exposing a stained and faded shirt and a pair of frayed braces holding up patched trousers that flapped above his ankles.

'He means you too, Missus,' another rough-voiced male addressed Flora.

Flora's mouth dried as a two more figures emerged from beneath the staircase. One was smaller than the first, though all three looked to be no older than their mid-teens, their caps pulled down to hide the top half of their faces.

She clutched her purse tighter to her body, though the couple of pounds it contained would not be such a great loss. What she regretted, in her eagerness to leave, was allowing Sally and Abel to fall so far behind.

'C'mon. We ain't got all day.' The first youth stepped closer. His chin was chiselled and youthful with no stubble, but his voice was hard, pitiless as he hooked a grubby hand onto Flora's forearm.

She recoiled at his soiled hands, the fingernails rimed with black grime, while her attention went to something that glinted in his other hand.

'He's got a knife!' Lydia's voice was low and pragmatic but held no fear as she handed the first youth her bag.

Flora nodded, unable to speak as her throat closed with fear. Where was Abel?

The leader of the group gave an impatient grunt and lunged, his hand closing on Flora's bag. Instinct made her clutch it tighter, creating an awkward tussle.

'Let go of it, Flora. It isn't worth it!' Lydia said beside her.

Her words made sense, but still Flora's fingers cramped onto the bag as if it were a lifeline, her gaze fixed on the youth's grime encrusted fingernails.

Vaguely the sound of footsteps intruded and with a furious growl, Abel lunged past her into the first youth and slammed him against the wall. One hand on his throat, with the other he shook a clenched fist beneath the boy's chin. The knife slipped from the youth's hand and clattered to the floor. Abel kicked it away, sending it skittering across the boards and out of reach.

With the grip on Flora's bag released, she clutched it tighter and eased closer to Lydia, unable to tear her gaze away from Abel. In horrified admiration, she watched him drag her attacker across the floor by his neck. With his free hand, he opened the main door, jammed it with one foot and hurled the youth outside.

The other two had backed into a corner, where they exchanged a look that contained a message. Apparently the pair did not lack courage, for in the mistaken belief they could take Abel on if they worked together, they lunged simultaneously. One latched onto Abel's back from where he aimed punches, the other grabbed his leg and hung on as if he hoped to bring the big man down.

Abel fended them both off easily, his answering blows more causal defence than an actual fight, resulting in a series of shocked yells, grunts and thumps as the youths hit the floor.

A movement brought Flora's gaze to the landing, where Sally stood motionless, though her face exhibited neither fear nor surprise, only a quiet confidence as she watched Abel deal with their attackers.

The youths' attempts at resistance ceased within a surprisingly short time. One scrambled away on all fours into the space beneath the concrete stairs, his face a picture of blind panic. He stared wide-eyed at Abel for a few seconds, then turned and bolted through the door that slammed back into place with such force, the frame rattled.

The third youth was on his knees, bent over and retching, though Flora didn't recall the blow which had felled him.

'Go on, get off out of here before I call a constable,' Abel snarled, his chin cocked at the door.

'Can't—' The youth bent double gasped. 'Can't-get-me-breaf.'

Abel grunted, grabbed him by the scruff of his neck with one hand and, holding the door open with the other, propelled him through helped on his way by Abel's boot connecting with his rear end.

'I should by rights tell you that was totally

unnecessary, Abel,' Lydia said, a shaky laugh in her voice. 'But in the circumstances they deserved it. Goodness knows what they might have done had you not arrived in time.'

'Oh, I don't know. I was horrified at first, but that last scuffle was quite exhilarating.' Flora smoothed down her rumpled coat, her confidence returned. 'I doubt you could have carried out your threat to summon a constable. We haven't seen one since we got out of the cab.'

'I heard them from the landing.' Abel retrieved the knife from the floor, a light, badly made, cheap object which looked far less threatening than it had a moment before. Abel's upper lip curled in disgust as he slipped the object into his pocket, pushing his other hand through his brown hair. It refused to stay in place and flopped over his forehead. 'Are you ladies both all right?' he asked, almost as an afterthought. His eyes lit with a keen intelligence she had not noticed before. There was evidently more to this young man than she had imagined.

'Perfectly, thank you, Abel,' Flora said, relieved. 'I'm surprised the entire building hasn't come running to see what all the noise was about.' She searched the upper landings for curious faces but no voices could be heard, not even the sound of a door opening reached them.

'Doubt it,' Sally descended the remaining steps, the basket held awkwardly in both hands. 'More likely they'd lock their doors and pretend not to notice.' Her eyes shone with admiration as she sauntered past Abel, throwing him a shy look from beneath her lashes.

Flora bent to retrieve Lydia's bag from where the youth had dropped it on his undignified exit. 'It's a bit grubby, I'm afraid, but will clean up again.' She handed it back to Lydia, unwilling to admit that nausea still gripped her lower belly at the thought of what might have happened had not Abel been there.

'I told you he'd be useful to bring with us, didn't I, Flora?' Lydia brushed dirt from the tapestry bag with her gloved hand, displaying no trace of nerves.

'You did indeed.' Flora stepped into the street, relived there was no sign of the three youths. Never again would she dismiss Bunny's repeated warnings that she not wander London streets alone as unnecessary fussing.

'I suggest you stay close to me, ladies.' Abel herded the three of them in front of him like a sheepdog. 'Tough neighbourhood is this.'

CHAPTER 12

'What did you think of that old woman at the last place,' Flora asked, her eyes on her feet as they negotiated the slippery front steps of a house they had just left in Tabard Street. 'She seemed more confident than the others.'

'Maybe,' Lydia said, sceptical. 'I still didn't believe her story about her son having been accepted into an apprenticeship. Robbie Homes is seven and she's sixty if she's a day.'

'I thought she looked scared.' Sally rested the basket on the ground, stooping to rearrange the parcels inside, separating the meat packages from the fruit.

'Abel might have been responsible for that,' Flora said. The way he lounged against the door frame and picked his fingernails with a file was enough to frighten anyone.

'It were more than that.' Sally threw a guarded look at the street behind them. 'Someone's told her not to talk.'

Flora's stomach shifted uneasily, one hand rubbing her upper arm with the other as small tremors ran along her skin. The morning had taken a sinister turn after the attempted attack in the stairwell. Now she longed to be back at home.

'You could be right, Sally.' Lydia had lost none of her composure. 'I had the same feeling. Although not everyone finds us unwelcome.' She cocked her chin at a girl of about eleven who leaned against a gatepost on the other side of the road, watching them. She wore a faded green dress a size too large for her beneath a shapeless cardigan that hung unevenly, caused by a rip above the pocket. Her scrawny legs stuck out from an ankle-length skirt, ending in bare, dirty feet. Shrewd brown eyes looked out at them from beneath toffee-coloured hair that was in dire need of a wash.

Flora assumed that any approach they made would send her off into the maze of alleys, but after a silent exchange that felt like a challenge, the girl pushed away from the low wall and sauntered towards them, her chin stuck out belligerently. She halted in front of Abel, her head tilted back as far as it would go without losing her balance.

'You was the one who saw off those Clay boys, didn't cha? Never seed 'em so scared. They won't stop till they reach London Bridge at the rate they was going.' She folded her scrawny arms across her chest without a trace of nerves. 'What they bin feeding you?'

Sally snorted and Lydia gave a ladylike giggle behind a hand.

Abel muttered what sounded to Flora like,

'cheeky mare', his face a picture of both surprise and admiration.

'You're from St Phil's aren' cha?' the girl addressed Flora. 'You here about Annie?'

'Who's Annie? ' Flora bent forward, putting her eyes on a level with the girl's.

'My friend who lives there.' She aimed a backward wave in the direction of a building with a lopsided wooden door that might once have been painted green but showed mostly bare wood. 'She's my friend, but she's not there no more. I bin looking for her.'

'What's your name?' Flora asked gently, though at the same time took a step back to avoid any lice which might have taken up residence in the girl's thatch of hair.

'Ada, Ada Baines.' She swiped a grubby sleeve beneath her nose, but her gaze didn't waver from Flora's.

Lydia consulted the list, but looked up and shook her head.

'What made you think we were from St Philomena's? Was this friend of yours ill and was taken there?'

'She took herself.' Ada's eyes glinted with scorn, her pointed chin jutted further. 'She don't need no nursemaid. She's twelve, like me.'

'I see.' Flora concealed a smile at the child's irrepressible confidence while at the same time the thought occurred to her that this Annie might have died and no one had thought to inform Ada.

'How long is it since you last saw her?' Lydia asked.

'Two weeks ago, or thereabouts.'

'She could have gone somewhere to convalesce,' Flora said, remembering Alice mentioning the home on the south coast where they sent children to regain their strength.

'Dunno what that is,' Ada shrugged. 'Huggins told me she'd gone, but he wouldn't say where.'

'This Huggins. Is he Annie's father?' Lydia asked.

'Naw. He's her uncle. Or that's what he calls hisself. Took up wi' Annie's mum a year ago but she scarpered last Christmas. Annie doesn't like him.'

'Is there a possibility Annie ran away because of this Huggins fellow?' Lydia asked.

'She wouldn't do that.' Ada's eyes narrowed as if Lydia had insulted her. 'She weren't scared of 'im, she just didn't take to him is all. Naw, the Sally Army bloke and some other chap came to see Huggins when she was in the 'ospital.'

'What Sally Army bloke?' Lydia pushed into the gap between Flora and the girl. 'What was he like?'

'I dunno. He didn't speak to me, but I saw them go into Huggins' place.' Ada's eyes looked suspiciously wet but didn't develop into full-blown tears. 'Annie never came back.'

'Did this Huggins say where she had gone?'

'He said she'd gone into service at some big house north of the river. I told him, Annie and me were

150

going into service together, but he didn't care. Said she was staying with her grandma for a few days before going to this big house. But he's a liar, Annie don't have a grandma.'

A single tear slipped down her cheek, forming a track mark in the grime on her face. 'Maybe Annie needed to work and didn't have a choice?' Flora suggested, though if Annie had gone into service, it wouldn't explain why she hadn't said goodbye to her friend, or been seen since.

'No!' Ada shook her head. 'She wouldn't 'ave left me. We're best friends.'

'Do you remember anything about this other man?' Flora asked. 'The one who was with the Salvation Army Officer?'

'Seen him about a few times.' Ada shrugged and swiped a hand beneath her nose. 'Short, stocky bloke in a brown coat and cap. Nothing special.' She seemed to give the matter some thought, then her eyes lit as she recalled a memory. 'He's got funny eyes. Like this.' With unnerving skill, Ada made one eye slide inwards.

Flora's pulse quickened. Could he be the man Lizzie Prentice saw at the hospital? A stocky man with a squint shouldn't be hard to locate. Or was she being optimistic?

'He drinks at the Corks.' Ada eyed the basket Sally held, prompting her to pull it protectively closer. 'But I dunno where he lives.'

'Corks?' Flora frowned. 'What's that?'

'The Corks Galleon, down that way.' She hooked

a none-too-clean thumb in the direction of the main road.

'She means The Antigallican,' Lydia said. 'It's what the locals call the public house on Tooley Street.'

'Alice mentioned that place to me at the tea room.' Surprised that Lydia not only knew of it, but was also aware of its colloquial name.

'His name's Swifty Ellis.' Ada brought all eyes swivelling in her direction. When no one spoke she blew out a frustrated breath. 'The man wiv the funny eyes.'

'Why didn't you say so at the beginning?' Lydia gripped the girl's upper arm, giving her a tiny shake.

'Di'nt ask.' Ada rolled out of Lydia's hold and rubbed the spot where her fingers had been.

Flora found Lydia's lack of sympathy puzzling. Firstly with Bertie's uncle and now this scrap of a girl, whose only concern appeared to be the whereabouts of her friend, but this wasn't the time to mention it.

'I see, well, thank you, Ada. We'll be sure to ask about Annie.' Flora turned away, dismayed that they had yet another name to add to their list.

'S'cuse me, miss?' Ada called her back. 'Can I have some o' them little oranges?' She indicated the basket hooked over Sally's arm. 'You're giving them away aren't cha?'

'Oh, yes of course.' Embarrassed she had not thought of it herself, Flora reached into the basket and retrieved four pieces of fruit, together with one of the paper-wrapped parcels. 'There are some sausages too, I expect your mother can cook those for you.'

'Don't be daft.' Ada gathered her skirt into a scoop to hold her prize. 'Me mum's doing a double shift at the pub. I'll cook 'em meself.' She shot Abel a steady stare before darting through a rickety gate into another faceless building opposite.

'Remind me not to patronize children again,' Flora said, tucking her free arm through Lydia's.

'They grow up fast round here.' Lydia sighed. 'She's probably older than she looks too. Their poor diet means they grow slower than most children.'

'That didn't occur to me.' Flora sighed. Her attitude to those less fortunate than herself needed some radical rethinking. Her own childhood had not been privileged by any standards, but she had never had to wear rags or go hungry. She realized then how she had taken her own advantages for granted and not paid enough attention to those who had so little. Poor didn't just mean a lack of luxury, fewer choices, and sparser homes. Poverty was insidious, it hardened the spirit, killed the joy of life and withered souls. Flora had the freedom to walk away, but that child and many like her had no choice.

'Are you all right, Flora?' Lydia asked. 'Not still worried about being robbed, are you?' Before she could answer, Lydia went on, 'Those three will have spread the word by now to give us a wide berth. No one will trouble us again.'

'I doubt we'll discover anything more here, so we may as well go back to Eaton Place.' Flora gestured to Sally to retrieve the basket.

'At least we *can* go home. We aren't trapped in this place like that poor scrap back there,' Lydia said, a half-joking remark that only increased Flora's melancholy. 'Are you sure you don't you want to go to the hospital first and tell Miss Finch what we have found out?'

'That was the plan, but this venture hasn't been as successful as I imagined.' Flora sighed. 'All I want to do now is go home. Do you mind?' She experienced an overwhelming need to retreat to her comfortable house where she could relax, cuddle her baby and feel safe in familiar surroundings. As they made their way back to the Old Kent Road and the promise of a cab back to Belgravia, she acknowledged this was a selfish need, but a real one.

'Have you thought,' Lydia said after a moment. 'That the girl, Ada, might have made up the story about this Annie so you would hand over some food?'

'Do you really think that?' Flora searched her face for signs she believed this herself, but Lydia's pragmatic calm persisted.

'I'm not saying she's deceitful, but you don't know these people. A stranger's finer feelings play no part in their fight for survival. Especially if that stranger is better off than they are. They do what they have to. I'm not judging, Flora, I'm simply stating the truth.'

'I don't really care if Ada did make it up, and at least she'll get a decent meal inside her tonight.' She slowed her steps as she gave the idea some thought. 'I don't think she made up the man with the squint. What was his name again?'

'Swifty Ellis, I wrote it down.'

Their walk had brought them to a short parade of shops with peeling paint, ancient posters and dusty windows which made it almost impossible to see what was stacked behind the glass. Wooden boxes of gnarled vegetables, fruit and racks of second-hand clothes were spread out on the pavements in front.

'Lydia? How do you know so much about this place and how these people live?'

She looked about to make some throwaway remark but checked herself and cast a quick glance behind her to where Abel and Sally followed as if establishing they were out of earshot. A few seconds passed as she appeared to come to a decision.

'I haven't always lived in Kinnerton Street.' She kept her gaze straight ahead so all Flora could see of her expression was her calm profile. 'I was brought up not far from here, in Peabody Buildings in East Lane where the rope factory is.'

'Really? I-I had no idea.' Flora stared round at the faded buildings, the piles of ordure at the kerbs and the too thin horses who pulled carts and even thinner children. She longed to ask how a soft-spoken, gentle soul like Lydia had escaped from this place to a neat little house in Belgravia.

'Why should you?' Lydia shrugged. 'I don't talk about it. I put the past behind me a while ago so it wouldn't colour the rest of my life. I got out. Many don't.' Her tone was flat, emotionless, as if she spoke about someone else.

'What was it like?' Flora couldn't resist asking as she tried to imagine Lydia as a child with wayward brown hair and dirty bare feet like Ada, but the image refused to form.

'My father was a foreman at the Peek Frean's factory on Clements Road when I was a nipper. He earned a regular wage so my parents qualified for the Peabody. We rented four rooms on the first floor.' Lydia paused in the road and lifted her face to the sky. 'Can you smell that?'

Flora took a tentative breath. 'Sulphur, soot and manure?'

'No not that.' Lydia laughed. 'That sweet baking smell is from the biscuit factory. It carries all the way back to Jamaica Road. It's stronger on some days, depending on the direction of the wind.'

Flora recalled something Bunny had said about this area being known as 'Biscuit Town' but had to concentrate on keeping up with Lydia who had not slowed her pace as she talked.

'In summer, my friends and I would walk home from school past the open doors of the factory. Rows of girls in white aprons packed the biscuits and we'd beg for broken ones.' Her smile turned wistful. 'I cannot look a garibaldi in the face to this day.'

'I'm sorry. Perhaps I shouldn't have asked you to come with me this morning.' Flora tucked her arm through Lydia's and pulled her closer.

'I wanted to. If children are being taken, I want to help. Most people here are honest, hard-working folk who live for their families and care for them as they should. Then there are the others. Those who can never hold down a job for more than a few weeks, who get poorer and less caring, but the children keep coming and they don't know how to stop it. Each year there's another mouth to feed, or in some cases, another pair of hands to send out to thieve for them. There's no one for them to complain to, much less care.' She slowed her steps, her chin lifted as she met Flora's gaze. 'I don't ask for sympathy, Flora, I thought I had left all this behind, but seeing young Ada reminded me of some things that are too much part of me to forget. I'm not saying it was that bad for me because it wasn't. I was lucky. My parents loved me, and I was an only child, so I didn't have to share a pallet bed with three or four others. Some of the children at the school where I taught came from homes like Ada's.'

'You taught school here?'

She nodded. 'I began my teaching career in Bacons Free School, founded by the guild for the tannery workers at Weston Street. If you want to know what life in a place like this really means, ask Sally. She was raised in Whitechapel, so her childhood must have been similar to mine. Probably worse, at least there are jobs to be had here.'

'Perhaps I shall.' Flora looked back over her shoulder to where Abel and Sally walked about ten paces behind; the top of Sally's head bobbed in line with Abel's shoulder, her face animated as she chattered with the basket slung between them. She had tended to dismiss Sally's outrageous-sounding claims as an exaggeration, or a call for attention. Something she would never do again.

'I wish you had told me, Lydia. Why did you feel the need to hide your upbringing from me?' Flora couldn't help feeling slightly hurt, and that she was being condescended to. 'I'm hardly gentry. I was raised in a servants' hall.'

'You were a governess, an upper servant, which isn't quite the same thing. You also lived in the country, with fresh air, clean water, space to run and play and the best food available. Now look at you. The daughter of a gentleman, married to a solicitor and your uncle is an earl.'

'I suppose you're right. But whatever you had told me about your past I wouldn't have judged you for it.'

'I know that, but it was more about me than you. I found it hard enough telling Harry.'

'How did he take it?' No wonder Lydia felt inadequate to Harry's previous fiancée, who had been a considerable heiress.

'Wonderfully well.' Lydia laughed. 'His family are high society now, but he told me when he was a boy, he discovered his great-grandfather earned his fortune from cotton mills and mining. He was a self-made man who treated his workers abominably. The family don't want it remembered or talked about, which is why they were so keen for him to marry Evangeline, whereas I'm a bad influence.

'You're no such thing, and Harry doesn't have anything to apologise for.'

'That's what *I* said, but somehow he feels he owes something to the common working man. He's an advocate for the Member of Parliament for West Ham, whose name escapes me for the moment. Keen something.' She tapped her bottom lip with a finger. 'No, Keir, Keir Hardie, that's it. He's Scottish, I think. Harry's parents were scandalized when he expounded the man's policies over dinner.'

'Oh dear, that must have been a difficult meal. Will Harry join the Labour Party?'

'I doubt he would go that far, but he might consider running for a Liberal seat. That way there would be less risk of him being thrown out of his club.' Lydia smothered her laugh with a gloved hand. 'Sorry, I'm being flippant, which isn't fair as Harry is quite serious. He feels the country will undergo vast social changes before long.'

They had reached the corner where the main road teemed with fast moving traffic, where no less than three road sweepers were kept busy clearing manure from the paths of pedestrians.

'I think that's enough about me for one day, don't you?' Lydia said, halting at the kerb. 'We have more important matters to deal with. I've been thinking about that Ellis character. He could be a local bully boy. He probably works for someone who can afford to hire henchman to do his dirty work.'

'What kind of dirty work?' Flora felt out of her depth, having only a vague idea of what Lydia was talking about.

'If he's the man who was seen outside the hospital, he might be what is called a procurer. What we need to know is, for whom.'

'Like a gang, you mean? That makes sense. How do we find out?'

'I don't know. We'll have to think about it more.' Lydia beckoned to where Abel and Sally had caught up with them and had paused a few feet away. 'Abel, could you flag down a cab?'

'Thank Gawd for that,' Sally released a heartfelt sigh, dropped the basket on the pavement and slumped onto a discarded packing case set against a wall. 'Me plates are killin' me.'

'What did she mean by that?' Flora whispered.

'I'll explain later.' Lydia smiled and patted Flora's arm.

CHAPTER 13

Locating a hackney in the bustle and clamour of Jamaica Road proved more difficult than Flora had imagined, even with Abel doing the hard work for them. Thunder groaned ominously overhead and a sudden burst of rain drove them to shelter beneath a shop awning.

Lydia indicated a horse bus that had pulled up several feet away. 'Never mind a cab, Abel. We can take that, it's going our way.'

'I've never been on one of those before.' Flora gazed at the open upper deck, where four men in suits sat beneath raised umbrellas against the rain.

'Regard it as a new experience.' Lydia dragged her by the arm through a rapidly forming stream of water that ran along the gutter and onto the rear platform of the horse bus. Flora worked her way along the narrow aisle, avoiding elbows and wide hats to the empty seat Lydia had selected near the front. Flora's rear end had barely touched the slippery upholstery next to Lydia before the driver pulled away.

'He appears to have taken a liking to your Sally.' She turned her head, nodding to where Abel had hoisted Sally onto the platform beneath one arm at the last second before the vehicle had moved off, somehow managing to keep hold of the basket with the other.

'Would it be selfish of me to hope I don't lose her too soon?' Flora sighed.

'Yes, it would.' Lydia pressed her arm in sympathy. 'Not that I don't understand your point of view. She's become your friend.'

'More than that. She saved my life last year too.'

Lydia smiled, possibly remembering the occasion the previous year when Flora and Sally had been trapped in a cellar waiting for a killer to come and finish them off. It was Sally's optimism and quick thinking that had saved them.

The thirty-minute horse bus ride proved to be more enjoyable than Flora had anticipated, despite frequent stops and the steady rainfall that flowed in rivulets down the windows, obscuring the view. By the time they reached Hyde Park Corner, the deluge had stopped as quickly as it had begun, carving a rainbow in the sky where clouds parted to reveal patches of blue.

'We'll walk the rest of the way.' Flora was appreciative of the cleaner air refreshed by the rain after the cloying atmosphere of the ugly, rubbish-strewn streets they had recently left.

At Eaton Place, she invited Lydia to avail herself of the well-appointed bathroom to remove the street grime from her face and hands, leaving Sally to entertain Abel in the kitchens.

'When we're married, Harry will have to make do with a bowl and pitcher to shave in at my house,' Lydia said. 'I wonder how he'll cope with the outside privy.'

'Won't the renovations to his uncle's property in Kensington be finished before the wedding?' Flora handed her a towel from the pile on her dresser.

'I very much doubt it. The property is in a poorer state than poor Harry imagined.'

'Even so, it's wonderful that you've been given a home in which to begin your married life,' Flora said as she led the way back down the stairs to the dining room.

'I know, although I shall miss my little house in Kinnerton Street. I love it, but Harry's mother thinks he's lowering himself by even visiting me there.'

'Your house is darling, Lydia, and that's a ridiculous attitude.' Flora sniffed appreciatively at the plate of hot, sliced pork and potatoes Stokes set out on the table between them. 'I must say, it's good to be home. I'm still shaky after that encounter in the stairwell. I don't know what I would have done had Abel not been there.'

'It was nice of you to invite him to take his midday meal in the kitchens with Sally.' Lydia spooned vegetables onto her plate.

'Sally looked fit to burst, didn't she? I expect she'll be on her best behaviour for the rest of the week. How long have you known him?'

'Abel? He's lived at the end of our street since

we came to live there and was so kind to Mother during her final illness. He would even look in on her on occasion when I was at the Academy.' At this mention of her mother, Lydia's mouth worked as she fought for control. Mrs Grey had been ill for over a year, but her death five months before had still come as a shock.

'I must remember to recompense Abel for his time,' Flora said briskly, aware Lydia was not the type to indulge in public emotion.

'You don't have to distract me, Flora. I'm all right, really.' Lydia applied her cutlery to the meat on her plate. 'I'm sorry I was so maudlin earlier, but I didn't expect Bermondsey to generate so many memories. This might sound odd, but I didn't see the filth and squalor in quite the same way when I was younger. It was simply home and I knew no better.'

'Don't feel you have to talk about it if you don't want to.' Flora slid the condiment dish towards her.

'It's hardly a dark secret.' Lydia picked at her food with a fork. 'Life wasn't so bad at the Peabody. Though as is the nature of philanthropy, they set strict rules. The worst one for me was having to be vaccinated against smallpox before we were allowed to move in. They scraped a layer of skin off my arm and rubbed it with a quill. Quite painful actually.' She rubbed her upper arm through her sleeve as if reliving the event. 'I still have the scar. It must have worked though, as there wasn't one case of smallpox in the buildings all the time we lived there.'

Flora toyed with her cutlery while contemplating whether or not she ought to have Arthur vaccinated. 'I expect the Peabody Buildings were more comfortable than one of those draughty little cottages?' She shuddered as she recalled the bare walls, cracked door frames and the insidious mildew smell that made her nose itch.

'We had what we needed,' Lydia said. 'There was a cast-iron range, an oven, and a boiler. We had to share a toilet block with other families. Our treat for the week was when Dad took Mother and me to the public baths built for the dockers in Spa Road,' she added without a trace of self-pity.

'You had to go elsewhere for a bath?' Flora asked, astonished.

'Oh Flora, what a sheltered thing you are. This is London. Even some well-off families use public baths. Better than a tub in the scullery. The hot water is pumped through pipes, not heated in pots on a range. Far more convenient, especially for larger families.'

'I suppose so,' Flora mused, wrestling with the concept.

'We had to walk through the railway tunnel to get there.' After Lydia's first hesitant steps into her past, she had got into her stride. 'If there was a train coming when we were on our way back, I refused to enter the tunnel until it had gone by in case I got dirty again.'

'It was the dirt which struck me too,' Flora said. 'The air felt thick with grime that clung to everything.'

'That's due to all the muck churned out by the factories. My clothes were always stiff from the soot and grit ingrained in the fibres. Washing could never quite get it all out. Mother had a friend who lived in the Peabody in Blackfriars Road where we would go on a Sunday afternoon for a visit. I loved those afternoons because they had a garden at the back for the children to play in. It was a modest square of green, but represented paradise to me. At East Lane, all I had was a triangular concrete yard.'

Flora gave her a weak smile, recalling the rolling fields and rose garden she had had to play in as a child; surroundings she had always taken for granted. 'When did you move to the villa in Kinnerton Street?' she asked carefully, unwilling to pry, but eager to know how Lydia's fortunes had altered so drastically. Bermondsey to Belgravia was quite a leap.

'That was unexpected.' Lydia pushed a carrot around her plate but made no attempt to eat it. 'When I was thirteen, Father's mother died. It seems they didn't get on, for reasons they never revealed to me. I knew nothing about my grandmother and we had never met, but Father was her only relative so her house came to him when she died.'

'The first time I saw that little townhouse, I thought we were rich.' Her eyes glowed at the recollection. 'Seven whole rooms for the three of us,

166

bedrooms with real fireplaces and a kitchen with a hot water geyser and a proper cooking range. Even the outside privy was a luxury as it was only for us. We could even afford to hire a maid. I was in heaven. I did so much better in school and Father was so proud when I became a teacher.'

'What happened to your father?'

'An accident at the factory. An oven door wasn't closed properly and—' She twirled her fork above her plate as if she needed time to compose herself. 'He-uh, he was burned. Badly. He took three days to die.' She looked up with a shaky smile. 'The factory took care of the funeral and looked after Mother and me. We didn't suffer.'

'I'm so sorry.' Flora reached across the table and covered Lydia's hand with her own.

'It was a while ago,' Lydia shrugged, sliding her hand from beneath Flora's as if embarrassed to have revealed so much. 'Now. You promised to let me see that lovely baby of yours. I expect he's grown since I last saw him.'

They adjourned to the sitting room, where Milly arrived promptly in response to Flora's summons, her arms full of a boisterous, beaming Arthur.

'Did you really name him after Arthur Conan Doyle?' Lydia held out her arms to take the baby.

'It was quite amusing how that came about,' Flora hesitated, unsure whether to reveal the real story behind her son's name, but settled on the version Bunny liked to tell. 'During the last few days of my confinement, I wanted to read "The

Adventure of Charles Augustus Milverton" in *The Strand Magazine*. I sent Bunny off to buy the latest edition and he arrived back to find the house in chaos. The midwife and a nurse had taken complete control of below stairs with Mrs Cope employing every pot in the house to boil water. It was a private joke at the time to call him Arthur, but the name quite suits him.'

'I agree, and he's adorable.' Lydia cuddled the baby on her knee. 'Goodness he's quite sturdy for six months isn't he?' Arthur had grabbed the lapels of Lydia's jacket in both hands, pulled himself into a sitting position only to collapse before trying again.

'He'll be standing in another month or so,' Flora said proudly. She glanced toward the door, where the nursery maid had faded into the background, reluctant to withdraw entirely.

'Milly, why don't you take a break and have a cup of tea in the kitchens?' Flora aimed for kindly dismissal.

'I've not long had my luncheon, madam.'

'Even so, I'm sure we can be trusted with Arthur for a short while.'

'As you wish, madam.' The girl dropped a grudging curtsey and fled, though her expression remained sullen.

'You still don't like her, do you?' Lydia indicated the closed door while at the same time she unbent Arthur's fingers from her bottom lip.

'I don't have to like her as long as she's conscientious. At least that's what Bunny says.' Flora was reluctant to give Lydia the impression her nurse didn't trust her with her own child. 'And Arthur is thriving, which William noticed when he was here the other day.'

'How is William, and how does he like being a grandfather?'

'He's a little bemused.' Flora smiled as Lydia caught Arthur's hand in mid-wave and planted kisses on his palm, eliciting delighted baby chuckles. 'But he's thrilled too. He not only gave me his mother's diamond necklace, but took me up in a hot air balloon the other day.'

'A hot air balloon!' Lydia's eyes widened, just as Arthur grabbed a hank of hair visible beneath her hat. 'Was it wonderful?'

'I expected you to ask how terrified I was. But yes, it was exhilarating. Almost like flying, but slower and quieter,' though that struck her as an odd remark as how could she know what flying felt like? 'Anyway, we could see for miles and the fact the balloon stayed tethered to the ground was reassuring. Although at first I kept having these images of the rope breaking.' She wasn't going to puncture her friend's admiration by admitting she had gripped the edge of the basket so hard her hands were sore when she got home.

'What an amazing gift. You're so lucky. I would love to do that. Perhaps I'll arrange it as a surprise for Harry. He's always eager for an adventure.' A triumphant smile slowly spread across her face. 'And it would horrify his mother.'

Their mutual laughter sent Arthur into a gale of happy giggles, as if he was the sole cause of their merriment.

'The owner, Mr Hedges Butler,' Flora said when the attention was off Arthur again, 'introduced me to his friend Charles Rolls, who is incredibly knowledgeable about anything mechanical.'

'That chap who wins all those motor car races?' Lydia broke off from blowing bubbles into the soft folds of Arthur's neck.

'The same. He races the cars in European competitions and is the tallest man I have ever seen. Handsome too.'

'I heard Bunny talking to Harry about him. That he and a man called Royce are planning to produce luxury motor cars. You'll need to keep a rein on your husband when that happens.'

'I wish I could.' Flora smiled, but she had no intention of thwarting Bunny's plans where motor cars were concerned. A year after they married, he had postponed his dream of starting a manufactory when it proved to be too risky a venture. Bunny had reverted to the law as a means of supporting them, and although he always claimed he did not regret his decision, she wanted him to fulfil his dream one day.

'Lydia,' Flora began, raising a subject that had niggled at her all morning, 'did you notice that none of the people we talked to this morning were the children's parents?' At Lydia's frown, she continued, 'Albert Fletcher lived with his uncle, and the second girl, Martha, with her aunt. Elsie with her grandmother and Ada told us her friend, Annie, lived with her stepfather.'

'Annie wasn't on the list Miss Finch gave you.'

'No, but that doesn't make her less missing, not if Ada is to be believed. Were they selected because it would be easier to persuade their families to take them if they were there under sufferance?'

'You think they were chosen? For what?' Lydia grimaced as Arthur grabbed her hat and pulled, dragging her head sideways.

'That's what worries me. I know we're supposed to be past the age of shoving small children up chimneys, but there are some equally awful occupations reserved for the vulnerable young.'

'There is also the shocking possibility that their relatives could simply have sold them?' Lydia reclaimed her hat from between Arthur's fingers and smoothed his wheat-coloured hair away from his face. 'Suppose this man Swifty offered them money to buy not only the children but their silence too?'

A cold hand grasped Flora's spine as Lydia's words slammed into her. She had not wanted to face the idea before but what other reason could there be for all six to have disappeared without a trace? Seven, if they counted Annie. Were those people so desperate, they believed it was a way out of the struggle to provide for children who had been foisted on them? Her thoughts went back to the sparse rooms with the ragged curtains like flaps on the windows, the worn rugs, scarred furniture and, in most cases, empty grates. Would she do the same in that situation?

'There's the other thing,' Lydia said, bringing Flora's thoughts back to the present.

'What other thing?'

'The Salvation Army man who went to see Annie's stepfather. Has it occurred to you that these children aren't missing at all? That they have taken legitimate posts in service?'

'I'm looking for shadows where there aren't any, do you mean?' Flora considered this for a mere instant before shaking her head. 'Miss Finch would have thought of that, I'm sure. She's convinced these children have been spirited away.'

Arthur started to grizzle and reached for Flora. She held out her arms into which Arthur lurched his plump body, only to demand immediately he go back to Lydia, where he padded his feet on her lap like a cat.

'Discounting Annie, have any of the others had a connection with the army?' Lydia tucked her hand beneath the baby's knees, giving him no option but to sit.

'Not that I know of.' She resolved to ask Alice Finch if she was aware the Salvation Army found posts for domestic servants. 'What do we do now?' Flora bit her lip as stark reality made her stomach knot.

'Not much, as no one has officially complained.' Arthur's eyelids fluttered closed and his head lolled against Lydia's bodice. In seconds, his lips puckered and his chest gently rose and fell in a gentle rhythm.

'How does he *do* that?' Flora gazed affectionately at her son. 'One moment he's wide awake and fussing, the next he's fast asleep.'

'I don't know, but I envy him.' Lydia cradled the baby in the crook of her arm. 'Now, what were we saying?'

'How do we get the police to open a proper investigation?' Flora broke off as the door opened to admit Milly.

'Shall I take him now, Madam?' She glided forward and relieved Lydia of the sleeping baby. 'It's time for his nap.'

'Miss Flora?' Stokes paused and stood to one side as Milly glided past him. 'There was a telephone call for you earlier. I'm so sorry but I was out and Mrs Cope answered the telephone, but she's not comfortable with the contraption and she forgot—'

'Please don't worry about it, Stokes,' Flora interrupted. 'Who was it who called?'

'It was from a Miss Finch,' Stokes replied. 'She said to tell you that another child has gone missing and she needs to speak to you urgently.'

'What?' She rose slowly from her chair, her mind racing. 'How long ago did she call?'

'I think about half an hour, madam. I apologise again, but—'

'Never mind,' Flora interrupted. 'Call me a cab,

would you, Stokes And call Miss Finch back and tell her I'm on my way.'

'I'm coming with you.' Lydia followed her into the hall, where they grabbed their coats and waited impatiently for Stokes to return with the cab.

CHAPTER 14

At St Philomena's, Forbes, the porter, had evidently received his instructions, for Flora and Lydia were hardly inside the front door before he carved a way for them through the crowded entrance to the office where Alice awaited them.

'Thank you so much for coming,' Alice leapt to her feet and greeted Flora with the warmth of an old friend, which in turn she extended to Lydia.

'Lydia Grey here was the friend I told you about who came with me to Bermondsey this morning,' Flora explained as they took their seats opposite the vast desk. 'She has a comprehensive knowledge of the neighbourhood that has proved invaluable.'

'How kind of you, Miss Grey.' The strain of the last hours was reflected in Alice's eyes as she grasped the younger woman's hand.

'It's a pleasure to meet you, Miss Finch,' Lydia said. 'In fact, I was treated here for bronchitis when I was eight. I'll always remember how kind the nurses were.'

'Indeed?' Alice's shrewd gaze slid over Lydia's

fashionable and expensive clothes, a question in her face. 'I'm always delighted to be reacquainted with former patients, even those who were treated here before my time.'

Flora fidgeted in her chair. 'Alice, do tell us about this child who has gone missing. I've been fretting in the cab all the way here.'

'Yes, of course. I apologize for involving you in this affair, but despite what some people might think I believe this latest disappearance is connected to the others.' Alice folded her hands on the desk in front of her. 'Her name is Isobel Lomax. Her parents went to Leeds to visit relatives and left the child with a nanny, who brought her to the hospital because she was running a fever.'

'What happened?' Flora asked.

'A misunderstanding, from what I can gather,' Alice said. 'Isobel had only a mild chest congestion, but frightening enough for the nanny. When she returned for Isobel yesterday to take her home, she was told she'd already been collected. Sister Lazarus thought she had been discharged, but the nurse on duty said there was nothing written in the discharge book. In the confusion, no one had missed the child for several hours.'

'Did anyone see Isobel leave?' Lydia asked.

'Forbes said a child matching her description was escorted through reception by a respectable-looking man he assumed was her father. They got into a hansom cab and left, but he had no idea where they went.'

'Matching her description? Isn't he sure?' Flora said.

'We have sixty to a hundred children being treated here at any one time.' Alice lifted both hands, palms upwards. 'He cannot possibly remember them all.' She leaned back in her chair, defeated. 'Isobel is a particularly attractive little girl of seven with fair hair and blue eyes. Somehow that makes me doubly concerned for her welfare.'

'That doesn't sound encouraging.' Flora chewed her bottom lip, the implications of Alice's words raising the hairs on her arms. 'Can the porter describe the man she left with in more detail?'

'All he could tell us was that he wasn't very tall, dark-haired with a moustache and he wore a black overcoat and top hat.'

'That description includes about half the men in London,' Lydia observed, unhelpfully.

'It doesn't sound anything like the stocky man with a squint Lizzie saw when the others went missing,' Flora said, adding, 'by the way, we think we've discovered his name. Swifty Ellis.'

Alice frowned. 'Not a name that's familiar to me. Perhaps one of the nurses knows who he is. It might be worth asking them.'

'Is the nanny certain this man wasn't a member of her family?' Lydia asked.

'She told no one Isobel was here,' Alice replied. 'She was too frightened her employers would find out she had let her fall ill.'

'She must be in a terrible state now the child is missing,' Lydia said.

'Indeed she is,' Miss Finch sighed. 'The police are dealing with her. The poor girl is only sixteen and this was her first position.'

A discreet knock at the door preceded the arrival of Sister Lazarus, who strode in without waiting for a response. 'Dr Reid wishes to speak to you, Miss Finch,' she announced shrilly, looking through Flora as if they had never met.

'Would you tell him I'll be along when I'm finished here?' Alice clenched her fists on the desk with barely suppressed impatience.

'He says it's important,' the nurse insisted. 'I told him you would come straight away.'

'Is it a case of life or death with regards to a patient, Sister?' A pulse jumped steadily in Miss Finch's temple, but she kept her expression bland.

'Not as I understand it, but—'

'In that case, I'll be there in due course. You may go.' She inflated her chest with a slow breath, thinning her nostrils.

Sister Lazarus glared at Flora through black pebble eyes and swung round abruptly, causing a jingling sound from the folds of her skirt as she hauled the door shut with a firm bang a fraction away from a slam.

Lydia widened her eyes in a 'what was that about look', to which Flora responded with a hand gesture that conveyed she would explain later. The woman not only possessed the demeanour of a bad-tempered nun, it appeared she equipped herself like a chatelaine. Did she jingle like a gypsy horse as she strode around the hospital? If so, at least the students could hear her coming.

'I apologize for that.' Alice cleared her throat while avoiding their eyes. 'Now, as I was saying, this time, the police are involved because Isobel has been reported officially missing.'

'What exactly are they doing about it?' Flora asked.

'They have begun door-to-door inquiries in Greenwich.' Alice fiddled with the buttons on one cuff with the fingers of her other hand.

'Greenwich? But that's miles from here,' Lydia exclaimed. 'Why did the nanny bring her to St Philomena's?'

'It seems Isobel fell ill whilst they were on a visit to the Tower of London. In a panic, she summoned a cab driver and asked for the nearest hospital. He brought them here.'

'But why search her own neighbourhood?' Flora asked. 'Whoever took her is hardly likely to take her home.'

'My dear, that's exactly what *I* told them,' Alice sighed. 'The police said they have procedures to follow. In the case of a missing child, they always begin in the home neighbourhood because children often simply wander off and get lost. They have latched onto the affluent man in the taxi theory and assume she did arrive home after leaving here, although the nanny refutes that.'

'Why are they wasting time?' Flora fisted her hands on her lap. 'Don't the police have any common sense?'

'It seems not,' Alice said. 'I got the impression they think the nanny is lying and trying to shift the blame. Nothing I have said will dissuade them, so we must hope they are right and find Isobel soon, though I have my doubts.'

'As do I,' Flora said slowly.

'Did you manage to find anything new out this morning?' Miss Finch redirected the conversation.

'I'm afraid we were received in the same way you were, with well-rehearsed stories and downright evasion. Without exception they were reluctant to talk to us.'

'Except Ada,' Lydia reminded her. 'A young girl, Ada Baines, asked us if we had seen a friend of hers called Annie who was treated here but went missing soon afterwards.'

'Oh dear. Another one?' Alice regarded them with dismay. 'Let me see if I can find this Annie in our records.' She consulted a thick ledger on her desk, flicked back a few pages and ran a finger down the left-hand page. 'There was an Annie Sims treated for influenza early last month. She was discharged after four days.'

'Annie lived in Decima Street,' Lydia said. 'Could she be this Sims girl?'

'It appears so, the address is the same.' Alice

released a long breath. 'This situation seems to be getting worse. Are we the only people who care about where these children are?'

'We need to find out more about this Swifty person,' Lydia said. 'If he's been hanging around the hospital, someone must know him.'

'What about that public house you told me about?' Flora turned to Lydia. 'The one Ada mentioned.'

'The Corks Galleon?' Lydia nodded slowly. 'Or rather, The Antigallican. Ada said he was a regular there.'

'I cannot see you young ladies going into *that* establishment,' Miss Finch rolled her eyes.

'Not us,' Flora said slowly, turning possibilities over in her head. 'But we know someone who might be able to go there unnoticed.'

'Abel!' Flora and Lydia said simultaneously.

A sharp knock at the door preceded the return of a grim-faced Sister Lazarus, who was apparently in no better mood than she had left. 'Dr Reid says—'

'I know, thank you, Sister, I shall be along directly.' Alice rose and eased around the desk. 'Sister, would you take Mrs Harrington and Miss Grey back to the main entrance? I'll ask Forbes to summon a hansom on my way through.'

'If you insist, Miss Finch, although I do have important work to do.' Sister Lazarus' eyes hardened as she watched Flora refold the list and return it to her bag.

'As do we all, Sister. However, I'm sure you can spare a few moments.' Alice turned away and grasped Flora's hands in hers. 'Thank you so much for what you did today. There's still much more we need to discover.'

'I agree,' Flora returned her firm grip. 'Though I'm not sure which direction we should take next.'

'Therefore we must stay in touch. And my thanks to you as well, Miss Grey,' she added over her shoulder as she closed the door behind her, leaving the three of them alone.

'Sister Lazarus,' Flora began, unable to rid herself of the feeling she addressed a nun, 'what do you think about these strange goings-on at the hospital?'

Lydia tactfully wandered a few feet away and studied a photograph of student nurses on the wall, though the set of her shoulders indicated she heard every word.

'I assume you mean those children Lizzie Prentice fussed about?' Sister Lazarus replied with a sniff. 'If Mr Buchanan was worried about them, there would be cause for concern, but he isn't. Miss Finch must have got it wrong.' She gathered files from the desk into a thick pile, apparently having forgotten the important work she had to do. 'As for those children, if their families didn't care about them, they wouldn't have brought them to the hospital in the first place.' She hefted the pile up in front of her like a shield. 'Better not keep that cab waiting too long, Mrs Harrison, it's difficult enough getting them to come here at all.'

'It's Harrington,' Flora corrected as she passed her into the hall.

'My mistake.' The ghost of a smile appeared on Sister Lazarus' face, confirming Flora's suspicion she had done so on purpose. Subtlety did not sit well on her sharp features. She looked more like a ferret about to pounce on a rabbit. 'We've seen a lot of you recently in our humble charity hospital.' She made it sound like a reprimand. 'I would have thought Guy's would have been a more suitable place for ladies like yourselves.'

'Miss Grey and I are considering making donations,' Flora lied, hurrying to keep up with the nurse's brisk pace as she strode along the corridor. 'You do such excellent work here and my husband likes the idea of a bed bearing his name.'

'Admirable, I'm sure.' She hugged the ledger close to her chest as she walked, but made no effort to slow down.

'Did you treat Isobel Lomax when she was here?' Lydia put on a spurt in order to draw level with her other side. They must have presented an odd sight with the stern sister flanked by two well-dressed ladies skipping to keep up.

'My job is mostly supervisory and I have a lot of administration to do. The actual nursing is done by others.'

'I can see you have a good deal of authority

here.' Lydia wasn't going to be put off, it seemed. 'What do you think happened to Isobel?'

'I have no idea, but I blame the parents for leaving her in the care of such a young and inexperienced girl.'

'Will you attend Lizzie Prentice's inquest, Sister?' Flora asked, determined not to let her ignore them.

'Whatever for?' They had reached the entrance hall, where she halted abruptly, the ledger held up to her chest like armour. 'It's a waste of my time when I could be doing more important work here.'

'You don't think it was possible she was attacked?' Flora asked.

'I haven't really thought about it.' Her thin lips curled. 'Members of the public come and go all the time through the rear yard. That gate is never locked.' Her narrowed eyes slid to Lydia and back to Flora. 'Now, if you'll excuse me. I have duties to perform.'

'In other words, she knows nothing,' Lydia murmured, her hard gaze on the woman's retreating back.

'Or everything.' Flora' attention was caught by a shiny gold ball that swung gently from the nurse's skirt as she walked, possibly the source of the jingling sound she had heard earlier. Her scrutiny appeared to be catching when Sister Lazarus halted, looked down in annoyance and tucked the object into her pocket before walking on again.

CHAPTER 15

'I do apologize, Mrs Harrington.' Forbes greeted them in the entrance hall with both arms held out in supplication. 'I'm afraid your taxi was claimed by another visitor. However, I sent a boy to fetch another one. He shouldn't be long if you wouldn't mind waiting.'

'It cannot be helped.' Flora concealed her frustration beneath a smile.

Lydia claimed a bench seat to the right of the porter's desk, but Flora was too restless to sit and paced a hall where nurses, hospital workers and visitors formed a constantly moving stream.

Who had collected Isobel from the hospital? Was he connected to the elusive Swifty? If so, were either, or both of them responsible for Lizzie Prentice's death? If the coroner decreed it was an accident, as Dr Reid had believed, how could the authorities be persuaded to take the case of the other missing children seriously? Without official help there was so little they could do.

Her thoughts were interrupted by the sound of the front door opening, followed by Forbes' enthusiastic greeting of an arrival. She turned in anticipation of the arrival of a hansom, but instead, Mr Buchanan strode into the entrance hall with the confident air of a man aware of his standing in the world. He lifted a hand to the porter in a distracted salute, pausing only when Forbes skirted the desk and handed him an envelope.

Buchanan tucked his walking cane under one arm and tore the envelope open with little more than mild curiosity, his chin lifted in greeting to a passing doctor. He withdrew two slips of paper, his brows knitted together and he gave a sharp gasp. As he read one, the second fluttered to the tiled floor, but Buchanan did not seem to notice, his focus on what looked to be a handwritten note.

Flora ran forward and retrieved the paper from the floor, reading it rapidly before handing it back. 'Yours, I believe, Mr Buchanan.'

'Uh-thank you, Mrs—' He nodded vaguely as he reached for it.

'Harrington,' Flora replied. 'Miss Finch introduced us the other day, if you recall.'

'She did?' His gaze darted to the entrance as he shoved both papers and envelope roughly into his pocket. 'Ah, yes, I think I do remember. Thank you, madam. Now if you'll excuse me.' He slapped a hand on the porter's desk to gain the man's attention. 'Did you see who left this for me?'

'No, Mr Buchanan.' The porter stared vaguely

at him. 'It was here when I arrived this morning. Is there no return address?'

'Never mind.' He pushed away from the desk, turned and headed along a corridor.

'Flora!' Lydia called from the open front door. 'Our taxi is here.'

'I'm coming,' Flora dragged her gaze away from the governor's back and hurried outside.

'What were you and that man talking about?' Lydia asked as the porter showed them to their cab and closed the wooden shutters over their legs.

'Passing the time of day, nothing more.' Flora's thoughts raced as the incident in the hall ran through her head. 'Do you like music, Lydia?'

'Of course, doesn't everyone? What sort in particular?'

'There's a concert recital at The Bechstein Hall tomorrow evening.'

'Ah yes, some German pianist who's reputed to be a musical genius.'

'Austrian, actually. It's his London debut with the Hallé Orchestra.' Flora grabbed the rail in front of her as their driver turned a sharp corner into Marshalsea Road.

'Really?' Lydia's right eyebrow lifted slowly and her lips formed a tiny smile. 'And do you happen to know what he will be playing?'

'Actually, I do. Brahms' Piano Concerto No. 2, Opus 83 in B Flat Major.'

'And you got all that from a slip of paper?' At

Flora's start, she laughed, 'I saw you hurl yourself across the floor towards whatever fell out of the envelope that gentleman was holding. Not very subtle, Flora.'

'Maybe not, but effective. It was a concert ticket. I only caught a glimpse, but it was enough to remind me of an article I read in yesterday's paper about Mr Schnabel, the pianist.'

'Are you going to tell me who the worried-looking gentleman was, and what does he have to do with a foreign pianist?'

'Mr Raymond Buchanan. And something tells me that concert is the last place he wants to be. When he saw that ticket just now, he looked as if all his worst fears had been realized.'

'You're confusing me,' Lydia raised her voice above the clop of hooves and the rush of traffic that passed them on both sides. 'What has he got to do with anything?'

'Alice Finch introduced us on our first visit to the hospital,' Flora said. 'He's on the Board of Governors, but Miss Finch says he dismissed the notion that children were going missing from the hospital'

'Which is understandable if the reputation of the establishment is at stake. Not something he would admit to unless it was uncontroversial.'

'That's what I hate about politicians,' Flora grunted. 'Nothing matters but appearances.'

'Has Miss Finch implied he might be involved in that nurse's death or the missing children?'

Lydia asked, as usual going straight to the heart of the matter.

'No, quite the opposite. She seems to admire him.' Experience had told her anyone could be a suspect until proven otherwise, so she was reserving judgement. 'I saw Mr Buchanan in a cab beside us when we left the hospital the other day and seeing him just now reminded me.'

'I'm sorry, I still don't see the connection.'

'He said he was in a hurry to keep an appointment but he was still at the hospital an hour later. Then he left in a cab within minutes of a dead body being found on hospital grounds. Wouldn't he have been eager to remain and take command of the situation?'

'Maybe he didn't know about Nurse Prentice? Or his appointment was local and he came back to the hospital to deal with the situation?' Lydia suggested.

'Maybe, but then if why get into a cab at the front entrance where everyone could see him when he had already established he wouldn't be there? Isn't he more likely to have slipped through the rear door?'

'Has that Sister Lazarus got anything to do with these instincts of yours?' Lydia tapped her gloved fingers against her lips. 'I ask, because your Mr Buchanan almost jumped out of his skin when he saw her just now.'

'Really? I didn't notice that.'

Lydia's powers of observation were evidently as keen as ever.

'I doubt you'll be able to spy on him at the concert if that's what you're thinking.'

'Why not? I'm sure Bunny would enjoy a musical evening. I'll get us a box so we can see everything.'

'I hate to say this, Flora, but I fear you'll be out of luck. That concert has been sold out for some time. Harry tried to buy tickets a month ago but found it impossible. And besides, there are no boxes at The Bechstein Hall,' Lydia added with authority. 'There isn't even a gallery. It's quite small with only five hundred seats on one level in front of a raised stage. Perfect for listening to music but useless for a play and not easy to watch someone without their noticing.'

'That's a shame.' Flora's shoulders slumped. 'It was such a good idea too.' She fell silent, the only sound the clop of hooves as they crossed Westminster Bridge, a sight she had seen a great deal lately. 'Lydia, what did you think of Miss Finch?' Flora asked after a moment.

'I thought her charming, and very professional. Though I couldn't help noticing some animosity between her and that Sister Lazarus. The way she put Miss Finch's concerns about the missing children down to fussing struck me as odd. I would expect a nurse to have more compassion.'

'I agree, about Sister Lazarus, but that wasn't why I asked. Do you think Alice and I look alike?' The hansom pulled sharply to the side of the road outside the *Harriet Parker Academy*, the abrupt halt slamming Flora's back against the upholstery. Wincing, she pushed up the wooden flap whilst rethinking her generous tip.

'Flora? Do you really believe Miss Finch could be your mother?'

'Is that completely ridiculous?' She let the half-open flap fall back into place.

Lydia chewed her bottom lip before answering, 'I thought about what you said the other day, and maybe you do bear a certain resemblance to her.'

'Do you really think so?' Flora's heart leapt for a second before settling again. Was it true, or was she too willing to latch onto anything, no matter how slight, which might link her to Alice?

'The shape of her eyes are similar to yours and you have the same height and build.' Lydia shook her head as if dislodging these details. 'No, Flora, it's not logical. Why would she leave you with Riordan,' she broke off and gave the street a swift glance, lowering her voice, 'a man she knew wasn't your father, never to contact you again?'

'I've asked myself that question, and more, since I first saw her.' Flora released a pent-up breath. 'Maybe I simply want her to be my mother in order to answer all the questions I still have about why she disappeared.'

'You might have to face the fact you may never have those answers.' Lydia rested her hand on Flora's forearm. 'Can't you leave the past alone and enjoy your life now? You have so much, Flora.'

'You make me sound ungrateful and self-pitying.'

A wave of shame sent a shuddering breath through her. 'I do have a good life, don't I? A lovely home, a wonderful husband and the sweetest baby in London. Perhaps you're right, and I should treat Alice Finch as a welcome new acquaintance, not a solution to the mysteries of my own past.' Even as the words left her, Flora's mind screamed a denial. No, it wasn't enough. She felt incomplete not knowing why her mother had abandoned her as a child. Did she not love her? What could a six-year-old child have done to drive her own mother away? 'As a concert appears to be out of the question, would you like to bring Harry to supper tomorrow evening?' she asked, forcing herself to sound normal. 'If we combine resources we might be able to come up with some strategy. I assume you have mentioned this case to him?'

'I have yes, but he seems as clueless as any of us. Supper would be nice though.'

'I would have asked you for tonight, but Bunny has some Lord Mayor's dinner. At this short notice it won't be anything elaborate but I'm sure Mrs Cope will be able to come up with something.'

'Anything would be most welcome, and make a nice change for Harry who has never quite mastered the tiny stove in his rooms.' The horse whinnied, shifting its hooves as if impatient to be off again.

'Now I really must go,' Lydia said. 'I have a deputy headmistress who manages competently without me, but I still have a mountain of paperwork waiting.' She signalled the driver to pull the lever to open the flaps allowing her to step down.

Flora raised her hand in a backward wave at her retreating figure as the cab moved off towards Eaton Place, her thoughts returning to Mr Buchanan's face when he saw the contents of the envelope. Something was going to happen at the Bechstein Hall tomorrow night, and it had nothing to do with the music.

'How did your visit to Bermondsey go this morning?' Leaving the door between their bedroom and his dressing room open, Bunny shrugged out of his shirt and slung it over a nearby chair.

'Not as successfully as I had hoped.' Flora perched on the end of the bed, her chin on her hands resting on the brass bedpost. 'The families all had explanations as to why the children aren't there.'

She relished these intimate moments in the day which were theirs alone, with no Stokes or Milly likely to interrupt.

'I gather you didn't believe their explanations?'

'Not just me, Lydia didn't either. Nor did Sally.'

'Oh well, that's conclusive then. If Sally—'

'Don't tease. Sally has good instincts about people. We all agree that they appear to have been warned not to talk about it.'

'I don't like the sound of that.' Bunny reappeared in the doorway, wiping his hands on a white towel slung over one naked shoulder. The short, blond hairs on his chest glowed gold in the flame from a wall light. For a man who spent most of his life at a desk, he was built like an athlete, with slim hips, a neat, tight waist and a washboard stomach.

'I met Abel Cain today,' Flora said. 'I see now what you meant about him, and he certainly proved his worth.'

Bunny swiped a dampened badger hair brush round a bowl of shaving soap and worked up a lather. 'What do you mean he proved his worth?' Frowning, he held the brush in mid-air.

'Um – only that people kept their distance with him there.' If she revealed their encounter with the youths in the stairwell, Bunny would forbid her to go anywhere near the place again. She slid off the bed and wandered closer, leaning a shoulder against the door frame. 'Lydia and I aren't sure what we should do next.'

'Maybe you should wait for the inquest verdict on that nurse.' His eyes met hers in the mirror as he spread a layer of creamy white suds over his chin with the loaded brush. 'What was her name?'

'Lizzie Prentice.'

'Yes of course. I should have remembered.' He retrieved a freshly sharpened straight razor from the box that had arrived from the barber's that morning. 'If the coroner decides it was an accident, there may be nothing else you can do. Unless you can find some connection between her death and those children to interest the police.' He stretched his neck and moved the razor upwards across his skin in swift, well-practised movements.

'Actually, there might be.' Flora's fingers itched to stroke his smooth back, but she pushed down the curl of desire that unwound in her belly, unwilling to startle him with a razor in his hand. He sent them to the barbers regularly to have them sharpened and were quite lethal. 'Alice Finch telephoned this afternoon to say another child has gone missing. Her name is Isobel Lomax and when her nurse went to fetch her from the hospital she wasn't there.'

'Oh no, really?' He twisted at the waist to look at her, shaking excess suds from the razor into the bowl. 'When you say missing—' He left the word hanging.

'Officially missing.'

'That's progress, isn't it? That the police are now involved.' He waved the razor in the air. 'I hope they find her, and soon.' He turned back to the mirror and reapplied the blade to his face.

'I hope so too.' Flora was about to tell him that did not help the other six children, when he said something she didn't catch. 'I'm sorry, what did you say?'

'I said, what made you invite Lydia and Harry to supper tomorrow?' His speech was slightly distorted by the finger he held against his nose, the thin blade applied to his upper lip. 'It's not like you to be so spontaneous.'

'I've been meaning to ask for ages and she was so kind coming with me today.'

'It's an excellent idea. I look forward to it.

Haven't seen Harry for too long. Though I hope the evening won't turn into a propaganda exercise. I hear he's considering standing for Parliament as a Liberal.' The razor clicked against the side of the ewer as he shook off the excess suds. 'And I'm sorry to desert you this evening, but I cannot get out of this dinner.'

'I understand. These social occasions are important to your career.' She delivered this sop to her conscience with a bright smile. 'Sally has the evening off, so I'll probably help Milly bath Arthur and have an early night.'

She decided this was not the right time to mention that she had inveigled Sally and Abel to pay a visit to The Antigallican to find out what they could about Swifty Ellis. Sally had needed little persuading with the promise of an evening in Abel's company in the offing.

'Much as I hate to admit it,' Bunny was still speaking, 'the chasm that exists between the affluent and the poor leaves the weaker members of our society at risk. Especially the children. London is a dangerous place.'

'Now *you* sound like a politician.' She drifted back to the bed, her hands on either side of her thighs, her gaze on the crease of his back which disappeared below his belt. At some point, the leather had dipped low enough to reveal the dimples on either side of his spine.

'Not me, though I admire Harry's principles. We condemn these activities as scandalous, but at the same time console ourselves that it's happening in Southwark and not on our own doorstep.' He flicked the towel from his shoulder and strolled into the bedroom, wiping traces of soap his razor had missed.

'Isobel Lomax didn't live in Southwark. She was there by accident.' Flora shifted position to face him, her feet dangling a few inches above the floor. 'Lydia has a theory that the children's families are being paid to look the other way. That's why they haven't been reported missing.' She decided not to mention Lydia's upbringing in Bermondsey, despite that she hated keeping secrets from him. Somehow repeating Lydia's story to anyone, even Bunny, would feel like a betrayal of confidence.

'If you're right about that,' Bunny paused in the act of withdrawing a clean shirt from a drawer, 'it's a well-organized operation and dangerous people are likely involved.' He shook out the shirt and slipped it over his shoulders. 'I don't want people like that even knowing you exist, and they soon will if you go around asking questions.'

'But what if Nurse Prentice knew something about who took the children?'

'Are you saying she was killed to get her out of the way?'

'Or perhaps because she knew something? It's possible, isn't it?'

'I'm afraid so.' He straightened, his eyes without his glasses looked soft and more vivid than usual. 'However, this time, I hope you'll be sensible and leave it to the police to discover who killed her and why.' He grimaced as he struggled to fasten his collar studs, but fumbled them and the left side of the collar came free. 'Damn.'

Flora slapped his hands gently away from the collar and fastened the studs for him.

'I'm serious, Flora.' He selected a silk bow tie from the dresser and slung it around his neck, the ends flat against his shirt like two squashed snake heads. 'It's not your responsibility to provide the police with evidence.' He pointed at his tie in a 'would you mind' gesture.

'Don't you see, that's exactly what I must do, or those children will be forgotten.' She knotted the tie beneath his chin into a symmetrical bow, folded his collar down over it and tugged the ends out gently. 'If we can make the police investigate not just Isobel but all the missing children properly, we may stand a chance of finding them.' She retrieved his spectacles from the dresser and slid them onto his nose, then placed her hands flat against his chest. 'Admit it, you want to solve this puzzle as much as I do, but you also want to keep me out of harm's way.'

'You know me so well.' His eyes darkened and he wrapped his arms around her, resting his chin against her forehead.

'I understand you worry about me,' Flora whispered against his chest. 'But if we do nothing, how can we live with ourselves knowing that young children have been taken from their homes and are—' her voice trailed off as unimaginable images crowded her mind. With an effort, she pushed them away. Sentimentality wouldn't help her now. 'Think of Arthur.'

'I *am* thinking of him.' He released a long breath into her hair. 'Perhaps I could find someone in authority willing to examine the case more closely. Someone who has influence and access to resources.'

'Oh, would you?' She jerked backward and stared up at him, incredulous and yet conscious she had been waiting for him to offer. 'Thank you.' Her eyes welled and she blinked away tears.

'I'm not promising anything,' he began gently, 'but the Chief Constable and half the senior-ranking police officers in the city will be at The Guildhall tonight. There must be someone among them I can convince this situation is worth pursuing. I only hope the criminal fraternity don't find out that the police stations will be empty this evening.'

'Well, *I* certainly shan't tell them.' Flora's arms slid up his back, her face pressed into his shirt where she breathed in the starched linen and shaving soap that, predictably, sent her blood rushing through her veins. 'I mustn't cry, or I'll ruin your shirt.' Suddenly aware her eyes were wet she pulled back sharply. 'Now, where's your dinner jacket?'

She turned in the direction of the wardrobe but Bunny caught her hand, pulling her back into his arms, his head bent and his lips against the skin below her ear.

'Forget the jacket.' His voice vibrated through her. 'We have a little time before the cab arrives.'

'Actually.' Her eyes closed as she wound her arms round his neck, 'I was thinking the same thing.'

'You'll have to retie my tie.' He lifted her a few inches off the ground and backed her towards the bed.

'I think I could probably manage that.'

CHAPTER 16

Flora ate her supper from a tray in her bedroom that evening in front of a glowing fire; a luxury she granted herself since Bunny chose to carouse with his lawyer colleagues. Despite his sympathetic understanding, they were no nearer to identifying who was responsible for Nurse Prentice's death, nor did they have any idea as to who could have taken the children.

Once Stokes had removed the tray, she attempted to read the latest H G Wells short story, 'The Country of the Blind' in *The Strand Magazine*, but was interrupted by the jangle of the doorbell that resonated through the hall and brought her onto the landing just as Stokes' brisk footsteps beat a smart tattoo across the tiled floor.

'Thank you, Stokes,' Beatrice Harrington's voice drifted up to where Flora stood, her hands tensed on the bannister. 'Inform your mistress I'll await her in the sitting room. I hope you've set a good fire in there as it's bitter cold outside.' The feathers on her voluminous hat bobbed as she glided across the hall. 'I shall require tea, Earl Grey and don't let it stew. Oh, and don't let that red-haired kitchen maid bring it, she always manages to slop milk in the saucer or drops the teaspoons onto the floor.'

Flora leaned against the wall, allowing a moment to compose herself before she dragged her feet to the sitting room, where Beatrice was comfortably ensconced in a wingback chair beside the fire.

'What an unexpected surprise, Mother-in-Law,' her bright greeting belied the stone that had settled in her stomach. 'How nice of you to call.'

'No need to take that sarcastic tone with me. I know quite well you didn't expect to see me. However with Ptolemy out for the evening I thought you would benefit from my company.' Beatrice tugged off her gloves, slapped them onto a side table and rushed toward the fire, her hands held toward the flames. 'I took an excellent early supper with April Groves in Lennox Gardens, so I don't need any refreshment other than the tea.'

'How thoughtful of you,' Flora said, her tongue firmly gripped between her teeth, catching Beatrice's sudden hard look. Bunny's mother might lack tact, but she could detect disrespect in a heartbeat. When their move to the city had become imminent, Bunny had suggested Beatrice share the charming villa she had bought in Chiswick with a widowed cousin to keep her company, an arrangement that suited them all, and where Beatrice revelled in her new-found independence and an ability to socialize with her friends whenever she pleased. The only disadvantage being that having the convenience of a private carriage enabled her to call on her son and daughter-in-law unannounced.

'I was about to go up and bath the baby,' Flora said. 'Would you like to come?' As the words left her, she knew they had been a mistake.

'Whatever for? That's the nursery maid's job.' She blinked in confusion, sending her black hat feathers quivering. Flora had seen grown men cower in her presence, not all of them tradesmen. With her penetrating blue eyes and perpetually pinched mouth, Beatrice Harrington could have given lessons in intimidation to the late queen.

'I enjoy bathing him myself.' Flora took a seat on a hard-backed chair, hoping her guest would take it as a sign not to get too comfortable. 'It helps me get to know him, and more importantly, for him to know me.'

'You do fret about the most unimportant things, Flora,' Beatrice sniffed as she left the fire and took a chair opposite Flora. 'Naturally, he'll know who you are. His nanny will tell him. A child's duty is to its parents, not the other way around.'

'I enjoy my time with Arthur.' She refused to be intimidated where her son was concerned. 'This way he'll know to come to me when he's upset or worried. He needs me.' Not for the first time, she wondered how Bunny had turned out to be the loving, considerate man he was with this woman for a mother. Perhaps he had a devoted nursemaid?

'It's enough to keep your child disciplined,

clothed and fed without worrying about how he feels, dear,' Beatrice went on, oblivious to Flora's stiff shoulders. 'A short visit before bedtime is quite adequate to check he is healthy and knows his manners. Anything else is merely fussing.'

'Don't you want to see your grandson?' Flora asked, a sharp edge to her voice she hoped Beatrice was too self-absorbed to miss. She could do without another lecture on disrespect of her elders.

'How can you ask, when you know how much I adore him? Tell the nurse to bring him down when he's been bathed and readied for bed.'

Flora rolled her eyes, an action she covered quickly as the door opened. 'Ah, here's Stokes with our tea.' She waited until he had set down the tray. 'Stokes, would you ask Milly to bring Master Arthur down when he has had his bath? I shan't be helping to bathe him this evening. Oh and take the cakes away, Mrs Harrington has already eaten.'

'Never mind, Stokes, leave them there.' Beatrice removed the plate of fancies from the tray and set it at her side. 'I might be tempted later.'

'As you wish, Madam.' Stokes' lips twitched at Flora in sympathy as he bowed and left.

Beatrice plucked an old copy of *The Strand Magazine* from a small pile on a side table. 'Detective stories?' She used the same inflection she might have adopted for the word 'Blasphemy'.

'I hope you aren't wasting your time on such nonsense, Flora? I was never allowed to read penny dreadfuls when I was your age.'

'They're very entertaining and penny dreadfuls is such an outdated term. Everyone reads fiction these days and Conan Doyle is well thought of as a writer. Bunny has a subscription,' she added, immediately regretting her blatant attempt to justify herself.

'Oh well, if Ptolemy allows such publications in the house, it must be acceptable.' Beatrice wrinkled her nose at her first sip from her cup, lifted the teapot lid and peered inside. 'How many scoops does that maid of yours put in this teapot?'

'I've never had a reason to enquire.' Flora stole frequent looks at the clock, whose hands seemed to crawl slower than usual while she listened with growing frustration during Beatrice's detailed account of her week, which seemed to consist of several excursions to her contemporaries, all of whom had allowed themselves to sink into desultory old age, with particular attention to those whose children had made less than advantageous marriages. The tirade finally ceased when Milly arrived with Arthur; his hair damp from his bath and his skin pink and sweet-smelling. Flora took immediate possession of this irresistible bundle of soft chubbiness, to which his grandmother appeared immune.

Beatrice's monologue changed to a tirade of criticism of Flora's disinterest in expanding her social circle. 'You should be seeking to enhance Ptolemy's career with the right people, not chasing around the city in search of spies and murderers.'

'Actually, Mother-in-Law, I don't—'

'—and to allow policemen into your home is the height of crass behaviour,' Beatrice interrupted her. 'What will your neighbours think?'

'Don't you agree that Arthur has grown since your last visit?' Flora said through gritted teeth in an attempt to change the subject. The last thing she wanted was an unseemly argument.

'Such a strong, handsome boy.' Beatrice smiled for the first time that evening, although her only display of affection took the form of holding his tiny hand between finger and thumb for a moment before removing it fastidiously in favour of one of the miniature cakes at her elbow

Once the baby had been cursorily inspected and declared hale and healthy, Beatrice pre-empted Flora and dismissed Milly with instructions on how many blankets the baby required, never to pick him up simply because he cries and a final warning to keep the windows tightly closed.

'October is a brutal month, I find. I can never get sufficiently warm.' She tugged her fur collar tighter round her throat. 'I like that girl,' she added as the door closed on Milly, who had shown no resentment to receiving orders from Beatrice. 'She's silent and yet both respectful and vigilant.'

'That's one way of putting it. More tea?' Flora asked, more out of politeness than a desire to prolong the visit.

Beatrice opened her mouth to reply just as the

rattle of the doorknob preceded the arrival of Sally, who burst into the room, her hat awry and her curly dark hair in her eyes.

'Miss Flora, you'll never guess—' she halted, blinking when she caught sight of Beatrice and gave a little bob. 'Oh, I'm sorry, ma'am, I didn't know you was here.'

'Really, Pond. Do you normally enter your employer's sitting room without knocking?' Beatrice snatched her gloves from the table and pushed herself awkwardly to her feet. 'You never could control your servants, Flora,' she said sotto voce, then louder. 'Speaking of which, would you ask Stokes to inform my driver I shall be out in a moment.'

'You've left the carriage in the road?' Flora signalled Sally to wait where she was while she escorted Beatrice to the door. 'It's freezing outside. Why didn't you send your driver round to the mews for a hot drink?'

'Whatever for?' Beatrice glared at Flora as if she were demented. 'How will he know when I'm ready to leave if he's dozing by the kitchen hearth? The very idea *I* should wait for *him* is quite ridiculous.' She swept along the hall to the front door, which Stokes had barely made ahead of her.

'That lamp is far too dim.' Beatrice pointed an accusatory hand at the porch canopy. 'I could easily fall and break an ankle on these steps. I'll talk to Ptolemy about it in the morning.' Without waiting for a response, she swept down the steps and glided along the path.

'Goodnight, Mother-in-law, and thank you for calling,' Flora called after her through gritted teeth, while trying not to shiver.

As soon as the carriage turned the corner into Belgrave Place, Flora sped back to the sitting room, where Sally had made herself comfortable by the roaring fire.

'It's bitter out there, Missus.' She blew into her hands and huddled closer, her feet braced against the brass fender. 'Sorry about barging in like that. If I'd known she was here I would have waited in the kitchen.'

'That's all right, Sally. Now what is it you have to tell me that I will never guess?' She chose not to bring attention to the fact Sally had reverted to the sobriquet 'Missus' after repeated instructions to call her 'Madam'.

'We found him.' Sally's eyes glinted and she hunched her shoulders. 'Swifty Ellis. The man that girl Ada told us about.'

'The man with a squint?' Flora lowered herself into the chair Beatrice had recently vacated. 'Where?'

'I'll start at the beginning.' Sally's cheeks and the end of her nose turning a soft pink as the fire warmed her skin making her quite pretty. 'We went to that pub in Tooley Street. The Antigallican.' She mangled the pronunciation, but again, Flora chose not to correct her. 'Abel bought me a port and lemon and we got talking to the barman about boxing. It turns out he used the same gymnasium as Abel when he was younger, the Lynn Boxing Club on Borough High Street.' She scooted backwards on her chair, evidently enjoying herself. 'Most of the local thugs use it as a meeting place for, well, their shady deals and such. Before long, someone mentioned Swifty, who is said to be handy with his fists.' Sally helped herself to one of the untouched cakes that resided on the tray, saw Flora looking at her and shrugged. 'Sorry. Wasn't thinking.'

'Shall I ask Stokes for a fresh pot and an extra cup?'

'Ooh, yes please. I could do with a cuppa.' Either Flora's sarcasm had passed Sally by, or she deliberately ignored it.

Sighing, Flora rose and tugged the bell pull. 'Go on with your story.'

'Well, when Abel asked if Swifty boxed in the tournaments, the barman said the fighting *that* bloke did wasn't in no boxing match. His fights had no rules. He's a bit of a bruiser by all accounts. And Swifty ain't his real name,' she said through mouthfuls of cake.'

'Isn't, Sally, and I had already gathered that. Not that it matters much if that's what everyone calls him.'

Stokes entered with a fresh teapot and cup, unable to hide his start of surprise when he saw for whom it was ordered.

'Thanks, Stokes.' Sally rubbed her hands together, gleefully. 'Just put it there would you?'

Stokes' shoulders stiffened but he obeyed without a word before he withdrew.

'You shouldn't goad him, Sally,' Flora chided when the door closed on him.

'Couldn't resist, but don't you worry about him. I'll talk him round. Anyway, as I was saying, Swifty got his name because he's light on his feet when the situation calls for it, if you get my drift.'

'I suppose that makes a kind of logic. What else did you find out?'

'The barman got a bit wary after a while, what with all the questions we was asking. He did mention Swifty's a docker at St Saviour's.'

'I don't know what that means.'

Sally eyed the cakes again, at which Flora pushed the plate closer.

'Dockers offload sacks and crates onto barges that bring the goods to the city from the ships at Tilbury and Gravesend.' Sally sank her teeth into a chocolate tart. 'They stand on the stones with dozens of others every morning for the call.'

'The call?'

'Do keep up, Miss-Madam, there's lots for me to remember. They don't work a regular job, only days when they are needed. The bosses turn away three times as many as get work. Swifty isn't big enough to be a stevedore, that's those who unload the ships, so he works on the docks.' Sally slurped her tea, grimaced and added two sugar lumps to the brew. 'Anyway, would yer believe it, just as we was about to leave, the barman came over and told us Swifty had come in and was in the other bar.'

'My goodness,' Flora sank down onto the edge of a chair. 'What did you do?'

'Nothing.' Sally shrugged. 'We got a good butcher's at him though. That girl Ada was right, he does have funny eyes.'

'I was worried for a moment that you might have become overenthusiastic and challenged him.'

'What do you take me for?' Sally jutted her chin, her eyes darkening. 'He's younger than we thought, but the way he scouted the bar told me he don't miss much. He has this look. Surly, like he'll challenge you to a fight as soon as look at you. He wore those funny gloves with the fingers missing and that coat he wears swings when he moves, like it was heavy. Like as not he keeps the tools of his trade in the pockets.'

'What sort of tools?' Their evening sounded dangerous to Flora, but Sally had apparently enjoyed herself.

'Who knows, but I'll wager there's a knuckle-duster in there somewhere.'

'I shan't even ask what that is.' Flora gave an embarrassed cough.

'Abel didn't like him much either,' Sally sniffed as if this vindicated her. 'He made me move my stool around so I had my back to him. Told me blokes like that have a sense for who's got their eye on them. We'll know him if we see him again.'

'I'm beginning to quite like your Abel. He sounds a sensible man and one who can be trusted. You did well, Sally.'

'There's more.' Sally's eyes gleamed, as if she was about to come to the good part and wanted to savour it. 'The landlord took a while getting our drinks the second time and when Abel mentioned the bar was busy, he was told they were short-handed due to his part-time barmaid having an accident a few days ago.'

'An accident?' Flora gasped when Sally's eyebrows rose. 'He meant Lizzie?'

Sally gave a slow, conspiratorial nod. 'She did the odd evening behind the bar to earn an extra few shillings, what with the wages at the hospital being poor.'

'Then why did she give Miss Finch the impression she didn't know who this Swifty was?'

'Probably because she wasn't supposed to be working in a pub. If the hospital knew about that they would have sacked her.'

'I wonder how well she knew him.'

'The barman didn't think she did,' Sally said, grimacing. 'Said a respectable girl like Lizzie wouldn't have had anything to do with the likes of him.'

'Yet she wanted to tell Miss Finch something. If it wasn't Swifty's identity, what was it?'

'Dunno,' Sally shrugged. 'Like I said, the barman

was getting a bit antsy with all these questions, so Abel said it was time to go.'

'Antsy?'

'You know, ants in yer pants. Fidgety.'

Flora cleared her throat, bemused by the wide education her maid was giving her. 'He made the right decision. Without an idea of what Swifty knows, we've reached another dead end and I don't—'

'I ain't finished, Miss Flora,' Sally cut her off. 'Lizzie had an up and downer with someone that night.'

'A what? Oh, you mean a fight? What night was this?'

'The last night she was at the Corks, working. 'Bout a week ago, he said.'

'I'm getting confused. What has this to do with Swifty, and with whom did Lizzie have an argument?'

'Dunno, as *I* weren't there.' Sally pulled a face as if this fact should be obvious. 'The barman didn't know either. They were in the scullery so he couldn't see them, but he heard a woman's voice, "going at poor Lizzie something terrible" was his exact words.'

'*Were* his exact words, Sally,' Flora said automatically. 'Did he find out what it was about?'

'He was too busy in the bar.' Sally shoved the last piece of cake into her mouth and slapped her hands together, releasing crumbs onto the floor. 'A Salvation Army couple were there that night rattling collection boxes. One of them was telling some drunk to change his evil ways, you know how the *Sally Anne* do, but the man didn't take kindly to him and a scuffle started. By the time the landlord had sorted them out, Lizzie was back in the bar. She was a bit shaken but refused to talk about the row or who she was arguing with.'

'Was the barman sure it was a woman?'

'He said he thought so, but didn't see her. Next thing he heard, Lizzie was dead.'

'Did he tell the police about this argument Lizzie had?'

'You're such an innocent, Miss Flora.' Sally's raised eyebrow conveyed disdain. 'Nobody says nothing to the police without being asked first. And maybe not even then. That's the way it is in Bermondsey.'

'That's unfortunate.' Flora relaxed back in her chair. 'We don't know even know what the argument was about.' Was it a woman who had killed Lizzie in the hospital yard?

Sally's face fell. 'I thought me and Abel had done a good job.'

'You did. I don't mean to imply otherwise.' Flora's thoughts raced. 'In fact, how would you like to do a bit more investigation for me?'

'What sort?' Sally pressed a finger to the remaining crumbs on the plate and brought it to her mouth.

'Tomorrow evening, I want you to follow someone. See who he talks to and what he does.

214

I cannot go as he's likely to recognise me, but you'll be invisible.'

'Oh, thanks a bunch.' Sally looked up sharply, a ring of almond crumbs around her mouth.

'Sorry, but you know what I mean.'

'Can I take Abel with me?'

'Excellent idea. A couple will raise fewer questions. We'll finalize the details tomorrow when I've thought it through.'

'You'll have ter put it straight with Stokes, what with me having two nights off in a row. I know I'm your maid but he likes to think he runs things below stairs.'

'Don't worry, I'll handle him. Now, Bunny won't be back for hours, so I think I'll go to bed.'

'Well then,' Sally rose slowly, 'I'd better be going up and get your night things ready.'

'I'll be up presently. Oh, and Sally, there's an envelope on my dresser. It's something to thank Abel for his help tonight. Could you have it sent round to him in the morning?'

'No need for that, I'll take it meself.' Sally's broad smile told Flora that aside from the discovery of 'Swifty', Sally's evening had gone remarkably well.

She sat for a while after Sally had gone, watching the fire burn down to glowing red coals that shifted and hissed in the grate.

Was the argument Lizzie had had in the pub been what she was going to tell Alice about, but was killed before she could do so? Was that why she was killed? What was the connection between Mr Buchanan and Lizzie Prentice, if there was one? Eventually, Flora's head began to feel filled with cotton wool, so she gave up and went upstairs to bed, her internal debate having produced far more questions than answers.

CHAPTER 17

The fire in the bedroom Flora shared with Bunny had long since burned to silvered ash, the temperature rapidly dropping until her nose felt cold to the touch. The nocturnal noises of the house combined with a strong wind that rattled windowpanes and moaned down the chimney. Shivering, she wrapped the thick counterpane between her bent knees, fighting to stay awake so she might relate everything Sally had told her when Bunny returned from his evening out.

Sometime after the hall clock struck twelve, she must have fallen asleep, for she woke to the sound of Sally's arrival with her morning tea.

Groaning, Flora turned over to where a dent in the mattress and a lingering smell of her husband's favourite cologne was the only evidence he had slept there.

'Where's Mr Bunny this morning?' She yawned and stretched her arms above her head. A glance at the mantelpiece clock made her gasp. How had she slept so late?

'He's downstairs with a visitor.' Disapproval

stiffened the girl's shoulders as she tugged open the curtains on a rattle of brass rings.

'Who?' Flora bolted upright and threw off the coverlet and shielded her eyes with one hand, observing Sally's pinched mouth with amusement. It wasn't often her maid took an instant dislike to anyone, but when she did, there was usually a reason. The last man who elicited that look had proved to be a Serbian spy.

'It's that Inspector Maddox.' Sally moved the tray from where she had placed it on the dresser, repositioning it on the nightstand. 'Him who gave you all that earache in the Evangeline Lange case. Not that he would have caught the fella if it hadn't been for us.' She scooped Flora's negligee from the bottom of the bed and nodded in the direction of the dressing room, 'I've run yer bath, Madam. Best get to it before it goes cold.'

'Thank you, Sally,' Flora said absently, her thoughts elsewhere.

If Inspector Maddox was prepared to come to the house, surely he must have some information to give them? That or he was prepared to open an investigation. Curiosity, together with the layer of ice on the window made Flora rush her bath and she tried not to fidget while Sally pressed hairpins into the soft sausage curls piled on her head and fastened the tiny row of buttons on her dress.

Finally released from Sally's deft hands and admonitions to keep still, Flora hurried downstairs. A lingering smell of hot fat and coffee emanated from the dining room containing only a maid stacking plates and dishes onto a tray.

She returned the way she had come and entered the sitting room, where a handsome man in his early thirties, with coal black hair and eyes to match beneath fine arched brows, leapt to his feet as she entered.

'Ah, Flora, there you are.' Bunny approached from beside the fireplace. 'You remember Detective Maddox.' As he passed her on his way to a chair, Bunny whispered, 'Sleepyhead' in her ear.

'You should have woken me,' Flora whispered back, moving to take the inspector's outstretched hand. 'A pleasure to see you again, Inspector.'

'I was hoping we wouldn't meet again, Mrs Harrington.' At Flora's raised eyebrow he shifted in embarrassment, but his handshake was firm and confident. 'I meant, not on this end of an investigation.'

'We happened to run into one another at the Law Society dinner last evening,' Bunny said, making Flora wonder just how much of a coincidence that was. 'He works out of Camberwell Church Street these days, don't you, Inspector?'

'Camberwell?' Flora frowned.

'Bermondsey and Southwark are in his patch. He's investigating the disappearance of Isobel Lomax.' He gave her a pointed look that conveyed clearly how hard he had worked to instigate that particular conversation.

'Oh, I see.' Realization dawned and she perched

on the edge of the sofa, her attention on the policeman's face. 'And how far have you got?'

'I'm not supposed to discuss ongoing investigations, you understand.' Maddox flicked up his jacket flaps as he resumed his seat. 'We're working on the theory that the nanny hasn't been candid with us. Other than that, I cannot comment.' Flora was about to disagree but he forestalled her with an upraised hand. 'Your husband was quite insistent we also look at the case of children missing from St Philomena's Hospital. You are friends with the Matron, I understand?'

'I am, Inspector. Though I hope you aren't going to tell me we share a fertile imagination and they aren't really missing?'

'My dear,' Bunny interrupted with a noisy clearing of his throat. 'Shall I ask Stokes to bring you some coffee?'

'No, that's all right.' Flora waved him away. 'I'll have something later, I—' She broke off as she caught his warning look. 'I'm sorry, Inspector. I understand you have procedures to follow, but many aspects of this case don't fit.'

'Indeed, but please don't think I'm unsympathetic.' Maddox's voice softened, losing much of its clipped formality, his eyes darkening to a deep chocolate colour. 'I'm not immune to the plight of these children. I've dealt with many cases where minors are treated by their own families like commodities to be disposed of as they will. We had a similar incident last year when I worked out of Canon Row, but the investigation went nowhere as the families refused to talk. As far as we're aware, the children never returned. I'm still haunted by what might have happened to them.'

'What *do* you think happened to them?' Flora asked.

A look of mutual understanding passed between Bunny and the policeman but was gone in an instant. Bunny fidgeted and Maddox cleared his throat, but no one ventured an answer.

'Detective,' Flora began with an inward sigh, 'I realize you feel the need to protect my sensibilities, but there really is no need.' She directed an accusing glance at Bunny to include him in the statement.

'I beg your pardon, I'm sure.' Maddox rubbed both hands along his thighs and leaned forward until he was perched on the last four inches of his chair. 'I don't mean to patronize you, but these cases are never straightforward. These children have apparently been taken with the consent of their families.'

'Consent? You mean they were given away?' Bunny's confirmation of what Flora had already surmised made her stomach churn.

'Surely that cannot be legal if the authorities have no idea where they are being taken and for what purpose?' Flora demanded.

'It's complicated, Mrs Harrington.' He cleared his throat before continuing. 'In fact, until last year, unless there was specific proof of abuse, we had no powers.'

'Last year?' Flora asked, shocked. 'You mean, taking children from their homes for some nefarious purpose wasn't a crime?'

Maddox ducked his head, embarrassed. 'If a family came to an agreement with a third party to send their child away to work or live elsewhere, even if they took money for doing so, there wasn't much the law could do about it.'

'And what if one of those children were found dead in a ditch at a later date?'

'Ah, now that would be a different crime altogether.' He spread his hands out in front of him. 'Murder is always murder.'

'That's outrageous,' Flora muttered, the silence stretching as the weight of their combined thoughts mounted, broken only by clearing of throats and the ticking of a clock.

'What about the death of Nurse Prentice?' Flora asked after a moment. 'She was the one who brought these children to Miss Finch's notice.'

Maddox nodded. 'I'm acquainted with the Matron; a very intelligent woman. I've also spoken to Mr Raymond Buchanan, both about Nurse Prentice's unfortunate accident and the Lomax girl. He mentioned nothing about other missing children.'

'Miss Finch said he didn't see any cause for concern,' Flora said. 'Though that doesn't mean there shouldn't be.'

'I agree. Maybe a second visit could result in something I could take to my superintendent to expand the investigation. You are acquainted with Mr Buchanan?'

'Only briefly.' Flora hesitated, reluctant to expand on her theories. Apart from a vague feeling of unease, she had no proof the hospital governor knew anything. Perhaps that might change after that evening? 'Miss Finch is also convinced Lizzie Prentice discovered something, but was killed before she could say anything.'

'That Miss Prentice's death was anything more than an accident hasn't yet been established,' Maddox said. 'The inquest has been set for later this morning. As for what she may or may not have been about to impart to Miss Finch, I—'

'I understand, Inspector,' Flora waved him away. Evidently, she would get nowhere with that line of questioning. 'However, Isobel Lomax was seen leaving the hospital with a stranger. Surely that changes things?' Her sharp tone elicited another warning glance from Bunny.

'Indeed it does, and as I said, we are pursuing a line of enquiry.' He exchanged another angst-filled look with Bunny.

Flora cleared her throat and waited for Maddox's full attention, which came after a heart-beat. 'Inspector, have you heard the name, Swifty Ellis?'

Maddox's eyes narrowed. 'That name is known to us. Might I ask how you've heard it?'

'Yes, do enlighten us.' Bunny rose one sardonic eyebrow.

'I'm sorry, Bunny, but you weren't here, so I couldn't explain. Sally and Abel Cain were in The Antigallican last night, and—'

'That's more my patch than yours, Mrs Harrington.' A nerve beside Maddox's left eye twitched, but he swallowed whatever he had been about to say next. 'I doubt a character like Swifty Ellis has the nous required to traffic a group of children without someone knowing about it.'

So the police did know him.

Flora frowned, unsure what the word 'nous' meant and resolved to ask Sally later.

'Go on with what you were saying, Mrs Harrington.' The inspector removed his ubiquitous notebook and pen from an inside pocket and scribbled something.

'Lizzie Prentice,' Flora began, 'worked at the same public house on occasion and just before she was killed, or died whichever you prefer, she had an argument with a woman in the kitchen there.'

'My, you have been busy, Mrs Harrington.' He raised his gaze from the page and regarded her steadily. 'However, if I investigated every confrontation in a South London pub, I would have no time for anything else.'

Flora suppressed a frustrated sigh at his patronizing tone. Didn't he see that argument could have been important?

'I'm sorry to disappoint you,' Maddox said, catching her audible sigh. 'And I'm aware you like to dabble in solving crimes, but—'

'Dabble?' Flora stiffened, knowing what was coming next. 'You make it sound like a hobby. And so there is no misunderstanding, Inspector, I specialise in murders.'

Bunny brought his fist to his mouth to cover a laugh, but ignoring him, Flora continued, 'what about this Swifty Ellis?' Had Bunny told Maddox about her and Lydia's foray into Bermondsey the day before?

'He's more of a small-time crook who fences stolen goods,' Maddox said. 'He pretends to be mentally incompetent when questioned, so we rarely get much out of him, but he's got a steady network of thugs who dare not defy him.'

'Isn't that contradictory?' Flora asked, irritated. 'On the one hand, he's too simple-minded to be involved, then you say he has the acumen to run a successful team of crooks?'

'Ah, yes I see your point.' He gave Bunny a how-do-you-manage-her look which Bunny returned with a brief widening of his eyes.

'I urge you to be very careful, Mrs Harrington.' Maddox's voice softened. 'And keep away from Swifty Ellis. If he *is* involved, you can be sure he's working for someone more powerful and better connected than he is.'

'What about the man in the top hat who was seen with Isobel Lomax the day she disappeared?'

Flora asked, although she couldn't help feeling that Maddox was indulging her for Bunny's sake.

'I'm afraid no other witnesses have come forward regarding that individual. Now if you'll excuse me,' Maddox slapped his knees and rose. 'I had better get back to the station. However, I assure you that if there is a connection to these cases, I'll find it. Good morning, Mrs Harrington. Mr Harrington.'

Bunny handed Maddox over to Stokes, who showed him out, the sound of male voices in the hall cut off by the closing of the front door.

'He thinks he's got the nanny for the Isobel kidnapping and has no more idea than we do how to look for the others,' she said.

'Don't be too sure,' Bunny said, slowly. 'He wasn't as dismissive as you imagined.'

Flora wasn't convinced. 'Anyway, thank you for persuading him to come here when you were supposed to be consorting with other lawyers over fine wine.' She scooted along the wide sofa to make room for him. 'And I apologize for annoying him when you went to all that trouble to get him here. Not that he told us anything we didn't already know. Why does he have to be so formal?'

'You underestimate him, Flora.' Bunny plucked her hand from her lap and enfolded it in both of his. 'He couldn't tell us anything. Not officially. At the dinner last night he explained the police now have authority under the Human Trafficking Act to look for children believed to be at risk. He also has this Swifty Ellis character in his sights, which tells me they are doing far more than you assume.'

'I suppose you could be right.' Flora straightened. 'Perhaps I'm so conscious of the fact he regards me as a meddling nuisance, I get very defensive with him.'

'I *had* noticed.' Bunny's lips twitched. 'However, I'm sure you're quite wrong about his disliking you. He's been more than complimentary about your past efforts.'

'You surprise me, when he loses no opportunity to tell me when I get it wrong.'

'That's because you do tend to rush into situations without thinking. Look at it from his point of view. Having a civilian poking about in his cases could be embarrassing for him.'

Flora shrugged. She wasn't used to people taking such an active dislike to her, which made her uncomfortable. Only one other person treated her dismissively, but she had put Beatrice's attitude down to jealousy. What did Inspector Maddox have to be jealous about? Or did he feel threatened by her?'

Bunny released her hand, giving it a final pat before he rose and poured himself a cup of coffee from a tray on the sideboard, that despite Flora's refusal Stokes had delivered. 'I hear you're sending young Sally out to pubs to scout the local colour now eh? I hope you aren't becoming a bad influence on her.'

'Me?' Flora threw him a sharp sideways look. 'It's more likely to be the other way around. She couldn't wait to go, possibly because it meant an entire evening in Abel's company.' The fragrance of coffee from his cup nudged her senses. 'Might I change my mind about that coffee? I could do with some.'

'You haven't had any breakfast either.' Bunny set his cup and saucer on the table and obliged. 'Maybe I could take you out for luncheon sometime this week?' He set a cup in front of her, from which an enticing wisp of steam rose.

'I would like that.' She lifted the cup to her lips, inhaling the rich aroma before taking a sip. 'And maybe you're right and Maddox didn't come here simply to oblige you in return for a good breakfast.'

'Cynic.' Bunny smiled. 'I see him as more a sponge than a fountain, which makes for a good policeman. Give him a chance, he'll work it all out.'

'Is that your way of saying you want me to take a step back and let the professionals take over?' She directed a hard look at him over the rim of her cup.

'As if *that* would make any difference.' He returned to the sofa, cup in hand, the cushion dipping as he lowered himself onto it. 'But please be careful, my darling. I know how passionate you are about this affair, but the sort of people who do this sort of thing won't think twice about putting a stop to any meddling on your part.'

'Is that what you think I'm doing? Meddling?' Her stomach rumbled, reminding her of her missed breakfast. 'Maybe the case will become clearer if the coroner decides Lizzie was murdered.' She caught his sideways look, adding, 'That's a horrible thing to hope for, isn't it?'

'Whatever you say about Lizzie cannot hurt her now. Now tell me again what Sally found out last night, and this time I want the long version.'

Flora sipped her coffee, the strong taste an aid to her whirling thoughts as she recounted Abel's conversation with the barman.

'I agree, that argument could be important,' Bunny conceded after Flora had shared her story in full. But even if you find this woman, I doubt she would admit to a confrontation with someone who died soon afterwards. By the way, when are you seeing Miss Finch again?'

'I hope to see her this afternoon at Martell's, although we've made no firm arrangement. Why?'

'I acknowledge that you aren't using this case purely to stay close to Miss Finch, it's too important for that. But take care where she's concerned, Flora, the likelihood of her being your mother is infinitesimal.'

'I know, and I promise not to rely on that possibility too much, although I cannot help admiring her. If nothing else, I'll have made a friend.' She crossed the fingers of her other hand inside the folds of her skirt. The more she saw of Alice, the conviction they shared a connection became more real.

'As long as you are prepared for disappointment.' He ran his knuckles gently across her chin. 'Now, I have some paperwork to do so I need to call into the office.' Bunny returned his cup to the tray and made for the door. 'I'll be back in time to get ready for our supper party. A pity William isn't available to join us. Did he drop any clues as to where he was going on this trip of his?'

'No. I believe he made a point of not doing so.' Renewed worry flooded through her at the mention of William's name. That he had not confided his intended destination to Bunny either convinced her he had embarked on something secret, even dangerous. She twisted on the sofa, both arms crossed along the back. 'Speaking of William, I—'

'Yes?' Bunny halted and turned back, peering at her over his glasses.

Her words froze on her tongue as she experienced a glimpse of the future. There would come a time when he would look at her just like that, when his hair was no longer wheat gold but sparse and grey, the creases on his forehead had deepened and the lens of his spectacles were as thick as the base of a whisky glass.

'What about him?' Bunny frowned. 'And why are you staring at me like that?'

'Oh, nothing.' Pushing down the sudden rapid thrum of her heart, she summoned a smile. 'It can wait. I'll see you this evening.'

CHAPTER 18

Martell's tea shop was unusually busy that afternoon, but the waitress who had served Flora on previous occasions assured her there would always be a table for her. 'Mr Martell insists we never turn you away, Mrs Harrington.'

'How kind.' Flora took the seat she indicated, located on a table with a panoramic view of the street through the bay window. From there she could observe the rest of the room; specifically a lone woman in an alcove in unrelieved black, who greeted every male patron with a wide smile but ignored the women. She reminded Flora of what Lydia had told her of a Piccadilly tea room that ran a house of ill repute on its upper floor.

Flora's private smile must have been taken as encouragement by Mr Martell, who bustled towards her with purpose in each step.

'Ah, so we have the pleasure of your company yet again, *ma chère madame*.' He held his right hand extended, bent at the wrist, his slight paunch straining an embroidered waistcoat, this one of peacock blue with green parrots. 'Do you await the delightful *Mees* Grey, or perhaps *Mees Feench* will join you today?'

'I'm both surprised and flattered that you should take such a personal interest in my activities, Mr Martell.' Did the man keep notes? The Frenchman had always struck her as solicitous, but lately, his attentions had become cloying, even intrusive. Perhaps his days spent over teacups and cream cakes made him long for some more sophisticated society?

'I like to *theenk* of myself as a good proprietor, dear lady with a keen interest in my patrons.' His oily smile persisted. 'I see you and the elegant *'ospital ladee* have become firm friends since coming *'ere.*'

'We didn't actually meet in your establishment,' Flora replied, unwilling to give the man too much credit. 'You are right, however, in that she's an exceptional person. We find we have a great deal in common.'

'I agree, she is *charmante*.' He gave a theatrical sigh too contrived to be genuine. 'What a *tragedie* about that poor nurse who was killed. Such things will do nothing for the hospital's reputation.'

'A tragedy indeed, but not one that could be put at Miss Finch's door.' Flora fidgeted, uncomfortable with the subject. 'As far as I know, the nurse fell and hit her head.'

'I did not seek to imply *ozerwise*.' He blinked repeatedly, his eyes surrounded by wrinkles that put her in mind of a myopic turtle. 'And yet that does not disappoint you, Madame?'

'I beg your pardon?' Flora frowned up at him from beneath the rim of her hat. 'I don't understand.'

'*Mais non?* But are you not famous! Is not murder of special interest to the brave heroine who confronted the killer of Mademoiselle Evangeline Lange last year?'

Taken off guard, Flora floundered for a response. He must have seen the report in the newspaper, though it struck her as indelicate to mention it. Alice was right, the man was an inveterate gossip.

The harsh jangle of the doorbell distracted him. 'Ah! Here is your companion, if I am not mistaken.' He nodded to where Alice had entered the tea room.

A crash of china brought the Frenchman's attention to where a waitress had swept a plate of cakes onto the floor behind the counter. Martell gave a sharp, horrified cry and scurried away to castigate the mortified girl.

'You arrived at exactly the right moment,' Flora said as Alice joined her.

'So I see.' Alice swung her bag onto the table and took the chair opposite. She wore a beautifully cut ankle-length wool coat in a flattering shade of sage green that clung in all the right places. Her pert hat and the way everything matched made Flora hope that she would look as elegant and youthful as Alice when she reached her forties. And why shouldn't she? Daughters often resembled their mothers, didn't they?

'Flora?' Alice's eyes widened in enquiry. 'Did you hear what I said?'

'Oh, sorry, I missed that.' Distracted, she cast an oblique look at Mr Martell, who was still occupied with the distraught waitress.

'I said, I haven't been to the hospital today as I attended Lizzie Prentice's inquest this morning.'

'I had completely forgotten. How did it go?' Flora waylaid a passing server and issued a request to replace their half-empty teapot.

'Dr Samuel's testimony was categorical, in that Lizzie couldn't possibly have injured herself so badly in a fall.'

'He's certain about that?' Though her sympathy for Lizzie was unchanged, the verdict might make the police take things more seriously.

'His explanation was quite technical, but in simple terms, the fracture was too high in the parietal bone to have been caused by a fall. She was hit with something extremely heavy and with some force.'

'She *was* murdered.' Flora nodded slowly. 'Someone hit her over the head with a stone and arranged it to make look as if she had fallen.'

'How did you know?' Frowning, Alice poured milk into her tea. 'It was only announced at the inquest.'

'Because the bloodstain was on the side of the

kerb stone, there was none on the upper surface Also, the side with the blood on it was already wet from the rain. When she was killed it had stopped, so when the killer moved the stone, he placed it dry side upwards. He was clever enough to put it back, but didn't have time to arrange the scene properly.'

'Perhaps I should have let you talk to the police that day.' Alice propped her elbows on the table, her chin balanced on her folded hands. 'Now, I can see you are longing to tell me something. I take it you have news?'

Flora waited until the waitress had set the replacement teapot on the table and left.

Over hot, strong tea and a plate of Martell's famous almond biscuits, Flora explained all that she had told Bunny about Sally's visit to The Antigallican.

'That certainly clarifies a few things,' Alice said when Flora had finished. 'I'm not surprised Lizzie didn't tell me. The student nurses live in quarters to which we attach certain rules. One being a curfew. Had I known, it would have been cause for her dismissal.'

'Have you no idea of what Lizzie was going to tell you that day?'

Alice drummed the fingers of her right hand on the table. 'Apart from matters connected to her patients, I don't think – oh wait, there was something. I passed Lizzie outside the basement kitchens a day or so before she was killed. She was upset, well, more shocked actually and she didn't respond when I spoke to her.'

'What was it that had upset her?'

'I asked her, but she said it was nothing. I took the stance that if she wished to tell me she would choose her own time.' Alice sighed. 'I wish I had insisted because she obviously changed her mind. Now it's too late.'

'I see.' Flora released the breath she held. 'That doesn't tell us much, does it?'

'No, I'm sorry. But just before Lizzie went off to her ward, she said how odd it was that something you see every day changes with one small detail.'

'Something or someone?'

'I have no idea. Two patients had been booked for the same bed, which put Sister Lazarus into a muddle trying to sort it out, so I stepped in. I wish I had paid more attention to Lizzie.'

'If she was referring to something at the hospital, something she had seen that she shouldn't have, that could mean someone at the hospital wanted her dead.'

'Not necessarily,' Alice countered. 'Members of the public have access to the building and grounds, not to mention tradesmen, clerical staff, and families. We have visiting doctors frequently of course, as well as the Board of Governors. Not that any of *them* could have been responsible.'

'No, of course not,' Flora mumbled, unconvinced. 'Did Mr Buchanan attend the inquest?'

'Yes, he did. He and Dr Reid were called to give evidence. I think they were both shocked, as Mr Buchanan had been content to go along with Dr Reid's conclusion that it was an accident.'

'Is he a good doctor? Reid, I mean?'

'Um-yes.' Alice blinked as if the question confused her.' He's an exemplary young man, if a little overenthusiastic at times. I don't think he misread the situation on purpose if that's what you're implying.'

'I wasn't implying anything,' Flora assured her. 'Only that we need to look at everyone involved with this affair as a whole. Is Mr Buchanan now convinced these children are genuinely missing? Or does he still dismiss your concerns?'

'I'm not sure, as I haven't discussed it with him since my last attempt. I don't wish to upset him more than necessary.' Alice sighed, replacing her cup slowly. 'The Isobel Lennox disappearance has affected him badly, and now, what with a murder, having the police on the premises casts a shadow over the whole hospital.'

Alice's reluctance to press Buchanan was a puzzle. She did not strike Flora as a woman easily distracted from a cause that mattered to her. Or was there more to her relationship with Raymond Buchanan than she had confided? He was a widower in his fifties, and not unattractive, so perhaps it wasn't out of the question Alice might be interested in him romantically. 'Have the police learned anything more about the Lomax girl?'

'It transpires the nursery maid has a gentleman friend. The police think he was the man who collected Isobel from the hospital.'

'Then why isn't she there?'

'Because with the girl's parents away, the police believe the nanny and her suitor were, er-otherwise occupied when Isobel left the house and became lost. It seems the child is known to have sleepwalked on occasion. When the pair discovered she wasn't in the house the next morning, they decided to say she was taken from St Philomena's to cover their own indiscretion. Not to mention negligence.'

'Can the police prove that?' Flora's estimation of Inspector Maddox took a dip.

Alice shrugged. 'She and the young man are still being questioned at the police station. Oh, look out, Mr Martell is coming over. Serves me right for smiling at him.'

The Frenchman paused beside their table, his head tilted and with a comedic expression that lacked subtlety. 'I was just saying before you arrived *Mees Feench*, that you and *Madame 'Areengton* have become especial friends. As usual, you seem to have so much to talk about.'

'You provide such a charming ambiance, sir, how could we not?' Alice's response was accompanied by a definite tightening of her jaw.

It seemed Flora wasn't the only one who was uncomfortable in his presence.

'I was saying to *Madame 'Areengton* before you

arrived, dear lady. About the murder. What a trial that must have been for a professional lady such as yourself.'

'News travels fast, Mr Martell,' Alice exchanged an incredulous look with Flora. 'I don't believe it has reached the latest edition of the newspapers as yet.' She thrust the hot water pot towards him, leaving him with no option but to take it. 'Would you mind refilling this for us?'

He blinked, his chin jerked back in mild shock. He glanced round quickly for a waitress, but none were in calling distance. Left with no choice but to perform the task himself, he bowed and with a murmured, '*Certainment, Madame*,' backed away.

'That was clever,' Flora said when he was out of earshot. 'I always regarded his nosiness as ingratiation before. Now it seems he has ears everywhere. I dread to think what he knows about us.'

'Those ladies don't appear to mind his fawning ways,' Alice indicated to where Mr Martell, the hot water pot still in hand, stood deep in conversation with three matrons at another table. 'But perhaps their lives are less interesting than ours. By the way,' Alice said, 'do tell your charming husband how grateful I am for his influence with the local constabulary. I got nowhere, though according to them I'm an impressionable spinster with an overactive imagination.'

'You are anything but that,' Flora had to raise her voice over the clatter of crockery and a burst of feminine laughter that rose from the table where Mr Martell entertained the ladies. 'What I don't understand, is why these particular children are being taken, and why after they have spent time in the hospital? There must be plenty of homeless waifs these people could—' Flora realized what she had said and brought a hand to her mouth in embarrassment. 'Oh dear, that was callous of me. I didn't mean anything by it.'

'I know, my dear,' Alice waved her away. 'I too have also given that question some thought. The treatment we offer at St Philomena's extends beyond immediate illness. The children are checked for conditions like rickets, skin diseases, eyesight problems and malnutrition. They leave us healthy, or as much as they can be, given their living conditions.' She balanced her full cup in both hands and took a sip. 'None of those who were taken are malformed or chronically ill. Without exception they are also good-looking convincing me they have been carefully chosen. For what, I dare not imagine.'

Flora's stomach knotted, her eyes fixed on the tiny spoon Alice used to stir her tea as a myriad of horrors ran through her head. How naïve she had been. Those poor mites taken from their homes with the promise of a better life only to be forced into – what? Slavery, even prostitution? The intermittent jangle of the shop bell as customers came and went jarred uncomfortably with the thoughts in her head. How could life be so cruel?

By the time Mr Martell had despatched a waitress to their table with the hot water, their conversation had dwindling to small talk, with neither willing to broach the subject that hung between them.

'Goodness,' Alice looked up at the wall clock. 'It's later than I thought, I must go.' She summoned the waitress to settle their bill. 'Mr Buchanan is expecting me.'

'Are you going back to the hospital?' Flora gathered her bag and together they made their way to the front desk where the waitress took Alice's money and proffered her change.

'No, I often assist him with paperwork in connection with his other business at his home. He had a secretary at one time, but when she left to get married, he didn't hire another. I think he prefers to work with people he knows, so I agreed to spare him a few hours a week.'

'Thus the hospital isn't Mr Buchanan's only interest?' Flora tucked a sixpenny piece under the plate on the counter set aside for gratuities.

'His role as a governor only occupies him briefly,' Alice explained as they emerged onto the street. 'His fortune was made in importing items from abroad, especially when Chinese furniture and porcelain became popular. When his wife was alive they travelled everywhere together. Since her death, he sends his agents to buy for him and has the goods sent home in his ships. I doubt he has the heart for foreign travel without Mary.'

They took their farewells on the pavement, and on the short walk back to Eaton Place, Flora's thoughts turned uneasily to her arrangement with Sally for that evening's concert; an excursion she was glad she had not mentioned to Alice. How could she admit that she had set her spy team onto the man Alice thought so much of? She would face that dilemma later, and if nothing came of it, she wouldn't have to.

It wasn't until she reached the path leading to her own front door that something Alice had said about Mr Buchanan scraped at her brain, though she couldn't recall what it was.

Flora held her sapphire pendant up to her throat, her head tilted and lips pursed at her reflection in the dressing table mirror as she assessed the effect it made against her gown. Frowning, she returned the item to the velvet lined box.

'Are you sure it's a good idea having Sally watch this Buchanan chap while he's at the concert, Flora?' Bunny joined her in the bedroom, his skin pink from his bath while rubbing his damp hair vigorously with a towel.

'I thought I had explained,' Flora sighed. 'She's going to sit in the café opposite for the evening. She and Abel will look to all the world like a courting couple having supper. They won't alert anyone's suspicions and if Mr Buchanan is inno-cent, they will just have enjoyed a pleasant evening.'

'I suppose so.' He lowered the towel and frowned

at her reflection. 'Why aren't you wearing the sapphire pendant? It's my favourite.'

'It's the wrong shade of blue.' Flora indicated the deep turquoise silk of her dress.

'I'll bow to your superior taste.' He discarded the towel and shrugged into a clean shirt.

'Sally's quite excited about helping with a real investigation,' Flora added, in case Bunny thought she had forced her maid to co-operate against her better judgement. 'Especially when I agreed that she should take Abel with her.'

'I gather you're paying for their supper?'

'Of course. And the hackney fare there and back. It's the least I could do.'

'I'll wager five shillings she takes the omnibus so she can pocket the difference.' He raised one perfectly arched eyebrow.

'I shan't take that bet as I am likely to lose. Sally is nothing if not enterprising.' A light knock came at the door, prompting Flora to hold up a finger in warning to be discreet as she went to open it.

'I'm ready to go, Madam.' Sally slapped her gloved hands together. 'Abel's waiting for me on the steps.' Smart and pretty in her best maroon outdoor coat buttoned to the neck, she had arranged a pert felt hat jauntily on her wild curls.

'Here's a prospectus for St Philomena's.' Flora handed her a pamphlet she had placed close to hand in readiness. 'There's a photograph of Mr Buchanan on page six. Do you think you could pick him out in a crowd from that?'

244

'Nice-looking man.' Sally held the page at arm's length as she squinted at the picture, her chin tucked in as with the other hand she pocketed the five half-crowns Flora handed her with lightning speed. 'Shouldn't be difficult.'

'Make sure you and Abel arrive well before the performance to lessen the chances of missing him. If he speaks to anyone going in or coming out, I need to know what they look like – in detail. Especially if you see Swifty again, but under no circumstances are either of you to approach him.'

'Cor, this feels like a real investigation. Do I get paid extra?'

Bunny's amused chuckle reached her from inside the room.

Flora threw him a backwards look, grasped Sally by the arm and eased her into the hall, pulling the door to. 'No, but you can have whatever you like for supper. If Mr Buchanan leaves the perform-ance early, I expect you to notice the time.'

'Got it.'

As Sally's footsteps receded down the stairs, Flora turned to find Bunny stood with his hands propped on his hips, grinning at her.

'Twelve shillings and sixpence? That's twice what she needs. You spoil that young woman; she'll be getting notions above her station if you aren't careful.'

Unwilling to get into an argument, Flora unhooked Bunny's jacket from a hanger and held it out.

'What exactly has a perfectly respectable businessman done to make you believe he's involved with these missing children and a murder?' Bunny eased his arms into the sleeves and swivelled round to face her.

'I'm not sure he's done anything.' Flora smoothed the fabric over his shoulders. 'However, when he opened that envelope with the concert ticket, he looked as if the whole world had descended on him. I know a worried man when I see one.'

'Which might have nothing at all to do with what is happening at the hospital.' Bunny eased his neck inside his upright collar. 'Besides, if he is involved, he's hardly likely to show his hand at a concert.'

'I disagree. It's the last place anyone would expect strange goings-on. Besides, all you have to do is enjoy Lydia and Harry's company this evening. I'll sort out everything else.'

'That's what worries me,' Bunny muttered as he retrieved his spectacles from a side table and polished the lenses with a handkerchief. The chime of the doorbell sounded from the floor below.

'That will be Lydia and Harry.' Flora plucked the spectacles from his fingers, slid them onto his nose and brushed her lips across his newly shaved cheek. 'We'd better go down.'

CHAPTER 19

Flora and Lydia took their seats in the sitting room, replete from a supper no one had enjoyed more than Harry.

'I told you he would appreciate a home-cooked meal after dining in cafés and restaurants every day,' Lydia whispered when he had delivered yet another effusive compliment. She wore a shade of chartreuse that complemented her fair hair and delicate features. A single drop pearl hung from a gold chain round her throat, her eyes sparkling with happiness rivalling the diamond on her left hand.

'What were you saying about postponing the wedding, Lydia?' Bunny dismissed Stokes in order to preside over the brandy decanter and coffee tray himself.

'Indeed, it's a shame when you were set on a festive ceremony,' Flora added.

'That's what *I* say.' Harry lounged against a chair, his forearms draped over the high back. 'I've made it quite clear I don't care a fig for my parents' disapproval.'

'Is that what this is all about?' Flora asked, angry

that the Flynns regarded intelligent, sweet-natured Lydia a poor candidate as a wife for their son.

'They were so set on me marrying Evangeline,' Harry said. 'It rather threw them when she died.'

'She was murdered, Harry. By her half-brother.' Lydia accepted the cut-glass balloon Bunny held out. 'Your mother was very fond of Evangeline.' That she felt less than affection for Lydia was implied. 'It must have been a shock for her to know her plans for you had been shattered.'

'More like horror that I wouldn't have access to her fortune.' Harry straightened in order to take a glass from Bunny, from which a rich spirit smell emanated. 'I've told them countless times I only went along with their plans to appease them.' He took a mouthful of brandy, giving a slight shudder.

'Is the spirit not to your liking?' Bunny asked, his forehead creased in a frown.

'Not at all. It's excellent.' Harry lifted the glass so it caught the light, the transparent gold liquid glowing through the crystal facets. 'Perhaps I should have sipped it.'

'That would be my advice. It's a rather fine Otard XO, matured in the lower vaults of Chateau Otard on the banks of the River Charente. The cellars provide a constant temperature and humidity perfect for the ageing of eaux-de-vie.' He smiled broadly at the row of astonished faces turned towards him.

'*Eu de vie*? Isn't that what the Scots call whisky?' Lydia asked.

'Funny you should say that.' Bunny took his seat

in his favourite leather studded chair, one ankle crossed over the other. 'The family originated from eleventh century Vikings and settled in Scotland, later becoming Jacobites. They followed James II into exile after the Glorious Revolution of 1688.'

'I had no idea you were so knowledgeable, Bunny.' Lydia's eyes shone in admiration.

'Not really. I spent a very boring holiday in Cognac when I was fourteen with an aunt who dragged me on a tour of the chateaux. Surprising how certain things sink in.'

'Don't spoil it.' Flora pouted. 'I prefer to think I married a man of the world.'

'Then you might be interested in the only other fact I remember.' Bunny ignored Flora's eyebrow dance indicating that he was about to risk boring their guests. 'Baron Otard was condemned to death in the French Revolution, but the night before his execution, the villagers of Cognac broke into his prison and freed him.'

'That's fascinating.' Flora held his gaze in challenge. 'However, we were discussing the post-ponement of Lydia and Harry's wedding.'

'Oh, yes, sorry. Didn't mean to be a bore.' Bunny visibly shrank in his chair.

'Which is something you most certainly are not.' Lydia's eyes flashed through her lowered lashes. 'As to the wedding. Harry's father is a dear, but I wanted to give his mother and sisters a chance to get to know me better. They always look as if they are sucking lemons when they see me.'

'Believe me, Lydia, my love,' Harry snorted, 'unless you inherit a fortune from a lost uncle with a dukedom, nothing will change.'

'Entirely their loss.' Flora patted her friend's hand. 'not to mention a real Jane Austen moment.' At Harry's confused frown, she added, 'You know, Charles Bingley's sisters disapproving of Jane Bennett.'

'Not a reader or romantic novels, I'm afraid,' Harry muttered, his nose buried in his brandy glass.

'When we are married, I'll simply have to educate you,' Lydia said.

His lower lip dropped, his discomfort greeted with a guffaw of laughter from Bunny. 'You might not find Austen as bad as you imagine, old chap.'

While Lydia scolded them gently, Bunny for his teasing and Harry for an aversion to her favourite author, Flora's mind drifted, her gaze going back to the clock on the mantelpiece for the third time in as many minutes. Surely Sally should have returned by now; it was after eleven.

'Flora?' the sharpness in Bunny's tone made her jump. 'Harry's coffee cup is empty'

'Ah sorry, of course. Anyone else want more coffee?' In response to murmurs of assent she rose and refilled their cups, the action giving her something to do, but it failed to reduce her growing anxiety. The concert wouldn't go on much after ten thirty, so where was Sally?

'I hear you've been flirting with politics, Harry?'

Bunny held up the brandy decanter in an open invitation.

Harry accepted, as did Lydia, but Flora declined. Baron Otard's brandy might be the finest but it was too fiery for her.

'Indeed he has,' Lydia said. 'He's become quite an admirer of Keir Hardie.'

'I take it you approve?' Bunny addressed Lydia, returning the decanter to the tray.

'I do, actually,' Lydia replied, enthusiastically. 'Hardie champions women's rights, free schooling and pensions. He's not a supporter of the monarchy either, which upsets the Conservatives.'

'I can see why your parents think Lydia is a bad influence.' Bunny aimed a wink at Harry making him laugh. 'Hasn't he come in for some criticism for attending the Commons in a tweed suit instead of formal dress like the rest of the House?'

'There are far more interesting things to say about him,' Harry said. 'Like the fact he's a man who would be sympathetic to the plight of these children of whom you and Lydia have become champions, Flora.' Harry saluted her with his coffee cup. 'At least now the Police have the authority under the Human Trafficking Act to make whoever is responsible account for their crimes in a court of law.'

'We'll need to find them first.' Lydia's comment was greeted with a sigh from Flora and murmurs of agreement from the men. 'I don't suppose this—' Lydia broke off as the door opened revealing Stokes.

'Excuse me, sir.' His eyes darted the room before settling on Bunny, while one hand made a vague pointing gesture to his right. 'There's a . . . person outside who insists on speaking with you.'

Flora's stomach knotted with disappointment it wasn't Sally. 'Who could be calling at this hour?' she asked no one in particular.

'You'd better admit them, Stokes. It might be important,' Bunny said, but before the butler could comply, Abel Cain shoved past him and strode into the room. Stokes gave a shocked protest, which Bunny interrupted. 'It's quite all right, Stokes. You may go.'

The butler bowed and backed away, his reluctance evident in the way he pulled the door closed far slower than normal.

'Abel?' Flora asked, as everyone's attention fixed on the newcomer, whose impressive build made the room suddenly crowded. 'What is it? What's wrong?'

He stood with slumped shoulders, his thick brown hair disarranged by the swift and last minute removal of his hat. 'Apologies for disturbing you, Mrs Harrington, Mr Harrington.' Abel's brown eyes widened in distress as he looked from Bunny to Flora and back again. 'Has anyone seen Sally?'

'Isn't she with you?' Flora rose slowly from her seat as dread turned the uneasy fluttering in her chest to panic.

'No, Miss. I hoped she might have come back

here.' Abel scanned the room with nervous darts of his head, as if he expected Sally might be concealed behind a sofa.

'Well, she hasn't.' Bunny placed his brandy glass on the mantelpiece with a click and came to stand at Flora's side. 'What happened tonight?'

'We did exactly what you said.' He repeatedly twisted the brown cap in both hands in front of him with a force that threatened to rip the material. 'We sat in that café across the road from the concert hall and saw Mr Buchanan arrive. He didn't talk to anyone from what we could see, but we saw him come out again during the interval. He stood on the street smoking a cigar.'

'I gather nothing unusual happened and he went back in again?' Bunny prompted, evidently irritated by Abel's slow, contemplative way of speaking.

'He didn't go back in, sir' He gave his hat another mangling.

'Where did he go?' Flora clenched her hands together to remind her not to snap.

'That's what I'm trying to tell you.' Abel swallowed. 'We followed him into the Lamb and Flag in St James' Street, where he bought a double whisky. The pub was very busy, so Sally and me had trouble keeping an eye on him without drawing attention to ourselves.'

'Are you saying he gave you the slip?' Bunny asked.

'No, sir. Only we daren't get too close in case he spotted us, and what with all the comings and

253

goings, it was hard to keep him in sight all the time.'

'We understand, Abel,' Flora said gently. 'It was a difficult situation. Did Mr Buchanan talk to anyone?'

'Not at first. We hadn't been there long when a man and a woman from the Sally Army turned up with collection boxes. I didn't think much of it at first, I mean, them God-botherers like to catch people in pubs and tap them up for a few shillings.'

Lydia giggled, but sobered when she caught Flora's hard look and mouthed an apology.

'Abel,' Bunny interrupted him, 'where is all this leading?'

'Sorry, sir.' He ducked his head, embarrassed. 'Sally told me she saw the woman give Mr Buchanan a note.'

'What woman?' Lydia asked, impatient.

'I didn't see her properly, Miss, she was wearing one of those poke bonnets.'

'The Salvation Army woman?' Flora finally made sense of what he was trying to say. 'Why didn't you say so?'

'I thought I did.' Abel's brows knitted together. 'They all look the same, those people. Same clothes, same expressions. Can't tell one from another,' he muttered this last almost to himself. 'The note seemed to make Mr Buchanan angry because he crumpled it up and shoved it into his pocket. The officer tried to speak to him but he waved him off. I couldn't hear what he said.'

'Interesting,' Bunny mused. 'I don't suppose we'll learn what that note was about?'

'I would like to know too,' Flora said.

'Well that's the thing.' Abel twisted the hat in his hands, his neck turning a dull pink. 'Sally told me to do it, but I wasn't sure about it.' He rubbed the back of his neck with one hand as if working up to something. 'I went to the bar and, well, I-I picked Buchanan's pocket.'

'Without him realizing?' Flora asked, both shocked and admiring at the same time. How did a man like Abel, who stood over six foot and with shoulders as wide as a door, go unnoticed?

'After three double whiskys?' Abel gave her an ironic, sideways look. 'I doubt he would have noticed if I'd taken his ruddy coat off his back.' In response to Flora's shocked expression his cheeks flushed a deeper red. 'Beggin' yer pardon, missus. He barely noticed me, just stared into his glass looking all grey and drawn.'

'Might we see the result of your sleight of hand skills, Abel?' Bunny held out his hand.

'Um yes, sir. Sorry.' Abel delved into his coat pocket and drew out a slip of paper which was little more than a mass of creases.

'What about Sally?' Flora was eager to see what the note said, but her maid was her main concern just then. 'Why didn't she come home with you?'

'I-I went to the gents. And well, I was only gone a minute or two, but when I came out, Sally wasn't in the bar. I ran outside, but there was no sign of her.' He pushed one hand into his hair and left it there. 'I told her to stay and wait for me, but you know how she is.'

'I do indeed.' Sighing, Flora closed her eyes briefly. 'Where could she have gone?'

'I doubt there's cause for panic, Flora. Sally isn't likely to get lost.' Bunny moved closer and laid a hand on her shoulder; a gesture meant to calm her, but only made her more agitated. 'London is her home, so let's not worry about her until it becomes necessary.'

Flora couldn't help worrying. Sally had plenty of money for cabs and should have been home by now.

'Abel,' Bunny's grip on Flora's shoulder stayed firm. 'Think. What did Sally actually say?'

'I'm not sure.' Abel's handsome face twisted in anguish like a small boy chastised for some misdemeanour, his brow furrowed as he tried to remember. 'Something about having seen him before, but it was really noisy in that pub.'

'Perhaps *this* will tell us more?' Bunny unfolded the note and peered at it. '*Eighteen hundred hours, SS Lancett, Tilbury, October 4th,*' he read aloud. He turned the paper over and back again. 'That's all.'

'My goodness,' Lydia gasped. 'October 4th! That's tomorrow.'

'The *SS Lancett*,' Harry said slowly, joining the conversation for the first time. 'That sounds like a steamship, with the time and date of its scheduled departure.'

'Mr Buchanan's a ship owner.' Flora's throat dried as she recalled what Alice had told her. 'It must be one of his. Can they be planning to take those children out of the country?' The blood rushed through her veins making her suddenly light-headed. 'We must *do* something, Bunny. We have to tell Inspector Maddox.'

Harry stood, placed his glass on the mantelpiece beside Bunny's and rubbed his hands together. 'Flora's right, but even they cannot go barging onto a ship when they feel like it and demand to know if they have children on board. Not without some sort of warrant.'

Bunny tapped the slip of paper against his top lip. 'It's almost midnight. We'll have to wait until the morning to do anything. I'll speak to Maddox first thing tomorrow, though he might not take action on the strength of the scant evidence we have at the moment.'

'What about Sally?' Flora fought back welling tears. 'The police need to be out looking for her.'

'I know it's frustrating, Flora.' Bunny's voice was infuriatingly reasonable. 'Sally hasn't been missing for long enough to necessitate a police search. In any case, I doubt a lowly night desk sergeant would be willing to drag Inspector Maddox out of bed on our say-so.'

'No, I suppose not.' Flora's thoughts raced. 'Why did Sally go after Mr Buchanan? How could she have seen him before? Unless he was at The Antigallican the other night?'

257

'She didn't, Mrs Harrington,' Abel's soft voice at her side made her jump.

Every eye in the room rounded on Abel, who swallowed before answering.

'Mr Buchanan was still in the bar. She followed the Sally Army couple.'

CHAPTER 20

With still no sign of Sally, it was almost two o'clock by the time the party broke up, having conceded that nothing more could be done that night. Abel was reluctant to leave, only agreeing when Bunny promised to let him know the moment they heard anything.

'Chances are she'll be back before morning with a colourful tale to tell,' Bunny said in an unsuccessful attempt to reassure both the dismayed young man and Flora.

'I do hope so,' Flora whispered unable to dislodge the knot of dread twisting her stomach. Sally wouldn't leave her worrying deliberately, meaning she had been taken and thus had no choice.

With a tentative promise to talk again the next day, Bunny and Flora took their leave of their guests on the front step, held open by a visibly flagging Stokes.

'Lydia is a very progressive young woman, isn't she? Even more so than you,' Bunny raised his hand in a wave as the couple disappeared round the corner. 'Who would have thought Keir Hardie would be her hero?'

'Times are changing, Bunny.' Flora gave an exaggerated shudder and hurried back inside the house. 'Which is as it should be. Women shouldn't be considered beyond the pale because they are interested in social issues. They affect us all.'

'Try saying that to my mother and see what she says.' Bunny ushered her inside where he blew into his cupped hands. 'When she discovered I wished to marry a girl who had travelled on a ship from New York without a chaperone, she almost had to call for the smelling salts.' He trailed up the stairs, chuckling to himself.

'Your mother, my love, is from a different age.' Flora followed wearily in his wake, her concern for Sally growing more intense by the minute. 'The Stone Age.'

After a fitful night, when Flora jumped at every creak of the floorboards or scrape of a branch on the window glass, she woke to the clack of the curtains being drawn across the brass pole, flooding the room with sharp white daylight accompanied by the whoosh of running water from the bathroom across the hall.

She bolted upright in anticipation, only to slump back against the pillows when she saw it was one of the maids with her morning tea.

'Has Sally returned yet, Nell?'

'No, Madam. Sorry, Madam.' Nell placed a cup of steaming tea on the nightstand but instead of withdrawing, she hovered by the bed, evidently in the hope of hearing something of interest she could report downstairs. 'We're all that worried downstairs. It ain't like her to stay out all night.'

'I know.' Flora sighed, propped her elbow against the bunched up pillows and lifted the cup to her lips. The tea revived her, helping to order her fuzzy thoughts and dispel the remains of a disturbing dream.

Sally had been missing half a day, but was that long enough to prompt Inspector Maddox to instigate a search? Probably not. She could hear his voice in her ear explaining patiently that Sally was a grown woman and free to do as she wished; even imagining the moralistic tone of his voice when he did so.

'Flora, I've been thinking—' Bunny emerged from the dressing room garbed in only a white towel wrapped around his hips to mid-thigh. 'Oops, sorry,' he halted at the sight of Nell. 'I didn't think anyone was—'

Nell gasped, her eyes wide above the hand she brought to her mouth. With a sharp scream she turned and fled the room.

Flora rolled her eyes, mildly irritated. In the same position, Sally would have smirked and stood her ground, not run away screaming.

Bunny let the towel slip to the floor and patted his flat belly. 'I suppose she'll scurry into corners whenever she sees me in the hall now?' He sighed and held up a pair of underpants for inspection before putting them on.

'Very likely. And if she gives notice, I'll hold *you* responsible.' Flora returned her cup to the night-stand. 'Now, what was it you were thinking?' She pushed back the covers and swung her legs onto the floor.

'That I shall telephone the police station before breakfast and talk to Inspector Maddox.' He pulled on a pair of socks and fastened them to red elastic gaiters. 'If he tries to fob me off with platitudes, I'll demand an interview with his superior and go and see him personally.'

'He's bound to be sceptical about our story of children being smuggled in ships by the Salvation Army. That sounds like something from a penny novel.'

'Well, I shan't let him put me off. Not with the weight of evidence that's piling up.' He peered down his nose into a mirror as he clipped his collar to his shirt.

'I appreciate that, thank you.' Emotion thickened her voice. 'I wasn't sure whether or not you would be willing to go against Maddox if the need arose.'

'Did you think I wouldn't support you in this?' He looked up from fastening his belt, his expression of fierce concentration softened. 'Look, Flora, I know I tease you about Sally being pert and disrespectful, but she isn't stupid. She went after that man in the army uniform for a reason. If she hasn't come back, it's because she's being prevented.' He shrugged into his jacket and blew her a kiss from the door. 'I'll see you downstairs.'

Flora's dressing ritual took on a certain poignancy without Sally. Not that Flora had ever minded shifting for herself, but she missed the bright-eyed whirlwind of a girl who lapsed into a chirpy East End accent in times of stress or excitement. Despite Beatrice Harrington's warnings of Sally's scant regard for her superiors, Flora enjoyed her company. Thus, when the tiny buttons on the back of her dress proved too much that morning, necessitating she summon a maid to help her, Flora was close to tears.

When she emerged from their room, she heard Bunny's low tones as he spoke on the telephone in the rear hall. In order not to interrupt him, she ascended to the floor above, where through the half-open nursery door she heard Nell in conversation with Milly.

'Even the mistress don't know what's happened to 'er.' Nell's sense of the dramatic clear in her high-pitched voice. 'Vanished without a trace, she 'as.'

The maid gave a tiny gasp on seeing Flora. Cheeks flaming, she dipped a quick curtsey and hurried past her into the hall.

'Little master was up at the crack of dawn, Madam.' Milly did not acknowledge Nell's rapid exit and continued to fold a pile of baby linens. 'He's teething just now, but he copes with it like a trooper.'

'I shan't wake him.' Flora leaned over the cot and gently stroked the fuzz of dark blond hair in tiny curls at his neck, just like his father's. Arthur stirred beneath her hand, flailed a dimpled arm, but settled again immediately, his thumb jammed firmly into his mouth.

'Oh, he won't mind.' Milly snapped a baby vest and folded it against her chest. 'He likes seeing you.'

Flora looked up sharply, her gaze on Milly's turned back as the nurse placed the clothes in a drawer. Had Sally's plight engendered such unexpected kindness? If so, she hoped it would last.

Downstairs in the dining room, no aromas of breakfast were evident, other than the trail of steam that rose from the coffee cup on the table at Bunny's side.

'I told Stokes not to serve breakfast in case we had to go to the police station,' Bunny explained when he saw her look. 'There's coffee, though.'

'That's enough for me, I'm too worried to eat.' She approached the coffee pot set over a paraffin flame on its stand. 'What did Maddox say? Are they going to search for Sally?'

'Actually, he was remarkably helpful. He's going to liaise with the River Police to organize a search of the *SS Lancett* before it sails tonight.' Bunny pushed back his chair and began pacing the room, cup in hand.

'That's something, at least.' Flora relaxed her shoulders as the tension of her difficult night flowed out of her. 'Waiting is so frustrating. What did he say about the Salvation Army man and Sally?'

'Ah.' Bunny pinched the top of his nose above the bridge of his spectacles. 'That was the less successful part of our conversation. He seemed to think Sally must have misunderstood the situation in the Lamb and Flag. I got the impression he's an admirer of that organization and, in his opinion, they're above reproach.'

'Probably a Quaker,' Flora murmured to herself as she set down the coffee pot with a thud. 'You said yourself Sally isn't stupid. If she was wrong and the man really was genuine, where is she?'

'Which is exactly what I told Maddox. Finally, he conceded I had a point, and will make enquiries. However he also said there are a large number of missions in London and tracking down one man in uniform will not be easy. He has asked to be informed if Sally returns on her own.'

'She would be here by now if that were possible.' Flora sloshed milk clumsily into the coffee. 'I'll wager she's on this ship, the—'

'The *SS Lancett*.'

'Why can't I remember that name?' She flapped her free hand in agitation and took the chair opposite him at the dining table.

'Flora,' Bunny's tone dropped to one of conciliation. 'I know you're upset, but I might as well tell you what else Maddox said.'

'Go on.' She stirred her coffee slowly, her eyes fixed on his face, aware she wasn't going to like what came next.

'He agreed to pay a discreet visit to Mr Buchanan this morning. He's not entirely convinced a man of his standing could be involved in anything . . . untoward.'

'Discreet?' She snorted at Bunny's benign look. 'Buchanan should count himself fortunate he isn't being arrested. That man has some explaining to do.'

'Maddox is being cautious, Flora. He cannot demand an interview or expect Buchanan's co-operation without first referring to his superior officer.'

'How long will that take?' Frustrated, Flora's voice rose. 'Buchanan could be selling children? Has Maddox told his superior that?'

'Calm down, Flora. There are still several hours before the *SS Lancett* is due to leave. We're going to have to be patient and trust Maddox knows what he's doing.'

'I don't suppose I have much choice.' She took a gulp from her cup, wincing when it burned the roof of her mouth. 'I feel I ought to call on Alice at her lodgings this morning. She'll want to know about Sally.'

'I'll come with you. But before we do that,' Bunny rose, took the cup and saucer gently from her hands and returned it to the table, 'I'm going to take you out to breakfast. No, don't argue. You need your strength to catch dangerous villains.'

'That's not funny,' she snapped, though at the same time his concerned smile sent a ripple of warmth through her. He was only being Bunny. Worried, protective and loving all at the same time but without being patronizing. How many women enjoyed those qualities in a husband? At times she even suspected he admired her determination not to let killers and spies go unpunished, or he wouldn't be so willing to jump in and help her. 'All right,' she agreed, though the thought of food still nauseated her.

'To be honest, sitting round here waiting for news is making me restless,' Bunny said as he guided her into the hall. 'I didn't like to mention it before so as not to upset you further, but I'm rather fond of Sally, and her extended absence is a worry.' He unhooked her coat from the stand and held it out for her while waving in dismissal to Stokes, who had appeared like a ghost to perform his front door duty.

'That doesn't upset me. In fact I'm glad you feel that way.'

'Has it occurred to you this ship might not be one of Mr Buchanan's?' Bunny asked, shrugging into his own overcoat. 'Even if it is, have you considered that your Miss Finch might know more about this matter than she admits to?'

'I don't believe that for a moment.' Flora concentrated on fastening the buttons of her coat, mainly to avoid having to look at him. 'Alice tried to get the police involved, but they refused to do anything. Which is why she asked for my help.'

'That's the story she gave you. Have you thought

that she might have had her own reasons for involving you?'

'To what purpose?' Flora put on her hat in front of the hall mirror, staring back at his reflection in the glass from beneath her hat brim. 'No, you're wrong. I know you are,' she snapped, though the surge of anger receded quickly. Bunny was simply being cautious, not accusing.

'Which is exactly why I feel you're too involved. In a case such as this, everyone is a suspect until proven otherwise.' He lowered his voice to a whisper as Stokes, unwilling to be robbed of another of his duties, rushed forward to open the front door. 'No exceptions because one of them might be your mother.'

Flora pouted, but had no answer to that. Bunny could be so equitable at times.

Out on the front step, the crisp morning air stung her cheeks and the smell of burning leaves filled her nostrils, evoking afternoons of heavy skies and bonfires in the Gloucestershire countryside.

'I do hope Sally's all right, wherever she is.' Flora pulled on her gloves. 'I should never have involved her. She has no idea how serious this could become and takes unnecessary risks.'

'Really? I wonder who she learned *that* from?' Bunny cast her a sideways look. 'Don't blame yourself, Sally makes her own decisions. It also strikes me that that collection box bandied about last night was evidently a drop.' At Flora's puzzled frown, he explained, 'A drop is a method of exchanging secret messages.'

'You see what you've learned by being married to me?' Flora tucked her arm through his, her shoulders hunched as she leaned into him.

'Some of which I could have lived without,' he murmured as they reached the corner of Belgrave Place where they were more likely to find a passing hansom. 'Didn't the barman at The Antigallican say he was unable to find out who Lizzy was talking to due to a disturbance in the bar?'

Flora cast her mind back to her conversation with Sally. 'He said the Salvation Army arrived and he had to deal with a disturbance so he didn't see the woman who argued with Lizzie.'

'Could it have been the same couple who met with Mr Buchanan last night?'

'The barman didn't say anything about the woman being part of the army. In fact, he said he didn't even see her, only that he heard her and Lizzie arguing.'

'Which doesn't discount my theory.' Bunny paused at the kerb, placed a thumb and finger between his lips and issued a piercing whistle. An idling hansom driver parked on the other side of the road touched the peak of his cap to show he understood. He flicked the thong of his whip, turned the cab around in the middle of the empty street and guided the horse to a halt beside them. 'It might all be conjecture, but I have an idea about this Salvation Army theory.' Bunny handed her into the cramped interior of the cab that smelled of saddle wax and damp wood. He slid in beside her just as the driver closed the wooden flaps over their knees with a dull thump.

'You're being unusually mysterious. What sort of idea?'

'All in good time.' He opened the trap above their heads. 'Claridge's Hotel, if you please, driver.'

CHAPTER 21

'Are you sure this is the correct house?' Bunny stared at the double black-painted doors with gleaming brass furniture of the Georgian mansion on Birdcage Walk. Reclining stone lions sat atop a pair of gateposts that flanked a wide carriage drive. 'It doesn't look much like a lodging house to me.'

'Me either, but I'm sure this is the address Alice gave me. Of course it's possible I wrote it down wrong.' Flora bit her lower lip and cast a worried look back to the panoramic view of St James' Park behind them. 'Maybe we could leave before anyone knows we're here?'

'It's too late now, I've pushed the bell.' Bunny sniffed. 'And it's been a considerable time since I've played *knock down ginger*.'

The left-hand door opened with a click, revealing a butler in a black coat and striped trousers who scrutinized them both. 'May I help you, Sir? Madam? Though I should inform you that my master is not at home, but if you would care to state your business with Mr Buchanan, I shall—'

'Mr Buchanan lives here? Mr Raymond

Buchanan?' Flora blurted before she could stop herself.

'Indeed,' the man drawled, his curious expression changing instantly to boredom. As if he had no time for unexpected callers.

'Who is it, Fielding?' A familiar voice interrupted from behind him.

The butler continued to block the door, his head turned to address the unseen the figure. 'Visitors, Madam. They wish to see the master without prior arrangement.' His tone implied it was a minor inconvenience he was capable of handling. He made to close the door.

Alice appeared in the gap between the double doors, forcing the butler to step back. 'It's perfectly all right, Fielding, these are friends of mine. Please let them in.'

Flora gaped and exchanged a shocked look with Bunny, whose eyes widened but neither spoke.

'If you say so, Madam.' With obvious reluctance, the butler stood aside, allowing Flora and Bunny into a marble hall large enough to encompass the entire ground floor at Eaton Place. In front of them, a grand staircase split to either side at the top and veered off in opposite directions along a long gallery on the level above them. Gilt mirrors graced the walls, reflecting light from crystal chandeliers on a ceiling twelve feet high.

Flora's upbringing in the opulence of Cleeve Abbey had not made her immune to the tangible evidence of wealth at every turn. Not just the impulsive expense made amongst gaudy items offered in the London department stores, but the ancient and polished affluence of generations handed down with pride displayed on every wall and polished surface.

'I'm delighted to see you both, and how unexpected.' Alice pressed each of their hands in turn, giving Flora the impression she would have embraced them had their acquaintance been longer. Her slate blue dress brought out her eyes; her hair, similar to Flora's own in thickness and texture but several shades lighter, was piled in soft curls atop her head accentuating her delicate neck.

'You live *here*?' Flora said once they were out of earshot of the butler. 'That man said this was Mr Buchanan's house?'

'Come along inside and I'll explain.' Alice led them down a hall to where a glazed door opened onto an orangery that stretched across the back of the house. The ornate metal frame of leaf green with glass walls looked onto a walled garden, its pathways, statuary and mature trees redolent of a country estate.

'This is certainly unexpected.' Bunny's eyes widened behind his spectacles. 'What a magnificent house.'

'Indeed.' Alice gestured for them to make themselves comfortable in the arrangement of four wickerwork chairs with peacock backs. 'St James' Palace is next door. I believe that during the late fifteen hundreds, the first King James kept aviaries of exotic birds in this very spot, thus the name Birdcage Walk. I believe there were camels, crocodiles, and an elephant too, together with a flower garden.' She took a chair opposite, the wide circular wickerwork providing a frame to her head. 'Might I offer you both some refreshment?'

'Ah, no thank you,' Flora replied, including Bunny in her refusal. 'We have just had breakfast.' She almost regretted the fact. The idea of drinking coffee beneath an ancient vine that wound round the ornate wrought iron supports above their heads appealed.

'I can see you are both shocked,' Alice paused to allow her words to sink in, her hands folded in her lap. 'I feel I owe you an explanation.'

'You owe us nothing, Miss Finch.' Bunny flicked up the back of his coat and sat. 'It is we who should apologize, having no idea you and Mr Buchanan were . . . um—' He broke off, flushed a deep red and coughed into a fist. 'I mean to say we—'

Flora concealed a smile behind a gloved hand at this change of roles, when in most cases it was her runaway tongue which caused them embarrassment. 'Suffice it to say we are both intrigued,' she said, hoping to save his blushes. Her conviction that Alice Finch was her mother took another dip. Lily Maguire had been a rector's daughter and therefore unlikely to move in the circles the Buchanan's occupied.

'Naturally, though I wish you to know I am not Mr Buchanan's mistress.'

'Oh, but we didn't think—' Bunny said.

'We would never assume—' Flora added.

'I wouldn't blame you if you did.' Alice cut them both off with another, rich, deep laugh. 'Our domestic arrangements appear unconventional to most people. Not those who know us, of course, but to the world at large we are an odd pair. Our only redemption comes from Mr Buchanan's well know devotion to his late wife makes him above reproach.'

'Have you been acquainted long?' Flora offered a weak smile. How could they imply Mr Buchanan might be involved in child trafficking after such an endorsement? The police were also notorious for believing vast wealth bestowed respectability.

'I've known Raymond and his wife for many years.' Alice leaned forward slightly as if conveying a confidence. 'When Mary died five years ago, Raymond was lost. He couldn't contemplate leaving the home where they had spent their married life and raised their children, but the house is too vast for him alone. At his request, I moved in, but it's quite respectable. I occupy a separate suite of rooms on the top floor with my own front door. It's an arrangement which suits us both.'

'Is Mr Buchanan at home this morning by any chance?' Bunny asked.

'Actually, I'm not sure.' Alice stared round as if

puzzled he had not joined them. 'I haven't seen him since yesterday. We had planned to attend a lecture on bronchial diseases this evening, but when I came down for breakfast this morning he had already gone out. He left me a note saying he couldn't attend the lecture after all, but there was no further explanation. It's most unlike him.'

'Has his behaviour been unusual in any way recently?' Bunny asked. 'Perhaps he is distracted, or has changed his regular habits?'

'Now you mention it, I believe he has.' Alice fiddled with the clasp of a delicate silver bracelet on her left wrist. 'I thought it was because of Isobel Lomax's disappearance. She hasn't been found yet and it's most worrying.'

'How exactly has his behaviour changed?' Bunny asked.

'Forget the enigmatic questions, Bunny.' Flora became restless with this careful dance he insisted upon. 'Just tell Alice what we came to say.'

Alice straightened in her chair and split a slow look between them. 'I assume then that this is not simply a social call?'

'I'm afraid not.' Bunny cleared his throat. 'Mr Buchanan attended a concert at the Bechstein Hall last evening.'

'To hear Mr Schnabel play?' Alice's blue-green eyes sparkled with interest. 'Yes, that's correct. How did you know?' She caught the hard edge of Bunny's smile and paused. 'I gather your mentioning it isn't a coincidence?'

'No.' Bunny cleared his throat. 'He missed part of the performance because he relocated to the Lamb and Flag where he was given a note about a certain ship.'

'Which ship?' The hand Alice brought to her throat trembled slightly.

'The *SS Lancett*.'

'I see.' Alice swallowed. 'I shan't ask how this note fell into your possession.' Her steady gaze contained no malice. 'How can I help?'

'The person who observed this exchange was my maid, and she has since gone missing,' Flora said.

'Should I ask what your maid was doing?' Alice's eyes darkened. 'No of course not, she was spying on Mr Buchanan.'

'I wouldn't say spying, rather—'

'Yes, that's exactly what she was doing,' Flora cut across him. 'We asked her to do it, but she hasn't been seen since last night. We're becoming quite concerned as it's not like her.'

'I'm very sorry to hear that. But then if she is missing, how did you know she was following Mr Buchanan? And do you think he had something to do with it?'

'Not with Sally's disappearance,' Bunny said. 'Not directly. She followed the man Mr Buchanan went to meet and her companion reported she has yet to return.'

Flora relaxed slightly, hoping that he too believed Alice was an innocent party in this affair. Either that, or he was waiting for her to fall into a trap of some sort yet to be revealed.

'There's something else, Alice,' Flora said carefully. 'You'll remember that I told you Lizzie had an argument at The Antigallican, the night before she died, with someone who might have been with a Salvation Army man. Well Mr Buchanan talked to a Salvation Army officer in the Lamb and Flag last night.'

'Then there was the girl, Ada Baines. She also mentioned a Salvation Army man who was with Swifty Ellis when her friend, Annie left home.'

'You think these incidents are connected?' Alice asked, puzzled. 'The Salvationists visit pubs all over London, it's part of their mission. It could mean nothing.'

'That's true,' Bunny nodded. 'However, they do appear to play a role in all this which cannot be ignored. I'm afraid we'll have to face the possibility they, and Mr Buchanan are involved in human trafficking of some sort.'

'Not some sort, Bunny,' Flora interjected. 'It's quite clear they are selling children.'

'It's certainly beginning to sound ominous.' Alice twisted her hands in her lap. 'And this reference to the *SS Lancett* confirms it.' She rose slowly to her feet. 'Come with me, I need to show you something.' She led them back the way they had come through a side hall and into a room that contained a massive oak desk, its top inlaid with tooled leather. A wide window with a view of the front drive and the park beyond. A very masculine room smelling of pipe smoke and furniture polish.

'Raymond never keeps his study locked,' Alice said in response to Flora's admiring look. 'We trust each other, you see. Or rather we did – before.' She shook her head as if dislodging an unwelcome thought and strode to a glass-fronted cabinet that stood on the far wall. On a high shelf behind the bevelled glass sat a framed photograph of a harbour scene, a handsome steamship with a blood red mast in the centre.

'This is the *SS Lancet*.' Alice indicated the photograph. 'Raymond's first ship.'

'He owns it?' Flora gaped as another piece of the puzzle slid into place in her head.

'Miss Finch.' Bunny scanned the photograph briefly. 'You must know how this looks? I—'

Flora halted him with a hand on his arm. 'Are you sure you want to do this, Alice? We wouldn't want to make your position more difficult.'

'On the contrary,' Bunny interrupted. 'We need to know everything, and this vessel is at the centre of it. I'm afraid loyalty and privacy have no place here.'

'You aren't in a courtroom now, Bunny,' Flora snapped. 'Alice is being very open with us, we ought to respect that.'

'No, Flora, he's quite right,' Alice cut across her. 'I'm not a fool, Mr Harrington. We have to consider all possibilities, including that this ship is being used to transport children. Yet somehow I'm confident the truth will exonerate Raymond. However, *if* he is involved, he must face the consequences of his actions.'

Flora stared out of the window so Alice would not see the doubt in her eyes. If Mr Buchanan was so innocent, what was he doing sharing information on his ships with a Salvation Army officer in a public house? If their business were legitimate, wouldn't their meetings be conducted in an office with documents as opposed to scraps of paper?

As they talked, Bunny developed a sudden interest in the contents of the cabinet, which apart from a series of framed photographs, contained a selection of curiosities; with small jade statues jostling for space with bronze figurines and china ornaments.

'But there is still the fact that Sally followed them and now she's missing.' From the corner of her eye, Flora watched Bunny him try the cabinet door handle without success, and her face flamed briefly.

'I realize that.' Alice didn't appear to notice Bunny's interest in the cabinet. 'But I still cannot accept Raymond is involved.'

'He means a lot to you doesn't he?' Flora asked in an attempt to reconcile her persistent belief that she might be Lily Maguire, although hope was fading fast. Her mother had been a rector's daughter and did not move in the circles the Bannerman's occupied.

'Mary and Raymond Bannerman were very good to me at a time when I needed a friend,' Alice began slowly, as if debating the extent of what she should reveal. 'A year before I met them, they lost their twelve-year-old daughter. Their nephew, who was a little older, had taken her onto the Serpentine in a rowing boat. The boy started messing about and somehow the boat capsized, trapping the girl beneath it. Raymond saved his nephew, but his daughter drowned. Raymond always believed that Mary blamed him for the loss of their child, although I know she neither believed nor implied any such thing, but guilt is a powerful master.'

'How awful,' Flora said. 'I can see why you wouldn't think he was capable of abducting children.'

'Exactly.' Alice brought her hands to her cheeks. 'I *don't* believe it. There must be some other reason for his actions. Raymond is a fierce advocate for the hospital and proud of the work we do there, none of which fits with what you are suggesting.'

'Excuse me, Miss Finch,' Bunny tapped the locked glass door with his knuckles. 'Do you happen to have a key to this cabinet?'

'Um, yes of course.' She slid open a drawer in the desk and removed a small bunch of keys, selected the smallest one and unlocked the cabinet.

Ignoring Flora's hard look, Bunny withdrew one of several wooden trays arranged on a lower shelf and laid it on the desk. Arranged in indentations in the velvet lining sat small ivory and metal objects; a fish with carved scales sat beside a pair of miniature binoculars complete with mother-of-pearl handle. A perfect replica of a violin, a tiny house complete with intricately carved windows and even a silver dolphin. All of them less than two inches long, some even smaller.

'They're miniatures,' Flora said. 'Pretty, but why are you interested in those?'

'Raymond collects them,' Alice said, frowning. 'They've been here years, but I've never taken much notice of them.'

'That's not all they are.' A superior smile played on Bunny's lips. 'They have one thing in common, do you see?'

'Not really, but I know you're longing to tell us.' Flora plucked a tiny fish from the tray, with carved scales and bulbous eyes, turning it over in her hand. 'What's special about them?'

'See that tiny metal circle on one side?' Bunny pointed to a tiny circular metal ring that formed the fish's eye. 'Hold it up to the light and look through it.'

'How can you see anything through that tiny hole?' Flora turned the fish over in her hand.

'There's a lens inside which acts as a magnifier. Go on,' he urged. 'Give it a try.'

Squinting, Flora held the fish to one eye. Instantly a transparent-coloured image jumped out at her. A grey stone church in minute detail with the words 'Eglise de St Madeleine' below in black script. 'It's beautiful.' She twisted the fish slightly to take in every detail. 'Like a kaleidoscope with the way the light shines through it, but much smaller.'

'They are called "Stanhopes",' Bunny said with a triumphant grin. 'After Charles, the third Earl Stanhope, who invented the lens. They've been around for forty years or so. Some people call them "peeps".' He ran his fingertips over the line of objects, finally selecting a miniature violin that he held up to his eye. 'I wonder what this one—' He jerked his chin back, snatching it from his eye as if it burned him.

'What is it?' Alice asked.

'Something I suspected when I first saw them, but wasn't sure about until now.'

'What *are* you talking about?' Flora reached for the object in his hand. 'Let me have a look.'

I don't think—' He jerked his hand away, but she was too quick for him. Taking the tiny instrument from him she held it up to the window and peered through the tiny hole.

'I can see it now. It's a woman with . . . oh!' She pulled back her chin, lowering the object quickly. 'She has no clothes on!'

'Really? How intriguing.' Alice's lips twitched with the hint of a smile. Selecting a peep shaped like a ship's wheel, she took it to the window and looked through the tiny hole in the centre. 'Goodness me,' she murmured, making no attempt to remove it from her eye. 'I would say this . . . lady

283

is a professional model. The photograph was evidently taken in a studio of some sort. The background is carefully staged.'

'It's not appropriate for either of you ladies to be looking at these.' Bunny plucked the ivory fish from Flora's fingers and returned it to the box, avoiding her eye. 'This is a gentleman's private collection.'

'I've been a nurse for fifteen years.' Alice laughed. 'It will take more than a naked lady or two to shock me.'

'Really, Bunny,' Flora tutted. 'It was your idea to look at them, though I don't see what they have to do with—' She broke off as a memory resurfaced, but it was vague, like a blurred picture she couldn't hold onto. 'Anyway.' She shrugged, embarrassed to have intruded into a man's personal possessions. 'It's not *that* unusual Mr Buchanan would collect rude pictures. You can buy similar postcards in the Old Kent Road.' At his oblique look, she shrugged. 'Sally told me.' The mention of her name made her throat burn with emotion.

'Now I know why Raymond kept them locked away, but I don't think these have anything to do with why you came here.' Alice returned the ivory key and the violin into their allotted places and carried the tray back to the cabinet. She re-locked the door and slid the bunch of keys back into the drawer. 'What are you going to do with regards to the *SS Lancett*?'

'Well,' Bunny began. 'We've informed Inspector

Maddox of the contents of the note. He's liaising with the Marine Police to organize a search of the ship before it leaves tonight.'

'And Raymond?' Alice rubbed her hands down her skirt with shaking hands.

'It depends on what they find,' Flora said gently.

'I understand.' Alice led them back into the hall. 'This is all very awkward, but I must keep an open mind.' She halted and turned to face them. 'Are you sure I cannot offer you some—'

'No, I think we should go.' Flora bit her lip. How could they sit over cups of coffee and make small talk having given Alice such devastating news? Not only had they implied Mr Buchanan might be involved in trafficking children, but had instigated an investigation that could condemn him to a prison sentence. Flora pressed Alice's arm when they reached the front door. 'I hope you're right and Mr Buchanan is quite innocent.'

'I have faith in him.' Alice's eyes looked suspiciously wet. 'You will let me know what happens this evening about the ship? Even if it's bad news?' Bunny looked about to say something but Alice held up a hand to forestall him. 'Don't worry, if he returns home in the meantime, I will say nothing of our conversation.'

'We appreciate that,' Bunny said. 'Although we're aware this puts you in a difficult position.'

Alice nodded, her eyes softening with compassion. 'You will tell me when your maid is found, won't you?'

'Certainly, we shall.' Flora noted she did not say, '*if* she is found'. What Flora had tried to recall before suddenly came to her in a flash. She tugged Bunny by the arm in the direction of the front door. 'Goodness, it's later than I thought, and Bunny has an appointment. You don't wish to be late.'

'Beg pardon?' Bunny turned to stare at her.

Flora brought her foot down lightly on his instep and he jumped. 'Oh yes, appointment. Of course. I had quite forgotten. This has been a most enlightening morning, Miss Finch.'

'I'm glad you think so, but I don't see that I have been of much help.' Alice escorted them to the front door, where she set Fielding off in search of a cab.

'That wasn't exactly subtle, Flora,' Bunny said when they had settled inside a motor taxi they had hailed near the Cockpit Steps. 'You hurried me out of there like my coat was on fire.'

'Sorry. Perhaps we ought to establish some sort of code alerting the other to the fact we need to make a rapid exit.'

'And why exactly did we need to leave in such a hurry? Or was it sheer embarrassment that we had suggested Raymond Buchanan was a child trafficker?'

'I feel dreadful. I had no idea they were so close. But it wasn't that. No, there was something I didn't want to mention in front of Alice.'

'Fair enough, and what was that?'

When we were looking at the tray of peepers or whatever they are, I remembered I've seen one before, quite recently. Sister Lazarus has one.'

'They are called "peeps", Flora.' His head swung towards her. 'Sister Lazarus? Are you sure?'

'Positive. She wears it on a chain attached to her pocket. I saw it two days ago.'

'Interesting, but what does that prove? Not all Stanhopes contain dubious images. As you saw from Mr Buchanan's collection, some are quite innocent.'

'Call me cynical, but I doubt this one is.'

'Even so, it might simply have been a gift from Buchanan. No don't glare at me like that, it's quite possible. Just because you don't like the woman doesn't make her a villain.'

'I suppose not.' Although she couldn't imagine Sister Lazarus and Raymond Buchanan being anything other than distant colleagues.

'Maybe we could find out about this Salvation Army couple? The ones who were at The Antigallican that night?'

'How? The Salvation Army are in just about every public house in the city at one time or another. Identifying them would be almost impossible.'

'Not necessarily.' He drummed the fingers of one hand on his knee. 'Actually, I might have an idea about that.'

'Another one? You're certainly full of ideas today, what with your extensive knowledge of Stanhopes.'

She sliced a hard look at him, but before he could respond, the taxi took a sharp corner, forcing Flora to brace against the door to stay upright while a cacophony of hoots, shouts and wheels passed within inches on either side of their vehicle.

'I'm not ready to reveal it as yet,' Bunny said when the taxi righted itself. 'It needs more thought.'

'Bunny,' Flora pursued her earlier thought, 'how did you know what a Stanhope was?' She narrowed her eyes at him. 'And I'm not referring to the ones with pictures of churches in them.'

'I've been wondering when you were going to ask me that,' Bunny chuckled. 'They aren't that uncommon. Any number of respectable public servants and wealthy businessmen own private rooms full of erotic artwork for the benefit of male guests at dinner parties.'

'Is that so?' Flora raised an eyebrow at him. 'And how many such parties have *you* attended?'

'A few, although I'm not going to go into that here and now.' He drummed his fingers on his knee. 'It occurred to me that if Buchanan is as respectable as Alice claims, there might be another reason why he hasn't gone to the police with what he knows.'

'If he knows anything.' Flora said, although Bunny could be right, in that there was a reason for Mr Buchanan's co-operation with these villains. But why would they require his ship, if not to transport children?

CHAPTER 22

When they arrived back at Eaton Place, Stokes informed them with a grave shake of his head that there had been no callers all morning, and that Sally had still not returned. His usually inscrutable expression remained but Flora detected a slight tremble to his mouth as he answered their question.

Bunny thanked him gently before he collected his post from the hall table. Sifting through the pile, he halted, frowned at a slim envelope and tucked it into his pocket before disappearing into his study. Helpless to do anything but wait, Flora took to walking past the telephone in the rear hall, willing it to ring, though the contraption remained obstinately silent.

During an early dinner that evening, the chime of the doorbell brought them both into the hall without waiting for Stokes' announcement.

'Hope you don't mind my stopping by.' Harry stood passive as the butler relieved him of his cashmere overcoat. 'Lydia is still frantic and asked if I would call in. She would have come herself but she has a meeting at the school.

Have heard anything from Inspector Maddox yet?'

'No, nothing,' Flora said, returning his brief hug and gestured they go along to the sitting room.

'I should think they are still at the docks.' Bunny waited for Flora to sit, while he and Harry took chairs on either side of the fireplace. 'The ship is due to leave in a couple of hours. If they've found anything we should learn of it soon.' He proceeded to bring Harry up to date on their discovery of the curios Mr Buchanan kept in his home, and that one was in Sister Lazarus' possession.

'It occurs to me there might be some sort of relationship between this Sister Lazarus and this Buchanan chap,' Harry said when he had finished. 'If not, why did she have one of his Stanhopes?'

'You know what they are?' Flora raised an enquiring eyebrow at him. Did all young men have a secret code they shared with only their friends?

'Well, um, I know *of* them. Put it that way.' Harry exchanged a loaded look with Bunny.

'I see. Perhaps she collects naughty photographs as well?' This remark attracted embarrassed looks from both men which made her sigh. 'There's the possibility Buchanan might have given it to her as a gift?'

'I cannot imagine that.' Bunny strode to the sideboard where he poured the coffee Stokes had brought in. 'And if it does contain something embarrassing to Buchanan, why wear it at the hospital? What if she lost it?'

'To taunt him?' Flora turned to face him, one arm draped along the back of the sofa. 'She looks the sort to go rummaging through other people's belongings.'

'Sounds to me that you want her to be guilty of something purely because you don't like her.' Harry suggested.

'Of course not.' Flora frowned, embarrassed by his perception.

'I find her cold and well, not very civil. Not at all like any nurse *I've* come across.' She sipped from her cup without enthusiasm. She wouldn't sleep tonight if she drank too much coffee. Not that she expected to with Sally still missing.

'Now we are into character assassination as opposed to evidence.' His gaze slid to Harry and the mood between them shifted, as if they had allied themselves against her.

'I know that.' Flora shrugged. 'Though I'm still keeping her on my list of suspects.'

'I still cannot see a man like Buchanan becoming involved in child abduction over a few risqué photographs,' Harry said.

'You've heard of him?' Flora asked, surprised.

'Only by reputation.' Harry shrugged. 'I believe he's quite the philanthropist. No socialite, but with wealth enough to live the rest of his life like a king. Why would a man like him get involved with people trafficking?'

'He also doesn't care that the whole of London is aware he shares his home with a single lady,' Bunny added.

'Single lady?' Harry's cup froze in mid-air. 'That sounds interesting, what have I missed?'

'Oh, nothing,' Flora interjected glaring at Bunny.

'Something tells me there's more to this affair than risqué photographs,' Bunny said.

'What then?' Harry returned his cup to the table in front of him. 'Unless you think he was also responsible for that nurse's death. What was her name?'

'Nurse Prentice,' Flora supplied. 'I cannot imagine him committing an actual murder.'

The room fell strangely silent as they fell into their own thoughts, interrupted only by the rhythmic tick of the mantelpiece clock.

'We appear to have exhausted the subject.' Harry slapped his thighs and rose. 'I'll leave you both in peace to enjoy the rest of your evening.' Flora looked up at him quickly and his face clouded as he realized his mistake. 'I'm so sorry, Flora, that was insensitive of me. I know how fond you are of Sally. I sincerely hope nothing bad has happened to her.' He paused beside her chair and pressed her shoulder. 'You will let us know immediately you hear anything, won't you?'

'Of course, I'll call you—' she broke off at a ring of the doorbell, followed immediately by a loud pounding on the front door, followed seconds later by the appearance of Inspector Maddox who barged past a protesting Stokes.

'It's quite all right, Stokes,' Bunny forestalled the butler. 'Do come in, Inspector.'

'Have you found Sally?' Flora demanded when he was barely over the threshold, tension making her voice high. 'Were the children on the ship?'

'All in good time, Mrs Harrington, Mr Harrington.' Maddox declined Bunny's invitation to take a seat, his hat and coat still firmly in place. He sent an enquiring look Harry's way and, in response, Bunny made a brief introduction. 'Ah yes!' Maddox nodded sagely. 'Thought I recognized you, sir. I questioned you in relation to the Evangeline Lange case.'

Harry's features hardened but he didn't respond, his discomfort at having been treated as a suspect in his own fiancée's murder still evident.

'Well? What have you to tell us?' Bunny demanded.

'Only that the raid on the *SS Lancett* was a total fiasco.' Maddox turned his burning gaze on Flora. 'And I hold you, Mrs Harrington, entirely responsible.'

'What *do* you mean?' The anticipation that had knotted Flora's stomach all day turned to crushing disappointment.

'Before you castigate my wife, Inspector,' Bunny said from the window that looked onto the street. 'Would you kindly remove your men from my porch? Having two policemen outside my door will do nothing for my reputation. This is Belgravia after all.'

'I'll ask Stokes to take them to the kitchens and give them a cup of tea.' Flora skirted Bunny and pressed the bell, aware he had managed to dilute Maddox's anger, if temporarily.

'Now we are calmer, what exactly happened, Inspector?' Bunny asked, having re-established authority in his own house.

'Nothing at all.' Maddox sniffed. 'There was no sign of either Miss Pond or any children, only a cargo hold full of farm machinery destined for New Brunswick.'

Flora kneaded her forehead with one hand and slowly paced the room. She had been so convinced they would find Sally on that ship. Where was she?

'Based on the flimsiest of evidence,' Maddox continued in a low tone that did nothing to conceal his frustration, 'I took a dozen policemen off the streets this evening to no purpose. Not only that, but my superintendent has demanded I issue a formal apology to Mr Buchanan for inconveniencing him.'

'You talked to Mr Buchanan?' Flora halted and turned to face him. 'What did he say?'

'Naturally, I did.' Maddox clasped both hands behind his back and rocked on his heels. 'As the legal owner of the vessel, his permission was sought to visit the ship.'

'You asked him first?' Flora slapped her skirt with both hands in frustration. 'Then he must have warned them. How could you be so—' Bunny came to her side, his arm circling her waist and tightened. She released a slow breath and swallowed her next remark.

'If you would allow me to finish, Madam,' Maddox went on. 'Even had he intended to do so, Mr Buchanan had insufficient time to make any such arrangement.'

'I see,' Flora murmured through gritted teeth, unconvinced. Buchanan must have found a way to send his cohorts a warning.

'A complete waste of time, in fact.' Maddox growled. 'This escapade of yours has caused me no end of trouble, not to mention upsetting a respectable pillar of the community. Are you aware of the vast amount of charity work that hospital does in—?'

'Escapade?' Flora interrupted, meeting his furious gaze without flinching. 'Is that all you think this is?'

'I understand the raid proved ineffective, Inspector,' Bunny interrupted him. 'However, I don't appreciate your haranguing my wife over a perfectly reasonable concern over these missing children.'

Maddox flushed an unbecoming red, studied his feet and cleared his throat. 'Well – um, I didn't mean to be disrespectful, and I'm not unsympathetic to your wife's desire to be a good citizen.'

'It's more than that!' Flora snapped. 'And you seem to forget, my maid is still missing. And please don't say she's run off on a whim to join the circus.' She swallowed against the tightness in her throat.

'I understand that, Mrs Harrington,' Maddox said, his voice brittle. 'However, you can have no idea as to what taking a dozen men off routine duties could mean on the streets? Word gets around fast in that part of the world. I imagine all sorts of crimes were committed tonight, and I had no men available to deal with them.'

'I'm sure Mrs Harrington regrets the inconvenience.' Harry lounged in his chair, one sardonic brow raised. 'After all, Inspector,' he drew out the words slowly, 'I'm sure you have enough to deal with from your superiors at all levels.' He picked a bit of fluff from his sleeve, his gaze averted. 'I was only saying to Sir Edward Henry the other day how overstretched your resources are.'

'Is that so?' Maddox narrowed his eyes. 'I take it the Commissioner of Police is a friend of yours, sir?'

Harry's response was little more than the mere ghost of a smile, while sending a swift wink in Flora's direction.

'The fact remains, Mr Harrington,' Maddox softened a little as Harry's remark went home, 'this venture was entirely ill-advised. We could have spent our time in the search of the Lomax girl, although we doubt her disappearance is connected to these other children.'

Flora's anger dissipated as she realized he was

right. There was nothing to link Isobel to the other children, who as far as the police were concerned weren't officially missing.

'That was a low blow, Inspector. These children are all under ten and no one has seen them for more than a week.' Bunny's eyes flashed fire as he squared up to the man. Flora could have hugged him.

'Uh-well, my apologies, and of course we're concerned.' A flush crept up his neck as he coughed into a fist. 'I've had officers visit all the addresses Miss Finch supplied. Their families maintain their relatives are alive and well and living elsewhere. Without checking every county in the south, for which we have neither the resources nor the authority, we cannot verify their stories. In any case, without an official report, we have no cause to investigate.'

'I know all that, Inspector,' Flora said through gritted teeth. 'But the families are co-operating with these people.'

'As I said, I'm not unsympathetic, but my hands are tied.' He eased his collar away from his throat. 'I'm afraid we also appear to have lost track of Swifty Ellis. He hasn't been seen in any of his usual haunts these last few days.'

'Doesn't that tell you something?' Flora asked, no longer apologetic. 'He's been alerted to your investigation and he's gone to ground.'

'His non-appearance could be for any number of reasons.' Maddox appeared determined to gain some professional superiority. 'We'll keep an eye out for him as we wish to question him about the Nurse Prentice murder.'

'Why?' Flora asked. 'Have you evidence he was involved?'

'I'm not at liberty to say, Madam.' He twisted his hat in both hands and cleared his throat. 'I'll, uh, take my leave now.' He nodded to each of them in turn, with a particularly direct glare at Harry before returning his attention to Flora. 'If you should come across any more conspiracies, I would advise you to be sure of your facts before coming to the police.'

Flora waited for him to be out of earshot before muttering, 'I *am* sure of my facts.'

CHAPTER 23

'How could we have got it so wrong about the ship?' Flora addressed Bunny's reflection in her dresser mirror as she got ready for bed. 'I was so certain they were keeping the children there.'

'Ignore Maddox, he's simply posturing.' He dropped a kiss on top of her head. 'More importantly, why didn't they find anything on the ship when the gang, or whoever is responsible, went to all that trouble of giving that note to Buchanan?'

'Is it possible they were too clever for them and hid the children somewhere they didn't search?' Flora pulled pins from her hair, releasing the heavy tress down her back.

'Either that, or they were never there at all,' Bunny murmured.

The doubt in his voice brought her twisting round on her chair towards him. 'You still have faith in my theory, don't you?'

'I do, but so much of this case thus far is supposition.' She opened her mouth to contradict him but he forestalled her. 'That's not to say there isn't some sort of conspiracy going on, but we don't have much evidence.'

'Sally is still missing.'

'I'm aware of that, but I can understand why Maddox was angry.' Bunny perched on the bed and untied his shoelaces. 'That he raided the *SS Lancett* on our word alone will have his subordinates nudging and whispering to each other for some time.' A shoe hit the floorboards with a dull thump as if it took Maddox's reputation with it.

'We had that note, and the fact Lizzie is dead must count for something.' Flora propped her elbows on the dresser and dropped her chin into her palms. 'The ship has probably sailed by now, so we'll never know what happened to those children. What annoys me most is Maddox thinks Buchanan is the injured party.'

'We're missing something.' Bunny draped his trousers over a chair, dropped his socks on the polished floor and kicked them aside. 'Did the Buchanans have other children apart from the daughter who died?'

'I didn't think you were listening as you were so absorbed by that cabinet with the peeps.' Flora halted her hairbrush in mid-air as she pondered the question. 'Alice hasn't mentioned any other children. What made you ask that?'

'You said Buchanan told her he couldn't bear to leave the house where they had raised their children, indicating more than one.' He climbed into bed, his arms folded on the pillow behind his head, the covers bunched at his waist.

'It's possible, but why would it matter?' Flora laid down her brush and slid beneath the covers, her back facing the room as she rearranged the pillows. 'Pass me that pillow under your elbow would you?'

'I don't know, but it all contributes to what we know about him.' Bunny obligingly handed over the pillow.

'Maybe he's listed in Debrett's.' Flora bunched the pillows into a soft pile and wiggled her shoulders backwards. The fire had been banked up, making the bedroom a warm and cosy haven.

'I cannot be bothered to go back downstairs and look.' Bunny sighed and leaned back against the piled up pillows, sighed and closed his eyes. 'It can wait till morning.'

'No need.' Flora slid open a drawer in the nightstand. 'I have a copy right here.' She balanced the book on her tented knees and flipped through the pages. 'Banderlege, Bander, Bannalea, ah, here it is. "Buchanan, Raymond E. Married Mary Frimley daughter of Bishop and Mrs Frimley of Wisbech, 7th May 1868, son Victor born 1873, daughter Alice born 1876, died 1888."'

Alice. His daughter was called Alice. Did that mean something? Was it a coincidence that Alice Finch shared their dead daughter's name, or could their symbiotic relationship be a romantic liaison when his wife was alive?

'Flora, are you listening to me?' Bunny nudged her gently. 'I said, the son must be about thirty now, although you say that Alice has never mentioned him.'

'Not to me.' She turned to the next page. 'There might be an entry for him here as well.'

'Never mind that.' Bunny took the book from her, returned it to the nightstand and turned down the wick of the oil lamp until it guttered and went out. 'I didn't suggest an early night so we can sit in bed and read Debrett's together.'

'It was your idea, about the book I mean.' She trailed her fingers lightly down his bare breastbone into the soft skin of his belly. 'You know, you really ought to start wearing pyjamas. I'm sure Stokes is scandalized when he counts the laundry and doesn't find any.'

'To the devil with Stokes.' He released a soft grunt and lunged sideways, pulling her into his arms. 'I hate to waste the moonlight.' He flicked a glance at a harvest moon visible in a shaft of silver beyond the casement window. He slid down the strap of her nightdress, ran his lips lightly down the side of her neck and across her bare shoulder.

'I cannot stop thinking about Sally.' A tremor ran through her as the thin garment fell to her waist in a whoosh of silk, her lower belly pulled in anticipation of familiar sensations as his lips nuzzled her neck, his hand sliding across her now naked back.

'I know this is difficult for you, Flora,' Bunny whispered into her hair. 'But Sally is tough and resourceful. She won't give in without a fight. In fact, I expect whoever took her is regretting it already.'

'That's what worries me.' Flora wiped her cheek with a cold finger that came away wet, offering a silent prayer that Sally would have the strength to survive whatever faced her, wherever she was.

'I won't let Maddox forget about her. I promise,' he whispered as his lips slid across her cheek and claimed her mouth.

Her throat prickled with tears as she returned his kiss, and relaxed into the comforting circle of his arms.

Later, she lay staring up at the moonlight playing on the ceiling, with Bunny's even breathing and the odd creak and thump of the house in the darkness. Everything had begun to make perfect sense until Inspector Maddox had barged into the room with his foul temper and accusations. The note Buchanan was given had to mean something. Why detail the *SS Lancett*'s departure time? Or had they wanted Buchanan to lead the police to the ship? No, how could he have known he was being observed and why not go to them himself? There was also the man in Salvation Army uniform Sally had recognized. Or did she? Perhaps she only thought she did and was mistaken? Even so, that doesn't explain why she had not come home. Abel's concern for Sally was clearly genuine as

Stokes reported he had called at the house several times asking for news of her.

Her instincts couldn't be wrong, could they? Admittedly she could never have guessed Alice Finch lived in Mr Buchanan's house, but if they were in it together, whatever this was, why involve Flora in the first place?

Or could she trust only what she had seen for herself? Sister Lazarus had been within earshot when Lizzie Prentice asked Alice for time alone to talk. What did Lizzie want to tell Alice that the nurse didn't want her to hear?

'Lizzie had to know something,' Flora said aloud. 'It's too much of a coincidence that she was killed within an hour of that conversation.'

Bunny turned over and mumbled something sleepily but thankfully didn't wake.

Images circled in Flora's head of the time when she and Sally had been locked in a killer's cold, damp cellar huddled together for warmth, with every expectation of becoming his next victims.

At least there had been the two of them on that occasion. This time, Sally was alone and facing a second night in captivity, who knew where? If only the police would find her. And if not the police, then who?

Flora had fallen into the semi-consciousness languor that preceded full sleep before she remembered that on arriving home, Bunny had slipped a letter, which appeared to have caught his interest, into an inside pocket of his jacket.

She had been about to ask what it was, when Harry had arrived, followed by an angry Inspector Maddox. As she drifted off to sleep, she resolved to ask him about it in the morning.

The motor taxi trundled along the Victoria Embankment and into Queen Victoria Street, the dome of St Paul's Cathedral visible between the buildings.

'Where exactly are we going?' Flora asked Bunny the third time since leaving Eaton Place. 'I don't wish to be ungrateful, but I'm not in the right frame of mind for an outing. I ought to be at home in case Sally returns.' *If she does.*

'You cannot hole yourself up inside the house forever, my love. We have to have faith that she will be found, safe and well.' He removed the letter that had arrived the previous day from inside his jacket. Written on plain paper in a rough brown envelope, it was unlike most of Bunny's correspondence, making it all the more intriguing.

'I meant to ask you about that last night, but things got a bit heated and I forgot,' Flora said. 'Who is it from?'

'I recently wrote to a friend of mine whom I thought might be able to help.'

'What sort of friend?'

'A Captain in the Salvation Army.'

'Really?' She twisted on her seat to face him. 'I didn't know you had such connections.'

'The Blakes were neighbours of ours in Richmond

when I was younger, but we haven't been in touch recently.' He returned the letter to his pocket. 'Captain Blake works in one of their shelters and has agreed to see us.'

'Where is this shelter?' Flora had never been to a Salvation Army Mission before. Their work among the poor and powerless was valuable although many believed the lower orders didn't deserve special treatment; a sentiment Flora abhorred.

'In Whitechapel,' he replied without looking at her.

'Whitechapel?' Her enthusiasm lifted a notch. 'Isn't that where the Ripper killed his victims?'

'That's not the only thing that happens in Whitechapel.' Bunny eased his collar away from his throat, telling her he was uncomfortable discussing the most famous murderer in London.

'It was over twenty years ago. I doubt he's still lurking about the place,' she said in an attempt to reassure him.

'Don't joke about it, Flora. He was never caught, remember?'

'Sorry.' A thought struck her and she turned to face him. 'Are we going anywhere near where it happened? The murders I mean?'

'Actually, yes.' He tugged at his collar again. 'Captain Blake works at the Hanbury Street shelter, near where his second victim, Annie Chapman, was found in a yard behind number twenty-nine.' His lips twitched into a smile. 'I thought *you* were the expert on murderers and their victims.'

'Not *all* of them.' She tried to look offended but the idea of seeing the house intrigued her.

As they left Threadneedle Street and Bishopsgate behind them, the shops and houses took on a run-down, unkempt look with broken windows and piles of rubbish in the streets that reminded her of her recent visit to Southwark.

Brushfield Street took them past the chaotic clamour of Spitalfields Market, where men in overalls wielded brooms and buckets of water in a valiant attempt to clear spilled blood and offal that littered the road and around the busy market shed.

Bunny closed the cab windows against the smell as their driver made a left turn into Commercial Street, followed by a right into a narrow road only wide enough for two hackneys to pass.

'Is this it?' Flora looked up at a line of red-brick buildings with the gable ends over the street, shaped like a row of tiny steps leading up to a single window in the peak.

'Hanbury Street.' Bunny nodded. 'The shelter is further along here on the right.'

Flora was about to say that wasn't what she meant, but thought better of it. Instead, she searched for a sign with a number on the centre panel and counted along until she identified the one she was looking for.

Number twenty-nine was a shabby shopfront with a red wooden door to its left and a black one beside it. Flora assumed this must lead to the rear yard where the poor woman's body was found.

The shop had been roughly boarded up some time before, the two rows of windows on the floors above giving every sign of the property being vacant.

'How many did he kill?' Flora kept her gaze on the red door as they passed along a street that didn't improve much in appearance and smelled of cooked cabbage and manure.

'Ah, back to Jack the Ripper are we?' Bunny sighed. 'If you must know, five were attributed to him, but between '88 and '91, eleven murders occurred in this area. The body of a woman called Martha Tabram was found in George's Yard Buildings in August '88. She had been stabbed thirty-nine times, but the police refused to attribute her killing to the Ripper.'

'Why ever not?'

'Because,' Bunny said reluctantly, drawing out the word, 'her throat wasn't cut like the others.' He slewed a sideways glance at her. 'Do you wish you hadn't asked?'

'Of course not.' Flora swallowed as unwanted images crowded her head. 'I can be objective about violent crime. I've had more than a little experience.' *Even if Inspector Maddox does treat me like a useless novice.*

The taxi came to a halt and they alighted onto a narrow, cracked pavement in front of a red-brick building. Despite its unimposing façade, the shelter stood out among the surrounding dilapidated shopfronts and houses. A hardware store stood two doors away, its goods piled into wicker baskets on the pavement beneath a torn awning. Several ragged women huddled near the entrance to the shelter, some of whom carried bundles, though there was not a pair of shoes between them. They certainly looked in need of charity. One woman's skirt was badly torn and barely covered her modesty, while others were no better clad, their clothes patched and darned, the colours faded to an indistinguishable shade of murky green. A young woman of about eighteen in the distinctive black bonnet and cape of the Army conversed with a woman who held a small child in her arms.

'Why are they standing out here?' Flora whispered, aware of the odd sideways looks they had attracted. 'If it's a shelter, why don't they go inside?'

'This is a night shelter,' the female in the bonnet had apparently heard her. She turned from her conversation with the group to address Flora. 'They have to leave in the morning, but are permitted to return at night.'

'That sounds harsh,' Flora said without thinking. 'I'm sorry, I didn't mean to sound uncharitable, but where do they go all day?'

'Flora,' Bunny warned.

'It's quite all right,' the woman actually smiled, though it was a reserved crack in a stony façade. Not conventionally pretty, the girl possessed clear olive skin and wide brown eyes that glowed with good health, in stark contrast to the sad, weather-beaten figures clustered on the street. 'It's understandable. But if you think about it, allowing the homeless to laze about all day in front of a fire simply makes them more dependent. At least outside they have to make some effort to make a living.' She turned away to address a figure with a badly faded scarf tied over her wispy grey hair. 'Now, Peggy, you know the rules. It's past eight, so you shouldn't be here.' The woman called Peggy mumbled something Flora couldn't catch, but the girl remained unmoved. 'If you've three pennies you can come back at six tonight. But not a minute before, mind.'

Grudgingly the woman moved away from the door, taking the other women with her. The child began to grizzle and was rewarded with a rough jiggling on the woman's hip. This didn't appear to help matters as the mewling turned into a full-blown wail.

The girl's expression softened. 'Is there something I can do to help you?'

'I hope so.' Bunny cast a final look at the creatures who had paused a few paces off. 'We've come to see Captain Blake.'

'Kindly follow me.' She stood aside to allow them into the main part of the building comprising of a long hall of bare, but recently swept floorboards, with a large fireplace at one end. The girl slammed the door and shot the large bolt on the inside. In response to Flora's surprised look, she added, 'We

310

have to keep this locked or they'll sneak back in when we aren't looking.'

Flora exchanged an uneasy frown with Bunny, but the girl seemed unmoved as she took them into a hall where rows of long wooden benches covered the entire floor, each with a number painted roughly on the end. Apart from an odour of damp wood and dust, the room was surprisingly clean without any of the unpleasant smells she had detected outside.

'Where are the beds?' Flora murmured, only half expecting an answer.

'This used to be a women's shelter, but now is known as a "sit up",' the girl explained. 'For a few pennies the poor get a bowl of soup, a warm fire, and a bench to sit on.'

'They sit up all night?'

'Did you think they were given feather beds and bathrooms?' The girl's smile faded, and with a gesture that they were to wait there, she disappeared through a door.

'She didn't have to be sarcastic,' Flora snapped. 'I've never been to a mission before and didn't know what to expect.'

'I suppose this place is something of a shock,' Bunny said. 'Was I wrong to bring you?'

'No, I'm glad you did, but it's so—' She broke off as the door opened again to reveal an attractive young woman of about Bunny's age. She wore her plain uniform dress with obvious pride, her dark hair pulled back from her face in a perfectly smooth bun. Her wide forehead and widely spaced hazel eyes above a mobile mouth broke into a broad smile as she approached.

'Bunny.' She ran the last few steps and took both his hands in hers in a relaxed, almost intimate gesture. 'How wonderful to see you again. It's been so long.'

CHAPTER 24

'And you, Emily.' Bunny grasped both her hands in his, the skin on his neck flushing slightly. 'Er-allow me to introduce you to my wife. Flora, I would like you to meet Miss Emily Blake. Or should I say Captain?'

'I can see by your expression that Bunny hasn't mentioned me, has he?' She turned a smile on Flora as natural and charming as her lilting voice.

'Indeed, he has not.' Flora shot him an accusing look, her hand thrust out, forcing Miss Blake to release one of Bunny's. 'I'm delighted to meet you.'

'We lived next door to each other in Richmond,' Bunny said. 'When we were about, oh, how old were we, Miss Blake?'

'Ten. And when did you stop calling me Emmie?'

'Have you been in the Salvation Army long, Captain Blake?' Flora asked.

'Oh, please, do call me Emily. I joined my brothers and sisters almost ten years ago now. My army ones, I mean. No one else in my family understood my calling.' She tilted her head and looked into

313

Bunny's eyes with the easy warmth born of long intimacy. 'Only Bunny understood.'

'I thought if anyone could help with our problem, it would be Emily.' Bunny bestowed yet another smile on the girl, who still retained one of his hands.

Flora fidgeted, beginning to feel like an outsider.

'I admit to being intrigued by your letter.' Emily gestured them into a small rear room where a welcoming fire crackled in the tiny iron grate. A plain pine table surrounded by four wheel backed chairs and a rag rug brought colour into an otherwise stark room. The younger girl who had shown them in acknowledged them with a nod as she stacked blankets on a set of racked shelves. 'Perhaps we could take tea while you tell me what brings you here. Hannah will look after things while we talk.'

When the girl inclined her head in assent and left, Emily gestured two high backed chairs set in front of a black leaded range where a fire was visible behind a grille in a small door.

Bunny held out a chair for Flora, but she sidestepped him and took the second, pointedly not looking at him, though from the corner of her eye she caught his wry smile as he took the chair himself.

Emily set a kettle on top of the range before joining them. 'Now, how can I be of assistance?' She folded her hands in her lap and sat in contemplative silence while Bunny explained about the death of Lizzie Prentice and her possible connection to the missing children.

'I've heard of St Philomena's,' Emily said when he had finished. 'It has an excellent reputation.'

'At the moment, however I fear this affair will do nothing to enhance that,' Bunny said.

'I appreciate that.' Emily twisted her hands on her lap as if nervous. 'You say the children went missing from the hospital? They weren't taken from their homes?'

'We aren't sure,' Flora said slowly. 'Some were collected from the hospital on discharge, but others went home first. In one case a man took an eight-year-old girl away in a taxi. It's not certain that particular case is connected.' Bunny gave Flora a warning look. 'However if not, it's an oddly timed coincidence.'

'And your maid?' Emily asked. 'How is she involved?'

'That was *my* fault.' Shame heated Flora's face. 'I asked her to watch someone whom we believed was involved. This person met with a man in a Salvation Army uniform. Sally followed him and she hasn't been seen since.'

'You think one of our soldiers is involved?' Emily's face paled slightly but the look she split between them was guarded rather than surprised. 'Is that why you came here?'

Bunny's response was interrupted when the kettle rattled on the range and spat a stream of steam into the air.

'Keep talking while I make the tea.' Emily rose and filled a plain brown teapot with a grace that would not have looked out of place in a Kensington drawing room.

'We don't know for certain,' Bunny said carefully. 'And I don't wish to insult your organization, I—'

'You cannot insult us in any way I haven't already heard.' Emily held the kettle in the air, a smile playing over her full lips. 'Simply say what's on your mind, Bunny.'

'As you wish.' He rubbed his hands across his thighs. 'Is it feasible that someone, maybe even more than one person, is impersonating your officers?'

Emily seemed to give his question some thought as she returned the kettle to the range and brought the teapot to the table, her expression not betraying what was going on behind her clear hazel eyes.

'I'm so very sorry about your maid,' Emily said, at last, handing Flora a full cup of murky brown liquid. She set a small jug of milk and a sugar bowl on the table between them, her enigmatic expression giving nothing away.

Flora added milk into her cup, though it made little difference as the brew remained a dark brown. She took a tentative sip and choked.

'Oh dear, is the tea all right?' Emily's eyes widened in alarm.

'It's fine,' Flora's voice lifted, but she recovered herself quickly. 'Perhaps a little stronger than I'm used to. Might I have some sugar?'

'Of course.' Emily pushed the sugar bowl across the table towards her before she lowered herself into a chair opposite.

Bunny frowned at a point somewhere on Flora's chin, pulled a handkerchief from his pocket and held it out. Wordlessly, she took it using it to wipe her face though she stoically refused to look at him, certain he was grinning at her.

'I'm not avoiding your question.' Emily's knuckles whitened on the table top as if she was summoning courage to speak. She took a deep breath and seemed to make up her mind. 'Have either of you heard of the Emigration Bureau?' Without waiting for an answer she continued. 'Our founder, General Booth established the bureau twenty years ago. He advertised in the *Social Gazette* offering free passage to domestic workers who were prepared to travel to Queensland, Australia, for work. Recently the bureau has made arrangements for children to be relocated in rural homes in Canada. Farms mostly.'

'Where do these children come from?' Flora asked.

'All over London.' Emily fiddled with her teaspoon. 'The reason for our . . . circumspection is because we have our enemies in Government who disapprove of sending our labour force abroad. Thus, we tend not to publicize the service too freely so as to avoid scrutiny. We keep records of the adults, but statistics for children were not begun until last year.'

'Isn't that somewhat lax?' Flora fought to keep her voice neutral but doubted she succeeded. 'To send children thousands of miles from their homes without knowing much about them or where they came from?'

'It's not quite as arbitrary as that. Very few children have been sent without their parents.'

'Even so—'

'Flora.' Bunny placed a warning hand on her forearm. 'Where is this Bureau? It might be worth paying them a visit.'

'I doubt it.' Emily shook her head. 'They don't have a proper office, just a few clerks working out of a corner room at our headquarters. It's a philanthropic practice, so I doubt any of our members would be involved in anything untoward.'

'Isn't kidnapping maids considered untoward?' Flora snapped, only to find herself on the sharp end of Bunny's angry look. 'I'm sorry, she blurted, horrified to find her eyes welling. 'I'm finding this more emotional than I thought. Sally means a lot to me and she could be anywhere, even hurt, and—' Her throat closed and she took a deep breath in an effort to compose herself, aware of Bunny's arm sliding across the back of her chair, his fingers moving gently across the nape of her neck.

His touch calmed her and her breathing slowed as she became conscious she was embarrassing herself in front of a young woman who shared a past with Bunny.

'I apologize, I don't mean to sound accusing,' Flora began. 'How can you be sure these children are going to good homes? That they are not simply being used as cheap labour on farms treated no better than slaves?'

'Isn't a life of hard work in healthy surroundings preferable to being maimed in a badly equipped factory, or even starving to death in a city slum?' Emily's tone became defensive. 'I assure you we only have their future welfare at heart.'

'Is that true for your entire organization?' Bunny asked.

'The Bureau searches out candidates among the poorest, it's true,' Emily set down her cup with a firm click. 'Although I can assure you we have never recruited from hospitals. Which leads me to your original question.' She leaned forward, her hands clenched on the table top. 'A little while ago, a woman arrived at another of our missions with a request. She asked if her nephew might be added to the list for emigration. At thirteen, the boy was a bit of a handful. He had joined a street gang known to be involved in local burglaries and she wanted to prevent his being sent to a training ship.'

'I'm sorry, I'm not familiar with that term,' Flora interrupted. 'What exactly is a training ship?'

'They are prisons for young men,' Bunny said. 'Decommissioned navy vessels are moored on the Thames at Purfleet and Chatham. Boys in their teens convicted of less serious crimes are sentenced to what is euphemistically called, training.'

'Euphemistically?' Flora raised an eyebrow at him.

'The regime is intended to be beneficial to their rehabilitation.' Emily sighed. 'But life on board those ships is harsh. To be plain about it, those young men are sent to be broken. They are worked relentlessly and suffer punishments for minor infractions, almost like the sailors were in the Napoleonic Wars. This woman I mentioned cared for her nephew enough not to let that happen, but she had no income to support the boy and came to us for help.'

'Couldn't he have been employed at one of the factories or a foundry?' Bunny asked. 'I believe they are the main employers in this area?'

'She tried, but he was dismissed after a week.' Emily's wry look indicated it was not a good experience. 'He hated being inside, so his aunt thought life on a farm would suit him. Anyway, the reason I mentioned her is because she appeared under the impression that the Army paid a fee in exchange for sending young people to positions in Canada where they were wanted.'

'I take it that isn't the case?' Bunny asked.

Emily shook her head. 'It's true the Bureau pays their travelling expenses but never offers money to families. When my colleague asked her where she had learned this, she insisted a friend of hers had been given money from the Bureau to send her daughter to a farm in Canada to work as a lady's maid two months before.'

'A lady's maid? On a farm?' Flora said, sceptical.

'Exactly. This woman had been sworn to secrecy, due to the demand, apparently. She was told there was a waiting list. If she revealed she had been given preferential treatment, the offer would be withdrawn.'

'And the fee paid for the girl subject to return, I gather?' Bunny stroked his chin with his free hand, the other arm still rested against Flora's shoulders. 'Quite an effective way to keep their activities secret.'

'Indeed,' Emily said. 'And if this woman hadn't come to us, we might never have discovered the fraud. Word has gone out to our other missions to keep an eye out for the couple involved, but as I am sure you can imagine, it's not easy. Most of our work is done on the streets, so looking for one couple is proving nigh on impossible. The pair wear authentic-looking uniforms and carry collection boxes. They have only been seen a few times and by the time word gets back and we go looking, they have gone.'

'The couple who were in the Lamb and Flag the other night were imposters?' Flora turned a shocked look on Bunny.

'You know who these people are?' Emily split a look between them.

'Not exactly,' Bunny said thoughtfully. 'Though your account fits in with what I have begun to suspect myself.'

321

'We must tell Inspector Maddox,' Flora interjected.

'In good time, Flora. We'll have to tread carefully. We aren't very popular with Maddox at the moment.'

'You mean *I'm* not.' Flora sniffed. 'Captain Blake – Emily. Has your organization reported this to the police?'

'Ah, no.' Emily glanced down, as a flush bloomed in her cheeks. 'We were hoping to discover the culprits ourselves. I'm afraid the police disapprove of our methods in the spread of God's word. They claim that our bands and parades cause disruption in the streets and anger from the more conservative denominations. If the story about this couple gets into the newspapers, the scandal could ruin us.'

Flora was about to ask if the army's reputation was worth more than the children, but caught Bunny's imperceptible shake of his head and thought better of it.

'Thank you for being so candid with us, Emmie.' Bunny rose, retrieved Flora's still full cup and placed it with his own on the tray. 'I would have understood had you refused to tell us anything at all.' A remark, Flora assumed, was aimed at her. 'If we discover any more about this couple, we'll be sure to let you know. And conversely, if you receive any intelligence—'

'I would like to say I would inform you immediately.' Emily rose with them, a doubt in her eyes.

'However, I'm obliged to obey the tenets of the army, and my superiors might insist on total privacy.' She must have seen the disappointment on their faces and her expression softened. 'But I will do what I can.'

'Our address is in my letter,' Bunny said. 'As is our telephone number.'

Emily laughed, a girlish, charming laugh which made her quite lovely. 'I'm afraid we don't run to such luxuries here in Whitechapel.'

As she showed them back the way they had come, Flora noticed she didn't promise to get a message to them by any other means either.

Once out on the street again, their presence acted as a source of entertainment, prompting Flora to regret not having asked the cabbie to wait for them. Doors opened and ragged children spilled onto the street to stare at them as they passed by. Women in none-too-clean creased and darned clothes leaned against door frames, aiming half-threatening looks their way, while others held contempt or hopeful expressions.

'You didn't tell me Captain Blake was a woman. And a very attractive one at that.' She eased closer to Bunny as two urchins ran past her, both being shouted at by an indignant greengrocer. The boys disappeared into an alley, leaving the disgruntled shopkeeper to retrieve the apples the boys had dislodged from a pyramid on a trestle outside the shop.

'Would it have made a difference?' The corner of Bunny's mouth twitched without becoming a smile.

'Maybe, maybe not. How would *you* feel if I produced a presentable young man, held his hand and called him by a babyish name and announced we had known each other for years?'

'Challenge him to a duel in Hyde Park at dawn, naturally.' He cast a sideways look at her from beneath lowered brows, though his eyes behind his spectacles glinted with amusement.

'Don't mock me.' She pouted, aware there was no real threat from Emily. 'I'm simply unaccustomed to having your former paramours, or whatever you call them paraded before me.'

'Hardly a paramour, and I refute having paraded her. We haven't seen each other since we were sixteen.'

'Old enough for the pangs of first love.'

'*You* are my first love, Flora. My only love, so you have nothing to worry about.' Bunny took her hand in both of his. 'Although I also adore the fact that you are jealous, therefore I forgive you for being less than your normal polite self.'

'I'm not jealous!' Her cheeks flamed, though at the same time she acknowledged to herself that she had been sharp. A little.

'Silly me.' He increased the pressure of his hand on hers. 'I must have misunderstood. Oh, there's a cab.'

'Thank goodness.' Flora sighed. 'I thought we

would have to walk all the way to London Bridge.'

The tension left her as she settled on the seat of the glass cab, relieved to be inside and separate from shabby streets that made her feel exposed and vulnerable in a way she had not experienced since Southwark.

'I accept that your Emily Blake is an intelligent, dedicated young woman.' Flora ventured the doubt that had niggled at her as they sat in the plain little room at the mission, 'But I suspect her loyalties aren't the same as ours.'

'I got that impression too.' Bunny adjusted the blanket provided over Flora's knees.

'It looks as if we'll have to find and expose these imposters ourselves.' She eyed the slightly musty smelling object, unable to help wondering about its origins, and resolved not to touch it more often than necessary.

'I agree, but the fact Emily told us about them means she is also aware we would have to pass the information on to Inspector Maddox.'

'I didn't think of that.' Flora sneaked an admiring look at his profile with a rush of pride. She liked to think his willing participation was because children were at risk, although perhaps, like her, he was finally beginning to enjoy the excitement of the chase?

Preoccupied, Flora stared out of the hackney at the shabby buildings where most of the shopkeepers' goods spilled onto the pavements and manure sweepers were few and far between. Whitechapel possessed an air of desperation, where no one smiled, and every eye Flora met glared back expressionless or slid away. Everything from the buildings to the clothes people wore merged into an amalgam of black or brown as if all the colour and life had been leached from its inhabitants and buildings.

How could a young woman like Emily Blake, who was attractive, intelligent and should have been mistress of her own home by now, bear to spend her days in such a depressing, joyless place? As soon as this thought occurred to her it was replaced with another. If not Emily and people like her, who else was there to help such unfortunates?

'You've gone quiet,' Bunny said after a few moments. 'Yet I can sense a growing excitement that you believe we might be close to solving this mystery.'

'Not solving, but what Emily told us about this couple is important. At first I thought they were Sister Lazarus and Swifty Ellis, but had that been the case, surely Abel would have recognised him?'

'That's the conclusion I came to. So where does it take us?'

'The woman could still be Sister Lazarus. And I only say that because I cannot think of anyone else whom it could be.'

'Not to mention the fact you don't like her?'

'Well, yes, but apart from that she's in possession

of a Stanhope which I'm convinced must be one of Mr Buchanan's. Imagine this.' Flora twisted on the seat to face him. 'Sister Lazarus and an accomplice went into The Antigallican dressed as Salvation Army officers with no idea Lizzie worked there. Sister Lazarus saw Lizzie and knowing she could cause trouble for her, warned her to keep her mouth shut. Lizzie, however, had a conscience and the day you and I were on our tour of the hospital, she asked to speak to Alice to tell her what she had seen, but was overheard by Sister Lazarus.'

'You think Sister Lazarus killed Lizzie to keep her quiet?'

'Is that so hard to believe? When she arrived with the tea tray that day, her skirt was wet. Why? She had no reason to go outside as the kitchen was next door to Alice's office.' He opened his mouth to speak, but she forestalled him with a hand on his arm. 'I know she said she had to find a handyman to fix the boiler, but we only have her word there was anything wrong with it.'

'Goodness, Flora, you've quite an imagination, the worst of it being there's every chance you could be right.'

'I don't know how we will expose them, but cannot help thinking if anyone knows where Sally is, Sister Lazarus does.'

'Maybe, but under no circumstances must you confront her. If she did kill Lizzie Prentice she's dangerous. If you come across her at the hospital, promise me you'll be discreet and not even hint you suspect her.'

'That won't be easy.' She caught the look on his face and sobered immediately. 'No, you're right. I won't say a word. But it won't stop me looking for proof of her involvement.'

CHAPTER 25

When Flora woke the next morning, a curtain of yellowish-grey fog pressed against the bedroom window, almost completely obscuring the houses opposite. Costermongers guided their horse drawn carts through silent deserted streets. Slow moving shadows whose disembodied calls were quickly swallowed up by the cloying mist.

Her morning visit to the nursery did not improve her state of mind with Arthur made fretful by the oppressive atmosphere that crept beneath the doors and the sides of window frames. He would not settle on Flora's lap, his chubby body rigid in her arms, dimpled fists clenched as he made his unhappiness evident in a long, unrelenting scream.

Conscious she was making things worse, Flora left him to Milly, whose murmured endearments followed her out of the room, turning almost instantly to happy gurgles. By the time Flora reached the ground floor she had sunk into self-pitying despair, though common sense told her Arthur's response was to be expected when Milly was the one who cared for him all day.

The sound of raised voices in the rear hall drove her onwards in the hope that there was some news of Sally, but she walked into a quarrel between the housekeeper and laundry maid. At Flora's approach, Mrs Cope waved the maid back towards the kitchen. 'I'm sorry, I didn't see you there, Madam.' She brushed both hands nervously down her skirt.

'Is something wrong, Mrs Cope?' Flora sighed, her question perfunctory. She was not in the mood for domestic squabbles today.

'Just that the silly girl hung the washing out this morning thinking it would be a good idea as the rain had stopped. Now it's all covered in blacks and she's giving me gyp about her having to do it all again. She's threatening to give notice and go home.'

'She's a country girl,' Flora replied, referring to the Sussex-born maid. 'This will be her first winter here, and the fog can come as a shock. She'll get used to it.'

'Well I 'ope she does, at least afore them sheets are scrubbed to ribbons.' The woman dropped an awkward curtsey and returned to the kitchens, mumbling to herself as she left.

'This fog is relentless.' Flora said to Bunny as she entered the sitting room, her hands outstretched to the crackling fire until her cheeks stung, though her toes remained numb with cold. 'I cannot bear the thought of Arthur's tiny lungs being attacked by thick, choking fumes that make it difficult to breathe. He's already fretful and it's going to get worse as the days get colder. Perhaps it wasn't a good idea leaving Richmond.'

'Don't be so hard on yourself. Arthur is well cared for.' Bunny looked up briefly from a newspaper that looked suspiciously damp. 'Everyone in the house is miserable today. I've instructed Stokes not to bother with any outside work and keep the fires banked up. I also said the staff can make tea whenever they feel inclined. At least we'll all be warm and comfortable indoors.'

'You're too generous.' Flora shivered, both hands held out to the flames though she didn't bother to add that the kettle was always on the boil in the kitchen. What he didn't know wouldn't hurt him. 'What would your mother say if she knew?'

'Whatever she likes, she's not here,' he mumbled. Discarding the newspaper, he rose and advanced on the sideboard where he riffled through the pile of letters on a silver tray. Selecting a stiff white envelope, he expertly slit it open with a paperknife.

'I'm sure this fog has thickened since breakfast.' She nodded to where the maids had lit the gaslights to lift the gloom. 'The butcher's boy hasn't brought the delivery this morning either.'

'I'm sure we'll not starve to death.' Bunny replied, distracted, his forehead creased as he focused on the letter in his hand.

Flora turned to look out at the street again as, unbidden, an image of Sally entered her head. Was she warm and being fed or out in this dreadful weather? Surely if she was still alive they would have heard something? 'I don't suppose Inspector Maddox called when I was upstairs?'

'Unfortunately not.' Bunny pulled a face. 'Shall I telephone him? Though I doubt it would make a difference other than remind him we still expect some effort on his part.'

Flora was about to say that might annoy rather than encourage him, but was forestalled by Stokes, who announced that Alice Finch was on the telephone asking for Mr Harrington.

'Are you sure she said *Mr* Harrington, Stokes?' Flora asked when Bunny had gone to take the call.

'Absolutely, Madam.' Stokes gave her a look as close to a glare as he dared before he withdrew.

'What did she want?' Flora asked when Bunny returned shortly afterwards.

'She would like us to call in at the hospital tomorrow. I could only just hear her. Goodness, it's freezing out there in the hall.' He strode back to the hearth and rubbed his hands together over the flames.

'The rain must have affected the lines,' Flora said, though with no idea whether this was true or not. 'Did she say what she wanted to talk about?'

'No.' Bunny sank onto the sofa Stokes had thoughtfully pulled closer to the fire. 'She sounded nervous and kept dropping her voice. As if someone was listening.'

'Perhaps we should go now?' Flora cast a quick look towards the window. 'Although it would take us a while to get there. That is, if we could find a cab willing to take us.'

'And I have no intention of driving, not in this.' Bunny flapped a hand at the window. 'Plus Miss Finch said St Philomena's has had an influx of patients with chest infections since yesterday, and insisted we go tomorrow.'

Anxiety tightened Flora's chest but she kept her voice neutral. Why was Alice being so mysterious? What was it she needed to say that she couldn't tell them over the telephone?

Flora woke the next morning with a mild headache, her multi-layered nightgowns twisted round her in an uncomfortable tangle. The sight of Nell with her morning tea sending fresh dismay through her that she was not Sally, her enquiry for news eliciting a shaken head and a rapid retreat.

After a desultory breakfast, she counted the minutes until it was time to go to St Philomena's, her head full of questions as to why Alice wanted to see them. Had the police found Isobel Lomax? If so, there would have been no requirement to inform her or Bunny. Or had something else come to light in the hospital?

Dressed in a thick navy blue gown that buttoned to the neck against the damp October cold, Flora descended the stairs into the hall at the same moment Stokes hurried from the rear hall to answer the door.

'I'm sorry for the intrusion.' Lydia burst inside.

'Abel is frantic about Sally. We wondered if you had any news?'

Abel hovered in the door frame, until Stokes gestured him to move so he might shut out the cold. Reluctantly, he stomped inside, leaving large wet footprints on the tiled floor.

Flora experienced a surge of sympathy, knowing Abel felt guilty for having 'lost' Sally. 'I'm sorry, Abel. I wish things were different, but we haven't heard anything new.' His unkempt hair and evidence of a careless shave made Flora's heart ache for him.

'It ain't your fault, Miss Flora.' Abel took a deep breath. 'I mean, *not* your fault. I was the one who was supposed to be looking after her.' Flora was about to protest but he waved her away. 'I went back to The Antigallican yesterday. Not sure why, but I couldn't think of anything else to do. The barman recognized me so I didn't ask too many questions, but I heard someone say the police had been looking for Swifty Ellis.'

'I know.' Flora walked down the last few steps into the hall. 'Inspector Maddox told us they were looking for him but he's not been seen.'

'Not by them, maybe.' Abel sniffed. 'But some blokes in the pub said he was at St Saviour's dock yesterday, so I went down there to take a look.'

'Where is this dock?' Flora's heart skipped at the thought they might be getting close.

'It's in the Jacob's Island area near Tower Bridge,' Lydia said. 'Not that it's a real island anymore. After the cholera outbreak in the middle of the last century, part of the Neckinger stream was built over. It's where they used to hang pirates long ago. That's where the name came from. Neckinger means, "Devil's neckcloth", another name for a hangman's noose.'

'Was there any sign of Sally or the children?' Flora asked, mainly to interrupt Lydia's impromptu history lesson. Although her question was redundant, for if Abel had found anything, he would have said so.

Abel shook his head. 'Swifty's barge was all locked up and empty.'

'Did you say he has a barge?' Flora asked. 'How does a small-time crook afford to buy a boat, not to mention cover the mooring fees?'

'I was gettin' ter that.' Abel split a look of frustration between the two women. 'A couple of the bargees told me Swifty stopped signing on for casual work a year ago. He bought the barge cheap from a river man who was injured.'

Flora briefly wondered if Swifty had anything to do with that injury.

'My guess from what was being implied,' Abel continued. 'Is that Swifty has a side line in stolen goods from the ships. The crews have been known to help themselves to bits and bobs from the cargo and sell them privately.'

'You are sure this boat of his was empty?' Flora hoped he was wrong, but if Sally was there, she was clever enough to let someone know. If she still could.

'I'm not daft.' He glared at her from lowered brows. 'It's one of those flat barges, like a narrow-boat but wider, sits low on the waterline and has a cabin on it. That's what made me think he could be keeping the nippers there, but I kept watch for hours and it was empty all right. No one came near.'

'An interesting idea, though how could Swifty have kept them hidden with dock workers and bargees coming and going? Children don't sit still for long, they make noise.'

'Then where?'

'Good morning, Miss Grey, Mr Cain,' Bunny said, wandering into the hall. 'I had no idea you were here. Have you brought news?'

'They came to ask *us* that.' Flora cut him a sharp look, removed her coat from the stand and shrugged into it while Abel repeated his story for Bunny's benefit.

'Ah, I see. How disappointing.' Bunny said when he had finished, placing a comforting hand on Abel's shoulder, a gesture Flora assumed was prompted by the man's downcast expression. 'We were about to leave for St Philomena's, summoned by the inimitable Miss Finch. Perhaps she has something new to impart.' He gave Abel's shoulder a final pat and reached for his hat.

'You're going now?' Lydia split a hopeful look between them. 'Could we come with you?'

The heavy rainfall forced their motor taxi to little more than a crawling pace so it took them over an hour to reach Southwark. Flora began to feel claustrophobic as the steady downpour drummed the cab roof where she was squashed into the seat beside Abel Cain.

'She'll think we aren't coming,' Flora fretted.

'Miss Finch will understand with the rain this heavy.' Bunny wiped condensation from the window, the annoying squeak making Flora wince.

It was past noon when Bunny paid off the driver outside St Philomena's Hospital. Flora stepped out of the taxi into rivulets of water that reached mid ankle, her dash for the main door sending water into the hem of her coat. 'Miss Finch is expecting us,' she explained to the porter who attempted to delay them. Her boots squelched as she pushed open the door to the corridor leading to Miss Finch's office. She glanced back to where Abel hovered by the porter's desk. 'Aren't you coming, Abel?

'I'll wait here if it's all right with you, Miss Flora.' He held his cap in one hand and brushed water off one shoulder with the other. 'I don't much like 'ospitals.'

'I sympathize.' Bunny patted his arm as he passed. 'We shouldn't be long.'

Alice rose from her desk as they entered, a look of relief mixed with anxiety on her face. 'I apologize for summoning you here like this.' She nodded in acknowledgment to Lydia, but before they had taken their seats, Alice handed Bunny a small silver globe. 'After what we discussed the other day, I thought you should see this.'

'Where did you get it?' Bunny weighed the object in his palm.

'It looks like one of Mr Buchanan's peeps.' Flora peered at it over his shoulder. This one was different to the one she had seen in Sister Lazarus' possession, in that hers was spherical and gold. The one Bunny held was egg-shaped and silver, about the size and shape of a quail's egg, with a thin silver chain attached to the wider end.

'That's exactly what it is.' Alice wandered to the window, her gaze on the far distance as if removing herself from the situation. 'I was given Lizzie Prentice's things this morning. She has no family to speak of, so the poor girl will be buried in a pauper's grave. This,' she indicated the object in Bunny's hand, 'was among them.'

Bunny turned the object over in his fingers before holding it up to the light, squinting while he talked. 'This is indeed similar to the others, and—' He halted, blinked and jerked his chin back. 'Ah! This is more what I expected.'

'What is it?' Flora went to take it from him, but he jerked his hand out of her reach.

'Nothing you should be looking at, Flora. It's rather, er, explicit.'

'Don't be silly.' Flora blew air through her lips in an impatient tut. 'It cannot be worse than the ones we saw in Mr Buchanan's office.' She wrestled the silver object from his hand, and lifted it to her eye. The edges were fuzzy, but the image showed two naked figures wound round one another, making it impossible to see which body parts belonged to whom. 'It's a photograph of a couple.' Flora twisted the peep, her eyes focussing on the picture inside slowly. The image jumped out at her and she blinked, removing it quickly from her eye. When she realized what she was looking at, she lowered it again quickly. 'I-uh, I see what you mean.'

'Precisely.' Alice exhaled slowly, her eyes closed.

'This puts an entirely different slant on the matter,' Bunny added, retrieving the object from Flora's limp fingers.

'Well?' Lydia demanded. 'Isn't anyone going to explain?'

'It's a picture of two naked men,' Flora whispered, uncomfortable heat flooding her face.

'Surely not?' Lydia gasped, with more surprised fascination than shock. 'Let me see.' She extended a hand towards Bunny and gestured he hand it over. He didn't.

'The contents of this item are hardly suitable for a married woman, Miss Grey, let alone an unmarried one.'

Lydia pouted but gave in with a resigned shrug.

'I've never heard—' Flora broke off as she tried to form the appropriate words, 'I mean, I knew about . . . men and other men, of course, but as to a photograph of them actually—'

'Indeed.' Alice's tone declared the subject closed.

'However, the existence of this object convinces me that Mr Buchanan is no child trafficker.'

'What makes you say that, Miss Finch?' Bunny asked gently.

She gave the silver egg a severe glance but made no move to touch it. 'Because one of the men in that photograph is Victor Buchanan, Raymond's son.'

Her words seemed to suck the air from the room, and whilst they processed the implications of her statement, the door was flung open and Raymond Buchanan strode into the room.

'Miss Finch, might I have a word with—'

CHAPTER 26

Buchanan's spaniel eyes widened as they locked on the object in Bunny's hand, his face drained of colour. He closed the door hurriedly and leaned against it.

'Raymond, I—' Alice hesitated, her face ashen.

'It's all right, Alice.' He gestured her away with one hand. 'I knew this was bound to come out sooner or later.' He regarded the object in Bunny's hand with resigned disgust. 'Is that what I think it is?'

Flora had taken him for a younger man, however closer inspection revealed his hair was thin showing areas of pink scalp together with spidery lines beside his eyes and mouth not visible from a distance. 'You don't recognise it?' Alice frowned but offered no further explanation. Instead, she pulled out her chair and gestured him into it. 'Might I suggest we all sit down?'

Buchanan complied, albeit reluctantly, glaring at each of them in turn. 'I recognise you, Mr Harrington, and your lady wife.' He narrowed watery blue eyes at Lydia. 'Though I don't believe I'm acquainted with this young lady?'

'This is Miss Lydia Grey,' Flora interrupted Lydia's flustered apology. 'A good friend of mine who has been of invaluable assistance.'

'I see.' He looked about to add something else, but changed his mind. 'In answer to your question, Alice, no, I've never seen it before. Where did you get it?'

'It was among Lizzie Prentice's belongings,' Alice replied. With Buchanan occupying her chair, she wandered to the window.

Flora observed her profile from the corner of her eye as she stared out at the walled garden as if distancing herself, her posture strong, erect and graceful as a dancer.

'How the devil did *she* get hold of it?' Buchanan's shoulders sagged, as if aware he had lost any chance of regaining command of the situation. 'And how many of the blasted things are there?'

'An interesting question,' Bunny said. 'I realize you don't owe us an explanation, sir, but am I right in assuming these items are what began your current – difficulties?'

'You could say that.' He adjusted his cravat as if giving himself time to form a response. 'As I am sure Alice has told you, I collect them. Churches, landscapes, that sort of thing. More recently I acquired some of a more, well, risqué nature, shall I say, but I assure you in no way illegal.' He searched their faces for disapproval, and apparently seeing none, relaxed. 'Purely for myself you understand.'

'Which brings us to this.' Bunny held up the silver egg. 'I'm sure I don't have to tell you it contains something more controversial than a picture of a church.'

'I assumed as much, or why would you all be here?' Buchanan massaged his forehead with one hand. 'My son gave me one quite similar. He thought it might amuse me.' His harsh laugh caught in his throat. 'Victor is – uh – less than discreet as to his proclivities. In fact he appears proud of them in a way no decent person should be.'

'Excuse my interrupting,' Lydia spoke for the first time since his arrival. 'Considering the uh – subject matter, why did you keep such a thing in your possession?' She gave the room a swift, embarrassed glance. 'Or is that crass of me?'

'Entirely my own fault.' Buchanan sighed. 'Victor handed me a presentation box as I was getting into a hackney to attend an appointment with the Board of Governors. I opened the box in my office. It was a small gold ball on a chain. I had no idea what it contained, or I would not have examined it with Sister Lazarus in the room.' He took a deep, ragged breath as if the next words pained hm. 'She saw how it affected me.'

'You didn't tell her what was inside?' Alice leaned her hip on the sill and turned towards him.

'No, of course not!' His flush deepened and he had trouble meeting her eye. 'I dismissed the thing completely and locked it in my desk. A day or so later, it went missing. I suspected Sister Lazarus had taken it but I dare not confront her.'

'She used the existence of the Stanhope against you?' Flora asked.

'Not at first,' he said carefully. 'Later, she took to wearing it on a chain at her waist, a triumphant smile on her face.'

Alice sighed and turned back to the window, the conversation evidently a difficult one for her.

'It was when she brought an officer from the Salvation Army to see me, that things became – well strange,' Buchanan added.

'In what way?' Bunny exchanged a look with Flora, who lifted an eyebrow.

'This chap – a Lieutenant Brodie, claimed to be part of the Emigration Bureau set up to help poor families relocate to places like Australia and Canada. They advance passage money to the poor and indigent to build more prosperous lives abroad.'

'I know of it.' Bunny nodded slowly, though made no attempt to introduce Captain Blake into the conversation. 'They operate quietly as the government disapprove of sending our much-needed workforce abroad.'

'That's exactly why he said I needed to be discreet. Normally, the passage money is refunded once the main breadwinner secures employment. However, Brodie was in the process of establishing a new scheme involving charitable donations.'

'Oh, Raymond!' Alice turned from the window,

her arms crossed over her chest. 'You didn't give the man money?'

'Not exactly.' He swallowed before continuing, 'that's when things became strange. I was asked, well more instructed to make the *SS Lancett* available to transport a group of emigrants to Canada. I told him it was a cargo ship and not equipped to carry passengers, but he brushed that aside. He suggested that part of a lower deck could be fitted out as bunks and washing facilities for a small number of travellers. When I suggested that would be expensive and impractical, he simply told me I would find a way to comply.'

'Thus his request became an outright threat?' Flora said.

'Exactly.' His face suffused with red. 'I was hardly in a position to refuse when Ruth had that disgusting object.'

'You did not inform the police she was blackmailing you?' Bunny asked.

'No. It would have been too shaming, not to mention disastrous for Victor.'

'Was Sister Lazarus aware of who was in the photograph?' Bunny asked.

He shook his head. 'That was never mentioned. As far as I know she had never met Victor. The fact I owned such an object was enough for her. If it was only my reputation at stake I would have told her to do her worst, but I could not take such a risk with regard to my son.'

345

'What did you think when Alice told you about the missing children?' Bunny asked.

'I spoke to the police, but they said they had not received any complaints, so I assumed you had misinterpreted the situation.' He directed a look at Alice that contained a plea for forgiveness. 'At that stage, I believed this scheme of Brodie's was legitimate.'

'Or you hoped it was,' Flora said, sharper than she intended. 'What changed your mind?'

Buchanan shrugged, but more in resignation than uncertainty. 'Lieutenant Brodie assured me he was not involved.'

'I wish you wouldn't keep calling him that,' Alice snapped. 'Surely you must have known by then he was nothing to do with the Salvation Army?'

'Perhaps you're right. I didn't want to admit I had been manipulated. I thought I could control it.' Buchanan massaged his forehead with one hand, his expression that of a man trapped by his own bad judgement. 'Then that student nurse was killed and everything got out of control.'

'Lizzie Prentice,' Flora enunciated slowly. *He could at least remember the poor girl's name!*

'Ah, yes, of course. Nurse Prentice.' He cleared his throat. 'After the inquest, I confronted Brodie, but he denied all knowledge. What could I do as I had no evidence against him.'

'How many times did this Lieutenant Brodie use your ship?' Bunny asked.

'This was to be the first voyage, and I made it quite clear it would be the last.'

'How do you contact him? Bunny's expression showed he didn't believe that any more than Flora did. Once Brodie had his claws into Buchanan he would never let go as long as his scheme remained lucrative.

'I don't.' He swallowed. 'He sends me a note via some scruffy-looking chap in a brown coat and a greasy homburg.'

'Swifty Ellis,' Flora murmured.

'Beg pardon?' Buchanan blinked, confused.

'Nothing. Do go on, sir.'

'I spotted him a few times hanging about the hospital, and assumed he had come to check up on me.'

'Is that where you meet him, here at the hospital?' Bunny kept his voice level, with no hint of accusation.

'It's never the same place. The last time was in the Lamb and Flag off Wimpole Street. We met so Brodie could give me details of sailing. Can you imagine the humiliation of that? *I* own the ship and he told *me* when he planned to leave.'

'Brodie had taken control of your ship?' Bunny sounded incredulous, whether at the audacity of this Brodie person or Mr Buchanan's duplicity wasn't clear.

He nodded. 'He brought in a new crew and negotiated the cargo. I had no say in the arrangements.'

'And you just went along with it and kept silent?'

Flora began to lose patience. He appeared more concerned for his own status than those poor abducted children.

'What could I do without putting Victor in danger of prosecution?' He spread his hands on the desk in a gesture of resignation. 'It wouldn't take the police long to work out who was the subject of the Stanhope. That sort of practice is a criminal offence.'

'You were being blackmailed,' Flora said. 'The authorities might have been willing to make allowances.' It occurred to her that the *SS Lancett* was being used to transport more than a few children.

'I couldn't risk it.' Buchanan's eyes took on a haunted look. 'Then when that Inspector Maddox chap asked to search the ship, I agreed in the hope that Brodie would be exposed. But there were no children aboard, so I still had no proof.'

'Brodie must have been aware that you co-operated with the police?' Bunny pushed away from the desk and began pacing the room, his hands clasped behind his back. There was scant room in an office with five occupants, but Bunny liked to walk as an aid to his thought processes.

'Exactly. I've been waiting for the shoe to drop these last few days. I haven't heard from him at all since the ship was searched, but I cannot see that lasting.' Buchanan fisted his hands on the desk and glared at the silver egg. 'I also had no idea there were others of those – *things* – floating about. How many do you think there are?'

'Maybe you should ask your son?' An edge crept into Flora's voice. How could a man be so sensitive to the plight of his own children and yet ignore that of someone else's?

'Why didn't you tell me any of this, Raymond?' Alice came to stand beside his chair, her hand on the back support. 'I would have helped you.'

'How could I?' His shoulders hunched in defeat beneath her uncompromising gaze. 'When I realized what kind of people they were, I couldn't risk involving you. If all this came out, Victor could go to prison. I couldn't take that chance.'

'Victor's a grown man,' Alice's voice hardened, 'you aren't responsible for his choices.'

'He's still my son.' Buchanan sighed.

The atmosphere grew heavy with embarrassment, the only sounds the odd cough and a shift of a chair on the floorboards, made more ominous by Bunny's thoughtful pacing. Even Lydia fidgeted in her chair as if she had no wish to be there.

That these revelations were hard on Mr Buchanan was obvious, though at the same time he seemed relieved to finally share what had become an unendurable burden. Perhaps Alice was right and he was simply a man one who had lost control of an impossible situation.

'What about the Lomax girl?' Alice broke the silence, apparently not finished with Raymond. 'Is this Brodie responsible for her disappearance too?'

'I thought so at first, but then the police told

349

me she had most likely wandered away when her nanny was distracted by a man friend.'

'Huh!' Alice threw away from him. 'A tidy, convenient theory enabling you to salve your conscience.' Ignoring his startled protest, she continued, 'and Ruth's complicity is shocking. She was a workhouse child, who under my mentoring became a good nurse,' she paused as if rethinking this opinion, adding, 'well, efficient anyway.'

'Not everyone can put their past behind them, Miss Finch,' Bunny said gently. 'Nor do they wish to. Perhaps whatever scars the workhouse left ran too deep. If she experienced no love in her own life, these children might be no more to her than commodities.'

'And how could you co-operate with such a scheme, even for Victor's sake?' She turned on Buchanan, who flinched.

'There will be a time for recriminations, Alice.' Bunny placed both hands flat on the desk, looming over Buchanan. 'If, as you claim, you wanted these men exposed, why give the police false information?'

'I-I don't understand.' Buchanan's eyes clouded. 'What false information?'

'That note Lieutenant Brodie gave you listed the date and time of the ship's departure. Yet according to the police, the *SS Lancett* is still berthed at Tilbury.'

'Perhaps they switched ships?' Flora suggested. 'Maybe they plan to take the children on another vessel?'

'They don't *have* another vessel,' Buchanan said. 'Brodie gave me that note so I wouldn't take on another cargo to spoil his arrangements.' His face cleared as he looked from Flora to Bunny and back again. 'I must have mislaid it somewhere between the concert and home that night.'

'I still have it here somewhere.' Flora retrieved her bag from the floor and rummaged inside.

'You found it?' Buchanan's eyebrows lifted.

'Something like that,' Bunny replied.

'I thought you had given it to the police?' Lydia edged her chair sideways, giving Flora more room.

'Bunny recited it to Inspector Maddox over the telephone, but I kept the original.' Flora continued searching her bag. 'Ah yes, here it is.'

She handed the paper to Bunny, who laid it on the desk and smoothed out the creases. 'The writing is spidery and difficult to read. What are these letters "TS" scrawled at the bottom corner?'

'I've no idea. As I said, I didn't write the note,' Buchanan insisted. 'I only had the thing a short time before I lost it.'

'There's nothing here other than what we told Maddox.' Bunny frowned. 'Only the name of the ship and the time of sailing. The 4th October.'

Buchanan straightened, frowning. 'No, that's not right. The *SS Lancett* was scheduled to sail for Halifax, Nova Scotia on 7th October.'

'It's a simple mistake.' Bunny ran his thumb beneath the writing. 'The horizontal line on the number four doesn't meet up with the top line.

This isn't a four, it's the continental way of writing a seven.'

Flora gasped. 'The seventh! But that's today!' She snatched up the paper and peered at it. 'You have to tell Inspector Maddox. He must go back to that ship and find those children. That might be where they are holding Sally too. If it leaves tonight, we'll never see her or them again!' Panic raised her voice an octave.

'Calm down, Flora.' Bunny's firm, but comforting hand on her shoulder kept her in her chair. 'We have to be logical about this. I doubt Inspector Maddox will instigate another raid merely on our say-so. Not after the trouble he got into last time. My guess is, they are keeping those children elsewhere until the last minute in case the ship is being watched.'

'But where?' Flora raised both hands, palms upwards.

'There must be any number of deserted buildings where they could be without anyone knowing.' Alice drummed her fingers on the desk in a steady, though irritating tattoo.

'They will need to get the children to the ship sometime before it leaves, so how would they do that?' Flora asked.

'My guess would be by water.' Bunny straightened, his gaze fixed on the window as he thought it over. 'Barges go up and down the river all the time.'

'And who do we know who owns one?' Flora directed the question to Lydia.

'Swifty Ellis does.' Lydia's face brightened. 'Abel knows where it's kept. Although he also said it was locked up and empty as recently as yesterday.'

'It's worth taking a look if I can persuade Maddox to come with us,' Bunny said. 'How long do we have before the *SS Lancett* leaves?'

Buchanan glanced up at the clock on the mantelpiece. 'Another five hours or so.'

'Which doesn't leave us much time,' Bunny said. 'Maybe if you told your story first hand to the police, it might help galvanize them into taking action.' That he should have done so before now was implicit.

'Is that wise?' Alice placed a hand on Buchanan's shoulder. 'The police aren't known for their capacity for forgiveness. You could be in a lot of trouble.'

'I'm aware of my culpability, Alice, my dear, and quite prepared to accept the consequences.' Buchanan gripped her hand for a few seconds before rising. 'Somehow, it's a relief to have it all out in the open. The most important thing is that we get those children back.'

'Is there something *I* can do?' Flora collected her bag from the floor in preparation to leave.

'You should remain here with Lydia and Alice,' Bunny said, halting her. 'If – when we find these children, they'll likely need medical attention, therefore we'll bring them back here.' Before he followed Mr Buchanan into the corridor, he swept the silver egg from the desk and slipped it into his pocket.

'Why did you do that?' Flora whispered, low enough for only him to hear. 'Surely, you don't intend showing it to Maddox?'

'Not if I don't have to.' He dropped a swift kiss onto her forehead. 'I'm not leaving it here for anyone to find either. We've got one of these things in rogue hands already.'

'Under normal circumstances, ladies,' Alice said when they had gone, 'I would suggest we have some luncheon, but I'm far too anxious to be hungry. Though I'm sure we could all manage some tea.' She moved to the bell pull beside the fireplace.

'I cannot eat either,' Flora said, a sentiment echoed by Lydia. 'What if neither Bunny nor Mr Buchanan can convince the Inspector to search the ship or the docks?'

'We'll have to hope they manage it somehow,' Lydia said.

Having issued instructions to the nurse who responded to the bell, Alice rubbed her upper arms with both hands. 'It's gone quite chilly in here.' She hefted the coal scuttle from the hearth and shook shiny black lumps onto the dying fire. 'I'm still angry with myself for being so wrong about Ruth Lazarus? I thought I knew her.'

'Perhaps she isn't directly involved?' Flora suggested. 'She could have been acting as a go-between.' Not that she believed that for a moment, but she longed to reduce Alice's distress.

'Which reminds me,' Lydia asked. 'Where *is* Sister Lazarus today?'

'I didn't think of that.' Flora's breathing quickened at the thought the nurse might walk in at any moment. 'Where is she?'

'It's her day off, and the reason I asked you to come.' Alice set the scuttle beside the grate, plucked a brass poker from the rack and gave the glowing embers a vigorous stir.

'Well that's something.' Flora relaxed, though at the same time wondered if she had accomplices in the hospital they were unaware of.

'That she should blackmail Raymond was cruel, when he's the kindest of men. However, that doesn't alter the fact I'm extremely disappointed in him.'

'He was trying to keep his son out of prison,' Lydia said, compassionate as always. 'When he realized what he had done it was too late.'

'It's never too late. He could have stopped it, though there's no point dwelling on that now.' Alice hurled the poker back into the rack, making it rattle.

A nurse arrived bearing a tray, giving Alice an opportunity to busy herself passing cups around and verify who wanted milk or lemon before finally resuming her seat.

Flora's composure finally cracked and she set her cup and saucer down hard enough to break the china. 'I hate sitting here just waiting.' She started at them both in turn, Lydia's face reflecting her own darkest thoughts, ones she could not bear to voice. Were the children still alive? Was Sally?

'With little choice at the moment, I suggest we keep busy.' Alice pushed back her chair and stood. 'I'll arrange for some temporary beds to be made up on a side ward.' She stepped into the corridor, calling over her shoulder as she went. 'Goodness knows where those poor mites have been all this time. At the very least they'll need a hot meal and a warm place to sleep tonight.'

'Flora.' Lydia halted her, waiting until Alice had put some distance between them before speaking. 'I hate to say this, but if this Brodie character thinks he and his gang are about to be discovered, they might decide to dispose of those children. Cut their losses as it were.'

'You mean they would—' Flora swallowed as the full meaning slammed into her. 'If those children die, this could all be my fault for meddling.'

'Don't say that. You did what you thought was right. *Is* right.' Lydia's words were comforting but her face reflected Flora's darkest thoughts.

Had she done the right thing? Flora wasn't so sure. Solving puzzles had always struck her as exciting, a challenge to her intellect and powers of observation. The thought that her meddling might result in such an outcome horrified her. Were the children still alive? Was Sally?

'Come on.' Flora linked her arm through Lydia's and hurried to where Alice had waylaid two workmen to whom she issued instructions.

The men touched their temples respectfully before hurrying away.

'I've asked them to fetch truckle beds from the stores and set them up in that room beside the recovery ward.' Alice said when they reached her, a finger pressed to her cheek, thinking. 'Next is linens.' She threw open the door of a cupboard, revealing rows of tightly packed shelves on three walls that smelled of bleach and sawdust. Having loaded their arms with sheets, blankets and pillows, she led them into a room not much larger than her own office, where the men had completed setting up temporary beds with thin ticking mattresses. 'It's not as salubrious as our main wards, but it will do very well.'

'It's been a while since I've made a bed,' Flora said, surprised at how easily she fell into a rhythm of tucking in bedding and plumping pillows. As she folded corners and tucked in blankets, memories returned of her morning ritual in the cosy attic rooms she shared with Riordan Maguire at Cleeve Abbey.

They had almost finished, when a knock at the door announced Forbes, who informed them that a gentleman was on the telephone asking for Mrs Harrington. 'He says he's your husband, Madam.'

Flora followed him back towards the main entrance, stopping every few yards to make way for a steady stream of patients with hacking coughs who arrived on foot, while others lay motionless on trolleys, their skin grey and chests barely moving. Doctors, porters, and kitchen staff flowed past on their way to the wards, kitchens and consulting rooms.

'Over there, Madam,' Forbes directed her to a three sided cubicle behind his desk where the telephone was located.

'What's happening, Bunny?' Flora demanded into the speaker without preamble, the earpiece pressed to her head. She placed her other hand over her other ear to shut out the ambient noises of the entrance hall where the doors opened and flapped shut repeatedly with a loud whooshing noise.

'The situation isn't quite as we had hoped,' Bunny's voice came down the line, clear but feint. 'Maddox is sympathetic, but he doubts he can instigate another search of the *SS Lancett* without more proof. A number on a note is not convincing enough to interest the Marine Police.'

'What about Mr Buchanan's version of events? Isn't that enough to take action?'

'Possibly, but the interview is taking too long and was becoming somewhat intense. The upshot being that Mr Buchanan feels threatened, so has asked me to be his legal representative.'

'But you aren't a criminal lawyer. Not yet.'

'Which I pointed out, several times. However, he was becoming distressed so how could I refuse? Now I've been engaged, I'm legally bound to protect him.'

'I understand you wish to help Mr Buchanan, but we're running out of time.' She turned around and glanced at the entrance hall clock. 'Even if Inspector Maddox convinces his superiors to help, you'll never reach Tilbury in time to stop the *SS Lancett.*'

'I know, which brings me to the real point of my call.' A high-pitched squeal came down the line. Flora snatched the earpiece away, wincing, returning it when it stopped.

'Sorry, Bunny, I didn't hear that. What did you say?'

'I said, if we could intercept Brodie and his cohorts before they reach the ship, we could still save those children.'

'And Sally? What about her?' If anything happened to her maid, Flora would always blame herself for having persuaded her to spy on Buchanan at the concert.

'We have to hope for the best where Sally is concerned. Now, I was thinking about this barge Abel Cain found? Where did he say it was moored?'

'St Saviour's Dock, or was it Jacob's Island. I'm not sure which, but I believe they are close together. Why don't you ask Abel yourself? Isn't he with you?'

'What do you mean? I left him at the hospital.'

'Oh, well, never mind.' She gave the entrance hall a brief glance but there was no sign of him although she couldn't worry about him at that moment. 'What are you going to do?'

'Maddox isn't being obstructive, he's as frustrated as I am. His superintendent doesn't like the

Salvation Army inference, so is blocking him.' The line crackled, making Bunny's voice sound as if he was a long way off, every fourth word muffled by background noise.

'Bunny?' She grimaced, her free hand pressed to her other ear to block out ambient sounds. 'What if we went to St Saviour's dock to see if the barge is being used?'

'That's isn't a good idea, Flora. It could be dangerous.'

'We shan't confront anyone, just observe until you and the police arrive—'

'No! Flora! I really don't—'

She returned the earpiece to the cradle, giving the instrument a pat with a whispered, 'Sorry, Bunny. This is too important.' She swung around, almost colliding with a young man, whose features solidified into that of Dr Reid.

'Oh, I'm sorry, Doctor. I didn't see you there.' He was dressed for the outdoors in a tweed coat with contrast stitching, though he no longer wore his ubiquitous leather apron.

'Mrs Harrington, isn't it? How nice to see you again.' His gaze roved her face slowly.

'And you,' she replied, mildly surprised that he had remembered her name. 'Did you manage to find a new home for your X-ray machine?'

'Unfortunately, no. But I shan't give up. Forgive me, but I couldn't help overhearing you on the telephone just now. You sounded distressed. Is there something I can do to help?'

'It's kind of you to ask, but I don't think so.' She tried to skirt round him, suddenly uneasy at the thought he might have overheard her conversation.

'Are you sure?' He moved into her path and grasped her upper arm. 'I'm quite resourceful.' He bent close enough so the fine stubble on his chin stood out clearly. 'I gather your husband is not here, so having a man on hand might be an advantage?'

'No, in fact that was him on the telephone.' She tried not to recoil from his touch but there was something insistent about it. 'Aren't you needed here? I mean what with all these new admissions.' She nodded to where the entrance was four deep with new arrivals.'

'I'm not officially staff. I'm a research scientist. So if there is any way I can—'

Just then Alice appeared through the double doors with Lydia, whose arms were full of what looked to be soiled linens.

'I really must go.' Flora looked pointedly at his hand that still encircled her arm. 'If you'll excuse me?'

'Oh, of course.' Releasing her, he took a step back, both hands held palms upwards in surrender.

'What did *he* want?' Lydia asked once Flora had reached them, her eyes narrowed at Dr Reid's retreating back.

'I'm not sure. Playing Sir Galahad, I think,' Flora replied. 'He offered to help, but I declined.'

'He wasn't bothering you, was he?' Alice hard

gaze followed him across the hall. 'I didn't like the way he grabbed your arm.'

'Perhaps you have an admirer, Flora,' Lydia said. 'He's quite a presentable young man.'

'Don't tease, Lydia.' Flora rolled her eyes. 'And it was nothing. Anyway we don't have time to worry about him. We need to get to Swifty's barge.'

'We do?' Alice frowned. 'What about Mr Harrington and Inspector Maddox?'

'Not good, I'm afraid. It appears the inspector has the enthusiasm but not the blessing of his superior. Bunny will do his best to persuade the river police to help us. They'll meet us at the dock as soon as they can.'

'They agreed to that?' Lydia frowned, sceptical as she tossed the linens into a nearby laundry basket. 'Even Bunny?'

'I suggested we find out if the children are there and if so, wait for them to arrive.' Flora avoided the question.

'By the time they went from Canon Row to the dock in this fog, we could be there.' Alice's eyes darkened as she mulled the idea over. 'It makes sense we should do some sort of reconnaissance if they are running out of time.' She stood aside, making way for a porter with a trolley on which lay a girl of about ten who coughed alarmingly into an equally soiled handkerchief pressed against her mouth.

Flora hesitated. Was she wrong to drag Alice away from where she was most needed? Perhaps

Bunny was right and they should leave everything to the police?

'I know what you're thinking, Flora.' Alice released the door and stepped closer. 'That I ought to be here, but my staff are very efficient and will cope without me. Right now, there are other children who need me.'

Flora made up her mind. Either they waited and worried, or did what they could to find the children themselves. 'All right. What do we do first?'

'We'll need some light to see by.' Alice clamped her hands together. 'It will be dark on the docks and the fog won't help.' She strode towards the front desk near the main entrance.

'Is this a good idea, Flora?' Lydia asked, as they waited for Alice whom they heard requesting some lanterns be fetched from the storeroom. 'It's not as if we're equipped to take on a gang of villains.'

'I'm hoping it won't come to that.'

Was she doing the right thing in encouraging Lydia and Alice to go rushing off into the fog with her? But what was the alternative? She had to do something, or this time tomorrow those children, and Sally could be mid-Atlantic. As always, she wavered between impulse and indecision as both took turns as her enemy.

CHAPTER 27

Once bundled up in coats, scarves and gloves retrieved from Alice's office, Flora and Lydia returned to the entrance hall that was busier than it had when they left moments before.

'A patient arrived in a hackney a few minutes ago.' Alice scooped three lanterns from the desk in one hand by their metal handles. 'A rare occurrence in this neighbourhood, so I've asked a porter to ask him to wait. We'll light these when we get there.' She shook a box of matches making the contents rattle, then slid it into her pocket.

Flora stepped into the chill, fog-laden air, experiencing a pang of regret as the heavy double doors closed behind them. Her boots splashed through streams of water that flowed into the gutters as they hurried towards a blurred dark shape of the hackney, confirmed by a whinny and the scrape of a shifting hoof, the twin lamps fixed to the front making a valiant attempt to penetrate the greyish fog.

'St Saviour's Dock please, driver.' Alice flung

open the carriage door and placed the lamps on the floor. 'It's urgent, so please hurry.'

'In this wevver?' He raised his cap and scratched his head beneath it, sending a trickle of water down onto his saturated cape. 'I woz on me way 'ome.'

'It's a mission of mercy,' Alice pleaded. 'We'll pay you double.'

'Why didn't you say so in't first place?' He retrieved the reins and mounted the step onto his perch. 'Where do you want, Missus? Shad Thames side or Mill Street?'

'Shad Thames will be fine, we can walk from there. It's most obliging of you,' Alice called up to him as they climbed inside.

'I don't blame him for wanting to be indoors on a day like this.' Flora settled into an interior that gave of the pungent smell of old leather and stale tobacco smoke. She had barely sat down before the driver urged the horse through the wrought-iron gates and into the road.

Although barely mid-afternoon, lamplighters were already out on the streets with ladders and tapers, a recent drop in temperature, combined with heavy rain precipitating more fires being lit belching gritty, dark smoke into the already misty atmosphere.

A high-pitched whistle cut through the air as the black snake of a train leaving London Bridge Station careered along beside them before veering off into the dark, belching black smoke into the already congested air.

Keeping the shadowy outline of Southwark Cathedral on their left, the hackney took a sharp right turn into the steep incline of Duke Street beside the approach to the railway station.

Flora fidgeted with impatience as they rumbled into queues of traffic on Tooley Street, their slow progress giving her time to study the shop fronts as they passed; the majority of which were river-related. Chandlers, candle makers, ships biscuit-bakers, block-makers, and rope sellers jostled beside second-hand clothes stores, grocers and bakers. Shopkeepers had set out lamps and candles by their doorways to help light the way of the pedestrians who scurried past, their heads down, some gesturing in apology when collisions occurred, while others shouldered past without a backward look.

'Of course!' Lydia gasped, straightening. She leaned across Flora and let down the window, allowing a gust of rain-laden air rush into the interior of the carriage. 'Driver, pull over.'

'What are you doing?' Flora braced her arm on the doorframe, her thighs gripping the edge of the seat to prevent her falling, the lanterns on the floor clattering together with a chink of glass.

Alice groped for the hand strap above her head as the horse halted at the side of the road, eliciting annoyed shouts and the blare of horns from other drivers.

'The note.' Lydia grasped Flora's arm, her eyes wide and staring. 'The one Abel took from Mr Buchanan.'

The driver's disgruntled face appeared at the window. 'Wot's wrong?'

'Would you give us a moment?' Lydia asked him, with a gracious smile.

'Your money.' His head disappeared again, though Flora distinctly heard him mutter the word, 'women.'

'I don't have the note.' Flora said. 'Bunny took it with him to show to Inspector Maddox. Why?'

'Apart from the date and time of departure of the *SS Lancett*, didn't Bunny say there was something else written on it?'

'The letters "TS" if I recall correctly.' Flora shrugged. 'But I don't know what that means.'

'I should have realized before.' Lydia groaned. 'I know where the children have been kept this last week.'

'Of course.' Alice slapped her thighs through her skirt. 'The Tower Subway. Why didn't I think of that? I used it regularly at one time.'

'What's The Tower Subway?' Flora split a look between them.

'It's an old tunnel that runs beneath the river this side of Tower Bridge,' Lydia said. 'A train used to run along it, pulled along a track on a cable. It became too expensive to run so was closed down and turned into a walkway, but when the new bridge was opened ten years ago, it was closed down for good. No one wanted to pay a ha'penny to walk a mile beneath the river if they could cross an open-air bridge for free.'

'You think they might have kept the children there?' Flora asked.

'Why not?' Lydia shrugged. 'It's half a mile underground and practically disused, although I believe the London Power Company run cables along it now. There are still several hours before the ship leaves, so we could take a look there first.'

'It's worth a try,' Flora said, willing to try anything at this stage. 'It will also give the police more time to get to the docks.'

Lydia poked her head out of the window and called up to the driver. 'Change of plan. Could you drop us at the end of Vine Lane? It's just before we reach Potter's Fields.'

'Right you are, Miss.' The cab nudged into the steady stream of traffic, the driver ignoring a repeat of noisy protests of carts, vans and taxi cabs that filled the road on either side.

'There's another reason I believe they might have used the subway.' Lydia pulled up the window with a bang. 'It's about a hundred yards away from The Antigallican.'

'Surely that cannot be a coincidence.' Flora's pulse raced that they had a real connection between the pub Swifty used and Lizzie Prentice. Perhaps this wouldn't prove to be a false trail after all? She clenched her fists on her knees and willed the driver to hurry.

A few hundred yards further along, the cab pulled into the kerb again, and they scrambled onto the road. Lydia and Flora emptied purses and pockets for change to cover their cab driver's inflated fee. The driver tipped his hat, giving them a gap toothed grin in response to Flora's overly generous tip as he left.

'The entrance to the tunnel is down there.' Alice nodded to where a narrow alley stretched to the river bank, the flicker of gaslights reflected in wet cobbles that tailed away into the fog.

She lined up the lanterns on a low wall, applied the lit end of a match to the wicks and handed one to each of them, the three of them set off into the fog, the orange glow of their lanterns swaying from side to side.

Damp cold seeped through the thick wool of Flora's coat, while drops of water fell onto her head and shoulders from broken gutters of nearby buildings as she trudged along after them, the collar pulled up around her neck as she tried not to think about the welcoming fire they had left back in Alice's office at the hospital.

Flora wrinkled her nose at the sour odour of silt, combined with coal smoke as they got closer to the river, her scarf growing damper against her mouth as she breathed into it.

The hairs on Flora's neck prickled and she cast a fearful look behind her, unable to shake off the feeling they were being watched; the massive concrete supports of Tower Bridge loomed up on their right, the top half invisible through a curtain of mist. The blurred outline of the ancient Tower of London lay squat and forbidding on the far bank.

'Hardly impressive, but this is the entrance.' Alice paused beside a structure that resembled a kiosk with a pitched metal roof; not unlike the green-painted wooden boxes the hansom drivers gathered in for meals and work breaks. She swung her lamp in an arc that illuminated a low door bordered by metal rivets, giving it a tentative push which sent it swinging inwards. 'Someone has been here recently. These hinges have been oiled.' Alice's lamp illuminated a metal staircase roughly seven feet across that dropped beneath them with no bottom in sight.

'There used to be lifts here when the railway carried passengers.' Alice peered over the rail into the darkness below. 'They were taken out some time ago, so we'll have to walk down.'

'I suppose it was too much to expect the gas lights would still be working,' Lydia said taking the lead.

'Careful,' Alice warned. 'The steps are likely to be slippery.'

Flora's stomach lurched and she felt dizzy at the thought of venturing into a cold, dark tunnel on a damp winter afternoon when she could barely see a foot in front of her face. Suppose it was flooded from all the rain that had fallen in the last hours? The alternative was to wait there in the empty street, alone and with the possibility of the rain starting again.

Flora placed her feet gingerly on the first step, and grasped the handrail with her free hand where the cold seeped through her glove. The sound of dripping water and the smell of mould and silt tickled her nostrils and brought back her fears of flooding. She bit her bottom lip, kept her gaze on Lydia's lamp as it bobbed below her like a disembodied yellow ball as they descended in single file, the metallic ring of their feet on the treads resounding off the brick walls.

'These steps have been swept at some point,' Lydia's voice drifted upwards. 'Though as far as I know, it hasn't been used in a while.'

'The Thames is inches away on the other side of this wall, with just sand and heavy clay beneath us, though it's been here forty years and hasn't leaked once.' Lydia chattered in a low whisper almost as if she was enjoying herself. Or was it bravado?

Flora tried not to imagine the millions of gallons of dirty water in such close proximity, just as her foot slipped on the next step down. Her stomach lurched and she grabbed the handrail tighter to steady herself, pausing to release a long, relieved breath. What none of them needed was a twisted ankle. Or worse.

It wasn't long before Flora found her rhythm on the triangular steps, her confidence returned and she increased her pace, just as a shadow rushed past her foot, disappearing so fast she couldn't be sure what she had seen. She froze. Was it a rat? No, she mustn't think of rats.

'What's wrong?' Alice asked at Flora's back.

'I thought I saw—' she broke off, listening, but the only sound that reached her was an intermittent drip of water and her own steady breathing. 'It's nothing. I'm fine.'

'I think we're too late,' Lydia called up to them. 'There's no one here.'

'Really?' Flora's gut churned with disappointment as she hurried down the last few steps to where the shaft opened out into a room roughly twelve feet square with a barrelled ceiling. The walls on either side contained a high-backed wooden bench like a church pew. Several candles in clay holders were scattered around the floor. Most of them had burned down to an inch or so, the flames doing little to lift the gloom. Lydia was right, the room was empty but for a blanket discarded in the middle of a bench.

'This was once the waiting room before boarding the train.' Alice moved slowly between the benches where thin mattresses covered with striped ticking had been arranged on the seats. On the floor at one end stood a chamber pot, which by the acidic smell had been used recently and not emptied; a stack of plates scraped clean of food sat on the floor beside it. 'They were here.' Alice held her lamp to shoulder height. 'For some time by the look of it as these benches have obviously been used as beds.'

A cool wind blew across Flora's cheeks, and frowning, she lifted her lantern towards the far end of the room, and gasped. A vast circular hole took up the entire wall, opening into what resembled a metal tube that stretched away along the bottom of the river. Curved walls formed by circles of iron about two feet wide bolted together with rivets reached into a tunnel that undulated to the right, dipped down and up again, disappearing into the darkness.

'It's like walking into the bowels of the earth,' Alice said, coming to stand at her side. 'The floor moves beneath your feet so it's quite a relief when you reach the waiting room at the other end.'

Flora turned to face her. 'How long is the tunnel?'

'About a mile. The walls sweat and you could swear you can hear running water, but it's just the echo. When it was used as a walkway, there were lights all the way along, but the feeling of being totally alone beneath the river is still daunting.'

'I would hate it.' Flora shuddered. 'I don't like enclosed spaces.'

'Which means you have likely never been on the "tuppenny tube"?' Lydia asked from behind them.

Flora shook her head. The first and only time she suggested they use it, Beatrice Harrington had made clear her aversion to going underground with crowds of what she called, 'unwashed working people.'

Flora nudged something with her foot, bent and retrieved a small metal object from the floor that she held beneath the lamp.

A toy soldier.

'We must have just missed them.' She blinked away frustrated tears, turning the tiny figure over in her fingers, marvelling at the detail on the face. 'Do you think Sally was here too?'

Memories returned of the night Flora was locked in John Lange's cellar, cold and alone. Had it not been for Sally's quick thinking in calling the police before she too was caught, who knew what their fate would have been.

'Oh, Flora, I'm so sorry.' Alice gave her a one-armed hug. 'Wherever she is, we have to believe she's alive and well.'

'I know, and I realize the children are the most important thing.' Flora fought back welling tears, her voice scratchy. 'But I so hoped we would find Sally here.'

'How long ago do you think we missed them by?' Lydia asked

'Possibly the last hour or so as that leftover food is still relatively fresh.' Alice sniffed the air, her head tilted to one side. 'I can also smell laudanum.'

'Let's hope they haven't been given too much,' Lydia said. 'It's too easy to administer too high a dose.' Flora turned to stare at her and she shrugged. 'My mother needed it for pain towards the end. She hated it at first, said it was bitter. However, after a few weeks of regular dosing she began to like the taste. A bit like spicy apples, she said. I had to ration her carefully.'

'Ruth Lazarus would know how much to use.'

Bitterness sharpened Alice's voice. 'She wouldn't want to damage the children after all the trouble she went to taking them.'

Flora remained silent, aware that Sister Lazarus represented a failure for Alice which rankled.

'The dock is only a short walk from here.' Lydia lifted the lamp up to shoulder height and adjusted the flame before making for the steps. 'We'd better get going.'

Flora hurried after her, glad to be leaving the chill, dark space beneath the fast-flowing river, hoping Bunny and Inspector Maddox had decided to go to the dockside with his men when she had intimated that was where she would be.

'If the men who took the children are at the dock, how do we get past them?' she asked as they emerged from the tiny kiosk by the river where a layer of grey-brown mist formed a hazy curtain that hovered mid-river.

'Perhaps we don't.' Alice turned up the wick on her lamp. 'We have no real idea of how many of them there are, so we should keep our distance until the police arrive.'

'If they've got Sally, I'm not waiting for anyone.' Flora set off towards the concrete archway that formed part of the Tower Bridge supports, her lamp swinging.

'Flora, please don't do anything stupid.' Lydia hurried to catch up with her. 'If those men are there you might get into trouble, which won't help Sally.'

'She's right, Flora.' Alice loped along beside her.

'I suppose so, but I'm so angry. How can these people think what they are doing could be acceptable. And I'm worried about Sally.'

After her burst of angry enthusiasm, their pace slowed as they fell into an uneasy silence along a path that took them past the end of Potters Fields; the slap of waves against the quayside walls from the river beside them.

'The pathway runs out here,' Alice said, veering through an alley into a cobbled street. 'This is Shad Thames which comes out again further downriver opposite St Saviour's Dock. Watch out overhead and mind your feet for muck and spillages.'

'I don't like the sound of that,' Flora murmured as they entered a long alley filled with shouts, bangs and clattering of machinery.

Wharves, storehouses and granaries loomed above them into the gloomy sky on both sides. The alley filled with horse-drawn carts loaded with unknown goods being moved into and out of wide open doors by men in overalls and cloth caps, barely distinguishable from one another. Pallets of dry goods sat piled up beneath the openings ready to be hauled up the side of the buildings on pulleys to the floors above.

The Hay's and Butler's Wharfs loomed above them on either side of the narrow road, between which ran a lattice of spidery walkways high above their heads that rattled and banged as sacks and wooden cases rumbled from one opening to another at different levels. Mingled with the clatter of machinery, rumble of wheels and bang of doors was the occasional whistle of a train leaving London Bridge Station on the other side of the buildings.

Flora picked her way around piles of hay, horse manure and discarded pallets, narrowly avoiding being mown down by loaded trolleys, while porters called harsh warnings to them to mind their backs. Twice, she was forced against a wall to avoid a load of hessian-wrapped sacks as they swung from gantries above her head. Her nose stung from a mixture of sulphur and silt mixed with the tang of manure, overlaid with the spicy, sweet smell of cinnamon and pepper.

'Is it always this busy?' Flora buried her nose in a handkerchief to muffle the earthy smells of manure, animal sweat and ancient grease as they passed wide doors designed to accommodate heavy vehicles. An array of metal ladders fixed to the brickwork overhead disappeared through arched openings in the walls, from which gantries hung precariously over the alley.

'The dock workers start early and once the barges are loaded, their work is done, so most of these men are packing up ready to go home,' Lydia replied. 'They'll all be back again at the crack of dawn tomorrow.'

Flora ducked just in time to avoid a pallet on a tent of ropes that swung close to her head, caught by the figure in a doorway and hauled inside. 'It's quite dangerous.'

'Accidents are common, I'm afraid.' Alice led them through a narrower alley that opened out onto the quayside, revealing the wide expanse of water in front of them. To their right, a smaller stream joined the Thames, bridged by a wooden walkway to a building with the words *New Concordia Wharf* painted vertically from the roof to the ground.

'We'll approach from the beach so as to avoid being seen by anyone on the dock.' Alice paused at an arched opening which Flora would have missed had she not been warned it was there. 'These are the Horselydown Stairs.' Alice's lantern revealed a long flight of shallow concrete steps that dropped to the river. 'Watch your feet. The bottom six feet is covered with slippery green algae. The tide is on its way in and will rise at least six feet from the bottom in a couple of hours.'

Flora's lower belly tightened, one hand on the metal handrail, and her lantern held out in front of her over a long flight of shallow steps made smooth and indented in the middle from generations of feet.

At the bottom, Alice turned to the right and led them along a shingle foreshore that opened out into a wide beach of greyish-brown mud and sand.

A wooden jetty ran from the quayside into a pier where an inlet flowed into the main river Thames;

a footbridge linked the Shad Thames wharves to Mill Street side, where more rows of wharf buildings and warehouses lined the inlet.

When Flora had first heard about Swifty's barge, she had consulted a map, from which she recalled that the inlet was once part of the notorious Rookery which Charles Dickens wrote about so vividly.

The quay lay deserted, with no sign of any policemen. Even the clamour from the wharf buildings sounded a long way away, possibly because they were at least ten feet below Shad Thames. 'What exactly are we looking for?' Alice nodded to where rows of flat-bottomed barges tied to mooring posts on the pier rocked gently against their ropes like horses eager to start a race.

'Most of those are open, so I'll wager it's that one. The one with the long cabin on the deck.' Lydia pointed to a black-hulled boat at the end of the pier that bore the name *The Bermondsey Boxer* in red letters.'

'Which pretty much settles it,' Alice said nodding. 'I'm willing to bet they won't arrive until it's time to leave for Tilbury. They won't be hanging about here or risk being seen.'

'I hope you're right, though what do we do if the gang are on board with the children?' Lydia said. 'We don't even know how many of them there are. Swifty, Brodie and Ruth Lazarus are a safe bet, but there could be others.'

Flora groaned inwardly as Alice and Lydia went

back and forth, debating. Were the gang there on the barge, and if not, did they have time to get the children off before being discovered? Were the children there at all? There was also the chance she had miscalculated and Bunny had not been able to persuade the Inspector to come to the docks? She shook her thoughts free. No, Bunny knew she was coming here. He wouldn't leave her.

'We cannot afford to wait.' She made up her mind. 'If the children are alone, we either take the *Bermondsey Boxer* back upriver ourselves, or we get them off and hide them until the police get here.'

'We cannot operate a barge!' Lydia gasped. 'Thames watermen have *years* of training before they know how the currents work. I've no idea how to start up an engine, let alone navigate this river.'

'What do you suggest?' A combination of fear and panic made Flora's voice rise. 'I'm not going to stay here and watch them take those children, or Sally downriver.' She wrestled the lantern handle from Lydia's hand, adjusting the valve so the flame guttered out.

'What are you doing?' Lydia snapped.

'We need to leave these here, or we'll be seen by anyone who walks onto the pier.' Flora did the same with her own lamp, reached for Alice's and tucked all three into the base of the quay wall. 'We'll come back and fetch them later.'

'You think working in the dark will make this easier?' Lydia asked, bemused.

'There's still some daylight left, so we'll use the fog to our advantage.'

'Even if the children *are* there, where are we going to take them?' Alice waved an expansive arm toward the river. 'We're out in the open with no vehicle of any sort.'

'We could use that rowing boat.' Flora nodded to where a dinghy tied to a mooring post had slewed to one side on the shingle.

'Which won't be big enough for seven children and three adults. Four, if Sally is on board. Not only that, we couldn't move fast enough on the river. They would catch us in minutes.'

'*If* they see us.' Flora chewed her lip, silently acknowledging she was right. 'We could hide them in the Horselydown Stairs, or take them up to the quay. We might be able to get as far as Tower Bridge before the gang notice they are gone.'

'We'll have to get them off the barge first,' Alice sniffed. 'And we don't even know if Swifty and his men are already here.'

'I know, but the longer we stay here second guessing ourselves, the more chance they will get away.' Flora said. 'I'm banking on the fact we are dealing with thugs, not master criminals and they won't think that quickly.'

'Then there's the tide,' Lydia said. 'See that metal ladder up to the pier. If we time it right, we can use that instead of walking all the way round the quay, which would leave us more exposed.'

'Good idea,' Alice said. 'We'll have to hurry as the tide is moving fast.'

Flora saw she was right. The waterline had crept forward several feet since they had arrived, the rowing boat that had been beached a few minutes ago was a foot underwater at the bow end.

'Then what are we waiting for?' Lydia hitched her skirt and set off across the beach, her boots crunching on shingle.

Flora followed, the heels of her boots sinking into loose shingle that soon turned to wet, sucking sand littered with scraps of drying seaweed and stones. The sour silt smell grew stronger and the soot-filled mist made her cough. She held her scarf over her mouth with one hand, and with the other hitched the hem of her coat out of rivulets of water that crept across the beach.

Hampered by her long skirts and petticoats, Flora's feet slipped on the narrow rungs as she climbed, though she tried not to look down at the water that lapped the pier supports beneath her. She emerged onto the pier and turned to help up a sprightly Lydia, followed by a more tentative Alice, who declared in a whisper as she released a relieved breath. 'I like water, but prefer it to be somewhat more remote.'

While Flora hauled on the rope that anchored the barge to the pier to prevent the boat moving, Alice hitched her skirt in one hand, and dropped onto the narrow deck of the *Bermondsey Boxer*, landing with a soft thump, followed a second later by Lydia.

Before she followed, Flora checked the quay-side and the river, but the shore lay silent and deserted, with only an occasional wail of foghorns in the distance. No lamps split the falling light, nor did any running feet cross the quay to stop them.

Flora took a deep breath, gathering her courage for what they might find and dropped to the deck where Alice was crouched, her head on one side and one ear pressed to the wooden cover.

'I can't hear anything.' Alice looked at Lydia, who shook her head in confirmation. Alice twisted the metal catch that held the hatch shut. Slowly, she slid the cover open.

Flora clenched her teeth in anticipation of a screech of wood that might alert someone below, but the hatch moved without a sound on well-oiled runners, revealing a short flight of wooden steps that led to the dimly-lit main cabin.

'Wait here a moment, and if you hear me shout, make a run for it.' Alice turned sideways, stepped down onto the top step and ducked through the hatchway.

Flora braced for a furious shout or even a scuffle, but silence reached them from below, apart from Lydia's nervous breathing beside her, the slap of water against the hull and a series of gentle clunks as the barges alongside them bumped hulls and bounced away again.

'Anything there, Alice?' she whispered, impatient.

Alice reappeared at the bottom of the steps, her wide smile in evidence. 'The children are here. Isobel is too, but there's no sign of Annie, I'm afraid. They're sleepy, but seem well enough.'

'Thank goodness.' Flora scrambled forward, her hands braced on the edge of the hatch as she lowered herself onto the short flight of wooden steps. She pushed aside her disappointment that Annie Sims wasn't among them, aware there was nothing she could do about that.

Below her, the cabin opened out into a comfortable sitting area. Instead of the cold, dark and damp space she had expected, a row of burning oil lamps hung from hooks set between each of four shuttered windows on either side which made the space cosy. The walls were painted a deep sunflower colour and the floor had been laid with grey linoleum, which quickly became slippery beneath her wet boots. A low door sat at the far end, beside it a pot-bellied stove with a metal chimney that took a crooked path through the barge roof.

Upholstered benches lined one side of the cabin on which the children sat or lay, head to toe in a silent row. Wide eyes in youthful faces stared at them, initial confusion turned swiftly to growing interest as they stretched and eased upright, their knees drawn up to their chins.

'No sign of Sally, I'm afraid,' Alice whispered.

Flora nodded, but couldn't trust herself to speak.

'Don't fret, Flora, we'll keep looking.' Lydia crept closer. 'You mustn't lose hope. She's still alive somewhere. I know she is. Sally's a strong person.'

'We'd better get started.' Flora cleared her throat and straightened her shoulders. 'We don't have much time.'

Alice crouched beside a tow-headed boy who had emerged from a blanket at the far end of the bench, his eyes wide and alarmed. He looked about six but could have been older.

'Who're you?' he demanded, though his voice was tinged with fear.

'It's Albert isn't it? Albert Fletcher? Don't you remember me? I'm the matron from the hospital.'

'Matron,' he slurred the word. 'Yeah. Didn't recognize yer wivout that funny 'at.' He yawned and his head slumped back against the seat, his eyelids drooping.

Flora recognized him from the photograph in his uncle's sparse sitting room with its surly occupant. Would he be happy to be returned there, or had he been told he was going somewhere much better?

'Flora,' Alice's urgent whisper told her it wasn't the first time she had tried to get her attention. 'We'll have to wake them up, there are too many to carry. Lydia, you stand on the steps and Flora and I will pass them up. Can you manage two of them?'

Lydia nodded, climbed through the hatch and onto the deck.

A small girl started to whimper and a boy protested, but quieted again when Alice spoke gently to them.

'It's a game.' She tugged the boy to his feet. 'We're going up as quietly as we can. Can you do that?' she said, coaxing a girl with pre-Raphaelite hair into a sitting position.

'Are those blokes out there?' Albert directed a quick look towards the hatch and away again. 'They said we was going on a big ship.'

'The men who brought you here told you that?' Flora asked.

'Yeah. The one with the squint and this big bloke who brought us food in the tunnel. And the nurse lady.'

Somehow Flora didn't think he meant Brodie, who had been described as a stocky man, so this was probably another person she had to worry about.

'Was Sister Lazarus here with you? Or earlier, in the tunnel?' Flora asked, unsurprised when Albert returned her gaze, his eyes empty. 'Never mind. All you need to know is that we're getting you out of here.'

A girl of about seven sat with her back pressed into the bench seat, staring at them with wide, frightened eyes beneath a mass of dark ringlets.

'What's your name?' Flora asked gently, so as not to alarm her.

'That's Isobel,' Albert replied for her. 'She don't talk much, but she cries a lot.'

'A lot of people have been worried about you.'

Flora reached out to brush the hair from the child's forehead, her throat prickling with emotion when Isobel flinched away from her touch. 'You don't need to be frightened.'

Her wool coat had lost a button and smelled of stale food and a more earthy smell on which Flora didn't like to speculate. A grubby blouse lay beneath a delicately embroidered pinafore which was clearly expensive. Her heeled boots looked new, but although the soles were barely worn, the uppers were badly scuffed from her sojourn underground.

Two boys began a minor squabble at the end of the seat, their trousers halted at half-mast, while a third's flapped over his feet. Two girls perched on the edge of the seat, their feet swinging, skirts and cardigans ending before they reached ankles and wrists; as if their clothes might have been made for someone else.

'Gather them near the steps and pass the first two up to me,' Lydia poked her head through the hatch. 'The coast is clear.'

'Is the monster coming?' asked a girl with vivid blue eyes who had gravitated towards Alice.

'What monster?' Alice asked, exchanging a look with Flora.

'The bloke said the monster would come out of the tunnel and get us,' a boy slightly taller than the others replied. His attractive green eyes were fringed with thick lashes and a smattering of freckles crossed his nose.

'There's no monster.' Alice finished fastening the bigger boy's ill-fitting jacket and gave him a shove towards the steps. 'And you aren't in the tunnel now.'

Flora silently condemned whoever had left them alone in a dark tunnel with tales of non-existent monsters; unless they meant themselves.

Alice ushered the children towards the hatch, where the boys nudged each other and muttered as they became more responsive. Isobel hung back, one hand gripping the folds in Flora's skirt.

'That's me foot.' Albert aimed a light punch at a larger boy who had shoved past him to be the first up the steps.

'Hey!' Another cradled his arm in the opposite hand and glared at a girl next to him. 'You pinched me.'

'Well get outta the way then,' the girl shoved him backwards, hard.

'Hush!' Flora's fierce whisper had little effect and her frustration grew that they had no sense of urgency, though she baulked at reminding them the men were coming back. 'I would have thought they would be terrified by being down in that tunnel.'

'Maybe being in a group helped.' A wry smile curved Alice's lips. 'Children are pretty resilient.'

Flora manoeuvred a small boy through the hatch. 'Is the coast still clear?'

'So far.' Lydia hauled the child through and onto the deck. 'But hurry, they could be back any moment.'

'Don't wait for us, take them to the Horselydown Stairs.' Alice handed a girl into Lydia's waiting arms. 'We'll follow as soon we can.'

Lydia's footsteps sounded across the roof of the cabin, followed by a crushing silence.

'I'll go next.' Alice climbed out onto the deck, followed by the taller of the boys, then lifted the girl Flora handed up to her. 'Follow me as soon as you can.'

Flora nodded, pulled aside the shutter on the window closest to the steps and peered out. Lydia had become no more than a vague shadow moving rapidly past the footbridge beyond which stood the curved wall of the quay leading to the Horselydown Stairs.

Alice waited at the top of the ladder for the boy to descend onto the strip of beach. She gave the pier a swift, sweeping glance, then hitched the girl onto her hip and followed.

Flora resumed her vantage point at the window and watched Alice hurry across the sand, the boy leaping puddles at her side. Twenty yards ahead of her, Lydia turned the curve of the quay wall out of sight. Alice and the boy were now no more than blurry shadows hurrying after them.

The little rowing boat was almost afloat as the river encroached further up the beach.

With no more time to lose, Flora gathered the two remaining boys together with Isobel at the bottom of the steps, just as a shadow loomed above the hatch, shutting out the remaining foggy daylight.

Flora's heart jumped in her chest and she gasped, grabbing Isobel, who released a short, high-pitched shriek. The two boys gave frightened yells and scrambled back into the cabin.

CHAPTER 28

'Lydia! You scared me.' Flora released her held breath in a rush as her friend appeared at the hatch above her. 'I thought you'd gone.'

'Sorry, I didn't mean to startle you.' Lydia bent closer. 'Alice has taken the children to the stairs, so I imagined you could do with some help with these three. Send them up one at a time, but hurry, there's a launch coming this way.'

'How do you know it's them?' Flora asked, alarmed.

'I don't, but I prefer not to take the chance. It's moving faster than a barge and will be here in a minute so. Hand the children up to me.' She waggled her fingers in a come-on gesture.

The smaller of the boys was clumsy and uncoordinated, taking each step with agonising slowness. At the top, he tripped on the edge of the hatch, the ensuing bang and distressed wail indicating he had fallen on the deck.

'Is he all right?' Flora asked and tried not to snap. These children had been captive in a dark tunnel for days, so were bound to be unnerved.

'He's fine, it was only a little bump. Quickly, send up the next one.'

'Come on Isobel, you're next.' Flora prised the child's clinging hand from her skirt and eased her forward. 'It's all right, I'll be coming straight after you. Albert's coming too.'

'Hurry, Flora. That boat is definitely coming this way.' Lydia's fierce whisper sounded from the hatch.

'Could it be the police?' Hope flared as Isobel's scuffed boots disappeared through the hatch.

'I don't think so. I can't see any helmets.'

'What are you doing?' Flora frowned. The boy had hung back at the bow end, darting furtive gazes at the door beside the pot-bellied stove. 'Albert! It's time to go.'

Albert didn't move. 'What about Sal?'

'What did you say?' Flora swung around on the steps and almost missed her footing.

'Sally. Ain't she coming wiv us?'

'Where is she?' Her stomach knotted, conscious of Lydia waiting on deck and was exposed to whoever was aboard that launch.

'In there.' Albert nodded at the door, which Flora had assumed was a storage space.

'Come on, Flora.' Lydia beckoned frantically from the hatch where she had just received Isobel. 'What are you waiting for?'

'I'm sending Albert up.' Flora grabbed the boy and gave him a shove that propelled him toward the steps. 'Go with Lydia, I'll follow as soon as I can.'

'What do you mean follow? Aren't you coming too?' Lydia said.

'Sally's down here. I can't leave her.'

'What?' Lydia cried, panicked. 'Flora, there's no time. That boat is coming straight for us.'

'You have to. Once Albert is out, close the hatch and get the other off this barge.'

Giving Albert a final shove, she made her way to where the single lantern threw deep shadows into the corners. The pot-bellied stove clicked as it cooled, the metal warm to her touch as she passed it and grabbed the wooden handle. The door refused to budge, but after several sharp tugs it finally gave with a scrape of warped wood against the frame and swung outwards, revealing a space hardly large enough for the enclosed bunk it contained. A window covered by a square of canvas nailed to the frame sat high up, through which streaks of weak grey light leaked through the edges.

Sally lay with one arm flung over her head, her cloud of wavy brown hair fanned out on a stained pillow, a rough grey blanket carelessly thrown over her. She wore the same clothes she had left Eaton Place in on the night of the concert, although her prized wool coat was missing. The same, sweet, decaying apple smell Flora had detected in the tunnel clung to her.

'Sally, Sally can you hear me?' Flora whispered, shaking her gently.

She stirred, issued a groan and batted Flora's

hand away with an annoyed grunt before rolling onto her side.

'I'm so sorry,' Flora whispered, brushing her hair away from Sally's face as guilt swamped her at having sent her into danger. Not that Sally would have wasted time attributing blame or feeling sorry for herself. She would have had them singing songs to banish the dark and told them stories at night.

'She all right, Miss? They didn't 'urt her did they?'

Flora gasped and whipped around, her heart thumping. 'Albert! You shouldn't be here. I told you to go with Lydia. She isn't still up there waiting, is she?'

'Nah. I told her to go and I would follow, but I couldn't leave Sal. She looked after us in the tunnel.' He hunched on the floor beside the bunk and regarded Sally with scared eyes. 'Why won't she wake up?'

'Because she's been drugged, but not heavily. At least I don't think so.

The chug of an engine approached steadily, ground to a spluttering halt directly above, followed by a bump which made the barge shift beneath her with a creak. Heavy footsteps pounded across the deck making her heart thump uncomfortably, praying that Lydia had got the other children into the Horselydown Stairs unseen.

'They're back.' Albert slid his hand into hers, his neck craned as he scrutinized the ceiling.

There was no chance of getting Sally out now, not in her state and the tiny cabin could not accommodate all three of them. They would just have to brave it out and hope the police arrived soon.

'Albert, she grasped his shoulders and brought her face close to his, 'stay in here with Sally. Whatever you hear, don't come out. Do you understand?'

'But—'

'Do as I say.' Flora shut the door on him, just as the hatch slid open and a figure descended the steps.

A man of about thirty wearing a dun-coloured coat that swayed round his ankles as he walked towards her. The shabby garment looked old, having taken on the shape of the wearer, a once white shirt visible above an open frayed collar. Tiny white lines in his deeply tanned skin radiated from his brown eyes, above a receding chin covered with gingery brown bristles that did not quite constitute a beard. Beneath a shapeless cloth cap, tufts of dirty brown hair poked out above the ragged ears of a fighter.

Swifty Ellis.

'Who the 'ell are you?' He gave the cabin a swift, hard look. 'Where are the kids?'

Flora fought back the acrid taste in her mouth as a wave of nausea flushed through her body as Ruth Lazarus appeared behind him. She wore an old fashioned dark green dress that looked second-hand;

a necklace of black jet encircled her thin throat, her hair pulled back in the severe bun which stretched her eyes into a cat-like slant.

'What's *she* doing here?' She slid her arm through Swifty's in a slow, possessive gesture.

She looked different out of uniform, younger somehow, though her outfit did nothing to detract from her lanky awkwardness, nor the permanent sneer that twisted her mouth.

''Ow should I know? But it won't do her no good.'

Flora's fingers curled into fists at her sides, her rapid breaths pushing her corset to its limit until she thought she might faint. Vaguely, she speculated on the nature of their relationship. Lovers perhaps, or merely partners in crime? She didn't have time to wonder for long as they split apart, making way for a third person to enter the cabin.

'*Madame 'Arreengton*,' Claude Martell's shiny black eyes regarded her with the same gleam he used to tempt her to try his famous madeleines. 'I 'ave to say I did not anticipate your presence 'ere.'

She had always regarded him as an inoffensive, even harmless nonentity. His lack of height, a barrel chest and arrogant strut combined with sparse oily black hair he wore brushed straight back from a low brow and a thin moustache, which Flora always speculated he waxed into points. The shiny black eyes which regarded her held intelligent, if uncompromising coldness.

As always, his immaculate black suit and highly polished shoes were in evidence, as was his scarlet embroidered waistcoat, his effeminate hand gestures and oily smile were absent.

'And yet,' Flora's dry throat lifted her voice an octave. 'I've been expecting *you*, Mr Martell. Or do you prefer, Lieutenant Brodie?'

It had taken her a while to work it out, but who but a Frenchman would write a seven like a four?

'I can see that no matter how well one plans, one always misses *somezing.*' Martell regarded her with pained disgust, his hands spread in a Gallic gesture of resignation. 'Where are the *cheeldren*, Madame?'

'Do you expect me to tell you, when I know you planned to sell them?' Her voice came out high and scratchy, her fury overriding her good sense, but she couldn't betray those children now, no matter the consequences.

'You make it sound shameful, *ma chère.*' Martell's lips curved into a sneer. 'When I offer them a better life with people who appreciate them. What 'ave they 'ere but short lives and early deaths from lung rot and malnutrition in a Bermondsey slum?' His leering smile beneath his caricature moustache that had so amused her in the past now repelled her. 'Besides, I could not have persuaded their families to part with them so easily had they not been unwanted.'

'Isobel Lomax was wanted,' Flora insisted. '*Is* wanted.'

'Ah yes.' He clasped his unusually small hands beneath his chin, the index fingers pressed together at the tip. 'Such a pretty child. I could not resist. She will be the easiest to place.'

'Nothing you say will justify what you are doing.' Flora's fear turned to righteous anger as Isobel's frightened eyes loomed into her head.

'Don't bother looking for them.' Anger burned and she imagined smashing a fist into Martell's sneering, arrogant face, the image strangely satisfying. 'They'll be miles away by now. You'll never find them.'

'Liar!' Ruth jutted her chin, her face so close, the yeasty smell of ale on her breath making Flora wince. 'We've only been gone from here a half hour. Tell us where they are!'

'I apologize for my associate's uncouth manners.' Martell gestured Ruth aside, his tone gentle, almost reasonable. 'I so dislike unpleasantness, but Ruth takes rather too much *plaisir* in such things.' His gaze flicked to Swifty, who smirked as if they shared a private joke.

'Buchanan must have talked.' Swifty glowered. 'S'pose the coppers are waiting for us at Tilbury docks?'

'After the fiasco of the other day?' Martell snorted. 'They 'ad twenty policeman crawling all over that ship and found *nozing*.' Martell scratched the back of his neck in agitation. 'I cannot *reesk* staying in the city another night, and if we don't leave now, we'll *mees* the tide. I have another lucrative cargo on that *sheep*, one which doesn't need to be fed or kept quiet. *Non,* we shall have to cut our losses this time. Forget them.' He took a step closer to Flora, his black eyes glittering with malice. 'Your interference has cost me a great deal of money, Madame.'

Flora braced herself for some sort of retribution, her teeth gritted so hard, her jaw ached, but nothing came.

'Claude, you can't!' Ruth exchanged a panicked look with Swifty. 'We need those other kids. That money would have set me and Swifty up.'

'She's right, Mr Martell, we have to—' Swifty cut across her, though he had hardly got the words out before the Frenchman lashed out, delivering a vicious slap to the man's face that echoed in the small space.

'What do you suggest?' Martell inhaled sharply, inflating his barrel chest, his eyes glittering with anger, 'wait 'ere for the police to arrive?'

A tell-tale red mark appeared above the stubble on. Swifty's cheek. He clenched his fist, then relaxed as if he fought an impulse to retaliate.

'We don't know as she's told anyone. She might be here on her own,' Ruth said. 'But I'll wager Miss Finch had something to do with it, Claude.' Ruth folded her arms across her diminutive chest. 'You said their cosy little talks in your tea room looked suspicious.'

'We cannot know who she has told. And I can always rely on you to piece things together, Ruth *ma chère.*' He patted her cheek with one hand, though Ruth's grimace indicated his touch was less than gentle. 'I trust you 'ave taken care of the mouthy one who was unwise enough to follow me the other day?'

'Don't worry 'bout her.' Swifty touched the peak of his cap, more in a gesture of pride in a job well done than respect. 'I've got her stowed nice and safe.'

Flora stiffened. *He meant Sally.*

'What do you mean stowed?' Martell's eyes flashed fire. 'I told you to get rid of that *beetch* two days ago. If she's still breathing, *zere* will be consequences.'

'I've got plans for 'er.' Swifty tapped the side of his narrow nose and winked. 'She's crafty, that one. I can get a good price for her from a madam I know in Kentish Town.' He aimed a gap-toothed grin at Flora. 'And if I take this one far enough out of London, I could get even more for 'er. Seems only fair when we won't get our cut for the kids.'

Flora's knees threatened to give way as the implications of his threat settled into her head. How had she got herself and poor Albert into this situation? Why had they wasted time at the Tower Subway? Had they come here first they might have got Sally and the children far away by now.

'Don't be *stoopeed*!' Martell cuffed Swifty's ear, another attack to which he barely responded. 'This woman is not a nobody.' He stroked his thumb and forefinger down either side of his moustache. '*Non*, you must dispose of her. Do it in the tunnel, then take her where no one would ever find her.' Without sparing Flora another look, Martell mounted the steps and disappeared through the hatch.

Flora swallowed at the thought of that dank tunnel and what might happen to her made her heart flutter, though hope remained that Bunny would arrive with the police while there was still time.

'What do you intend to do with Sally? Flora demanded of Swifty, recalling Claude Martell had told him to dispose of her. 'If you hurt her, I'll—'

'You'll what?' Ruth closed the space between them, her cat-like eyes narrowed.

'Ruthie, love, don't waste your time.' Swifty handed her a black leather sap, the lascivious wink which accompanied it did not enhance his unprepossessing looks. 'You stay here. Show this meddling bitch what we do to people who interfere in our business.'

'Where are *you* going?' Ruth stared at the object in her hand, then back up at him, the plea in her eyes confirming Flora's assumption about their relationship.

'Sod Martell and his cargo. I'm going to see if I can find out where the nippers are hiding.

'You won't find them!' Flora shouted in a final burst of defiance.

He turned back, leapt down the steps and shoving Ruth aside, pulled back his right arm and swung a clenched fist straight at Flora's face.

She jerked her head back, but not quick enough to avoid his knuckles connecting with the side of her jaw. Sharp agony reverberated through her teeth and down her neck, which sent her staggering backwards into the bench behind her. She bounced off it and landed on her rear end on the linoleum floor, catching her elbow on the edge on the way down.

Tentatively, she eased her jaw, but halted as pain sliced through her, accompanied by the sound of the hatch slamming shut.

Swifty had gone.

'That was daft, goading him like that.' Ruth perched on the bench, her skirt swishing as she moved it aside, tapping the ball end of the sap against her other palm. 'Don't you know he's handy with his fists?'

'Someone did mention it.' Flora pushed herself into a sitting position, her jaw supported in one palm, her gaze fixed on the wicked-looking object in Ruth's hand.

'Is that what you used to kill Lizzie Prentice?' Before the words left her lips, she regretted them. Though it occurred to her that she could hardly make the situation any worse.

'Think you're clever, don't you?' Ruth snorted. 'I'm not admitting to that, even if she did ask for it.'

'No one *asks* to be murdered, Ruth.' Flora was beyond calling her Sister Lazarus. As far as Flora was concerned, Ruth was not deserving of such a title.

She wasn't convinced of the woman's denial either. The day Lizzie was killed, Ruth had been a long time fetching the tea and returned to Alice's office with her skirt and shoes wet from the rain. She had both a reason and the opportunity to do the deed. 'From the way Miss Finch spoke about you, this isn't like you at all,' Flora said. 'Consorting with child stealers, blackmail and impersonation. You might have been raised in a workhouse, but—'

'Don't pretend to know anything about me!' Ruth's eyes flashed, the sap clutched in one hand, and a finger of the other pointed at her chest. '*This* is who I am. It was having to bow and scrape to the likes of you and that witch, what with all her, *yes Matron, no Matron.* That was the sham.'

'And Lizzie?' Flora unwound her legs and adjusted her skirt from where it had bundled round her hips as she fell. 'What about her?'

'She should have kept out of it. I had no idea she worked at the *Corks*, which was *against* hospital rules.' Her lips curled into a sneer, twisting her unremarkable features into near ugliness.

'It was you she argued with that night at The Antigillican? You threatened her.'

'When she saw us dressed in our Sally Army uniforms and knew something wasn't right. I warned her then not to breathe a word or she'd regret it, but she couldn't wait to run back to Matron Finch with her story.'

But you got to her first. 'Did Lizzie know you were blackmailing Mr Buchanan?'

'Don't know, don't care,' Ruth snorted, triumphant. 'Worked though, didn't it? Buchanan would have done anything to stop me showing that dirty picture to his Board of Governors. Thought he was such a gentleman, and all the time—'

'He was, I mean he is. For you for to involve him in kidnapping children was despicable.' She doubted an appeal to Ruth's better nature would work, but couldn't help herself.

'How could I not, more like?' Ruth snorted. 'Beats spending my life cleaning up after a bunch of whiney, snotty kids.'

A thump of feet came from above, followed by Swifty's voice ordering they cast off. Seconds later by the sound of the engine that roared into life, growing louder before settling into a low thrum that reverberated through the floor.

They were leaving! Swifty must have given up, or worse, he had found the children.

Flora cocked an ear but no lighter footsteps or children's voices followed. The hatch remained shut.

'About time,' Ruth snarled, scrutinizing the cabin ceiling. 'We'll be in Tilbury before you know it.' Her look reflected relief as well as triumph. 'Not that it makes much difference to you.' She reached beneath her and slid back a door in the side of the bench, from which she brought a black box about eight inches long and half as wide, placing it on the seat beside her.

'Don't you move.' She levelled the sap below Flora's chin, and using her free hand, flipped open the lid to reveal a metal and glass syringe half filled with an opaque pale orange liquid.

'Wh-what are you doing?' Flora scooted further along the bench, her pulse racing. She reached the end and scrambled to her feet, but there was nowhere to go in the small space.

'Exactly what I was told.' Ruth's thin lips twisted into a parody of a smile. 'It's something to make you sleep. Permanently,' she rolled the word on her tongue.

'I thought Swifty had other plans?' What was she saying? Life in a brothel was better than death? Maybe not. Her stomach lurched as an image of Bunny reaching the quayside, only to watch helplessly as the barge disappeared downstream.

Would he ever be able to find her in the stews Swifty frequented? Would he want to? No, she daren't not think like that.

'Best to follow Claude's orders. He's the boss.' Ruth tucked the sap into a pocket of her gown, removed the glass syringe and held it up to her eye, slowly pushing the plunger which released a drop of liquid onto the point of the needle.

'You don't want to do this, Ruth.' Flora's voice shook. She was about to add it would get her the rope, but what difference would that make when she had already killed Lizzie?

'You'd be surprised at what I want to do.' Ruth raised an eyebrow as if the idea appealed.

Flora's whirling thoughts clarified into one overriding emotion; the will to survive. Her son needed her. Bunny needed her. Pleading with Ruth was not an option; she had already showed she had no heart, but then nor was allowing herself to be killed. The seconds stretched interminably, when suddenly, the barge lurched to one side as the vessel changed course and went into a sharp turn with a grinding of engines.

Flora tensed, then in an impulse born of sheer desperation, threw her full weight at Ruth, slamming her back against the bulkhead.

Ruth issued an angry cry and swung the needle in a sweeping arc which missed Flora's eye by a fraction. Flora caught her hand in both of hers on the backwards swing, but doubled over as Ruth jabbed her other hand into Flora's ribs. Pain, sudden and excruciating made her gasp. One hand went instinctively to her midriff but she had the presence of mind to hang on with the other, keeping the syringe aloft and away from her skin.

Flora twisted her hand on Ruth's wrist as hard as she could until the tendons stood out with the effort to release herself. With a frustrated grunt, Ruth raked her fingernails of her free hand down Flora's face. At the last instant, Flora saw what was coming and jerked her chin back so that the blow ended uselessly in mid-air.

Flora's triumph was short lived when Ruth stamped hard on Flora's instep. Flora bit her lip hard enough to draw blood, the coppery tang on her tongue reminding her she had to gain the upper hand – and quickly as Ruth didn't appear to be tiring. She had shifted her grip on the glass phial, holding it like a knife that she brought down towards Flora's neck.

Flora grabbed her hand in mid-air and pulled sideways as hard as she could, bringing them crashing onto the cabin floor in a tangle of arms and legs with Flora uppermost; the sap in Ruth's pocket swinging against Flora's thigh hard enough to cause a bruise.

Ruth was taller, but her delicate, sparse frame was no match for Flora's slender strength, helped by the fact there was no space for Ruth to gain any purchase for her to wriggle out from beneath her.

Ruth cursed and issued dire threats through gritted teeth, her feet drumming the floor while refusing to release her grip on the syringe.

Flora realized that if she did manage to wrestle the object from Ruth's fingers, and the contents were as deadly as she had implied, using it against her was not an option. Flora had no wish to become a murderess. Self-defence or not.

An idea occurred to her and she shifted her knee on the elbow of Ruth's free arm while she tried to locate the pocket where Ruth had put the sap.

Ruth squirmed, grunting, and after two useless attempts, Flora's fingers closed around the end of the compact weapon.

Gritting her teeth, she tugged, only for the ball end to snag in the heavy material. Her fingers on Ruth's hand were slick with sweat but she hung on, gave a final, panicked yank with her other hand which pulled the object free, tearing the taffeta.

Ruth bucked upwards, partly throwing Flora off her, just as she brought the weapon down hard above Ruth's left ear.

She collapsed without a sound. The syringe dropped from her limp fingers, rolled across the stained lino and came to rest against the bulwark.

During the brief, but frantic struggle, Flora became vaguely aware of a rhythmic thumping and stared fearfully up at the ceiling. Had the men above heard the commotion and on their way down to see what was happening? She scrambled over Ruth's limp form and pushed up onto her knees, just as the door to the inner cabin opened outwards and Albert burst through, both fists raised and his feet splayed like a pint-sized prize-fighter.

'Blimey!' He straightened, dropped both his arms as his gaze went from Flora to Ruth. 'Wot 'appened?'

'She wasn't being particularly congenial.' Flora slumped back on the floor, her breath coming in short, shallow breaths as she fought for calm. 'I distinctly recall instructing you to stay in there, whatever happened.'

'I thought you was being killed what with all the racket. Then the door stuck and I couldn't get out. What's that?' He reached for the glass tube that lay on the floor close to his foot.

'Don't touch it, Albert!' Flora swept the object from beneath his reaching fingers. Carefully avoiding the point of the needle, she returned it to the black box and twisted the clasp, closed her eyes with a sigh.

'Is she dead?' The boy's dark eyes probed hers before sliding to Ruth.

'I doubt it.' Flora inhaled a ragged breath, followed by another. 'Would you help me find something we could use to restrain her?'

'Rest-what?'

'Tie her up.' She gave the cabin a sweeping glance but the small space was frustratingly empty, even the tiny cupboard the box had been kept in.

'Well why didn't ya say so?' He slumped onto the linoleum and started to tug at a pair of stout, if badly worn and scuffed boots. 'I've got these!'

'Shoelaces.' Flora smiled. 'Good boy. Help me tie her hands.'

Albert removed the narrow strips of leather from his shoe flaps, while Flora turned Ruth over, grunting with the effort. In repose, Ruth's face had lost all its cruelty, although she would never be pretty, and by the look of her misshapen nose, she had broken it when she hit the floor, face first.

'Pity we don't have anything to gag her with.'

Flora tied the final knot, rejecting the idea of tearing up her perfectly good petticoat.

'If she wakes up and yells for that Swifty, you won't 'alf cop it!' Albert said, exhibiting an unnerving talent for stating the obvious.

'If she does, you show her this.' Flora pressed the sap into his hand. Small but surprisingly heavy, she decided it must have a central core of some sort of metal wrapped in thick black leather.

'Can I 'it her wiv it?' His eyes widened.

'Just show it to her. She'll get the message.' Leaving them, Flora climbed the steps to the hatch and tugged the handle, but it wouldn't budge.

'They've locked us in!' She punched the wooden cover with a fist as frustration built, aware they were mid-river by now so there was no way to get off the barge without swimming. Defeated, she returned to the bench, pulled back one of the shutters and peered out.

'Where do yer think we're going?' Albert asked. 'To that ship the Frenchie told us about?'

'I imagine so.' She tried to keep the dread from her voice. 'Don't worry, Albert. The police will be here soon.

''Cept we won't be *here*, will we. We'll be at bloody Tilbury!' He lifted both arms in frustration, revealing his braces beneath a jacket that was too tight across his shoulders.

'I cannot argue with that.' Flora sighed, twisted round on the bench and slumped against the bulkhead. 'We'll simply have to hope and pray. Is Sally awake?' she asked to distract him.

'She was moaning before, but she's still sleeping.'

'I'll take a look at her.' Flora rose, and patted his head on her way to the rear cabin, but a distant shout from the river sent her scrambling back to the window. Out on the water a dark shape moved through the fog some twenty feet off the stern of the barge. No figures were visible in the mist, but someone must have been on deck as yellow glows bobbed from several lanterns reflected on the water.

Flora's breath begun to catch in her throat as hope flared. *Could it be the police at last?*

'Heave to starboard!' the same voice shouted, this time from much closer. 'This is the Thames Marine Police,' the loudhailer spoke again. 'We're about to board your vessel. Heave to, or we open fire.'

Rapid, heavy footsteps came from above, followed by blows and shouts of both authority and protest. The engines spluttered and died abruptly, the hull vibrating as the barge fought against the tide. Light thumps which could have been ropes landing on deck were followed by shouted instructions. A tattoo of footsteps tramped across the deck above their heads.

Flora wrapped an arm round Albert, her breath held as the hatch slid open slowly and a pair of legs in charcoal grey trousers descended the steps.

Bunny paused halfway down, both arms braced

411

on the opening above his head. His eyes widened as he took in Ruth, then flicked to Albert before coming to rest on Flora.

'Flora? What are you doing here?' He gaped.

Releasing Albert, Flora leapt to her feet and threw herself at him with a relieved sob. Taking his face in her hands, she planted a slow, resounding kiss on his lips that were soft, pliant and familiar. His arms closed round her and a sob rose to her throat beneath his mouth.

Finally, she pulled back, her hands clamped on either side of his face. 'You came after me. And in a boat! How romantic.'

His jacket was damp and scratched the skin of her cheek, the scent of his sandalwood cologne overlaid by coal smoke. He had smuts on his face and hair, and his glasses were askew, but nothing mattered other than he was there.

'I would have anyway, had I known you were on board.' He rubbed her back and shoulders in strong, comforting circles. 'We were coming after Brodie and the other two, but the last thing I expected was you to be on this barge.' He held her away from him by her upper arms, and stared into her eyes. 'What on earth are you doing here? I called you at the hospital and told you that under no circumstances were you to come to the river, but you hung up on me.'

'Hung up?' She shrugged, sheepish. 'Really? The line went dead, so I didn't hear.'

'Hmmm.' His eyes roved her face for long

seconds, then he released a relieved groan and wrapped her in a suffocating embrace. 'You're not hurt are you?' he asked, his lips against her hair.

'I'll have quite a bruise on my chin tomorrow, and in various other places, but no, not really.' Though she couldn't stop shaking. Now she was safe, the full implication of what might have happened hit her with full force. Her tightly wound knot of curls had loosened, lying heavily on her neck, though the six-inch hat pin had done its job well, and though askew, her hat remained firmly in place.

Behind them, Albert muttered what sounded like a snort of disgust.

'And who's this?' Bunny cocked his chin at the boy, whose brow was creased in a critical frown.

'Bert Fletcher.' He sniffed and swiped a hand beneath his nose. 'Are you 'er 'usband?'

'I am indeed.' Bunny grinned and hugged Flora closer.

'Just as well.' He folded his arms across his chest, the sap still held firmly in on hand.

Flora stepped smartly away from Bunny as memory returned. 'Sally's in the next door cabin. She's been drugged at some point.' A thought struck her and she lifted her chin and searched his face. 'Please tell me you didn't come alone? That *is* the police up there?' She scrutinized the ceiling, from where came a series of thumps and shouts.

He nodded. 'Between Buchanan and myself, we managed to convince the river police to help with the rounding up, though they were reluctant to go near the *SS Lancett* again. There are only four men on the launch, but more will meet us at St Saviour's dock with Black Marias and possibly hackneys, if they can find any in this weather.'

'I had this awful feeling you might get there and find we had already gone.' Flora shuddered. 'I've no idea where Abel Cain went either. We didn't see him when we left the hospital.'

'He'll be at the dock by now,' Bunny said. 'He turned up at the police station determined to help. Had he known you three were going to wade in like you did, I feel sure he would have stayed.'

'We could have done with him actually, but never mind. He'll be glad to know Sally is all right.'

Shouts from above steadily increased in volume, followed by a bump, which Flora assumed must be the police launch tying up alongside. Footsteps pounded across the roof and Inspector Maddox stuck his head through the hatch. 'Are you there, Harrington?'

'All safe and unhurt, Inspector,' Bunny replied without taking his eyes from Flora's face.

Maddox descended into the cabin, one brow lifted at Ruth, who had come to and pushed herself into a sitting position, her legs splayed out in front of her beneath her skirt. She didn't speak, but simply regarded them with rebellious eyes. Her bun had loosened in the struggle and she was intermittently blowing stray strands off her face with angry puffs through her lips.

'Nice work, Mrs Harrington.' Maddox tipped the edge of his hat in salute. 'I'm delighted to know you're safe, despite the fact you ignored all my advice to leave this matter to the professionals.' The look he exchanged with Bunny told her they had discussed this before.

'Thank you, Inspector, but I wasn't alone,' Flora assured him. 'Miss Finch and Miss Grey were with me. They took the other children to the Horselydown Stairs to await your arrival. Have you located them?'

'Not yet. Which Stairs did you mean? Old or New?'

'There are more than one set?' Flora frowned. 'The ones on the other side of the curve in quayside. They're quite close.'

'New.' Maddox gave a curt nod. 'We'll send someone to find them. Now, did I hear you say Miss Pond was down here as well?'

'In there.' Flora pointed to the door that swung lopsided on its hinges after Albert's assault. 'She's still suffering the effects of the laudanum and is in no state to be questioned.'

He accepted this with a nod, shoved his hands in his pockets and called up through the open hatch. 'Constable! Get a couple of men down here and fetch Miss Lazarus out would you? And bring the shackles.'

'I didn't know you were already acquainted with Ruth Lazarus, Inspector,' Flora said.

At the sound of her name, Ruth's eyes darkened

as she squirmed furiously against the bindings on her wrists but did not utter a word.

'I interviewed her at the hospital over the Nurse Prentice case.' Maddox sniffed, regarding Ruth as if she were a specimen in a zoo. 'Callous sort of woman. Didn't think much of her at the time. Dead eyes.' His hand came down gently on Albert's shoulder. 'Now, my lad. We'd best get you back to the shore.'

Albert remained where he was seated on the end of the bench, eying Maddox with suspicion.

'I don't talk to coppers.'

'Indeed?' Maddox sighed, making Flora wonder how many times he had heard that before. 'How would you like to go on a police launch?'

'Can I sound the 'orn?' The hostility drained from his face and he looked just like any small boy requesting a treat.

'I suppose so.' Maddox cocked his chin towards the steps.

'Goodbye, Albert. Maybe we'll meet again one day?' Flora bent closer and whispered in his ear. 'Where's the sap?'

'In me pocket. And it's not a sap, it's a blackjack.' He winked, ducked his head and sidled past her. 'Take care of Sal.'

Flora's stomach lurched as she watched him go, recalling the shabby sitting room of his uncle's house he called home. She chose not to dwell on his possession of the blackjack.

Following, Maddox placed one foot on the short

flight of steps, then checked himself. 'Oh, Harrington. You'll never guess who the boss of this villainous gang is.' Without waiting for a response, he stomped up the wooden steps and disappeared through the hatch.

Bunny frowned. 'What did he mean by that?'

'Our Salvation Army imposter, Lieutenant Brodie, is in fact Claude Martell,' Flora said proudly. 'Whom I sincerely hope is also in shackles by now.'

'Martell?' Bunny's frown deepened. 'The effeminate little Frenchman who owns the tea room?'

'There was nothing lady-ish about him earlier when he realized I had ruined his plans.'

'Oh dear.' Bunny wrapped an arm round her shoulders and drew her closer. 'You'll have to get your cakes from somewhere else now, I imagine.'

'Not funny.' Flora nudged him with an elbow.

'Sir,' a policeman stuck his head through the hatch. 'We're back at the pier now if you and the lady wish to disembark.'

'Indeed we do, thank you officer.' Bunny finally released Flora, and together they made their way up to the deck.

The incoming tide had lifted the river almost level with the pier, cutting off the route to the Horsleydown steps and the beach they had walked on less than an hour ago that was now in full darkness, the quayside just a blurred grey outline.

The river lapped at the quayside, on which two police vans and a hackney were parked. Several shadowy figures moved between them, the small orange flames of lanterns that swung from their hands gave an eerie but reassuring atmosphere to the dark riverside.

The Bermondsey Boxer had been tied securely to the pier, a police launch moored alongside, from which Claude Martell and a burly man in a shabby black overcoat were being marched off onto the jetty. A shadow detached from the fog and bounded along the jetty towards them.

Abel Cain leapt onto the boat in one stride. 'The Inspector said Sally was here!' His eager expression dissolved. 'Sorry, Miss Flora. I didn't think. Are you all right?'

'I'm fine, Abel, thank you for asking.' She couldn't help smiling as he shifted from foot to foot. 'Go on. Sally's down below.'

Beaming, he sidled past them and clattered down the steps into the cabin.

'I should be angry with him for leaving you at the hospital,' Bunny said as he disappeared through the hatch. 'But he wasn't to know you would come rushing down here.'

'You cannot blame Abel. Besides, all he was thinking about was finding Sally. I want to stay and see her brought out. She's been heavily drugged and I need to know she'll be all right.'

'Are you sure? I would be happier staying here with you.'

'No need. She nodded to where the boy sat with his feet dangling over the edge of the barge, the flaps of his boots turned outwards. 'Take Albert to the quay. I don't suppose they have found Alice and Lydia yet? They took the other children to hide from the gang.'

'I'll see what I can find out and see you on the quay later.' He approached Albert, urging him to his feet. 'Come on, old chap.'

Flora retrieved a lit lantern that had been left on the deck, its small flame comforting as she waited for Abel to reappear. The temperature had dropped in the last half-hour, and shivering, she stamped her feet to get her circulation going.

'Have we got them all?' Inspector Maddox spoke to one of his men from the deck of the police barge that had moored alongside the *Bermondsey Boxer*.

'I'm afraid not, sir,' a disembodied voice answered. 'Swifty Ellis pushed an officer into the drink and made a run for it. He must still be on the dock somewhere. I've sent a couple of men to look for him.'

Flora's stomach lurched. They couldn't let him get away.

CHAPTER 29

Flora's gaze remained on Maddox's retreating back as he stomped along the pier towards the quayside, her thoughts squarely on Swifty. She was sure he had returned to the barge, but how had he managed to elude the police when they reached the pier? Distracted, she didn't register the figure which approached out of the gloom until her features solidified into a familiar, and welcome face.

'Alice!' She released a relieved breath. 'I'm so glad you're all right. And the children?'

'They're fine. We heard the whistles as the police launch arrived, so we felt it was safe to bring the children out of the stairs and onto the quayside. They've become quite excitable after their adventure. Which might have to do with the fact I promised them cocoa and biscuits when we get to the hospital.'

'I *had* to make sure you were unhurt.' Her eyes glittered as if she was near to tears, but it might have been a trick of the light as the pier was filled with policemen carrying lanterns.

'Lydia volunteered to go to the hospital, but

she said to tell you that she'll call on you tomorrow at Eaton Place after we have all had a good night's sleep.' She crossed her arms over her chest and rubbed her upper arms. 'It's getting quite cold now. Are you sure you're not injured? Young Albert said you had had an altercation with Ruth Lazarus.'

'Oh, that.' Flora doubted that was precisely the word Albert had used. 'It was something and nothing.' She decided not to mention being punched, or the needle, which Maddox had removed from the barge. 'It was when the engines started up and we took off down river when things became frightening. I'm so relieved Maddox managed to talk the Marine Police into helping.'

'From what I heard, it was more Bunny's threat to go to the newspapers with the story if they didn't act.' She took a step closer, her face thrown into sharp relief by the lantern in Flora's hand. 'Is it true what I heard one of the policemen say? That Swifty is still out there?'

'I'm afraid so.' Flora turned towards the river as it flowed steadily upstream, the surface black and almost oily beneath a pall of yellowish-grey fog. 'The place is crawling with officers now, so he won't get far,' she said with more confidence than she felt.

'Don't underestimate him, Flora. He could just as easily disappear into the London underworld, never to be seen again.'

Flora shuddered, though not from the cold.

The sound of footsteps drew their attention to where Abel emerged from the open hatch with Sally draped over one shoulder, her dark hair hanging down his broad back. Despite her diminutive size, the manoeuvre must have proved awkward in the narrow space beneath the low roof.

'Goodness, is that your maid?' Alice crept closer. 'Is she all right? She's very pale.'

'I thought she was going to wake up a minute ago, but she drifted off again,' Abel said, his voice gruff with worry.

'We must get her to St Phil's to be examined by a doctor.' Alice placed one foot on the deck, the other still on the jetty, and extended a hand to help guide him off.

Abel raised a foot about to leap the narrow gap between the two, when Alice glanced past Flora's shoulder. She froze. Her eyes widened and she screamed 'Fleur!'

The seconds stretched as Flora processed what Alice had said, but immediately dismissed it as having misheard. A violent shove to her shoulder knocked her sideways, her hip glancing off the corner of the cabin as she fell. A sharp pain seared through her side as she hit the deck with both knees, her breath expelled from her lungs in a rush at the same time she heard a loud splash and a female cry.

The lantern slipped from her hand and shattered on the deck with a tinkling crash, the sharp smell of paraffin irritated her nostrils, followed by a whoosh as the flame drank up the pool of spilled oil on the wood. Instinctively she scrambled away from the flame, which bloomed briefly, but quickly guttered out.

She lay where she had landed on deck, her hands flat against the boards as she tried to inhale, but her muscles wouldn't work beneath the confines of her corset, leaving her gasping for breath.

Finally, she gasped in a lungful of sulphur-laden air – also soot laden and smoky but it was air. She exhaled in relief and taking another shallow breath, then one more as she eased upright, wincing at the pain which stabbed through her left side.

Abel had fallen onto one knee, Sally still draped over his shoulder. He started to rise when the figure raised his boot and brought it down on the back of the bigger man's knee. Sally slipped from his hold and dropped like a rag doll onto the deck, her top half hanging over the side.

There was no sign of Alice, until a movement on the water brought Flora's gaze to where, arms flailing, Alice's head broke the surface a dozen yards away from the pier.

Flora's pulse raced as she tried to decide who needed her most; Alice, in her heavy uniform dress and coat being dragged beneath the Thames, or Sally, who slipped further towards the water with each dip and heave of the barge.

'Flora!' Bunny's heavy footsteps pounded along the jetty towards her.

'Never mind me,' she screamed, a shaking finger pointed to where Alice struggled in the dark water. 'Get Alice!'

Bunny did not hesitate. He kicked off his shoes and shrugged out of his overcoat, flinging it over a nearby mooring post that stuck up from the pier. He raised his arms and dived into the river, surfaced within seconds and struck out, arm over arm towards the figure in the water.

Flora crawled, painfully and slowly towards Sally, who lay face down, one leg bent beneath her and her arms draped over the side of the boat, one hand trailing in the oily water.

Abel staggered to his feet, one hand held against his head as he gazed round, confused.

'It's Swifty!' Flora cried. 'He's trying to start up the engines!' When he hesitated, she shouted, 'go on. I'll help Sally.'

With a final, worried glance at Sally, Abel nodded, and took off after him.

Flora stared round in search of Inspector Maddox, who couldn't be far away, when a shape materialized out of the gloom. Swifty must have caught him unawares as he lay, face down and motionless on the pier. She debated what to do, when he stirred, raised a hand to his temple and eased into a sitting position. Obviously groggy, he climbed to his feet, his gaze searching the pier until he settled on Flora. 'You all right, Mrs Harrington?'

'I'm fine. Swifty's trying to start the engines.

Abel's trying to stop him.' One look at his swaying form told her he was in no state to fight anyone. 'You'll need more men. They probably can't see what's happening in this fog.'

He nodded, turned and took off along the pier in a rolling, unsteady gait while calling for reinforcements.

By this time, Swifty had reached the engine housing and was fumbling with the catch in an effort to get the door open when Abel lurched forward and slammed a hand down on the box, almost trapping his fingers. With a yell, Swifty ducked smartly to one side, plucked a pole from a line of cleats attached to the bulkhead and swung it to one side at knee-height, his lips drawn back from his teeth in a malicious snarl.

Abel saw it coming and swivelled his upper body so the pole whooshed past him, gouging a five-inch slice into the deck before rolling away.

Cursing, Swifty lunged for the pole, scrambled upright and hefted it again, but the blow must have been weak and ill thought out, for Abel caught it in mid-flight, tugged it from the smaller man's grasp, and threw it overboard.

Swifty put his head down and with a furious roar, charged Abel's midsection, bringing him crashing onto the deck inches from where Sally lay.

The fast-running tide heaved the barge on their right upwards, the mooring ropes pulled taut, then loosened again, bringing the two hulls together with a screech of metal on metal. The barge tilted alarmingly, halting Flora in her painful crawl towards Sally, who slipped a few inches further over the side.

When the boat levelled out, Flora braced her foot against the lip of the deck and extended a hand as far as she could reach but Sally was still too far away. She gritted her teeth against the pain in her hip and crept closer, hooked her fingers into the waistband of Sally's skirt and hauled backwards with all her strength. Her efforts were useless, as without leverage, Sally was a dead weight and wouldn't budge, but she hung on. If the barge tilted again, Sally would go into the Thames and with darkness closing in they might never find her.

From the corner of her eye, Swifty aimed a blow at Abel which he sidestepped, hooked his arm round the smaller man's neck and leaned backwards, pulling them onto the deck again where Swifty resisted with a frantic thrashing of legs and arms.

She prayed Bunny had reached Alice and had managed to get her out of the cold and unforgiving water, trying not to think of an article she had read once, that people rescued from the Thames often died from infections at a later date.

The two grappling figures of Abel and Swifty had worked their way to the bow end of the barge, both little more than blurred shadows in the fog, indistinguishable apart from their contrasting size. The smaller man lunged again, throwing both arms round Abel's thighs, and dragged him to the deck where the fight continued, interspersed with grunts and shouts of pain as blows landed.

Swifty twisted free from Abel's grasp and bounced on his toes in a boxer's stance, aiming shadow punches into the air.

Abel squared up to him, and with impressive skill, aimed a right-hand jab at Swifty that caught him full in the face. His arms dropped to his sides and he stiffened, but made no sound, simply tumbled backwards over the edge as the barge swung to one side and crashed against the hull of the one that lay alongside.

A deathly silence fell over the riverside, broken only by the slap of the water against the hulls as the barges bumped together, lifted slightly before they bounced apart again.

'I'm coming, Flora! Hang on!' Bunny yelled as he ran along the jetty towards her, leaving wet footprints on the wood. 'Don't let go of her!'

'That's easy for you to say, you're not wearing the corset!' she uttered through gritted teeth. Her arms felt pulled from their sockets as she strained backwards, terrified the material hooked round her cramped fingers would tear and Sally tumble over the side, but she held on, her ribs screaming with pain.

Bunny sank to his knees on the edge of the barge, leaned down and grabbed Sally around her waist and eased her onto the deck. Water dripped from his clothes and his hair was plastered to his head. His glasses were gone and he gave off a silty smell. In a series of slides and awkward lifts, together, they eased Sally onto the deck.

She had begun to wake and, disoriented, struggled feebly against the hands that lifted her onto the jetty. Her skin felt clammy, but she was warm to the touch, and shivering.

'That's good isn't it?' Flora asked. 'That she's shivering?'

Before he could answer, Abel staggered towards them, manoeuvred Bunny out of the way and dropped to one knee. 'Sally, Sally wake up. It's me.' He wrapped one arm around her and brushed her damp hair away from her face with the other, murmuring apologies for having left her.

'Her breathing is better and she's starting to come round. But, Abel, you're injured.' Flora indicated a dark trickle of blood that worked its way down the side of his face. 'You should have a doctor look at you.'

'Never mind me. I've had worse.' Abel waved her away, his attention on Sally as her eyes snapped open. She stared around for a few seconds, then moaned and scrambled into a sitting position, knees splayed beneath her skirt, and hands pressed against her forehead.

'How do you feel, Sally?' Flora asked.

'Got one corker of an 'eadache,' she slurred her words as if her lips wouldn't work properly. 'Where the 'ell are we? I'm freezing!'

'Take her to the hackney, Abel,' Bunny gestured vaguely towards the quay. 'She needs to be kept warm and they have blankets over there.'

Nodding, Abel scooped Sally into his arms and carried her along the pier as if she weighed nothing.

'You're soaking wet!' Flora said, grimacing at Bunny, who shook his head like a dog, spraying her with dirty water.

'It's not as if I could have had a bath in between rescues.' His voice was sharp, but the look he slanted at her was amused.

'Sorry, it was merely an observation.' She flexed her wrists to restore the circulation and rolled each shoulder in turn. 'And I wouldn't want you to catch cold. Is Alice all right?'

'Wet, cold and furious. The tide is in so I had to swim with her all the way back to the quay, which took me longer than I thought. Once we were on the quayside, she ordered me back here to check on you.' He caught Flora's sideways look and added, 'not that she need to of course. I left her bundled up in blankets in the hackney cab over there. Reluctantly, I might add.'

'Thank goodness.' Flora sighed. 'I was so frightened when I saw her go into the river. Are the police here yet?' She pushed herself to her feet, but her sore hip protested and she buckled.

'Careful.' His arms came round her waist in a firm, reassuring hold and he hauled her back upright. 'A Black Maria pulled up a moment ago with the hackney.'

'And Raymond Buchanan? Where's he?'

'What's with all these questions?' he gave her another oblique look, 'the superintendent wanted to get his story down from the beginning, so he's still at the police station. But never mind all that, we can talk about it later. I'm more worried about you. Are you in pain?'

'Aching and sore, but I doubt it's permanent. And I could ask the same of you.' She smoothed his wet hair from his brow. 'You're wet through and your teeth are chattering. And you've lost your glasses.'

'Not lost, I hope. I shoved them into my coat pocket at the last second before I jumped in. I found my shoes but I don't suppose you can see my coat anywhere?' He tucked his arm through hers, and in a series of hops and staggers, they made their way slowly along the jetty.

'I'm afraid I didn't notice. I expect one of the policeman has retrieved it.'

'Hold onto me, would you?' Water trickled from Bunny's trousers as he walked. 'It's quite slippery underfoot.'

'As long as we don't try to run, I shall be fine. You don't have to worry.'

'Actually, it's not you I'm worried about.' He dropped his voice an octave. 'I can't see more than six feet in front of me. Could you lean into me a little so everyone will think you're the one who needs assistance?'

'Like this?' She supressed a near hysterical giggle,

dropped her shoulder and dragged one foot. Though it occurred to her that by the morning she wouldn't have to exaggerate anything. Her hip was stiffening with each step.

'Perfect.'

CHAPTER 30

Bunny made himself known to the policeman in charge of a pile of blankets, and availed himself of a hip flask Inspector Maddox had produced. 'Purely medicinal, Mrs Harrington,' he called to her as she passed. Flora smiled in response and limped to the open rear of the police van. Sally huddled in a corner beneath a blanket, Abel's arm slung around her shoulders, an expertly stark white bandage wound around his forehead.

'How are you, Sally?'

'Me 'ead still hurts. You, madam?'

'I'll mend. How much of the last few days do you remember?' Flora braced a hand on the door frame to take the weight from her sore hip.

'I recall seeing that bloke in the Lamb and Flag.' Sally tilted her head back to look at Abel. 'I shouldn't have left you in the pub that night, but when I saw that Martell all togged up in a Sally Anne uniform, I knew he was up to no good. I followed him as far as the next alley when some bruiser came at me out of a doorway. The next thing I knew, I was in that tunnel with those nippers.' She looked up at Flora, her eyes wide. 'Did you find them? Are they all right?'

'We did indeed, and they are all safe and on their way to the hospital, which is where you should go too.' She was about to suggest they could find room in the hackney for them both instead of a police van, but by the way Sally gazed adoringly up at Abel they would probably appreciate the privacy.

'I ain't going to no 'ospital,' Sally sniffed. 'I've felt worse after a Pond family wedding.'

'Sally. You were drugged, shoved in a cupboard and dropped on your head. You should see a doctor,' Flora insisted. 'Oh, and Inspector Maddox will need to speak to you as well.'

'I'll think about it, though I ain't happy about talking to coppers. Not in my nature you might say.' She appeared to think of something and lifted her head. 'What about that bloke Swifty and his bint? Right bitch she was – er – begging your pardon.'

'Ruth Lazarus has also been apprehended.' Flora debated whether to tell her about Swifty, but without knowing if he would be pulled alive from the river or not, she would leave that for another time. 'If you're adamant about the hospital, I'll see you at home, but I'm going to summon a doctor to take a look at you.' Without giving her a chance to object, Flora signalled to the officer to close the van door.

★   ★   ★

Flora relaxed against the padded upholstery of the hackney, supplied courtesy of Inspector Maddox, her head against Bunny's shoulder. A thick, if scratchy blanket had been draped around her shoulders, her chilled feet resting on the cloth-wrapped hot brick someone had thoughtfully placed on the floor.

A movement at the door revealed Alice, her head and shoulders shrouded in an identical blanket, her hair hanging in rat's tails on either side of her face.

'I just wanted to say goodnight before I left.' She clutched the edges of the blanket together beneath her chin. 'That was brave of you, staying behind to save your maid. It could all have turned out so differently.'

'Indeed it could have.' Bunny's voice was muffled through the towel as he scrubbed roughly at his wet hair.

'I wouldn't say brave, as I was terrified at one point.' The moment when Alice had gone into the water, had been a moment she would never wish to repeat. seconded only by her sending Bunny after her. She patted the seat on the other side of her. 'Don't stand out there in the cold. Come inside and get comfortable. It's not perfect, but certainly warmer than out there.'

'Yes, do, Miss Finch.' Bunny jumped down onto the quay, one hand extended to help her up the step. 'I'll have a scout round and see if I can locate my coat.' He turned and strode off along the quayside, hailing a policeman as he went.

'He's very tactful, your husband.' Alice climbed inside and took the seat opposite, taking a moment to rearrange the blanket around her. Her hair hung in dark and straggly rat's tails round her face, but somehow made her look young and vulnerable.

'Isn't he.' Flora fidgeted, unsure of exactly what to say. She debated whether or not to ask about what Alice had said back on the pier, but refrained in case it only served to embarrass them both?

'Your delightful Miss Grey has gone to St Philomena's with the children,' Alice said after a pause. 'They appear quite well, if tired. Some are more shocked than others, of course. Isobel appears to have suffered the worst. It must have been quite a harrowing experience for her.'

'Is that where you intend to go now, the hospital?' Flora asked. 'If so, we could take you when Bunny comes back.'

'That's not necessary. It isn't far, and Inspector Maddox has offered to take me in his own cab.' She glanced down at herself and shrugged, a hand drifting to her hair. 'Fortunately I have a change of clothes in my office. It's a shame about my hat, but I'm certainly not going back to look for it.' She straightened, her hands arranged in her lap as if about to deliver a speech. 'Now, the Inspector has informed me that this all started with a simple fraud. Mr Martell and Sister Lazarus posed as Salvation Army officers to trawl the London pubs with collection boxes. Naturally they kept their spoils.'

'I imagine that must have been quite lucrative,' Flora said. 'Most people give the Army money out of guilt and to make them go away. I've heard they can be quite intimidating. Had they not decided to expand their operation to child abduction, we might never have found them out.'

'Oh, I think they would have been discovered eventually.' Alice caught Flora's eye but glanced away quickly. Tension hovered between them, as if she had something more important to say, but instead, she smothered it beneath an uneasy smile and stared out across the water. An uneven line of policemen were strung along the pier, their lanterns held out over the edge, presumably in search of any signs of life.

'Swifty's gone, hasn't he?' Sympathy rose in her throat, though when she recalled what he had planned for Sally as well as herself, her heart hardened.

'I doubt he survived.' Alice sighed. 'His body will probably wash up somewhere downriver.'

'Alice, I—' Flora blurted, then hesitated.

'Yes?' Alice's eyes slowly roved her face.

She lost her nerve, and instead, voiced a thought she had struggled with since Alice had first told her about the children. 'Do you believe they were going to be adopted by childless couples?'

'Do *you*?' Alice's smile wilted around the edges, confirming Flora's own fears. 'What distresses me the most, is that they preyed on youngsters who had been foisted on family members, all of whom could ill afford another mouth to feed thus were relieved to part with them. It was so brutal and calculated.'

'Alice,' Flora said, keeping her voice low, 'when you fell into the river, you—' she broke off as the solid bulk of Inspector Maddox loomed into the open carriage door, his face wreathed in smiles.

'Well that's that, Mrs Harrington.' His smile was one of self-congratulation. 'It's been quite an eventful afternoon, don't you agree?' He tipped his hat back on his head, revealing an impressive lump the size of a quail's egg on his temple.

'That's one way of describing it, Inspector.' She exchanged a wry look with Alice.

'Your statements can wait, but I wanted to let you know that it was your persistence that finally broke this case.' He adjusted his bowler hat and jammed both hands in his pockets, rocking gently back and forth on his heels. 'Getting Buchanan to reveal his part in the whole mess was a bold move.'

'You'll have to thank Bunny for that, Inspector,' Flora said. 'What happens now?'

'My priority tonight is to get these characters to the police station.' He gestured to where a Black Maria stood, the profiles of Claude Martel and a sobbing Ruth Lazarus visible through the metal grille in the rear door.

As they watched, the vehicle pulled away from the kerb and drew level with their carriage. At the last second before it moved on, Martell's eyes settled on Flora and narrowed, holding hers for a chilling second before the van moved past them.

Refusing to be cowed, she told herself the Frenchman could always get a job making madeleines in the prison kitchens.

'Something amusing you, Mrs Harrington?' Inspector Maddox's voice broke into her thoughts.

'No, nothing. I was just thinking about cakes. Tea and cakes.' The thought was quickly followed by who would run his charming little tea shop now.

'Ah, well goodnight then, ladies, and thank you again.' Maddox slapped the side of the cab and turned to leave.

'Inspector,' Flora summoned him back, 'Ruth Lazarus intimated she didn't kill Lizzie Prentice. Though who else could it have been?'

'That doesn't surprise me.' His upper lip curled. 'She's not likely to admit to something that would be guaranteed to get her the rope. We had to tell her that Swifty is probably dead and she went into a fit of hysterics so we'll get nothing out of her tonight.' He tutted in annoyance and moved away.

'Are you sure we cannot take you to the hospital, Miss Finch?' Bunny asked brightly. He had found his coat, but despite the two blankets wrapped around his shoulders he was shivering.

'Thank you all the same, but no.' Alice eased forward to the edge of the seat and pulled herself onto the step, then turned back and patted Flora's hand, whispering, 'I'll see you soon.'

'Goodnight then, Miss Finch,' Bunny said. 'Thank you for everything.'

'Not at all, Mr Harrington.' She stood in the road, gathered the edges of the blanket round her with one hand, and pushed strands of damp hair from her face with the other. 'It's you I wish to thank for pulling me out of the river. You were quite the hero.'

The shadowy figures of policemen leapt from barge to barge along the pier, their lamps bobbing like fireflies as the search for Swifty Ellis' body continued, while the hackney rumbled off the quay, the mournful wail of fog horns on the river in the background.

A combination of pain, relief and weariness overwhelmed her as the hackney trundled back through Tooley Street, crossed London Bridge, taking the route alongside the remains of the old London Wall and into Thames Street.

'Bunny?' She began as they passed the northern end of Blackfriars Bridge, partly to distract herself from the pain that went through her ribs at every bump in the road. 'Why would Ruth deny killing Lizzie Prentice at this stage when they have all been—?'

'Hush.' Bunny placed a finger on her lips. 'Forget them. It's over now and all I want to do is to have a bath, eat a delicious dinner and spend the rest of evening in front of the fire with you.'

'The first thing I shall do when I get home is to hug Arthur,' she whispered, comforted when he squeezed her hand beneath the rough and musty smelling blanket.

Fear and shock gave way to weariness and she imagined how things might have turned out differently on that barge. How could she have been so reckless? Not only had she almost thrown away her own life, but she had risked never seeing Bunny or Arthur again. The thought that her son might have grown up, as she had, without a mother, made her hands shake.

What had she done? Had she saved those children from Martell, only to condemn them to life in the slums of London with little future and scant hope? What if Martell was right and they would have had better, healthier and more loving lives somewhere across the Atlantic?

Her throat felt scratchy and tears welled, dripping silently onto her cheek. She blinked and swiped them away before Bunny saw.

'I'm sure I spotted several curtains twitching when we arrived home.' Flora stood in front of the sitting room mirror and rubbed at a soot smut beside her eye.

'Which is hardly surprising,' Bunny said. 'The simultaneous arrival of a hackney cab and a police van is a notable occurrence in Eaton Place.'

'I suppose we'll be the topic of conversation over the teacups tomorrow.' The smut persisted and she gave up. 'I've asked Nell to run me a bath as I look such a wreck. I daren't go up and see Arthur like this as I'll likely frighten the poor child.'

Her hair had lost half its pins and hung in untidy ringlets down her back. Her dress was torn at the hem after her struggle on the barge, the wool damp to the touch. It also smelled of the river; a mixture of mud, silt and sulphur.

Apart from a ruined suit that gave off a lingering earthy smell, and a clump of seaweed clinging to the front of his shirt, Bunny had escaped with little more than a deep scratch on the back of his hand from a stray nail. His still damp hair promised to dry soft and straight with no unflattering kinks to the wheat-coloured locks.

'Of course he wouldn't. Besides, I quite like it when you look all tousled and less than your usual immaculate self.' Bunny grinned at her reflection.

'You worry me sometimes.' Flora cocked her head, frowning. 'Is that the doorbell?'

The sound of male voices reached them from the hall, one of which Flora didn't recognize. Seconds later, Stokes appeared at the sitting room door.

'A Dr Reid is here, sir, who insists on seeing you, sir, madam. I tried to explain it was not a convenient time, but he would not be dissuaded.'

'Here?' Flora directed the question at Bunny. 'How does he know where we live?'

'I've no idea.' Bunny replied just as Reid strode into the room and grasped Bunny's hand in both of his.

'My dear Mr Harrington, Mrs Harrington. I do apologize for turning up like this, but when I heard about what had happened I simply had to reassure myself you were both all right.'

Informally dressed in a tweed jacket with leather patches at the elbows, he was also hatless, his sandy hair blown about by the wind, as if impulse rather than intention had brought him there.

Reminded of how she must look, Flora raised a hand to her own hair, realized she would only make it worse and abandoned the idea.

'Indeed, it's been quite a day.' Bunny retrieved his hand from the doctor's enthusiastic handshake. 'May I offer you a sherry? Flora and I could do with some, couldn't we, my dear?' He caught her eye briefly, his eyebrow raised as he crossed to the sideboard.

'Talk at the hospital is all about how Miss Finch and yourself helped the police round up the villains who had kidnapped those children.'

'You say you heard all this at the hospital?' Bunny spoke over one shoulder, the decanter poised over a trio of crystal glasses. 'I'm surprised news reached there so quickly.'

'Why from Miss Finch, she told me the whole story herself.' He accepted the glass Bunny held out without looking at it.

'She told you what had happened?' Flora frowned, puzzled. *He must have come straight here within minutes of Alice arriving at the hospital.*

'Indeed, and what a dreadful experience it must

442

have been for her. And you, of course, Mrs Harrington,' he added, ignoring Flora's dishevelment. 'You were quite the heroine, I'm told. She also said that Mr Buchanan was at the police station and that this dreadful affair had something to do with his Stanhope collection.'

'You know about those?' Bunny lifted an eyebrow.

'I've had the privilege of dining at Birdcage walk on occasion and admired them greatly. He has some very interesting ones.'

'Is that why you are here?' Flora gestured him into a chair, but he remained standing, 'because you're concerned for Mr Buchanan?'

Or was he more worried about what Raymond might be telling the police?

'Only in that I cannot believe he could possibly be involved in anything like child abduction. However, there are all sorts of rumours flying around the hospital about Sister Lazarus and Lizzie Prentice. Something about a Stanhope being found among Nurse Prentice's belongings being used in blackmail. Miss Finch said it was now in your possession, although she didn't go into all the details.' Reid's hand shook slightly as he brought his glass to his lips.

'That's quite correct, Doctor. And yet the strangest thing,' Flora began, ignoring Bunny's warning frown, 'is that no one has any idea how poor Lizzie Prentice came to have it. In fact, Mr Buchanan claimed never to have seen it before.'

'He did? How odd.' Reid's glass halted halfway

443

to his lips. 'I expect he was confused. He has quite a large collection. Perhaps it's difficult to keep track of them all. He's also been under a great deal of strain lately.' He took a sip of the sherry, his throat constricting as he swallowed. 'If I might be of service, what with all you have been through today. I could return it to Mr Buchanan on your behalf.'

'That's a kind offer, Doctor, but won't be necessary,' Bunny said. 'Inspector Maddox has asked us to meet him at Canon Row in the morning. I expect they'll need the Stanhope as evidence.'

'Surely that isn't necessary?' A trickle of sweat ran down the side of his temple, though the room was barely warm from the newly laid fire. 'After all, they have the culprits in custody.'

'They're still investigating,' Flora lied, surprised at how convincing she sounded. 'It appears there are more elements to this affair than anyone imagined.' *You being one of them.*

'Would you like more sherry, Dr Reid?' Bunny headed back to the sideboard, and murmured, 'I know what you're doing,' to Flora as he passed, then louder. 'Oh dear, it's almost empty, I'll have it refilled. Won't be a moment.' Shielding the object with his arm, he summoned the butler.

Stokes must have been outside the door as he appeared immediately, and for once, Flora didn't resent the butler's busybody ways. Their exchange was too far away for her to overhear, but they exchanged only a few words before the butler stiffened, his expression inscrutable. With a single, swift nod, he rapidly withdrew, cradling the still half full decanter.

'Now, what were we talking about?' Bunny strode back to Flora's side, his closeness giving her confidence. 'Ah yes, I remember now. You seem unusually concerned about one of Mr Buchanan's peeps, Dr Reid.'

'I-I beg your pardon?' Perspiration beaded on his forehead, his gaze shifting rapidly between them. 'I was merely being—'

'Is it the Stanhope itself which interests you? Or the contents?' Flora interjected.

I really don't know what you're talking about. I—' Reid flushed and gave a high, short laugh that was entirely unconvincing.

'It was you in that photograph, wasn't it?' Bunny took a leisurely sip from his glass and pointed it at the doctor. 'Lizzie Prentice must have confronted you about it and you panicked.'

'Is that why you killed her?' Flora demanded. Ruth told the truth when she denied killing Lizzie.

'After which,' Bunny added. 'You gave evidence at her inquest that she died as a result of a fall to cover your own actions?'

The room seemed to empty of air. Suddenly nervous, Flora took a mouthful of sherry and gulped it down. Whatever happened next couldn't be good. The man was obviously trapped and by the expression in his eyes he knew it.

'Really, I—' Reid dragged his gaze from Bunny's

and looked at Flora. The mood shifted and he seemed to sense they had allied themselves against him. He retrieved his glass, drained the contents before setting it down on the table with a crack hard enough to crack the crystal.

'That *stupid* girl. If only she had minded her own business. The Stanhope was mine. Lizzie called at my lodgings to deliver a message and she saw it on my desk. She thought it was simply a pretty novelty and couldn't resist examining it.' His spat the words out, his tone low and angry as if talking to himself. 'I thought she would understand as we were friends, but—'

'Instead she was disgusted by you?' Flora said gently.

His lip quivered and he looked suddenly broken and yet defiant, as if he couldn't accept that his own choice had brought him to this situation.

'She refused to give it back. She said she was going to take it to the Board of Governors.' 'I confronted again in the yard the following day, hoping she had reconsidered. I tried to make her understand that my important work had to continue.' His eyes hardened as his arrogance returned. 'She said I deserved to be publicly disgraced. I offered to pay her, but she pulled away from me and—' He shrugged as if what followed was inevitable. 'I grabbed a stone from a flower border and hit her. I barely remember doing it. The next thing I knew, she was lying on the path, bleeding. I searched her pockets, but she didn't have the peep on her.' He laughed, a hollow, dreadful sound. 'Perhaps I should have made sure of that first.'

Flora closed her eyes, disgusted that he exhibited more frustration than remorse. Or as a man who helped save lives, did he believe he had the right to take them too?

'Then you slipped back into the building, and when the shouting started, joined the crowd in the yard and pretended you had no idea what the commotion was about,' Flora said.

'Something like that.'

'All that, and you still didn't have the photograph,' Bunny said calmly. 'The existence of which could cause a great deal of trouble for both you and Victor Buchanan.'

'If you give that Stanhope to the police, we'll *both* go to prison.' He brought a fist down onto the back of Bunny's favourite wingback chair, his eyes flashing. 'I'll never be able to practice as a doctor again.'

'Inevitable, I'm afraid.' Bunny sighed. 'Besides what the police refer to as indecent practices, let's not forget the fact that you murdered a young girl.'

'I was afraid you might be unsympathetic.' He slid his right hand into a pocket. When he removed it again he held a pistol, so small, Flora wondered if it was real or not.

'I hadn't anticipated that,' she whispered, her heart thumping against her corset.

'Nor me.' Bunny stepped smartly in front of her, his hands held palms outwards. 'I wouldn't if I were you, Doctor. This will simply make your situation much worse.'

Flora was about to tell him he was wasting his breath, as a similar plea had had no effect on Ruth either, but the tiny hole at the end of the gun barrel held her frozen.

'I have no alternative.' Reid eased towards the door, the weapon pointed at Bunny's chest. 'Now, I'll have the Stanhope, if you please.'

'We're not certain where it is just now.' Flora tried to distract him as she calculated how long it had been since Stokes had left. 'You'll have to allow us time to find it.'

'Don't lie.' The gun jerked. 'I'd be willing to wager it's in this very room. Now give it to me!'

Behind him, the door opened and a shadow loomed in the door frame.

Flora forced herself not to look in case she alerted Reid, but suddenly his eyes dulled, rolled up in his head and he toppled onto the floor at her feet. The weapon fell from his hand and skittered across the polished floorboards, coming to rest against the hearth.

'Stokes said you had a bit of trouble in here, Mr Harrington.' Abel Cain filled the door frame, a mildly puzzled frown directed at the prone figure on the floor.

'Not any longer, Abel.' Flora exhaled a relieved breath. 'That was most efficient, thank you.' Her knees went belatedly weak and she collapsed onto the nearest sofa. Her gaze drifting to his hands which were empty. 'What did you hit him with?' She had forgotten Abel had arrived home with Sally and insisted on getting her settled so was still in the house.

Abel shrugged and held up his clenched right fist, that was the size of a plucked chicken.

'Mrs Cope was making me a cup of tea and Stokes came to say a doctor was here. I thought he had come to see Sally, but Stokes started babbling about the police and insisted I come up here. The second he opened the door I recognised that chap from the hospital. I saw the gun – and well. I didn't have a choice did I?'

'For which we shall be eternally grateful Abel,' Flora said. 'Where is Stokes now?'

'He's gone to telephone for a constable.'

'Right, well I doubt Reid will stay unconscious for long.' Bunny pressed his fingers to the still motionless man's neck. 'His pulse is steady anyway so no permanent damage. We'll have to secure him until Maddox gets here. Give us a hand would you, Abel?'

'I've spoken to Inspector Maddox, sir.' Stokes returned at a run, smartly sidestepping Abel who dragged the unconscious Dr Reid along the floor by his ankles. 'He was a little resistant, but when I explained what had happened, he said he would be here shortly.'

'Most efficient of you, Stokes, thank you.' Bunny

untied a silk cord from the curtains and wrapped it round the doctor's wrists, securing it round the leg of the sofa.

Flora retrieved Reid's pistol from the floor. The weapon was tiny, no more than three inches long with a curved handle inlaid with mother-of-pearl etched with gold. The object sat neatly in her palm, the metal smooth cold, and comfortably heavy.

'Bunny?' she hefted the object in her hand admiringly. 'May I have one of these?'

'What the devil—?' Bunny's mouth opened in horror as he leapt forward, snatched the gun from her. 'Goodness, Flora, what do you think you're doing?'

'I wasn't going to shoot anyone!' She released the weapon reluctantly, her hand strangely empty without it. 'I thought it would be useful if I ever came across another Swifty.' It would also fit beautifully into any of her bags.'

'This, my darling, is a *Webley Bulldog*.' He held the gun in his open palm with something like reverence. 'Even the Americans have copied this model, though this ornamental handle suggests this one was custom made. Small but powerful, and certainly not for inexperienced hands.' Muttering to himself, he strode to the bureau, placed the gun inside a drawer, and his eyes narrowed at her over his shoulder, slid it firmly closed.

'Pity.' Flora sighed.

CHAPTER 31

Flora's only legacy of her struggle on the barge and the episode with Dr Reid were scraped knees, sore fingers, and a persistent ache in one hip. She had slept late that morning and enjoyed breakfast in bed followed by her second bath in twelve hours to rid herself of the residual smell of damp filth that clung to her from the excursion on the river.

'How are you feeling this morning?' Bunny entered from his dressing room and perched on the edge of the bed.

'Much refreshed, although it's taken until now to get the taste of soot and sulphur out of my mouth.' She smoothed her hair over one shoulder and gave the long tresses a surreptitious sniff, relieved it smelled lavender and not coal smoke and river water.

'Sally appears to have recovered from her adventure.' Bunny crossed to the window that overlooked the street two stories below. 'I heard her regaling the maids with her heroics when I came downstairs. I could have sworn I heard Abel's voice as well. Didn't he go home last night?'

'He did, but came back again this morning. I've given Sally a couple of days off to recover, though you would never know anything had happened to her.' Flora sifted through the mail the maid had brought up. 'Have you heard from Inspector Maddox yet today?'

'He telephoned first thing to let me know that we don't need to go to Canon Row until tomorrow.' He held back the curtain with one hand, frowning slightly. 'The Dr Reid episode means he has more paperwork to complete. He told me that the captain of the *SS Lancett* has also been arrested, something to do with a separate dubious cargo they discovered on board. Also that the children will be returned to their families this morning once they have been deemed fit and healthy.

This news did not please Flora as it should have. Having seen some of the homes the children came from, it occurred to her they had been saved from one type of horror only to be returned to the original one. The children had also been questioned, but none recalled a child named Annie.

'Isobel Lomax's parents wanted us to accept a reward,' Bunny continued, oblivious of Flora's disquiet.

'I hope you refused.' She looked up from the pile of letters.

'Naturally. I thanked them politely, but said that virtue was its own reward.'

'You didn't!'

'Of course not.' He chuckled. 'I suggested they

make a donation to St Philomena's Children's Hospital instead.'

'Excellent solution.' Flora tore open an envelope that bore Lady Jocasta's writing. 'I'm sure Alice will be very grateful. I can only imagine how she feels about harbouring a villain like Ruth on her staff.'

'I doubt anyone will blame her for Sister Lazarus' actions. Talking of Alice.' His gaze returned to his contemplation of the street. 'I've come to the conclusion you were right, and there's definitely a family resemblance.'

'What made you think that?' Flora halted in the act of unfolding the letter.

'Because I'm looking right at her. She's at the front gate.'

'What?' She dropped the letter she was holding and hobbled to his side as fast as her stiff muscles allowed and stared down into the street.'

Dressed in her elegant grey coat and matching hat Flora had admired before, Alice stood at the gate, her hand on the latch as if she was not sure whether or not she should step onto the tiled pathway.

Flora turned and swept out of the room, her movements markedly hampered by her hip. She braced her arms on the bannisters and eased carefully down each stair in turn, fearful that Alice would change her mind and vanish. Finally, reached the front door and yanked it open.

Alice stood on the top step, her hand reaching for the bell pull. She blinked in surprise on seeing

Flora and lowered her hand. 'Good morning, Flora. I-I think we need to talk.'

'So do I.' Flora stepped back to allow her into the hall, her heart thumping uncomfortably in her chest as she helped Alice out of her coat. Anticipation made her hands shake as she transferred the garment to the hat stand.

'Come into the sitting room. Have you had breakfast?' Flora's throat dried as she led the way, her voice higher-pitched than usual. Surely there could only be one reason for her presence? Or had she come simply to make sure everyone was all right after yesterday's adventures?

'Yes, thank you. I was up very early this morning, but I would welcome some coffee.'

Bunny appeared as Alice was taking her seat.

'Miss Finch, how delightful.' He greeted her with his usual charm, even to dropping a kiss on her knuckles, her hand held in both of his for a long pause. 'Actually, I have to leave you. Inspector Maddox requires a full written account of what transpired yesterday. I think I'll retreat to my study and do that now while it's all still fresh in my mind.' He backed away, but paused to direct a slow, conspiratorial wink at Flora.

'That was tactful of him.' Alice gave the pile of magazines scattered on the cushions an enquiring glance. 'Have I come at an awkward time?'

'No, of course not. Oh, sorry. Let me move these.' Flora gathered them into an untidy pile and dumped them unceremoniously onto a nearby table.

'Now I'm here, I'm not sure where to begin.' Alice made a show of settling onto the sofa, but kept her gaze averted.

'Then let me.' The question Flora had asked herself all night sprang to her lips, 'I might have been mistaken, but when Swifty appeared about to attack me on the deck of his barge, I could have sworn you called me Fleur.'

'I wasn't sure you had heard me.' Alice twisted the metal clasp of the bag in her lap. 'You are correct. I did call you that. It was the name I gave you when you were born.'

Slowly, Flora lowered herself onto the space beside her, falling the last few inches as the room seemed to recede around her. She had gone over the scene on the barge a hundred times since it happened, convincing herself she had misheard. That it was a meaningless slip of the tongue.

'Flora, are you all right?' Alice leaned forward in her chair. 'I didn't mean to upset you.'

'No, no, you haven't. *When I was born*, that's what you said isn't it?'

'It was, yes.' She gave a light, if nervous laugh. 'Riordan hated it. He said it was too presumptuous for people in our station. He insisted you be called Flora.'

'He did?' Flora frowned, recalling that Riordan had told her that her grandfather had changed her name, but perhaps, like so many things, she had misunderstood.

'When I saw that man loom out of the dark on

the pier, yesterday, I reacted purely by instinct.' The look Alice gave her held a plea. 'Yet at the same time, I was terrified I might have revealed something you wouldn't welcome. Or accept.'

Suddenly, Flora felt barely able to breathe. Her instincts hadn't betrayed her after all. Excitement rushed through her veins at the facts she was about to have every question that had plagued her all her life answered. Before she could summon any of them, Stokes arrived and set a tray on the table between them.

'Shall I leave you to pour, Madam?' His knowing smile indicated he knew this was no ordinary social call.

'Uh-Thank you, Stokes, I will.' Flora watched him depart through narrowed eyes. Had Bunny said something to him?

'A tactful manservant too. Alice said when he had left. 'My, you are a fortunate young woman.' She smoothed her skirt over her knees, set her bag carefully beside her. 'I think you know why I'm here.'

Flora concentrated on pouring the coffee, mainly to stop her hands from shaking. The rich aroma, which usually relaxed her, combined with the rapid fluttering of her heart had made her feel nauseous.

'Perhaps this isn't the right time?' Alice's smile did not hide the anxious question in her eyes at Flora's lack of response.

'No!' She looked up quickly, the coffee pot hitting the table with a thump. 'I mean yes, of course it is. I want to hear whatever you want to say.' *I always have.*

'Well then.' She inhaled slowly. 'I was sixteen when I went into service at Cleeve Abbey as Lady Vaughn's maid.' She accepted the cup Flora handed her with an unsteady hand. 'I was young and life at the Abbey was so different from that of a minister's daughter in a tiny village in Surrey. Lady Vaughn loved to travel and she took me with her everywhere. I was swept away by the grandeur of it all. Unwisely, I fell in love with a young man within the family. We were both young, and at that age you believe anything is possible.'

Flora smothered an impulse to speak William's name by taking a mouthful of coffee, but gulped too fast and it threatened to choke her.

'Are you all right?' Alice handed her a napkin from the tray.

'Yes, of course. Hot.' She flapped a hand. 'Do go on.'

'He was as impetuous and romantic as I was. When I think back to how reckless we were it was inevitable I should get into trouble.' She dropped her gaze to her cup. 'I'm sure I don't have to explain what sort.'

'No. You don't,' Flora said gently, hoping she didn't sound judgemental.

'He told his family we wished to marry. We even arranged the wedding.' Her smile reflected the joy she had obviously felt at the prospect, but immediately it withered to sadness. 'I'm sure you can

457

imagine how that announcement was received. Lady Vaughn persuaded him to change his mind and within weeks they had sent him to America to complete his education, though everyone knew it was to remove him from me.'

'You understand what I'm trying to tell you?'

'That Riordan Maguire was not my father,' Flora replied calmly, recalling a similar conversation she had had with Lady Vaughn after Riordan's death, when the secrets of her parentage had come out.

A small frown appeared between Alice's eyes, as if she suspected this was not news, but chose not to pursue it. 'Riordan was head butler at the Abbey, as you know. A kind, upstanding man, if proud. He was older than me but I knew he admired me, so when he offered to give you a name I was flattered. Not to mention relieved.' She sighed, and in that one sound, Flora heard a lifetime's anguish. 'I accepted him mainly to spite my young man. Your father.'

'Spite him?' Flora's cup halted in mid-air.

'Yes. I didn't see it at the time, but that's what it was. He had allowed money and social position to part us after claiming those things weren't important to him. I felt betrayed. I was fond of Riordan, but there was never love between us – not the kind I felt for—' She broke off, her lips pressed together in a hard line. 'Anyway, Riordan said that didn't matter and from the moment you were born, he adored you. We both did. To be honest, I felt pushed aside. Ignored.'

'Are you saying it was *my* fault you left?' Flora blurted. 'Because you were jealous of me?'

'No, oh no, that wasn't it at all.' Alice reached for Flora's hand with her free one, but after a light, brief touch, withdrew it.

'I was eighteen when you were born and despite what had happened I was still romantic, high-spirited and loved to dance. Riordan was kind and gentlemanly, but he was also possessive, over-bearing, and serious. If I joined in the country dancing at the summer fair, or talked to a young man, any young man, he would drag me aside and say my behaviour was inappropriate. That it reflected badly on him.'

'All the servants at Cleeve Abbey respected him.' Flora couldn't resist jumping to the defence of the man she still regarded as a parent. One she still missed. 'He most likely wanted to retain their respect, and if he thought his wife was—' She trailed off.

'Look, Flora.' Alice's eyes clouded. 'I'm not trying to cast him as a cruel or a bad man, he wasn't. Far from it.' She worried her bottom lip with her teeth. 'As you say, he was respected. Thus the other servants took their cue from him and treated me accordingly. They made it clear that I didn't deserve a man like Riordan, and ought to have been more grateful. He never defended me, so I felt very alone.'

Flora conjured up the man she had known in her head. A proud man, certainly, overly serious at times whose smiles were rare, but precious when they appeared. She couldn't' reconcile him with the person Alice described, but she had no reason to lie.

'I know the other servants whispered in corners about me.' She gave a light, if sad laugh.

'I wasn't aware of any gossip—' Flora broke off as memories returned of a summer's day when she was about nine or ten. A sun-lit corridor filled with conspiratorial voices of the housekeeper and governess had sent her ducking into an alcove to listen to words clearly not for her ears. *It's best she's gone. That Lily was never good enough for Maguire.* Words Flora had never repeated, but which stuck with her through the years, having interpreted 'gone' as being dead.

'Your father . . .' Alice's voice pulled her back to the present. 'Your real father, returned from America when you were small. He came to see me when Riordan wasn't there to say he had made a mistake in leaving me – *us*. He swore he had been bullied into it. He was doing well in America and begged me to return there with him.'

'I don't know why I refused,' Alice went on as if reading Flora's thoughts. 'I was tempted, but Riordan was my husband. I felt I had to stick with the choice I had made. Besides, I couldn't have shamed him in front of everyone he knew. I thought I was being noble.' She laughed, a self-mocking, hollow laugh, her fingers plucking at a fold in her dress. 'My pride had a lot to do with it. I mean, how dare he run away at the first sign of disapproval, only to crawl back almost three years later and say he was sorry?'

'This meeting – was it at the lodge?' Flora asked, unable to stop herself. 'You argued, didn't you?'

'How could you know that?' Her coffee cup hit the saucer with a sharp click. 'You were barely walking.'

'I remember. Bits and pieces mostly.' The cottage kitchen with its black leaded stove loomed into her head, along with the rainbow colours of the rag rug and a rectangular shaft of sunlight on grey flagstones. The thump of her mother hitting the floor and the metallic smell of blood.

'He pleaded with me to leave with him that day,' Alice continued, breaking into her memories. I refused, and he got angry, saying we belonged together, that we had a child. He lifted you into his arms and I was terrified that he intended to take you away. I-I flew at him and, in the scuffle, I fell against the table. My nose bled everywhere. I was lucky not to have broken it. Riordan arrived then and there was the most awful row.'

'I remember some of it,' Flora said. The images that had plagued her in dreams throughout her childhood returned. 'The feel of that rug under me and the blood. Especially the smell. There was shouting too. Lots of shouting.'

'I'm so sorry.' She reached for Flora's hand again. 'I imagined you would be too young to understand.'

461

'He returned to America alone. My father?' Flora let her hand lay passive in Alice's, the length of their fingers achingly similar. Even their nails were the same shape.

Alice nodded. 'Any disagreement I had with Riordan after that always ended the same way. He would accuse me of wanting to leave, demanding to know why I hadn't. Eventually, a rift developed between us; a polite, silent one, but a rift all the same.'

'Is that when you decided to leave?'

'I didn't decide exactly. It just happened. But no, not then. That was later.'

The sight of several strands of grey nestled in Alice's ash blonde hair was strangely poignant in that she spoke of the events of her younger self as if they were the present.

'I began helping at the women's refuge in town, mainly to get away from the Abbey.' Her gaze sought Flora's, but she looked away quickly. 'Riordan disapproved – naturally. He couldn't understand why I wanted to be with people who regarded me as a do-gooding busybody. How could I explain that despite the fact he never raised a hand to me, I understood those downtrodden and abused girls with their brutish fathers, many of whom saw them only as a means to earn money.'

'Like Amy Coombe?'

'You know her?' Alice's eyes widened.

Flora nodded. 'Amy is housekeeper at the Abbey now since Hetty retired.'

'Really?' Her expression transformed from anxiety to delight. 'You'll have to tell me how that came about sometime. Anyway, as I was saying, Riordan didn't understand that I too felt abused.' She brought her fist against her bodice. 'In here. Six years of being treated like an errant child made me feel worthless. When Sam Coombe raised his arm to me, it was all part of the same thing.'

'Everyone believed he had killed you and hidden your body.'

'He was a violent man, and Amy was such a scrawny, frightened little thing. I was determined to get her away from him. I wasn't expecting Sam to be there when I planned to take her and her sisters to the refuge that night. He had been laid off from the brewery and was drunk. When he realized what I was there for, he was furious and hit me with something. I don't know what, but I still carry the scar.' She lifted a curl away from her temple, revealing a raised white line a half an inch long.

'Either he threw me out or I ran away, I don't remember much about it. I can remember walking, though not where or for how long. It was snowing that night, but I hardly felt the cold. The next thing I remember, I was being shaken awake by a bad-tempered guard at Paddington Station who demanded my ticket. A kind lady who was passing spotted blood on the collar of my dress. She told the guard that I was hurt and he was to stop harassing me. She paid my fare and took me home with her. Her name was Mary Buchanan.'

463

'Raymond's wife?' Flora nodded slowly. *No wonder Alice wouldn't hear anything against him.*

'She summoned a doctor, who diagnosed a serious head injury. I was disoriented for days. Mary insisted I remain with them while I recovered.'

'Why didn't they contact Riordan? Did you lose your memory?'

'No, but for a long time I suffered with headaches.' Her smile had a twist to it, behind which something hovered. 'I-I didn't tell them about Cleeve Abbey or Riordan. I let them think I had forgotten who I was and where I came from. Raymond tried to help. He even hired a private investigator in Exeter to discover who I was.'

'Exeter? Why there?'

'That's where the train I was found on started its journey.' Bright colour appeared on her cheeks as if she recalled a shameful memory. 'I-I never corrected him.'

'You misled them? Why?'

Alice shrugged. 'Many reasons. When I was well again, the Bannerman's didn't want me to leave. Even Victor was delighted to have me there. Which, when I think about it might have had something to do with how he turned out later. He spent all his time with Mary and me.'

'I don't think you can take the blame for that.' Flora snorted.

'Well, maybe not.' A ghost of a smile lifted her mouth. 'Anyway, they never belittled me or suggested I wasn't worthy to be in their company. I almost forgot I had ever had a former life.'

'And me? Did you forget me?' Flora's throat burned with unshed tears, her voice bitter.

'No, never.' Alice's eyes pleaded for understanding. 'I was a weaker, more cowardly person in those days. Though even then, I knew there was a price to pay for deserting my family. You were that price.'

'Was that why you started nursing? To make amends?'

'I'm coming to that.' Alice drained her coffee cup, setting it back in the saucer with a firm click. 'I needed a name, so Mary suggested I use that of their dead daughter, a child they had lost a year before. Alice. Mary wanted the name used in the house again by a real person and not a ghost; which might sound maudlin to some, but I quite liked it. In some ways I was one myself. The ghost of Lily Maguire.'

'And Finch? Where did that come from?'

'When I was ill, I would watch greenfinches gather in a tree outside my window. Sometimes, the whole tree seemed alive with tiny green birds, as if it were breathing. It made perfect sense at the time, though perhaps seems odd now.'

'I don't think it's odd at all.' Flora imagined it was something she would have done herself. Greenfinches were one of her favourite birds.

'Life was good with the Buchanans,' Alice continued. 'But I knew I couldn't take everything and give nothing. Not after what I had done.' Her eyes filled with tears that she blinked rapidly away. 'I began helping Raymond with his work at the hospital, and decided to become a nurse. I trained at The London, which was very different from Birdcage Walk. Not that I'm complaining,' she added quickly. 'Those were good times and I worked hard in a profession I came to love. I became Head Nurse after a few years, then Assistant Matron and three years ago I was made Matron.'

'That's exceptional.' Despite a sense of loss at not having known her during that time, Flora experienced a surge of pride at what Alice had achieved. Not many young women could have left home with only the clothes they stood up in and not end up on the streets, or worse.

'The Buchanans became my family.' Her features softened as past memories ran through her head. 'When Mary died, Raymond was so lost, he begged me to move back into Birdcage Walk, which was one of the less difficult decisions I had to make.'

'I can understand that. It's a magnificent house.' Flora smiled. 'And you never considered marrying again?'

'How could I?' Alice shrugged. 'I was still married to Riordan.' Her eyes took on the meditative look of someone wrestling with a memory. 'In fact, I wrote to him ten years ago asking for his forgiveness for leaving and that I understood if he chose to divorce me for desertion.'

'He knew you were alive?' Flora gasped, going back

in time in her head. She must have been sixteen, about the time she became Eddy's governess.

'All I asked,' Alice's voice dragged her thoughts back to the present, 'was that I should be permitted to visit you on occasion. I offered to do so away from Cleeve Abbey if he didn't want anyone to know.'

'What happened?' Flora's throat tightened.

'That you have to ask tells me he didn't mention this to you' Alice sighed, resignation in her eyes.

'No. he didn't.' Flora's throat closed and a stone formed below her ribs. How could he have kept that from her? 'He told me you were dead.'

'That doesn't surprise me,' Alice said, nodding. 'He refused outright to divorce me and ordered me to stay away. In his eyes I didn't deserve to be part of your life.'

'I see.' All Flora's past loss and childish longings rose and threatened to overwhelm her, but she couldn't bring herself to voice them. Alice had her own conscience to wrestle with, and from her tone, those intervening years had left their own scars.

'Your letters weren't among his things when he died.' Flora shook her head. 'I don't understand. He did everything he could to find you when you went missing. He wrote to the newspapers and—'

'Are you sure about that?' She raised a sceptical eyebrow.

'Of course I'm sure. He always—' She started to say that Riordan always spoke kindly of Lily, but in fact he had never mentioned her mother at

467

all. That only two photographs of Lily had survived suggested her memory was flawed. Photographs Riordan had never looked at, and which had never been displayed in their home.

At the time, Flora had interpreted his reluctance as the pain of never having found her, but was what Alice said true? That Riordan had consciously wiped her from their lives?

Had the signs been there all along and Flora had simply ignored them? If so, then none of what she had always believed was real.

'Are you all right, Flora? I realize all this must be a dreadful shock to you.'

'I'm quite well, I . . . let's say I'm rearranging my memories.' Why would Alice lie after all this time? What had she to gain now?

'I was helping Raymond sort out Mary's things after her funeral,' Alice withdrew two yellowed newspaper clippings from her bag and handed them to her, 'when I found these.'

Both were from the Gloucestershire Echo, and one bore the heading '*Woman disappears from Cheltenham leaving, husband and child*'. The other dated a year later announced: '*Still No News of Missing Cheltenham Woman on One Year Anniversary.*'

'They knew who you were all along?' Flora stared at them in disbelief.

'It seems so, and yet they never said a word to me. Those reports stirred everything up again. What I had left behind, whom I had hurt.' Her eyes met Flora's for a heartbeat before sliding away.

'I returned to Gloucestershire once, although I had no idea what I would say to Riordan when I got there. As it turned out, I was too late.'

'Too late?' Flora sighed. 'This was after he had died?'

'Yes, though I didn't know that. When I got off the tram outside the Abbey, I saw some of the servants walking back from church. Among them was Bracenose, the Vaughn's estate manager. He had always been kind to me, and that day he sneaked me into the estate office and told me Riordan had died two months before. That a footman named Scrivens had helped a neighbour kill him. Bracenose said he coveted Riordan's position.' A frown appeared between her eyebrows. 'Didn't he take over after he died?'

'Yes, he did. It-it was an awful time.' Flora chose not to explain the full story of how Scrivens had killed Riordan on Grayson McCallum's instructions in order to gain access to William's fortune. Perhaps Bracenose had left that part out because he felt guilty at having revealed Flora's parentage, and by doing so had set the whole conspiracy in motion.

'Poor Riordan.' Alice sighed. 'He didn't deserve such an end, though if he died protecting you, as Bracenose said, then to my mind it wiped out every unkind thing Riordan ever said to me.'

Flora smiled, though at the same time a shudder ran through her as she recalled the day McCallum had also tried to kill her. That Riordan had found

469

out and confronted him, thus leading to his own death was something she hated to talk about. Alice was entitled to know the details – but not today.

'Bunny and I had been married almost two years by then, and I assume Bracenose told you I no longer lived at Cleeve Abbey? Why didn't you get in touch when there was no one left to object?' *Except maybe William.*

'I knew losing Riordan would be hard on you,' Alice said. 'So I decided to let things lie for a while. Also, I didn't know how much you knew about your past or mine. I risked making things awkward for you and the last thing I would wish was to cause you any more pain.'

'What changed your mind?'

'Your name was mentioned in the newspapers in connection with the Evangeline Lange case. Then there was this.' She delved into the capacious tapestry bag once more, from which she handed Flora a much-folded newspaper clipping. Newer than the others, it bore the announcement of Arthur's birth five months before, together with their London address.

'I tortured myself for weeks as to whether or not to contact you. I even walked past this house several times. Once, you came out pushing a baby carriage, but I hurried away before you saw me. I—' she faltered, as if she needed to pluck up courage for what came next. 'What I did then might seem a little, well sinister.'

'Why? What did you do?' Flora searched her

features for long seconds before the truth hit her and she drew in a sharp inrush of breath. 'You sent us that invitation to St Philomena's Hospital?'

Alice nodded. 'I instructed the porter to tell me when you arrived so I could be sure *I* was the one to show you round. I had decided to tell you everything over tea, and take the consequences of whatever you felt about me. When Lizzie Prentice was killed – well, in all the ensuing chaos, my story had to wait.'

'What if Bunny had known nothing of this? About my being the product of an affair between you and one of the Vaughns? He might have renounced me rather than face the shame that might have caused.' An image of Beatrice Harrington's disapproving pout loomed into her head.

'I pride myself on being a good judge of character, Ruth Lazarus notwithstanding.' She winced. 'I vowed that if I saw something uncompromising in your husband that day at the hospital, I would keep silent.' Her features softened as she went on. 'However, the moment I saw Ptolemy, I knew what sort of man he was. What a charming name by the way. It suits him far better than Bunny.'

'I agree, but he has always been called that, except by his mother.' Had Bunny been a different sort of man, Flora might have spent the rest of her life in ignorance. Would that have been worse? Or Better?

'I see, a schoolboy nickname, I assume?' Flora nodded, smiling as Alice went on, 'I knew then

471

there was nothing I could say which would change his love for you. Had it been otherwise, I would have never spoken. I also owe him my life as he jumped into the river and saved me last night. How can I ever forget that?'

'Something tells me you would have got out on your own, but I admit my heart turned over when you fell in.'

'You must feel so confused,' Alice said gently. 'I've had twenty years to reconcile myself to what I did, but all this is new to you. I hope you'll find it in yourself to forgive me for the past. Although I would understand if you wished to have nothing to do with me.' Her voice remained calm but the look in her eyes revealed what she really wanted.

'I'm not sure what I feel about you or Riordan – yet.' Flora's mind whirled with excitement, happiness and resentment as well as disbelief and even jealously. None of which lingered long enough to dominate, leaving her numb and confused.

Should she throw her arms round this woman or slap her? Rail against her selfish act all those years ago, or try to understand her reasons? Whichever she did wouldn't obliterate the misunderstandings that had grown over the years. Though what would be the point of making everything worse?

'Were you aware I recognized you that day at St Philomena's?' Flora fought to keep her voice steady.

'I wasn't sure, but I hoped you had. I used those missing children as a way to keep seeing you. Not that finding them wasn't important. It was. I imagined if we could do it together we could form a bond which would make it easier to explain everything.'

'And did it? Make things easier?' Her voice came out sharper than she intended.

'No.' Alice's lip quivered and she stared off for a moment, visibly overcome.

A brief, but heavy silence fell between them, interrupted only by the chink of china and the tick of the clock on the mantelpiece. The everyday sounds of the household appeared to have stilled. No chattering from the kitchens reached them, no doors slammed or footsteps sounded across floorboards.

Her thoughts went to Bunny, who was most likely pacing his study at that moment. Trying to decide if this woman deserved to be in his house, or would he be summoned to throw her out.

Flora's thoughts whirled and collided, but with no immediate solution, she rose and gave the bell pull beside the fireplace a sharp tug, taking refuge in practicalities. 'While we decide where we go from here,' she said, her voice scratchy with emotion. 'Would you like to meet your grandson?'

'I would, very much.' A flash of warm pleasure lit her eyes. 'I never dreamed I would become a grandmother.'

Flora's hand stilled on the strip of tasselled

brocade as she recalled that William had used those same words. Keeping her eyes averted, she swallowed the lump in her throat, taking wry comfort in the fact her son would receive more loving attention from Alice than he ever would from Beatrice.

'Did you know Arthur was my brother's name?' Alice said as Flora resumed her seat opposite. 'He died during the Ashanti war under General Wolseley.'

'Actually I did. Though don't tell Bunny. He thinks I chose it because I like Arthur Conan Doyle's detective stories.'

When Stokes arrived in answer to her summons, he found them in gales of delighted laughter, and startled, he froze on the threshold. 'Madam?'

'Ah, Stokes.' Flora wiped tears from her eyes while handing Alice an embroidered handkerchief as she did the same. 'Would you ask Milly to bring Arthur down?'

'He has an excellent nurse, who doesn't like me very much,' Flora said when they were alone again.

'That's not uncommon.' Alice smiled knowingly. 'A nurse who has sat up for four nights with a desperately sick child can become critical, even resentful of the child's mother when it comes time for the patient to go home.'

'But Milly knows how much I love Arthur,' Flora said, defensive.

'Of course she does, but with sole charge of a young baby, it's hard for her not to become attached. She might feel she's the only one who has his true interests at heart, with you as an intruder.'

'What should I do?' Flora asked. 'I don't want to dismiss her, she's a good nurse, but I cannot employ someone who disapproves of me.'

'Might I suggest you ask her advice from time to time? Even if you don't need it. She knows your son as well as, even better than you in some ways. Discuss his sleep patterns and teething remedies with her in a non-judgemental way. Involve her rather than treat her as if she should disappear into the walls when she isn't required.'

'I doubt any of my servants would accuse me of that. Ask Sally.'

'Ah yes, your spirited lady's maid. How is she after her ordeal?'

'Holding court in the kitchens from what I last heard. She's quite the heroine and enjoying every minute of it. She's even ordering Stokes around, demanding he serve tea to all her visitors. The poor man might never recover.'

Milly's arrival interrupted more companionable laughter, causing the nurse's eyes to widen a fraction at the sight of the stranger.

'This is Mrs Finch, Milly,' Flora said so as not to create more gossip in the servant's hall than was already circulating. 'You'll be seeing a great deal of her in future as she's Arthur's maternal grandmother.'

'Good morning, Madam.' Milly's astonished

gaze remained on Alice as she handed the baby to Flora.

Flora rested her lips against the baby's fluff of fair hair, and inhaled the sweet scent of his newly washed skin, his attention focussed on the garnet pendant round her neck. 'I'll warn you, he's heavy.'

'He's quite adorable.' Alice's eyes softened and she reached eager hands for Arthur, who went to her without protest.

Arthur's face creased in puzzlement at the stranger, but within seconds he had grasped the flowers on her hat in his chubby fingers and mouthed her cheek while making incoherent baby noises.

'I'll come back later, Madam.' Milly curtseyed and backed away.

Alice called her back at the door, 'One moment, Milly is it?'

'Yes, Madam.' Milly turned back, her eyes wary, her gaze flicking to Flora and away again.

'Might I ask you a little about Arthur as you know him better than most?' She held the baby's hand and bounced him on her lap in a miniature dance.

'He's a good baby, Madam,' Milly beamed, inflating her diminutive chest. 'He's a good sleeper and rarely fusses. He's never ill other than a cold and he's got five teeth now. I'm sure he'll be walking before his first birthday.'

Alice asked gentle, non-critical questions about

the baby's care, even congratulating Milly on the child's obvious intelligence, as if giving her credit for it.

For his part, Arthur was delighted with the strange new face, poked his fingers into her mouth and eyes and tried to gnaw at a gold locket around her neck.

Alice probed with more gentle questions, even congratulating Milly on Arthur's intelligence, as if giving her credit for it.

Flora observed them with growing emotion. This was what she had missed all her life; a mother's advice and gentle guidance on subjects she could never have broached with anyone else. Even Bunny, for all his practicality and kindness, didn't always understand that at times, Flora felt ill-equipped to be a mother. Like most men he regarded motherhood as instinctive; a skill that females were born with. How could she tell him that most of the time she floundered, with panic and doubt taking turns?

As Alice made baby noises against Arthur's plump cheek, rewarded with soft looks and endearing nonsense talk, the warmth left Flora and something else took its place.

Surely Lily had done the same for her when she was a baby? There must have been precious times when she held her close as a toddler and marvelled over the small miracle that was her child? When had that ended? With Sam Coombe's blow, or before? While Lily enjoyed the opulent life in the

Buchanan's house on Birdcage Walk as Alice, did she ever think of Flora growing up in the servant's hall at Cleeve Abbey?

Flora knew without doubt that *she* could never abandon her child, no matter what the circumstances. Or was she being unfair and Alice truly believed she had had no choice? That Flora would be better off without her, no matter how painful that decision was?

Among the sounds of female laughter and babyish chuckles, questions circled in Flora's head with nowhere to go. Perhaps they should be left in the past, or she would never be at peace with her mother's return. No one can truly guess the hearts of others, and all that mattered was that Alice was back in her life.

However, despite her calm reasoning, a worm of resentment sat at the back of her mind and repeated over and over. *How could she have left me?*

CHAPTER 32

Alice's visit lasted through luncheon and on into a pleasurable afternoon, ending only when she politely refused their invitation to dinner insisting she had overstayed her welcome. Giving promises to return soon and often, Bunny had asked Stokes to send a maid to summon a hansom to return her to Birdcage Walk.

Bunny said little as they changed for dinner, as if he sensed Flora's conflicting emotions. It wasn't until the maid who stood in for Sally had withdrawn did he venture a question.

'How do you feel now you know the full story?' He leaned a shoulder against the frame of his dressing room that adjoined their sleeping quarters.

'Truthfully? Strange.' She turned to look at him on their way out of the room. 'Do you really think I look like her?'

'I do, yes.' He studied her face, his head tilted as they strolled side by side along the hallway. 'Not so much in individual features, but the way you bite your bottom lip when worried, or have heard something outrageous and are trying not to laugh. Then there's that tiny hiccough when you—'

'Enough!' She elbowed him gently. 'I'm thrilled to have her back again, but I keep asking myself the same question.'

'How could she have left you?' He paused at the top of the stairs and turned towards her.

'Exactly.' She summoned a shaky smile, unnerved by his keen perception. 'Will I ever be able to look at her and not dwell on all those wasted years in between?'

'Knowing you. Yes. But it will take time. Your perception of your past and hers has been altered in the course of one day. Don't try and make sense of it now. Let your thoughts settle a while and see what happens.' He turned away from the stairs and tugged her towards the rear of the house. 'I have an idea. Why don't we call in at the nursery before the dinner gong sounds?'

'As long as you promise not to wake him. He's been thoroughly spoiled today and I suspect Milly had trouble putting him down.' Despite her mild protests she allowed him to lead her towards the nursery. 'So no tickling his feet, and then pretending he woke up on his own? Promise?'

'If you insist.' Bunny said over his shoulder as he pushed open the door. 'Though it's not as if he has school in the morning.'

'Be careful.' Flora winced as the hinges gave a tiny squeak. 'We don't want to alert Milly. Her room is only next door and she has impeccable hearing.'

'You say that as if I've never done this before.'

The nursey was a square room with a window at the far end that slanted a shaft of pearly light across the crib set beneath it. A heavy Victorian chest of drawers occupied one end, a waist-high set of shelves at the other, a neat row of soft toys lined up on the top; parodies of rabbits, dogs and elephants in inaccurate colours and textures and wide, staring glass eyes.

The lower shelves held children's books Arthur was years too young to appreciate yet, but which Flora could not resist buying. *Peter Rabbit* jostled beside *The Water Babies*, *Tom Sawyer*, *Treasure Island*, and a copy of a new story, *The Wonderful Wizard of Oz* that Lady Amelia, the Vaughn's eldest daughter, had sent her from America when he was born; all favourite tales of her own childhood she anticipated sharing with him when he was older.

Arthur lay on his back, knees bent like a little frog and both arms thrown back on either side of his head, his fingers curled into his palms.

'I could never leave Arthur.' Flora's voice cracked as she gazed at her sleeping son. 'She just walked out of the door and never went back.'

'She was injured at the time,' Bunny said gently, having been given Alice's complete story again over afternoon tea. 'How could she have taken you with her when she left? The courts don't favour women who leave their husbands, whatever the reason. Riordan would probably have kept you anyway, which is what he wanted.'

'She lied to the Buchanans as well.'

'Again, quite understandable. Had she told them she was a married woman with a child they might have sent her straight back to Riordan. She must have been desperate, Flora. In ways you couldn't possibly understand.'

'I know all that, but—' though she hadn't at all. Alice had told her story in a calm, pragmatic way, with little of the real pain she must have felt evident. Maybe there was time to revisit the past with her and examine those moments one day?

'No buts.' Bunny bent and ran a finger down Arthur's cheek. The baby's nose twitched and he batted it away with a fist before settling again. 'She suffered for leaving you behind. And you have to admire her courage for seeking you out again, which proves she never forgot you.'

Arthur's eyes fluttered open. At the sight of their faces staring down at him, his mouth curved into a smile and uttering eager mewling noises, he raised his arms.

'I warned you not to wake him.' Flora's fierce whisper only served to make Bunny smile.

'No harm done.' He lifted Arthur into his arms, propped him on one hip and swayed gently from side to side. 'Hello, young man.'

'Shh! Milly will hear you.'

'We're not scared of Nursey, are we old chap. No-we-are-not.' He bounced Arthur on his hip in time with each word, rewarded with a toothy smile and a sleepy burp.

Flora froze, listening, but when no sound of movement came from Milly's room, she relaxed.

'Now,' Bunny dropped his voice to a whisper, 'what should I call her? Mother-in-Law, Miss Finch or Mrs Maguire?'

'She wants me to call her Alice.' Flora softened at the sight of her son in his father's arms as Arthur's head slumped against Bunny's chest, his eyes open and his thumb in his mouth. 'She says she isn't Lily Maguire anymore.'

'Which makes perfect sense. Alice it is then. You need to get to know her, and—'

'To forgive,' she finished for him. 'Yes, I see that now. I was so bound up in the excitement of wanting her to be my mother, I forgot how I might feel if it turned out to be true.'

'I recognize that look on your face. Are you hoping she and William will get together again?' he asked over the top of Arthur's fluffy head.

'Is that so ridiculous?' She stroked the baby's neck where the skin lay in tiny folds as she pondered his question. 'They are in their forties with years ahead of them. Why shouldn't they spend them together?'

'It's been twenty years, Flora. Years which must have changed them both beyond recognition. Perhaps they aren't right for each other now?'

'I don't believe that.' She recalled William's face when he talked about Lily, and Alice's when she explained why she had parted from her child's father. Perhaps she could contrive a meeting between them once William returned from his mysterious trip.

'I know what you're thinking, Flora,' Bunny interrupted her thoughts. 'But you cannot write the end of their story for them. You'll just have to trust to luck and nature.'

'Luck and nature,' Flora repeated under her breath. 'And perhaps a little help from me.'

'What did you say?'

'Nothing. What did Inspector Maddox say when he called you on the telephone this afternoon?'

'Goodness, that's a rapid change of subject. Not a very subtle one either.' Bunny shifted position and wrestled his glasses back from Arthur's clutching fingers.

'I would like to reassure Alice that Mr Buchanan won't be prosecuted.'

'It seems his co-operation has abrogated any criminal responsibility, and with a child trafficking gang in custody, the police are feeling magnanimous. Not to mention Maddox getting his name in the papers as the lead investigating officer.'

'I hope Victor Buchanan doesn't have any more of those photographs floating about to cause trouble.'

'Not if he has any sense. Or he could find himself penning verses in Reading gaol.'

'Not funny.' Flora narrowed her eyes, but his mischievous smile persisted. 'What about the peeps?' She stiffened slightly, prepared for bad news. 'Sister Lazarus still has one.'

'Ah yes, the notorious Sister Lazarus.' Bunny's eyes flashed behind his horn-rimmed spectacles as a memory returned. 'She did break her nose by the way, which will make her police mugshots look very interesting. Maddox found the peep on her at the police station, which, as Mr Buchanan's property, has duly been returned to him.'

'As simple as that?' She widened her eyes in surprise, then narrowed them again. 'Or did you have something to do with it?'

'Whatever gave you that idea?' He took Arthur the two paces to the window and pointed to the garden, not that there was much to see in the fog-shrouded dusk of an October evening.

The baby yawned and flailed his arms, caught the window with a hand and let out a discontented wail. His small body went rigid and his face puckered as if working up to a full blow cry.

'Now look what you've done!' Flora took the baby from Bunny's arms and returned him to his cradle, rearranging the covers over him while hushing him gently.

Further along the hall, a door opened and Bunny grabbed Flora's hand and tugged her past Milly's door before she appeared. With no time to reach their room without being seen, he pulled her into an alcove halfway along. Squashed together in the corner, Flora giggled and he flapped a hand in a signal for silence just as Milly's voice drifted along the corridor.

'I don't recall leaving this door open. Aww poor Artie. Is that why you woke up?'

'Artie?' Flora mouthed at Bunny, who shrugged.

Once Milly had returned to her room, the pair fled back to their bedroom where they collapsed onto the canopied bed, laughing and hushing one another uselessly.

'In our own house,' Flora gasped between breaths. 'How ridiculous we are.'

'I know, but it was fun, wasn't it?' Bunny propped himself on an elbow next to her on the bed. 'And while we are on the subject of Stanhopes.' He drew from his pocket the silver egg that swung gently on the end of a fine chain.

'You kept it?' She was about to take it from him, but he moved it out of her reach at the last second.

'Call it a memento. Reid won't have any use for it now, especially when I have had the photograph replaced with something less – er, controversial. An image of my wife, perhaps?'

'Sounds interesting. With or without clothes?'

'Ah, now there's an idea.' He sent her a sideways look that sent her blood fizzing through her veins as he returned the object to his pocket. 'Or was that simply to tease me?'

'Actually, I was just thinking of whom we might engage to take the photograph.'

'Hussy!' He threw his arm around her and

hugged her close. 'Although,' he whispered into her hair, 'there's this place in Soho that claims to be very discreet.'

'Really?' She let the idea percolate for a moment. 'How discreet?'